BELOVED BETRAYER

"Meant you what you said?" Wulf's voice was husky. "That you have craved to be close to me one last time?"

When he lifted her braid to his lips and kissed it, Brianna could no more lie than cease breathing. "A-ay."

"Then I would make love with you if you will have me — and then 'twill be good-bye. I will not come to you again nor will I look back, Brianna. Not this time. You have said there can be naught between us, and I see 'tis so." When she made no answer but gazed on him with huge eyes, he asked softly, "What say you, my lady?"

She murmured, "I know not."

She was remembering his strength and tenderness, the way his hands had thrilled as they moved over her body. For that very reason, how could she make love and then give him up? Yet how could she not?

JOAN VAN NUYS

UNWILLING BETRAYER

LEISURE BOOKS ▌▙ NEW YORK CITY

This book is dedicated with love and admiration to my daughter, Suzanne, my golden girl.

A LEISURE BOOK®

May 1992

Published by

Dorchester Publishing Co., Inc.
276 Fifth Avenue
New York, NY 10001

What has become of the steed?
What has become of the warrior?
What has become of the seats of banquet?
Where are the joys of the hall?
O for the bright cup!
O for the mail-clad warrior!
O for the glory of the prince!
How that time has passed away
And grown dark under the cover of night,
As if it had never been.

From "The Wanderer"
(anonymous Anglo-Saxon poem)

GLOSSARY: UNWILLING BETRAYER

Ard Ri: the king of kings

souterrain: a subterranean passage

rath: a raised mound of earth surrounded by an earthen wall

dun: a fortified rath protected by two walls with a water-filled ditch between.

solarstein: a piece of cordierite through which a navigator looked at the sun's zenith to ascertain its direction

thrall: a slave

berserk: a Norse warrior who fought with frenzied rage in battle

Maun: Early Viking name for present-day Isle of Man

tuath: a territory of which there were over two hundred in Ireland, each occupied by a tribe under a chieftain

prime-signed: to be marked symbolically with the cross, enabling Vikings to live peacefully among Christians without forsaking their own gods

trews: close-fitting trousers

waif-word: a rumor

wattle and daub: a wall construction consisting of posts interwoven with twigs and branches and plastered with clay and straw

Prologue

Kincora, April 1012

The palace of the emperor of Ireland lay as peaceful as was the land itself in the setting sun. Atop a mast on its tallest watchtower, the scarlet and black lion-banner of Brian Boru hung limp, and the moat between the thick earthen walls shone red-gold and unruffled in the last shimmering sun-rays of an eve in early spring. In the dimness within the palace walls were heard only the soft footsteps of the servingfolk as they moved quietly through the fresh sweet-smelling rushes, lighting wall torches and banking fires for the night. Ay, all was serene in Kincora, the royal dun that Brian Boru had built for himself on the Shannon.

7

All, that is, except the thoughts of the Ard Ri himself.

He entered the bedchamber of his wife unseen and watched with veiled eyes as she combed out the mane of thick dark-red hair that hung down her back and over her breasts. It fell to below her hips, soft, lustrous, beautiful. She herself was beautiful. Her beauty never ceased to amaze Brian, for Gormlaith was no longer a young woman. The sight of her smooth-skinned, voluptuous body in the light of the flickering wall torches aroused a flame within him.

He dismissed it. It was mere passion stirring him now. The deep and desperate love he had felt for her in their first years of marriage was long gone. Too many things had happened between them, too many things said and done that could never be called back. He watched her turn as she sensed his presence, and saw contempt flare in her green eyes. It was quickly subdued.

"I am surprised to see you here, my lord," Gormlaith said coolly.

"You be my wife, lady," came the gruff answer. "Why should I not be here?"

She was furious with her husband this night for a hundred reasons, foremost of which was his treatment of her brother, Maelmorda. She was angry with Brian Boru most of the time now, yet it pleased her to see the flicker of desire heating the icy gray depths of his eyes. Slowly, seductively, she donned a green silken bedgown which displayed more than covered her magnificent body.

"You may be the Ard Ri," she said huskily, "but if you think to bed me after seeding every whore between here and Cashel, you are sadly mistaken."

Her languid gaze moved over his tall, muscular form as she placed scent between her breasts, on her wrists and throat, behind her knees, at her temples. She would fight his certain advances, ay, but she knew well she would yield. While she had come to hate him these past few years, she craved his lovemaking. She craved lovemaking with any man so long as he was taller and stronger than she and was comely.

"Take yourself to your own bedchamber, Boru, for you will not stay the night here." She lowered herself onto her silken bedcovers, fully aware of the ravishing sight she made.

Brian ignored her words. Devoid now of any desire, he observed the thrust of her breasts nearly tumbling out of her bedgown.

"Where have you been until now, Gormlaith?"

"Walking," she snapped. It was a lie. She had been with her lover in the souterrain beneath the palace since late afternoon.

Brian's icy eyes narrowed to slits. "So. Walking . . ."

"Is that so strange?" Her own eyes flashed emerald fire. "Since when does the Ard Ri care where I go or what I do?"

Brian did not lie. "You are right, I no longer

9

care. 'Tis Maelmorda who interests me. I would know what went on here that put him in such a towering rage."

He had learned from the palace guard that the king of Leinster had arrived late yesterday bearing tribute, and then had stormed off this day shortly before Brian and his men returned from the second royal residence at Cashel. Brian had sent a lieutenant to fetch him back, whereupon Maelmorda had slain the man on the spot and gone his way.

"I am waiting, Gormlaith. What happened?"

Gormlaith laughed, her little teeth sharp and white against her cherry lips. "As if 'twere some mystery why he constantly smolders. He be king of Leinster, yet you—"

Brian's forced smile held more fury than warmth. "He is king because I say he is king, lady. I allow him to be king."

Gormlaith went on as if he had not spoken: "—yet you hold him hostage as if he were some petty earl, demanding subservience and tribute. 'Tis an outrage, Boru, that you should drain the riches of his kingdom so."

Brian's bearded jaw tightened. The woman knew well why her brother was held hostage and made to pay such heavy tribute. He was a troublemaker, as was Sitric, her son by the Viking Olav Kvarnan. Brian himself had striven endlessly for peace and unity among Celts and Vikings alike and had attained it, whereas Maelmorda and Sitric fomented unrest to enrich themselves. In the last conflict they had begun, he had defeated them both soundly, yet he had been merciful. He had restored their kingdoms in return for their allegiance, and had even given Sitric his own daughter, Emer, in marriage. He himself had wed Gormlaith, for she was ravishing and he had craved her. He had even come to love her. Now she was a complainer and a whiner and a trollop, and her weasel of a brother was growing troublesome again. He said again, low:

"What happened whilst I was gone, woman? I would hear it and I would hear it now. I will not ask again."

Gormlaith was incensed, seeing there would be no lovemaking this night. She rose from her silken bed, disdaining to cover one full white breast now exposed to his angry eyes. She stood tall, six feet of haughty Irish royalty, lithe, graceful, more beautiful, more desirable than any other woman in Ireland, high-born or low, and well she knew it. She glared at him.

"He came yesterday," she said, her voice dangerously soft, "bearing the tribute you do outrageously require—three superb pine timbers from the forest of Fidh-Gaibhli to make masts for your damned ships."

"Ships he agrees we must build if we are to have a strong navy."

"Hah. 'Twas an idea you forced on him!" Her breathing grew heavy and her blood ran fast. It was always thus when she thought on Boru's subjugation of this weak but handsome brother of hers. "He himself helped carry the

11

timbers through mountains and bogs and in so doing, ripped a button from his tunic."

Brian answered stiffly. " 'Twould seem a small thing to put him in such a state. He slew the man I sent to fetch him back, lady."

Gormlaith's face was white. "I care naught for your man, Boru. As for the tunic, 'twas an elaborate silken thing banded in gold and buttoned with worked silver which he said you gave him. I trow 'twas worth a fortune, but I deemed it an abomination, a disgusting badge of vassalage. You give him expensive gifts to soothe the fact that he, the kind of Leinster, must carry your damned tribute on his own shoulders like a common thrall!"

" 'Twas his own choice to bear it thus, I assure you."

"Know you this, O great Ard Ri, I tossed the wretched thing into the fire, silver and all, rather than have it mended. And first I spat on it! Maelmorda sees finally that the time for tribute is ended. He is his own man now and will stand up to you. If he had any doubts as to the wisdom of such a move, they disappeared when your son insulted him over the game board."

"Insulted him? Murrough?"

"Murrough," she spat.

Brian looked on her in disgust. By the gods. Her damned brother had slain one of his favorite lieutenants in cold blood, and all she could talk about was silver buttons and an insult during a game of draughts. He was at the end of his patience. He allowed her to rant on only because he had been sucked into a deepening whirlpool of memories. What had happened to them and to the love he had once felt for her? Was it his doing that there was nothing but lust between them any more? His doing that she now took one lover after another? He shook his head. He did not know.

"Hear you what I said?" Gormlaith cried, her eyes wild. "Your miserable son called my brother a coward before a room full of men!"

" 'Tis best to stay off this subject, Gormlaith," Brian said grimly.

"Nay, I will not!"

She was magnificent in her anger, but Brian was unmoved. Beauty without loyalty or love to soften it was a harsh, too-bright thing. He felt empty, remembering his first wife, long in the ground. She had known of loyalty and love. Even a child knew more of loyalty and love than did Gormlaith. Into his thoughts skipped a sturdy little maid, her hair the color of autumn, eyes green, a laughing elfin face. Brianna. His own foster daughter and daughter of his dearest friend. Little Brianna who had declared her love for him and demanded he wait for her to grow up. He smiled at the long-ago memory. That little maid of ten winters had had more love and loyalty in her little finger than Gormlaith ever could summon in a lifetime.

"I demand an apology from Murrough," Gormlaith raged, pacing the floor. "And when next my brother returns, if ever he does,

Murrough will apologize to him, also."

"Murrough knows of what he speaks, Gormlaith. 'Tis common knowledge that the king of Leinster shows the white feather when the battle heats."

"Damn you, I will not hear it! The prince will apologize"—Gormlaith's eyes smoldered—"or you will answer to Maelmorda's Leinstermen. Methinks you will answer to them in any event."

Brian spoke between clenched teeth. "If there be any answering to do or apologies made, 'twill be from Maelmorda to me. 'Tis my man who lies with his skull split open."

"You accursed spalpeen." Gormlaith's face was whiter than white. She spat at his feet. "A pox on your beards, you and that scut-son of yours!"

As soon as she said it, she died inside. More and more she had hurled insults at Boru, but this was the ultimate, cursing his beard. She watched his handsome face blanch and then turn red. She straightened her shoulders and raised her chin high. Never would he know the terror she felt when he looked at her so.

Brian's voice was thick with his rage. "You have stirred the pot one last time, Gormlaith."

She gaped, her luscious mouth open. "Wh-what mean you?"

"You have interfered in my life for the last time. Get you gone from my sight."

"I—understand not what you are saying . . ."

"Methinks you do, lady." His gray eyes glittered. She had been a thorn in his side and an ache in his heart for too long. Out of mercy he had not brought her before the judges for her adultery, but now, now she had called down shame on his beard and on Murrough's. There was no higher insult a woman could offer her husband. "Get you gone from Kincora, Gormlaith," he said low. "I divorce you."

Gormlaith's heart stopped. "Brian, nay! Let us talk—"

"The time for talk is over. I want you out of here."

"My lord, you cannot!" She began to tremble. This could not be happening again, this being put aside. First Olav, then Malachi, now Boru. Suddenly her trembling was with rage, not fear. Men! She hated them all, for they had brought her nothing but grief. Her two former husbands, Boru, her son, her brother. Her flesh was seared by the flames of her hatred.

"I divorce you, woman," Brian declared. "Tomorrow you will attend to your affairs and get you hence. My men will accompany you to Leinster or Dublin, whichever you prefer, but at Kincora you will stay no longer, I promise you." He turned and strode toward the door.

Gormlaith leapt in front of him, her beautiful eyes ablaze. "You will regret this, Boru. Mind you that I have vast influence and connections. My lineage towers over your own. I am daughter of a king, sister to a king, mother of kings, and have wed none but kings. You will find no other to equal me."

The emperor shook his head. "You are wrong, Gormlaith. On any street corner, I can find such as you." He made no move to ward off the two stinging blows she dealt him on his cheeks.

"You bastard! Let the truth be known then— too long have I languished here at Kincora craving the embrace of a real man. I will go to Dublin and 'tis glad I am to leave!"

Brian's laughter erupted. She was making it easy for him to say goodbye. "By all means, go to Sitric and his Viking court. If you stir up but half the trouble for him that you made for me, he will be too busy to join Maelmorda in any mischief against me."

She could have slain him. In truth, Dublin was the last place she wanted to go. Sitric's moldering stronghold on the Liffey was a far cry from her luxurious quarters here at Kincora. The only bright spot in the whole dismal picture was that his warriors, tall, brawny Vikings and Norse-Irish, were lusty and virile and could be had with no effort whatsoever. Already she had sampled many of them.

"I hate you, Brian Boru." She was scarcely able to choke out the words. "You call yourself emperor of all the Irish, but to me you are naught but Brian of the Cattle-Tribute. Brian the Cow-King. Know that I will see you dead for this."

" 'Tis grateful I am to be forewarned," Brian said quietly. Gazing down on her from his great height, his hand on the door latch, he saw that her eyes glimmered. It was the first time he had ever seen her weep and he was touched. "You be a troubled woman, Gormlaith. I wish you naught but peace."

"Go!" she screamed. "Go, bastard! I hate you!" Her slipper hit the door as it closed.

Chapter One

At Sea, 2 November 1013, Midday

Wulf Thorsson stood beneath a thickening gray sky in the stern of the *Sea Serpent*, his hands gripping the steering oar and his eyes slitted against the wind and frothing walls of water. His beard, eyebrows, and lashes were matted with sleet, silvery crystals gleaming amid the gold. Despite his hooded fur-lined cloak and boots he was frozen to the core, as were his men. Gazing on their faces as they bent over the oars, he sensed their weariness and discouragement.

Shrouded as his vessel was in sleet and fog, neither the solarstein nor stars could be used for reckoning their course. They had been relying on instinct alone. Sail furled, they had been rowing directly into the gale since passing the Hebrides two days since. They had bailed from the great dragonship hundreds of buckets of the ever-moaning, ever-rising North Sea, and had pushed and pulled the heavy paddles endlessly. Yet it was as if the ship, now silver with ice, had stayed in the same spot all the while.

Wulf felt a growing fear for his men and his craft but did not let it show. Now was not the time to let any know of the despair he felt. Instead, he vowed to give this faithful crew of his every bit of strength and confidence he possessed. He shouted to his skald:

"Gardar! Leave off your bailing and fetch your harp. Let us hear a song or two to heat our blood."

As the skald moved to the half-deck to get his instrument, Wulf clapped the shoulder of his best friend. Leif Karlsen was in the stern with him, his booted feet pressed hard against the shuddering steering oar as he helped hold the vessel steady.

"Methinks you should slay us all when we reach land," Leif muttered, "if ever we do."

Wulf laughed, his iced beard pointing to the sky. "We'll be in the Orkneys before nightfall, I promise you, and you'll have a fine tale to tell your children one day."

Leif glumly shook his dark head in its fur-lined hood. His own beard and lashes were ice-coated. " 'Tis sorry I am I sided with fools against you, man."

"Nay, old friend, not fools. We all wanted to get back to Norway before Yuletide."

"You knew 'twould be best to winter over on Maun."

"No more than the others did I crave to stay the winter on that accursed isle with those bewitched Celts breathing down our necks."

His mistake had been made long before that, Wulf brooded. He had been as loath as his men to leave the pleasures of Byzantium earlier, thus pushing the inspection of his stronghold on Maun dangerously late in the season. But it was bootless now to have regrets. He barred them from his mind as he saw that Gardar had settled himself in the bow of the *Sea Serpent* and was strumming his harp to warm his fingers. The wind-howl and the wave-song were no match for his powerful voice when it was raised suddenly in a familiar song that told of battle and bravery and of a death more glorious than life—to live forever in Valhalla, the land of heroes. Wulf felt his spirits rise.

Looking on, Leif saw that fifty pair of eyes were fastened on their chieftain, this man who could have been king in their part of Norway's land had he but chosen to accept the crown offered. Wulf Thorsson was taller than the tallest of them, and the strength of his long-limbed body was evident even in the ice-covered bearskins he wore. His bravery was legend. But what would any of that avail them now, Leif thought glumly, as one fierce sea after another buffeted their ship. They were going to go down.

As he listened to his skald, Wulf's racing blood warmed his frozen body. He had but wanted reminding, as did they all, that a man need not die with a sword in his hand to go to Valhalla. He need only die unafraid. Now he joined in the song, and soon was laughing and chanting with Gardar. Leif and the others, gazing on his glowing eyes and serene face, took heart and began to chant also, their deep voices soaring over the storm-scream.

Wulf knew of a sudden, with every fiber of his being, that Valhalla was near. He marked that his men did not sense it as did he himself, but no matter, it was there waiting for them all. The great Val Hall, bright-shining, was hovering in the murk and sleet above ship and storm-howl, its walls aglow with the dazzle of the shields and weapons of fallen heroes. The Valkyries were there to welcome them while Odin, the Valfather, watched and waited. Wulf gazed upward, in a rapture, striving to see the glory, but then the moment passed, gone as quickly as it had come. Except that now his heart was at peace. If their time to die was now, Valhalla waited for them all.

" 'Tis all right, men," he shouted above the din. "All is well, I promise you."

Wulf gazed about him at his comrades and his vessel, and his heart swelled. Who needed anything more than this—sting of sleet, taste

21

of brine and danger, camaraderie . . . He was pushing against the steering oar with redoubled strength when a shout came from the bow. Gardar was on his feet, pointing.

"Landfall! I see landfall! 'Tis the Orkneys, men! We are saved."

Wulf grinned and gave Leif's shoulder a thump. "Now be you happy, old friend?"

Sitric Olavsson, king of Dublin, hid his rage. He had made a long and dangerous winter journey north to these damned Orkney Isles to gain help in overthrowing Brian Boru, and so far he had received nothing but yawns from their king. Damn the bastard. But he knew better than to make a display of his temper. Not while he sat in the seat of honor in Sigurd's great hall, stuffed himself with Sigurd's sumptuous food and drink, and enjoyed his women. And there was the extra boon of meeting chieftains from Iceland and Greenland. He sighed, his anger fast dissipating as he refilled his horn and heard the skald now singing about the conquests of Sitric's father, the late great Olav Kvarnan, Dane-king of Dublin.

Sitric locked a smile on his mouth and forced himself to make small talk with Sigurd and his nobles. At the same time, his eyes slid over those wenches sitting at the same board. The two he had bedded these past two nights, Icelanders both, had shown him pleasures he had never imagined possible. And now a soft black-haired little Celt was staring at him. Would she be the one opening herself to him this night? He touched his tongue to his lips and gave her a bold, penetrating gaze in return. She smiled. The tip of her own tongue, red and velvety as a little rosebud, shone between her parted lips. He felt himself rise. Ay. She was the one.

With that settled, he put the thought of women aside. He must concentrate more fully on Sigurd this eve, except that he knew not what else to say to convince the fat devil to join himself and Maelmorda. Thus far, his every offer had been rejected—gold, cattle, slaves, jewelry. Sigurd was balky as a mule, and no wonder. The bastard already had everything.

Thinking of his mother waiting for him back in Dublin twisted Sitric's gut into a knot. Gormlaith had bade him offer the king anything to gain his support. Anything. The most important thing in her life now was the humiliation and downfall of Brian Boru. But damnation, what else could he offer Sigurd Hlovidsson? Sitric stared resentfully at his host's well-nourished body and at his great hall which overflowed with every comfort, a luxurious shelter against the fury howling without.

Great logs flamed on the hearth, and there was wine, mead, and a delectable, never-ending supply of roast swine and mutton with a multitude of thralls to serve it. And the Orkney king had ships aplenty and sails aplenty and men aplenty. There was nothing more the smug devil needed. But wait, wait—could something be made of the fact that both of them had Irish mothers and Dane-king fathers? Both were half-breeds. Surely that counted for some bond between them.

Sitric was stewing over this when there came the sound of men's voices from without. The doors were flung open, and the hounds leapt forward baying. The wall torches blew and flickered as the gatekeeper burst in, bringing with him the storm-scream and a biting blast of snow and ice. He was followed by a towering figure clad in furs and skins and flanked by two berserks. The great hall fell silent as all gaped at the sight.

"Sire, 'tis Wulf Thorsson of Husaby," the herald cried. "He has come through the storm!"

Sigurd, deep in drink, rose unsteadily to his feet. He scowled. "Thorsson of Husaby? Through this gale? I can scarce believe it!"

"Believe it, old friend!" Wulf called, laughing. He removed his snow-caked bearskin and flung it to a serving-wench. "Can we shelter here this night or must we move on to the Shetlands?"

"By the gods," Sigurd shouted. "By the holy bones and blood of Odin, 'tis you, Thorwulf! Welcome!"

Sitric of Dublin stared at the newcomer and at his long, gleaming sword with the jeweled hilt which he now hung on the wall as was the custom. Both were fearsome sights. Sitric had heard of the Wolf of Husaby, and of his battle-feats against the Celts, but never had he seen the man. As he looked on, the Norseman strode toward the king, his arms outstretched to embrace him. He was brawny, taller than Sigurd by far, and his body, now clad only in supple leather leggings and tunic, was hard and muscular. More fit than his own, thought Sitric glumly. And the fellow was handsome, judging by the blushes and dewy eyes of the women.

Sitric looked with little enthusiasm on the stranger's rugged, strong-boned face, blue eyes, and Grecian-straight nose. So? What was so unusual? He himself had blue eyes, an aristocratic nose, and a lustrous blond beard which had earned him the name Silkbeard. As for these silly wenches who had trembled when he himself first looked upon them, damn their fickle bones. He rose, courtesy overcoming ire, as Sigurd brought the chieftain to him to be presented.

"Sitric Olavsson—Wulf Thorsson." The two nodded, each taking a silent measure of the other.

Sitric watched as Thorsson and his dark-haired comrade were seated at the high-board, and his great crew of Norsemen placed on wall benches farther down the hall. As the wenches flew to fetch horns and more mead and food for all, the Orkney king questioned Wulf eagerly, but Sitric's own thoughts were centered on new possibilities.

This Thorsson was a noble, a warrior of the first rank who held strongholds on Maun, the Hebrides, and the Shetlands, and who commanded great loyalty back in Norway. And he spoke the Celt tongue. It would therefore behoove him, Sitric, to enlist the fellow's aid in the conquest of Boru rather than resent his effortless conquest of the ladies present. And if Thorsson agreed, it might even follow that the balky Sigurd would follow suit and rally to the cause.

Sitric sat straighter. He had heard, too, that this Norseman was well-liked. If it were so, perhaps Wulf could win over these accursed aloof Greenlanders and Icelanders who sat with stony faces guzzling Sigurd's mead. By the gods, Sitric would make Thorsson a captain for certain if he accomplished such a miracle. He would then loose him on Brodir and Ospak of Maun, two Norse chieftains who took special delight in ignoring him. Sitric's thoughts churned as slowly he sipped his mead and studied the tall chieftain with hooded eyes. He would wait until Thorsson had eaten and was pliable before broaching the subject of alliance.

Maun, 2 November 1013, Midday

Brianna hugged herself and did a merry dance about her bedchamber. Boru was coming! She was going to see Boru again for the first time in thirteen years. She could scarce believe it—thirteen years! Would he look and act the same, she wondered, or would everything be different? What a foolish question, for everything was different. She was not a little girl any more, and this was not Kincora but her father's stronghold on Maun. As her thoughts drifted back to Boru's palace in Ireland, a tapping on the door pulled her abruptly into the present.

"You summoned me, lass?"

"Ay, Maeve." The young mistress of Carnane flew to the old woman and drew her into her bedchamber. Maeve was her friend, and more a mother than a serving-woman. "Will you arrange my hair for me, please?"

Maeve gave a cackle. "You, who won't let me near you with a comb?"

" 'Tis just that I hate to be fussed over—but this be different. I want to look nice, and I'm not as clever as you. Will you do it, please?"

Seeing that her mistress's beautiful green eyes were pleading, Maeve gave her a hug. Never could she deny Brianna Kinrade anything, not since that long-ago day when Maeve had been brought to Carnane to serve her, a wee motherless thing of ten.

"Ay, lass, of course I'll do it. Sit yourself and tell me how you want it."

"Coiled atop my head somehow or other, and mayhap some gold bands to bind it."

As Maeve tugged the comb through the snarls in her thick mass of dark-red hair, Brianna had thoughts for none but Brian Boru. He was her father's oldest and dearest friend and the man for whom she had been named. Lachlan Kinrade had first met the Dalcassian prince at school, at Clonmacnoise, when both were young lads. In later years, they had fought the Vikings

27

side by side in Ireland and Maun. Boru had been king of Munster when Brianna was sent to him for fostering, and now, now he was the Ard Ri, king of kings and emperor of all the Irish. And she was no longer a child . . .

Suddenly Maeve was scolding. "Stop your squirming, girl, else your head will look like a curlew's nest!"

"I'm sorry . . ."

It was just that she was so excited. She wanted to look years and years older than her twenty-three winters. She wanted to appear sophisticated and regal; as different as possible from those days when she had sat on Boru's knee and recited her lessons for him. Then he had been widowed, and the palace at Kincora overflowed with his many children and his foster children. Since then, she heard he had married a beautiful Irish princess, but it was said he was divorced now. A man alone. But what foolish idea was this? These past several years she had thought of Boru hardly at all, and she was certainly not about to think of him as a husband now. Besides, never would she wed . . .

As Maeve began twisting her hair into an auburn rope and arranging it in intricate coils about her head, Brianna was back at Kincora. In her mind's eye, it was a golden haze of perfection: lamps and candles flickering day and night; gold and silver and bronzeware winking from dark corners and ledges; tantalizing aromas wisping from the kitchen-house; the fragrance of warm perfumed baths; the caress of fine linen and satins and rich velvets against her skin; the glitter of the Shannon on a blue summer's day; playing with her friends in gardens filled with bright flowers and the drowsy humming of bees. Boru himself . . .

Brianna's eyes glowed as she recalled the dear copper-haired giant of her childhood. Her memories of him were the most golden of all: tall, strong, handsome as a god to her little-girl eyes; a warrior-king who took the time to be a father to her. She had not learned until later that her own father had been struggling at the time with her mother's last desperate illness. All told, Brianna had lived happily at Kincora for five years before returning to Maun, her island homeland in the Irish Sea. By then, she had fallen in love with the Munster king. Oh, ay, ten winters old and wildly in love. Her lips curved, remembering her parting command to Boru that he wait for her to grow up, for she meant to marry him! What an impossible child she had been.

"Who is't that comes tonight?" Maeve asked. "Never have I seen such bustle nor seen your cheeks so pink."

"Brian Boru is paying us a visit."

The serving-woman's wrinkled hands grew still. "The Ard Ri?"

Brianna smiled. "Himself."

"Holy Mary. I mind as if 'twas yesterday that day he brought you home to Carnane, him so tall and beautiful and every inch a king." She sighed and her hands grew busy again. "Now

29

there was a fine brute of a man . . ."

Brianna chuckled. "Ay, he was that."

But her amusement was mixed with a sharp resentment against her father. If she had not overheard Lachlan Kinrade and his kinsmen talking in the council chamber moments ago, she would never have known that Boru was coming. She knew of the great gathering of the chieftains of Maun this eve, ay. Being mistress of her father's manor, it was she who had chosen the food to be served and the quantities necessary. But why had he not told her the emperor was coming? Was there some secret war brewing against the Vikings?

There in her bedchamber with the November sun brightening the faded wall hangings and a fire dancing on the hearth, Brianna felt the cold creep through her. Her body tightened and a heaviness invaded her stomach. Nay! She straightened her shoulders and by sheer will forced the hated sensations and the images causing them to leave. She was all right. She had been all right for a long time now . . .

"What gown will you be wanting for the feasting, lass? The green one from Dublin is grand with your hair and eyes, but then the hall is so cold, you'll be bundled in your cloak anyhow."

"The burgundy satin will do." It was queenly. It was also warm and the sleeves long.

"And the jewelry?"

"The amethyst brooch." Boru had sent it to her as a gift for her sixteenth birthday.

Brianna stirred in her chair. Maeve did not know that Brianna needed more than a fine gown and coiffure to attend the feast. She needed for her father to see reason. He had forbidden her to attend. He had declared it was not for womenfolk, and that she could see the Ard Ri on the morrow if see him she must. But Boru never tarried long in one spot. He would be gone before the day dawned. Brianna twisted her slender fingers in her lap, her eyes distant. She would see him, there was no doubt of that. She would attend the feast and sit by his side in the seat of honor, she had not a doubt of it. It was just a matter of how to foil her father and accomplish the feat. It was then that an idea began to blossom . . .

"Can you not hurry, Maeve?"

" 'Tis done, lady"—Maeve gave her mistress's sleek hair a final pat—"and 'tis a beautiful thing you be with your white swan neck and your fine cheekbones showing. The emperor will be surprised at how you've changed." She moved to the great wooden chest that stood against a wall and removed the burgundy gown. "Will you be dressing now?"

"Not yet." Brianna rose and walked about the chamber, a plan a-building in her head. It would work. She knew it would, and it would amuse Boru. She remembered how deep his laughter had been and how easily she used to coax it from his lips. "Maeve . . ."

"Ay, love, what is't?"

"Forgive me, but—methinks 'tis braids I want after all."

Maeve stared. She put her hands on her bony hips. "Braids? 'Tis not to be believed! Braids, with you looking like a queen this way? Nay, lass, I'll not do it."

Brianna tapped her foot and crossed her arms. She was the daughter of a high chieftain of Maun and not accustomed to having her orders questioned. Maeve was her dear friend, ay, but she was also her body-servant.

"It saddens me to inconvenience you," she said pleasantly, "but I will have braids."

Marking that small tapping foot, Maeve gave her young mistress a look of outrage. Wordlessly she uncoiled Brianna's hair and combed it out into a lustrous flaming cape that hung to her waist. She parted it down the middle, made two thick ropes, and tied the ends briskly with cords of silk. As she began to add the customary golden balls for decoration, Brianna rose.

"Nay, I'll not be needing those."

Maeve sniffed. " 'Tis just as well, my lady. I trow none will be looking at you anyway with you plain as a pikestaff."

Brianna's lips twitched. Poor Maeve. It was a mean thing to have done, but it was necessary. She would hear why on the morrow.

"Will you need me for dressing?" Maeve asked stiffly.

"Nay, run along—and Maeve, I do thank you."

Chapter Two

Wulf was bone-weary. He had eaten and drunk his fill, and now he wanted only to stretch out on a bench and sleep. He had not slept for three days. In addition, his leg was throbbing. No more could it take the cold and the damp for days on end, not since he had received the long-ago wound which had nearly cost him his life. He drew a deep breath and drained his horn, his eyes inadvertently meeting those of a woman at the next board. He saw instantly that he could have her for the asking. Here on Sigurd's manor, such a thing was expected. Instead, he looked away. It wasn't that he did not hunger for an occasional lady to warm his bed, but not

33

tonight—although she was a lovely thing.

He sat quietly, mead seeping into his aching body. The music of the harpers and the rise and fall of voices washed over him like ripples on a shore, and smoke from the wall torches and hearth fire stung his sleepy eyes. Through his torpor, he marked that the Dublin king stared at him. The fellow had been silent throughout the meal, and just as well. Wulf had no desire for speech with a man who had traded his freedom and respect for a crown from the enemy. Sitric's allegiance had been to Brian Boru these many years now.

"Will you be continuing on to Norway?" Sitric Olavsson asked.

"Ay, after a stop at my stronghold in the Shetlands," Wulf answered brusquely. "We crave to be home by Yuletide."

Sitric drained his horn, his eyes never leaving the newcomer. Marking the long, pale scar that stretched from his right temple to his jawline, he said, "Long have I heard of your bravery and of your sword, the Shining Death, Thorsson of Husaby."

Wulf said nothing. He saw clearly, drunk and sleepy though he was, that this half-breed king of Dublin was a flatterer who wanted something of him. He made a quick guess. Sitric was embroiled in some local battle and craved Wulf's right arm, his sword, his men, and his vessel.

"What know you of Brian Boru?" Sitric asked low, pouring more mead for them both.

Brian Boru? Wulf's eyes narrowed. He knew what every Norseman knew about Brian-the-Hundred-Killer: The devil was the deadliest foe the Vikings had in Ireland and Maun. It was during a surprise attack by Boru's troops on Maun that he had received what was nearly his death-wound. Many of his men, good warriors and good friends, had gone to Valhalla that day. Ay, long and long Wulf had had a score to settle with Brian Boru. Now his curiosity stirred.

"Why ask you this, Olavsson?"

"Wouldst like to see Dublin in Viking hands once more? Mayhap all of Ireland in Viking hands?"

There was nothing he would like better, but Wulf masked his interest. His eyes remained sleepy and hooded. " 'Tis a strange thing, this, coming from you, Silkbeard. Methought you were content to be bound to the Hundred-Killer and pay tribute to him forever."

The contempt in the Norseman's blue eyes made Sitric's face burn. "Never was I content. I agreed to Boru's terms only so we would not lose Dublin to trade." It was not completely true, but this devil need not know it. "Now I deem his damned tribute and my self-respect too great a price to pay. I am going to overthrow him."

Wulf nearly laughed. "You and what others? Who stands with you?" He kept his voice low, for this talk seemed between himself and Sitric. Sigurd, sitting directly opposite him in the highseat, was in drunken dalliance with the woman next him. Leif, on Wulf's left, had dozed off.

"My uncle, Maelmorda of Leinster, stands with me and my Dublin Danes."

Wulf frowned. "None other?"

"Never fear, there are others. I trow I will have Sigurd's support before I leave here on the morrow." He hoped to Odin it was so, for where Sigurd went, his chieftains followed: men from every isle on the Scottish main. If only he could find the key to unlock the Orkney king's vast treasure trove of warriors. "Also we have sent the war arrow to Maun and Iceland and all Scandinavia. 'Twould do us honor, Thorsson, if you joined forces with us and brought in others."

Wulf studied Sitric's petulant, too-pretty face and his pale silver-blond hair and beard. It was an odd thing, Sitric's sudden urge for overthrow, when these many years he had been at the end of Boru's silken leash.

"I would know more," Wulf said. "After all this time, why do you talk war?"

Into Sitric's thoughts came Gormlaith's beautiful face twisted in fury. Never had he seen her so livid. And never would he admit to any that it was her wrath which was fueling the uprising against the emperor. It was she who had goaded Maelmorda into a frenzy of rage and self-pity; she who had goaded himself to join him.

"Ever since Boru set himself up as Ard Ri,"

Sitric muttered, "he has grown more and more demanding. Every king in every tuath is pledged to give him seven hundred men in battle."

"An emperor needs fighting men," Wulf said easily, "and Brian Boru has more than set himself up as Ard Ri. He has been the Ard Ri these many years now. 'Tis said the Stone of Fal screamed when he touched it—the sign of the true king of kings."

Sitric snorted. " 'Tis naught but a wild Celt tale, that. Boru usurped the throne—and his damned thirst for tribute involves more than men. Maelmorda is forced yearly to hand over thousands of domestic animals and bolts of linen and silver chains. Kincora is awash in luxuries whilst the rest of us go without." That, too, was not true. He knew well that Boru used the tribute of all to ease the lives of those who had little. But then what matter? "I myself give the same as Maelmorda in addition to a hundred and fifty barrels of the finest red wine and . . ."

Wulf listened in quiet courtesy to the trials suffered by the king of Dublin. Sitric complained on and on, with never a word of the shame of the once-proud Norse Kingdom of Dublin now Celt-ruled. Wulf was amazed. It was but their own selves that Sitric and Maelmorda cared about. They were two peas in a pod. But then it mattered little to him why they fought Boru. The important thing was that they fight him, and that the devil fall.

His thoughts drifted to himself, to how these

past two years he had grown impatient with maintaining his strongholds. Having long since tired of raiding, he had considered encouraging his men to follow the banner of another, but never had he done so. Had some inner part of him known that this day would come, this uprising against Boru?

He said to Sitric quietly: "I myself would join you in your fight, Olavsson. As for my men, I will speak with them now." He got to his feet and shook Leif by the shoulder. "Wake up, man, we have things to discuss with the others."

Sigurd of the Orkneys missed none of this. When Wulf and his captain departed, he ceased fondling the woman by his side and raised his horn to Sitric.

"Your trip has not been in vain, Silkbeard. They will fight, and in Thorsson you will have a brave and staunch ally. Many will rally to his banner when they hear he supports you."

" 'Twould gladden me even more were you and your followers to join us," Sitric answered. "Is there naught that will tempt you? I will give you anything you ask. Anything."

Sigurd smiled. "Why didst not say so in the beginning instead of jawing about cattle and thralls and such?"

Sitric stared at him. "What—would you have then?"

The Orkney king did not answer immediately. Sitric was made to wait while he consumed all of the food on his trencher, and washed it down with mead. Sitric began to sweat, and a sinking feeling filled his belly.

"I would have your throne," Sigurd answered finally, placidly. "The Kingdom of Dublin. Also, I require the hand of your mother in marriage. It has reached my ears that she be the fairest woman in Ireland."

"My mother!" Sitric gave a scornful laugh, but he was hammer-struck. What would Gormlaith do if he gave her to yet another king when she had vowed she would never marry again? "Man, Gormlaith is an old woman now! Why in the name of all the gods would you want her when you have all these fair wenches?"

The bastard! Damn his lustful bones. Sitric would have slain him where he sat, except it would have assured his own swift demise. He stared as the Orkney king wiped his mouth on his sleeve.

" 'Tis said the princess Gormlaith has the body and the eyes and the hair of a goddess," Sigurd replied. " 'Tis said also she has a hunger which cannot be quenched."

Sitric gave a snort and took another swallow from his horn. "I trow she be fair enough, ay, but as for the other, know you—such hunger has its disadvantages."

"Yet three kings craved and possessed her—"

"All of whom put her aside," Sitric snapped. He cared for his mother after a fashion, but had he been any one of her husbands, he would have put her in a convent long ago, not merely put her aside. "Gormlaith is a woman who must have her own way. All is fine as long as she is not crossed."

Sigurd's eyes glittered. "Such things matter naught to me. I will have her. I will have her and your crown in exchange for my help in putting down Boru. Decide you, Dubliner. If your answer be ay, this will be a secret thing betwixt us until this battle be won."

As Wulf Thorsson and his comrade threaded their way back to the high-board through the crowded hall, Sitric agonized. The Wolf of Husaby had as many followers in his own land as did Sigurd Hlovidsson in this part of the world. If Thorsson said ay, why then should he yield himself to Sigurd's greed? But then how could he not? It would take every man he could garner to overcome Boru's ever-growing strength—and this past year he had had sparse success in garnering any. But to give up his own kingdom? Sitric's stomach churned so violently he thought he would lose its contents. Gormlaith he could live without—it would be a blessing, in fact—but not his crown. He sucked in a deep breath. The trolls take this Orkney bastard.

Returning to the high-board, Wulf marked that Sitric looked wretched. It could mean one of two things: The Orkney king had turned him down, or had but driven a hard bargain. Wulf hoped it was the latter, for Sigurd was powerful. He would be needed if the battle were as great as this one promised to be. After he and Leif seated themselves, Wulf said to Sitric:

"My men and I have talked, Silkbeard, and have reached an accord. You have our help."

Sitric suspected that Thorsson, too, would suck him dry. He asked gruffly, "I trow you have great demands?"

Wulf laughed. "I have but one demand. Boru must die." He turned to Sigurd. "What say you, old friend, are you with us in this?"

Sigurd shrugged. "We have talked, Sitric and I, and now 'tis his decision. What say you, Dubliner? Am I with you?"

Until that moment, Sitric had been drowning in despair. If he agreed to Sigurd's outrageous demands, Gormlaith would flay him alive, and it would matter little if his crown were lost. But with Thorsson now on his side, he felt stronger and clearer in the head. In an eyeblink, he saw that neither need happen. He could strike hands in agreement with Sigurd, ay, but his mother would surely slay this fat bastard before she would let him lay one greedy finger on her. And before that might happen, he himself would make sure that Sigurd died in battle before he could claim the Dublin throne. Ay, it would all work out . . .

"What say you, Dubliner?" Sigurd asked again. "I am waiting."

Sitric, his heart filled with treachery, dared not look the other in the eye but gazed down into his horn. "You are with us, man. Of course you are with us."

All three struck hands then, sealing the bargain.

* * *

It was the middle of the night, and all was quiet within the stronghold of the Orkney king although it still stormed wildly without. In the great hall, the logs in the hearth had burned down to embers, and shadows flickered over the quiet forms of Wulf Thorsson and Sitric Olavsson as they lay with their men on wall benches and the straw-covered floor. They slept the sleep of the dead, for all had drunk overmuch.

Of a sudden, Wulf was dragged up from his deep dreaming by a hissing noise. Forcing open his eyes, he saw a sight he could scarce believe: swords, spears, and battle-axes leaping from the walls on which they were hung, and as if held by invisible hands, slashing at unseen foes over his head. He shuddered and sent a swift prayer to Odin as the air was filled with the terrible ringing clamor of metal striking metal. It seemed forever that the terror went on. And then as swiftly as it had come, it was gone, and Wulf, drenched in a cold sweat, was left to shake and to wonder what it had been about, or if it had been but a dream.

Likely it was a dream, he brooded, for his head spun still and his ears rang from too much drink, just as they had when he had first lain down. Or had it been a doom-portent such as they told about in sagas? . . . Another chill swept him in his fur sleeping bag, for whichever, dream or portent, such a strange thing was not to the good. Shivering still, he hunched down deeper into his bag and shut his eyes, but it was a long time before he slept.

He did not know then that Sitric Silkbeard and Leif Karlsson had earlier awakened to the same sight. Certain that it was but the result of too much revelry, they had closed their eyes and gone immediately back to sleep.

Maun, 2 November, Eventide

As Brianna moved about the bustling kitchen-house, she was relieved to see that there was food aplenty: crisped roast lambs, braces of fowl awaiting their turn to be served, and fresh-baked bread stacked high. The cooks and serving-folk were all so busy that none paid her a bit of attention or wondered at the plain blue linen kyrtil and apron she wore. So much the better, for her plan called for her to dally there until the gathered chieftains were well along with their meal and filled with drink. She would then slip into the great hall and greet Boru before her father could stop her. And Boru would never allow her to be sent away.

When she judged it time to put her plan into action, Brianna trod the covered corridor to the great hall and cracked open the heavy door. The cavernous room, usually cold and dark, now was aglow with light from wall torches and two central fire pits. Festive candles lit the boards at which the fur-clad chieftains sat. But she heard no shouts nor laughter nor harpers playing, only the deep drone of men's voices. Peering through the haze of blue smoke, she soon saw what she sought, the silken banner suspended above the seat of honor at the far end of the room. Three black lions on a field of scarlet. The banner of Brian Boru. She moved forward; there could be no turning back now. She stopped a maid carrying a small keg.

"I will take that, Niam." The girl stared, seeing it was the mistress herself, dressed in the lowly garb of a serving-wench. " 'Tis all right," Brianna said easily. " 'Tis but a small prank I am playing on my father."

At that, Niam giggled. "Ay, mistress, to be sure."

Brianna worked her way between the benches, carefully stepping around her father's great wolfhounds which were eagerly searching out bones. None of the chieftains looked at her, for all knew the rules at Carnane: The serving-wenches were inviolable. The maids themselves, flying between the boards to keep the men filled with food and drink, were too busy to look at her.

As Brianna approached the seat beneath the emperor's banner and saw the tall warrior sitting there, her heart began to race. He looked much the same, except that his coppery hair and thick beard held a glitter of frost now, and the grooves between his gray eyes and bracketing his lips were deeper. But his skin was dark and taut and young-looking and his shoulders were as broad and hard as ever. He still looked like a god. She took a breath and spoke:

"I have brought you a fresh keg, sire."

The Ard Ri looked up at the maid standing by his side. She was tall and slim and her coarse garb did not hide the exquisite shapeliness of her body. She was a beauty: skin like the richest cream, eyes like sunshine on the green Irish Sea, hair like flame, a face like one of God's angels. Brian gazed on her, intrigued, and when a familiar smile lifted her rosy lips, a memory stirred. He frowned.

"Do I know you, lass?"

"Ay, Boru."

The frown became a scowl. Who was this impudent wench who dared call him by name? Then Brian's deep laughter soared to the rafters. He leapt to his feet.

"Brianna!"

"Greetings, Boru."

He crushed her against his chest in a great hug, kissed her forehead, and then held her at arm's length, studying her. "Has it been so long then? By the saints, you be a woman . . ." He gave her another resounding kiss on the cheek and then directed a fierce scowl at Lachlan Kinrade. "What means it, old friend, that my foster daughter be a serving-wench on your manor?"

The high chieftain of Maun looked on his daughter with amazed eyes as all at the highboard began to laugh. He shook his head and spoke to Brianna sternly:

"Did I not tell you, girl, that this affair was for menfolk only?"

45

Brian himself was laughing still. "I mind the lass always was clever at getting her own way." He pointed to the seat of honor. "Sit you here by my side, Brianna. You, girl"—he beckoned to a serving-wench—"fetch a horn and trencher for your mistress." To Lachlan Kinrade, he said, "I would speak with Brianna for a moment."

As the wench hurried off, Brianna settled herself in the ornately carved throne alongside her foster father. For a brief happy time, she answered his questions, wondering all the while about the Irish princess he had wed. It was rumored that she was very beautiful, yet he had set her aside. Whose fault was it? she wondered, deciding instantly it was the woman's. Boru might be the fiercest of warriors, but he was ever gentle and yielding with women and children. She smiled, thinking of her own childish passions and tantrums at Kincora, yet never once had he laid a hand on her in anger or punishment.

With effort, she tore herself away from her memories and came back to Carnane where the most powerful chieftains in the land sat at her father's high-board and throughout the great hall. She marked that three of her uncles were there and her cousin Fin. She met his brown eyes and saw the laughing approval in them.

"As I was saying when I was interrupted," Lachlan Kinrade said, raising his voice, "all of the chieftains of Maun are here, Brian, and this night they will give you their allegiance."

Brianna's wide gaze went from her father to

Boru. "What is't?" she blurted. "Why wouldst need their allegiance?"

"Damn me, girl," Lachlan rebuked her, "had I wanted you to know, you would know."

Seeing the red staining her white cheeks, Brian said, " 'Tis all right, Kinrade. I see no harm in the maid's being here and knowing what we are about." He took Brianna's hand. " 'Tis war, lass."

Brianna's breath caught, seeing how grave were his eyes. She knew little of what went on in Ireland; only that since Boru had become emperor, there was unprecedented peace among tribes that had always warred. She whispered: "How came this to be?"

Brian stroked her silky cheek. " 'Tis not for you to worry on, child. 'Tis but a family matter gone agley. My former stepson and brother-in-law would run Ireland differently and have stirred up a bit of trouble."

Brianna was indignant. "How dare they! 'Tis said even the Vikings think you be a good ruler!"

Lachlan Kinrade said gruffly: "Brianna, we have not the time for this. Hush you now, girl."

Brianna obeyed. She had been warmed by food and drink and Boru's shining presence, but now she was chilled. It had been long and long since their part of Maun was attacked by Vikings. Her father had achieved much power in recent years and was held in great fear and respect by them. But other parts of the isle were Viking-harried still and forced to pay tribute.

And now the talk at the board was of Sitric, the Viking king of Dublin, sending out the war arrow, and of Boru planning a siege of the city. It was war. She yearned to help. She would do anything for Boru, but then never would she be allowed.

"Know you, Brian," Lachlan was saying, "that Sitric asked Ospak and Brodir of Maun to rally to him?"

"I knew he would, but I have heard naught of the outcome. My spy in Sitric's court, God rest his soul, was discovered and slain just this past month. I have as yet been unable to slip in another."

"Brodir will have a high price," Lachlan replied, "and Sitric must woo him. Ospak was not there when the war arrow came, but my spies say he will spit in Sitric's beard for an answer. 'Tis said he calls you the lesser of the two evils."

Brian laughed. "The man is right."

Brianna's interest was piqued, for these were names she knew. Ospak and Brodir were brothers, Viking chieftains who maintained strongholds on Maun and drew tribute. She recalled that one of them, she knew not which, had long ago forsaken his Norse gods and come to Carnane to be prime-signed by a priest. It was said he had grown so holy that he was a deacon in some Christian church, while the other wallowed in sin and was a notorious womanchaser. Which was it who favored Boru? she wondered. Surely the deacon . . .

"Tell this Ospak I will welcome him gladly," said Brian.

"He is told," Lachlan answered glumly. "Twice I have gone to him, but he will do naught to help you."

"Mayhap if I visited the fellow myself, except there be no time left me this trip. I will come again. 'Tis essential I garner every man I can. How many ships has he?"

"Ten."

Brian's eyes gleamed. "I will have them. I will return."

Lachlan shook his head. "It doubts me he would betray his own people and join us."

"We will find out," Brian answered gruffly. " 'Tis uncertain when I can attend to this, but 'twill be done." He rose and gazed down on Brianna. "Now 'tis as your father has told you, lass. The rest of this eve be for menfolk. I must greet and thank each of these chieftains."

Brianna, too, rose. She gave him a smile. "I—just wanted to see you again, just for a bit."

Brian tugged one of her braids, much as he had when she was small. " 'Tis glad I am that you came, child. 'Twould seem"—his voice softened—"you will always be ten winters to this old man."

"You are not old!" Brianna cried. Standing on tiptoe, she threw her arms around his neck and kissed his cheek. "You are just as I remember." Her eyes stung, and soon the tears would come. Never had he seen her weep, nor would he now. "Goodbye, Boru . . ."

As she climbed the narrow steps to her chamber and prepared herself for the night, his dear face floated before her. She lay awake in the candlelight, seeing him in every shifting shadow and thinking, thinking. . . . That Viking chieftain who had given up his pagan gods—it was Ospak, she knew it was. And such a Christian man would rally to the goodness of Brian Boru if he but knew of it. And who better to tell him about the emperor than one who had lived in his household when he was king of Munster? Why, she even spoke the Norse tongue. Boru had insisted on it. For three years the royal tutors at Kincora had drilled it into her.

As her idea grew, Brianna's heart thundered. It was perfect. She had yearned for some way to help Boru and here it was! She would go to Ospak. But should she tell Fin and have him along? She shook her head. She must think on it, and not be hasty. But that she herself would go was a certainty. Just as soon as she worked out the details, she would go to Valaberg and she would gain Ospak's allegiance and his ten ships for Boru. It was as simple as that.

Chapter Three

Brianna did not sleep well that night. Her head spun with all the things in it, and when morning finally arrived, she had a hundred questions for Fin. After breakfast, she found him in the dimness of the horse barn mending a bridle.

Hearing her approach, Fin looked up and grinned. "Ah, 'tis Lachlan's new serving-wench, I see."

Brianna's eyes sparked. "After last eve, we are unfriends, you and I, Finian Kinrade. You might have told me Boru was coming."

"Now, lass, I couldn't go against your father's orders." He chuckled then. " 'Twas priceless, the look on Boru's face when he finally recognized you—and Lachlan's mouth falling open.

'Twas exactly what I would have expected from such a one as you, Annie."

Brianna put her hands on her hips. "And what might that mean, pray?"

"Why, 'tis a compliment for your cleverness, darlin'."

Fin put his attention back on the bridle, musing that the maid was without an equal at getting those things she set her heart on. Like the time not too many years ago when she had fair pestered the life out of him until he taught her knife and sword-play and archery. Never had he discovered why she craved such unmaidenly skills.

"Fin—"

"Ay?"

Brianna sank into a straw heap and watched as her cousin hung up the new-mended bridle and took down a worn halter.

"What is happening in Ireland? Methought all were content with Boru's rule."

"Not all. There are those who will always be unfriendly toward him."

"Unfriendly? 'Tis more than unfriendly to be sending out the war arrow! Who be this damned Sitric that he should do such a thing?"

Fin shook his dark head. " 'Tis not for you to worry on."

"But it is! Tell me. What meant Boru, saying 'twas a family matter?"

" 'Tis too complicated to go into."

"I would know," Brianna insisted. "He is as dear to me as my own father."

Fin sighed, hung up the halter, and sat in the straw beside her. He would have no peace and get no work done until he did her bidding.

"Rumor is 'twas a family spat at Kincora that started the whole trouble. Brian's brother-in-law, Maelmorda, the king of Leinster, was insulted by—"

Brianna frowned. "Maelmorda? Be he brother to the beautiful Irish princess Boru wed?"

"Ay. Gormlaith be her name, and he has since put her aside. But to the point, Maelmorda received this so-great insult from—"

"What insult? 'Twould have to be huge to start a war!"

"By the saints, woman, I know naught of what 'twas about. Just let me tell the damned tale so we both can get back to our work. Maelmorda was insulted by Brian's son, Murrough, and he grew so wroth, he journeyed to Dublin and made his moan to Sitric. Sitric, too, got into a stew over it."

Murrough? Brianna's head was awhirl. She knew Murrough—but first things first. "Why would Maelmorda, an Irish king, go to a Viking to complain?" she asked.

"Because Sitric is his nephew. Sitric be Gormlaith's son by her first husband."

Brianna climbed to her feet and angrily shook the straw from her skirts. "You are telling me those two started a war because of some insult from Murrough?"

" 'Tis said it runs far deeper than that. The insult was but the final blow."

Brianna tapped her foot. "I can scarce believe this. I knew Murrough when I lived at Kincora; he flung insults at folk all the time, even Boru. 'Twas but his high-handed way." She was so upset that she commenced to pace through the straw. "This Maelmorda is Irish—why would he betray Boru?"

Fin laughed. "The king of Leinster is not known for his honor and loyalty. Always has he resented Brian's power and popularity, and 'twas an easy thing to stir up his men."

Brianna seethed at the unfairness of it. Suddenly it seemed more important than ever for the Viking chieftain Ospak to turn from his own people and rally to Boru. It would be a fitting repayment for Maelmorda's treachery. But could she sway Ospak, she wondered, or would she receive the same refusal as her father? But she must not allow herself to think of defeat.

"When will the war come to a head, think you?" she asked.

"Not 'til spring, for this promises to be a hard winter."

Studying her kinsman's face, Brianna saw his concern. And how much more he would worry if she confessed her plans to go to Ospak. She dared not. Yet the thought of going alone to a Viking stronghold made her heart tremble. Once more she experienced the chilling memory that had come when Maeve was dressing her hair— her rape by a Viking. Once more she faced it squarely, reminding herself as she always did when it gripped her, that it had happened long ago. She had been but a maid of fourteen then, and now she was tall and strong and could better defend herself. Fin himself had taught her how to protect herself with various weapons.

"Brianna, what is't?" Fin rose and turned her to face him. "You be white as a ghost."

She could not tell him. Her shame had been so great that she had never told any. It would be her secret until the day she died.

" 'Tis just that I fear for Boru," she murmured, "and for all of you."

Fin nodded. "I understand. So do I fear for Maun. Soon all of Ireland will be besieged by howling, frothing berserks waving their damned battle-axes, and methinks they will spill over here. God willing, we will have defenders enough to turn them back in both lands."

Berserks. Brianna had heard of those fiercest of the Vikings who went into battle only after they had reached a frenzy. Ospak would have such warriors to protect himself, all chieftains did. Yet he dared not let them harm her; she was a Kinrade. But he was a Viking, and though he might now be holier than Patrick himself, raping and sacking was in his blood. For certain, she must take Fin. To go alone without telling any would be the worst sort of stupidity. She swallowed, twisted a strand of hair about one finger, and then declared:

"Fin, I am going to Valaberg soon t-to talk with Ospak." She watched a dark flush spread over his face. His brown eyes burned under suddenly scowling brows.

Fin said quietly, "What mean you, you go to talk with Ospak?"

Brianna stood straighter. "Boru craves his men and his ten ships, and I trow I can get them for him."

"Woman, what nonsense is this?"

"Ospak be a holy man," she answered. "He has taken our God for his own and is even a deacon. Methinks I can make such a man understand that Boru is better than any other for Ireland." Her resentment flared as Fin hooted. "What is so amusing, Finian Kinrade? My father himself has spoken of this man's holiness."

"Ospak holy? Ospak? Damn me, Annie, you have got it all twisted. 'Tis Brodir who was the deacon, and that was long ago. He has since returned to his pagan gods and is a worse bastard than before. As for Ospak, he would take you on the spot."

"Nay, he will not!" Brianna cried, embarrassed and shocked. More than that, she was hugely disappointed. "This changes things, ay, but 'twill not stop me. It but means I must approach the man differently. I will make it clear that I be Kinrade's daughter there on his behalf. Ospak will not dare harm me." When Fin groaned, she added hurriedly, "We all know there is peace in these parts because no Viking dares stir the wrath of my father and his tribe."

Fin said sharply, " 'Tis true also that we Celts are careful to incur no Viking wrath. 'Tis an uneasy peace betwixt us, and what you propose holds danger. There could be misunderstanding."

"Or there could be understanding and agreement. Oh, Fin, you heard Lachlan—Ospak prefers Boru to Sitric!"

"Yet will not lift a finger to help him."

"Mayhap I could coax him . . ."

Fin stared as her lips parted in a soft smile and she fluttered her long lashes at him. By holy St. Lonan, might such a ploy work? Perhaps the devil would be so moved by her beauty, as was every man he knew, that he would yield to her blandishments. God knows, Boru could use all the help he could get against the Viking horde that was forthcoming.

He asked gruffly, "You would put yourself in such danger?"

"For Boru, I would."

"You would not be frighted?"

"Not if you were there," she lied. "And my father's name will protect us."

"Lachlan will not allow it, I tell you that right now."

Brianna laughed, her excitement rising. "But you will not tell him, for you think, as do I, that this has possibilities. I see it on your face, kinsman."

Fin scowled down at her. "I must think on it."

"Oh, ay, think on it, but we are going to do it. And if you do not, I will go no matter. Nothing you nor my father can say or do will stop me. I will tell Maeve I go to visit our cousin in Shenn Valley sometime soon. With Sinead nearing the end of her confinement, 'tis possible I will stay several days."

"Vixen!" Yet he could not help but admire such strategy.

"Ay," said Brianna, again showing her soft smile. She lowered herself once more to the straw. "Now, sit you here beside me and talk, kinsman. I would know those things the Ard Ri has done for Ireland, Celt and Viking Ireland alike, so that I can win this Ospak over. Nay, Fin, don't look at me so. 'Tis bootless . . ."

On Wednesday of the following week, Finian Kinrade was by Brianna's side as they rode north toward Valaberg. Inwardly he fumed. What in the name of all the saints ailed him, allowing her to do this thing? But then, it was not a matter of his allowing Brianna Kinrade to do anything. Not even her father could rule her—unless he was of a mind to put her in a cage and throw away the key. Nonetheless, Lachlan would have his hide when he learned of this. Fin's heart beat faster as they approached Valaberg. It was not a town but a rude outpost from which to launch raids; a few wattle-and-daub cottages clustered about a timbered stronghold with a stockade nearby. All looked out onto the Irish Sea, and in the bay were ten dragonships with their sails furled.

"Hold, Celts!" a sentry bawled from a distance. "Come no farther."

Fin raised his voice. "We come in the name of Lachlan Kinrade of Carnane to seek an audience with Ospak." To Brianna, he said low, "From now on, lass, 'tis all yours."

Brianna tensed as the ruddy-faced warrior drew near and scanned them, his sword and shield at the ready.

"Who be you?" His suspicious blue eyes moved from the hoods of their fur-lined cloaks to their tall skin boots.

"I am Brianna, daughter of Kinrade," she said, "and this be his nephew, Fin Kinrade. We come for peaceful talk with your chieftain." She saw that his eyes had lighted on the deadly longbows slung over their shoulders.

"Guard these two," he ordered his companion. "They would speak with Ospak. I will tell him." He leapt onto a shaggy pony and trotted in toward the stronghold.

While he was gone, the wind commenced to keen across the sea, lifting the green-gray water into spray and whitecaps. Snow was flying by the time he returned.

"Ospak will see you," he said. "Leave your mounts and weapons here."

Brianna opened her mouth to protest, but reading Fin's face, she desisted. They fastened their bows to their saddles, and Fin surrendered the dirk at his belt. Brianna's remained hidden beneath her tunic as they followed the mounted sentry into the fortress, and thence into a great hall whose only warmth and light came from a meager fire flickering in a central pit.

As Brianna's eyes adjusted to the shadows, she saw that several men sat on wall benches drinking from their horns. Ospak, fur-clad and horn in hand, was sprawled in his high-seat, two armed giants on either side of him. Her skin crept, knowing they were his berserk bodyguards. Marking the chieftain's pale eyes examining her, Brianna was thankful she had been wise enough to bring Fin. She saw instantly that she could not use feminine wiles and coaxing on such a man. She dared not act other than bold and unafraid, though her mouth felt dry as dust and her knees trembled.

"I am Brianna Kinrade," she said, dismayed that her voice sounded small and girlish. She thought of Boru then, of his golden dream for Ireland and his need for the dragonships in the bay, and she was strengthened. "I am the daughter of Lachlan Kinrade of Carnane"— now her words rang strong and clear—"and this be my kinsman, Fin Kinrade, nephew of the Kinrade. We come in my father's name and under his protection to talk to you of Brian Boru."

Ospak gazed on her with unconcealed amusement. When he spoke finally, it was a thunder-rumble. "Why does the Kinrade send a woman in his place?"

"Already he has come twice to rally you to Boru," she answered coolly, "and both times you have refused. 'Twas thought I might give you another perspective of the Ard Ri." Her body grew hot beneath her woolen tunic and trews and cloak as he continued to stare at her.

"What viewpoint might that be?" His tongue flickered suggestively across his lips.

Brianna lifted her chin. "Brian Boru be my foster father. I lived at Kincora for five years."

The bastard. He was undressing her with his eyes, and doubtless he would try to bed her before she left. But she had Fin by her side, and the name of Kinrade to guard her. And she had Boru to help. She drove all else from her mind.

" 'Twas thought I could tell you things about the emperor you might not know," she continued. "He be a good man, Ospak, and worthy of your allegiance."

Ospak laughed, another thunder-rumble before the storm. "It doubts me not you think so, my lady, but there are those of your own people who call him a usurper who forces tribute from all and sundry." His pale eyes blinked and moved over her ominously. "Nor will you find any Viking who disagrees with them. The sword of Brian-the-Hundred-Killer thirsts for Viking blood. It always has and always will."

"Sire, you are wrong!" Brianna stepped closer, praying she would remember at least some of what Fin had told her. "Brian Boru has mellowed. He did not start this war, and his thirst now is for a united kingdom, not for the blood of you Strangers. He thirsts for schools and good roads a-and food for all. That is where the tribute goes, not into his own coffers."

Seeing that she had captured the chieftain's attention, Brianna pressed on. "When Boru talks of uniting Ireland into one kingdom, he includes you Vikings who have Celt blood in your veins, are wed to Celt women, or have fathered Celt babes. He holds you as kin."

Once more Ospak's eyes seemed to undress and fondle Brianna's slender body beneath her fur-lined cloak. "I will consider what you have said, for your words please me. More than that, you please me. Are you wed to any, Kinrade's daughter?"

Brianna stepped back abruptly to where Fin stood, thankful for his tall form close beside her. "Never will I wed," she said crisply.

The words surprised herself even, for it was a thing she had mused on often but never voiced aloud. She might one day love a man, ay, but it would be unfair to wed him. Never could she enjoy him, nor give him enjoyment. That Viking who had stolen her maidenhood had also stolen any such happiness from her.

"Never wed? 'Tis a pity, that," Ospak said, and wet his lips again, "for you be a beauty. You and your kinsman will take food with us now. You will also spend the night. Tomorrow we will discuss Boru further."

"You have my thanks," Brianna said quickly, "but 'tis impossible to accept your hospitality. My father eagerly awaits our tidings. We will return again tomorrow for more talk if need be."

Ospak glared at the sentry who entered just then. "What is't, man? Can you not see I am at business?"

"Sitric Olavsson and Wulf Thorsson and their men stand without. They would speak with you."

The Valaberg chieftain gave a shout of laughter. "So, two more come to woo me! Send them in! You," he barked to his Celt visitors, "stand off to the side there."

Brianna met Fin's worried eyes as the Valaberg great hall overflowed suddenly with a swarm of armed Vikings. Never in her wildest imaginings had she dreamt that Sitric Olavsson might come while the two of them were there. Fearing she would erupt with laughter out of sheer terror, she bit her lip hard. She had come this far, she would not jeopardize her mission now. Pulling her hood forward to hide her face, she studied the two men who now stood before Ospak.

Sitric Olavsson was nigh six feet tall with a face as arrogant as it was comely. His pale silken beard was spread over a green and gold tunic, and atop his silver-blond head was a slim band of gold filigree. As Brianna's gaze next moved to his towering companion, that Viking threw back his hood. She could see little of Wulf Thorsson's face for the wild tangle of dark-gold beard upon it and his mane of golden hair—but what she saw was familiar.

She gave a muffled gasp. Holy Jesu, what game was being played here? Was it Boru? She put a hand to her suddenly racing heart and looked up at Fin. He shook his head.

When she returned her gaze to the tall warrior, Brianna's reason returned as well. Of course he was not Boru. In this dim hall, his height and tawny hair and rugged profile minded her greatly of the emperor, ay, but this was a Viking, of that there was no doubt. As she stared at him, fascinated by the resemblance, the Dublin king's voice rang out.

"Who be this beauty you hide from us, Ospak? I can see only that her mouth and her eyes are the fairest of the fair."

As Sitric smiled at her and stroked his beard, Brianna held her breath. Would Ospak divulge their reason for being at Valaberg? And why was he looking at her so strangely of a sudden? She watched uneasily as he heaved his bulk to his feet and lumbered toward her. Holy Jesu, what was he doing? She gasped as he seized her arm and cupped her chin in his big hand.

"I know not who the wench is, Olavsson," Ospak drawled, "excepting she be a Celt thrall. She belonged to another, but I craved her and had her stolen. She was brought to me but moments before your own arrival. In fact, you have interrupted my first inspection of her."

Brianna was too stunned for speech, but Fin moved instantly. He tore her from Ospak's hands and thrust her behind himself.

"You damned Viking bastard, there is no way you can do this. My people will lay waste this stronghold and mount your head on a pole!"

Ospak's great berserks were there instantly, wrenching Fin's arms behind him. It shocked Brianna to action.

"Don't harm him, please! Make them loose him!"

Ospak paid her no heed. He growled to his giants, "Throw him into the stockade."

Seeing her kinsman dragged, raging, from the great hall, Brianna thought to take her dirk and begin slashing, starting with Ospak himself. Before she could make a move, he caught her, tore off her cloak, and hurled it to the hard-packed floor.

"I would see what I have bought," he said.

"You snake!" Brianna hissed, "you have just asked for death by my father's hand!"

Ospak's pale eyes roved over her shapely breasts and buttocks as there came a rumble of approval from the watching men. Next he roughly loosed her long gleaming hair from beneath her tunic where it had been hidden. He laughed with satisfaction as it flamed down her back.

" 'Twould seem I have me a beauty. And look at those cat eyes. Be they green or gold, wench?"

Brianna's fury spewed forth. "Bastard!" She raked his face with her fingernails before he subdued her.

"A cat for sure," he laughed. " 'Twill be good sport to tame you."

Brianna kicked her captor's shins and struggled fiercely to escape, but he held her fast. As he slid a greedy hand over her breasts and his mouth lowered to hers, she shuddered. She was going to be raped again, only this time it would be worse. This time she had dragged Fin down with her and she had failed Boru. Nor would her people come seeking her as Fin had threatened, for none knew she was here. Tears of fright spilled from her eyes as Ospak's wet mouth sucked on hers and then trailed over her cheek to her temple, and thence to her ear. He said under his breath:

"Little fool, wouldst have me tell Sitric the truth?"

"N-nay," she choked.

"Then damn me, hide your claws and go along with me. 'Twill be all right, I promise you." He thrust her from him roughly and returned to his high-seat. He pointed to a spot at his feet.

"Sit you there, wench. You may don your cloak first."

Brianna quickly obeyed. It seemed that for the time being she was safe, but her body did not yet believe it. Her tears streamed still, and her heart pounded. Her breath came in harsh gasps. And she burned with mortification. She had been pawed and kissed while the enemy looked on, and now she, the daughter of Kinrade of Carnane, must sit at the feet of this damned Viking chieftain as though she truly were his thrall. As he and the king began their talk, she stared dully at the floor, but she vowed to remember every word.

Long moments passed before she remembered the warrior who had minded her of Boru. Ospak's brutal charade had driven him from her thoughts completely. Lifting her eyes slowly, cautiously, she found his wintry gaze upon her. She was stung by its anger and intensity, and by her own indignation. Why was he so wroth with *her*? What had *she* done? Did he hate women so much, or was it only Celt women? Or thralls . . .

She looked away, but his image burned in her thoughts. His height and wide shoulders, his strong, straight nose, the lion's mane of hair, a beard that grew wild and thick on a face that was as handsome as it was cruel. It was plain to see he was hard and cold as a pillar of ice. It gladdened her that she would not have to look at him or encounter him ever again.

Chapter Four

Seeing the maid beseeching him with streaming eyes and her soft mouth a-tremble, Wulf was struck by a thunderbolt of fury. He detested slavery. Men and women belonged to none but themselves, and she was a netted dove, a lamb about to be slaughtered. And she was silently, desperately begging him for help. As she lowered her gaze, he marked that she was near to collapse from fright.

He forced his ears to the war talk between Sitric and Ospak, but it could not hold his attention. His thoughts clashed in battle. He craved to bed the wench himself—she was the fairest thing he had ever seen—yet he craved to protect her from harm. And for one such as Ospak to own her was intolerable.

Wulf gritted his teeth. Somehow he must take her from here and he must do it this day, even if he had to come back in his own vessel with his own men. He vowed it. With that decision made, he put his full attention on his bickering countrymen. It was clear that Ospak was toying with the king, refusing to say either ay or nay to his request for aid. It was equally clear that Sitric was in a silent rage, and would soon hand the reins of talk over to Wulf. Wulf was therefore amazed when Sitric said to Ospak sharply:

"I will give you more time, Ospak, though 'tis a marvel why you would need it. I will return in two weeks."

Ospak shrugged his burly shoulders. "Even then I may have no answer for you, Dubliner.

"Then I will return again, and yet again," Sitric said. He was of no mind to give the devil over to Thorsson so early on. Nay, he himself would win this bastard. "Methinks eventually you will see the danger you face. If Boru overruns our cities in Ireland, think you he will stop there? I say he will not. The Viking strongholds on this miserable speck of an isle will be next."

Ospak's smile was placid. "Already I am surrounded by Celts who dare not attack me."

"Boru will attack, make no mistake," Sitric growled, and turned abruptly to Wulf. "We are leaving."

"Nay, nay, man." Ospak was jovial of a sudden. "You cannot leave without food and drink."

69

Sitric pursed his delicately etched lips before saying stiffly: "I would rather you offered your help than food and drink, Norseman." He clapped Wulf's shoulder. "We go."

"Ay," Wulf muttered, but his heart beat hard in his concern for the thrall. Having vowed to take her from this damned place, he craved to do it now rather than later. But how? At swordpoint? Could he buy her from Ospak? He was on reasonably friendly terms with him, but never would the fellow sell such a beauty before first sampling her. And afterwards, Wulf suspected he would never give her up.

Ospak raised his voice. "Hold, Dubliners! My men have just informed me 'tis storming and snowing so without they cannot see their hands before them. I must insist on giving you food and drink."

Sitric muttered to Wulf, "Rather would I eat and drink with swine than with this damned traitorous scut."

"Ay," Wulf said quietly, "Yet yarning with Ospak over his mead is preferable to going down in the storm." His own men and vessel he would trust to stay afloat, but not those of Sitric. And the delay would give him valuable time to plot his rescue of the maid.

Sitric grunted. "Upon reconsidering, 'tis my thought exactly. We stay." He directed a look of patronage toward the Maun chieftain. "We accept your offer, Norseman, but only for a brief time."

"Good, good."

Ospak had nothing but contempt for this pampered half-breed from Dublin, but it was unthinkable that any should leave Valaberg without receiving food and drink when he, Ospak, was known far and wide for his hospitality. He bawled to one of his men:

"Tell the wenches to mend the fire and bring ale and food. As for you, my pearl"—his eyes returned to Brianna—"you will come with me now." He grinned at the men looking on. "You will all understand my eagerness to show my new thrall what is expected of her . . ."

Wulf held himself rigid as Ospak yanked the maid to her feet, lifted her into his arms, and cruelly kissed her mouth to the accompaniment of the men's laughter. It took all of the discipline he possessed not to slide the Shining Death from out its sheath and press the point to Ospak's thick neck. But if he did, this hall would become a battlefield. And if he himself were slain, who then would protect her from those who were the victors? He watched impassively as Ospak carried her from the room, and shut his mind to her fate. He could not prevent it, but soon she would be safe in his hands. He turned to Leif and spoke under his breath:

"When we leave, she goes with us, old friend."

Seeing the deadly light in his captain's eyes, Leif knew better than to laugh at his strange words or to ask why he had uttered them. He had but one question:

"How?"

"I have a thought or two," Wulf muttered,

pushing toward the double doors of the great hall. "Sitric will skewer this devil Ospak if we stay here long, so we had best decide quickly. Let us go outside where we'll not be heard.

As soon as Ospak had carried Brianna from the great hall, she began to struggle in his arms.

"You damned Viking swine!" she hissed, "how *dare* you! Put me down!" She twisted, kicked, and pounded him with her small fists. She was enraged further to see that he was laughing.

"Oh, ay, I'll put you down, wench, but first I'll have me another kiss."

"Nay! I'll slay you! I swear I'll—"

His bearded mouth clamped down on hers again, silencing her, and when he began squeezing her breasts, Brianna grew afraid. His earlier words had raised her hopes, but now, alone with him in his bedchamber, she knew she had no reason to trust him. If eventually her father came to Valaberg seeking her, Ospak had but to say he had not seen her. And Fin he would slay, she was certain of that. Dear God, she could not bear the thought of Fin being harmed on her account.

"There, now, wench," said Ospak, setting her on her feet and beaming at her, " 'twas a thing we both enjoyed. Never will I believe otherwise."

Brianna's scorn overcame her fright. She wanted to spit in his eye, but dared not. She was at his mercy. She could not show her weapon until that moment when her life or Fin's was in real jeopardy. She said icily:

"Never would I have given freely what you took, Ospak, nor will I forget that you humiliated me before those men. Neither will my father take it kindly."

The chieftain gave a bark of laughter. "Had I not acted thus, you little fool, none would have believed you were my thrall. They know me. All in all, I thought 'twas exceeding clever of me." His eyes gleamed over her admiringly. "By all the gods, but you be a beauty, Brianna of Carnane. Marry me."

Brianna stared at him, wondering if he could possibly be serious. Her instinct said he was not. "I have told you, Ospak, never will I wed."

" 'Twould insure peace between our people, my pearl, and I know more ways of making love than—"

She said quickly: "Already there is peace between us."

When his eyes danced, Brianna knew that she was right. She was in no immediate danger from Ospak of Valaberg. She did not know how he treated other women or thralls, but herself he was going to treat with velvet gloves. Perhaps fear of her father held him in rein, or perhaps it was his admiration for her. Whatever, she was safe for the time being. She relaxed enough to give him a smile.

"Have thanks for not betraying me . . ."

Ospak shrugged. "There is naught to thank for. Rather would I have peace with Kinrade of Carnane than help that half-breed bastard make war against a man who has been good for Ireland."

Brianna blinked. Never had she thought to hear such words from his lips. "Then rally to him!" she urged. "Brian Boru needs you."

Ospak's grin was a wicked one. "Oh, nay, nay, not so fast, my pearl. What is in it for me? Know you, I am a man with strong cravings . . ."

"You will be well rewarded by Boru himself," she said firmly. "He will give you his loyalty and his protection."

"Ah, but 'tis not that which I crave. I crave a woman of beauty and bravery who will set my loins on fire." He grasped her face between his hands and gave her another hearty kiss.

Brianna gave him a resounding slap. "I am not that woman, Norseman, believe me!"

Ospak groaned in mock agony. "Even your blows excite me. I knew not that Celts grew such Valkyries."

Her eyes narrowed. "Methinks you are naught but an old clown, Ospak, and if you lay your hand on me one time more, I will bite it off."

His delighted laughter rang out. "Nay, you will not. You like me. I see it in those cat eyes of yours. Such beautiful eyes. Ah, holy Odin, I yield me. Tell your Ard Ri that my men and my vessels are his, wench. You have but to wed me."

Brianna smiled, certain now he would go running in the opposite direction if she agreed. He would bed her if he could, but never would he wed her. He loved women, all women, far too well.

"Nay, Ospak, be assured I will not wed you. We have naught further to discuss now, but methinks you can be made to see reason by and by. 'Tis time I left before my father lays waste this so-called stronghold of yours. Return Fin to me."

"Later. I forbid you to leave now. You will stay until yon Dubliners depart. 'Tis possible I will display you again. It gladdened my heart to mark Sitric and his tall captain slavering over you."

The captain slavering? Brianna hid her surprise. It was true that Sitric had ogled her and preened himself, but Wulf Thorsson certainly had not. He had wanted to break her in half. She could still see his wintry face and eyes.

"Now I return to my guests. You will stay here until I fetch you," Ospak ordered. "Hear you, woman?"

Brianna gave him a docile smile. "I hear."

After he left, she slowly counted to ten before looking out into the passageway. It was empty. He had returned to the great hall without leaving anyone to guard her. She quickly put on her cloak and hurried from the room. As she moved down the dim corridor in search of an outer door, her worried thoughts were on Fin. She knew she could not free him; she wanted only to call to him through the enclosure and tell him what was happening. He would be wild with worry, and it was only right that he know she was safe and that soon they would be returning home.

*   *   *

"So," Leif said as he and Wulf stepped out into the storm, "how mean you to get the wench away from here?"

Wulf pulled up his hood and shuttered his eyes against the flying snow. Gazing about him, he nodded, satisfied. " 'Tis as I had hoped. Because of the weather, few sentries are about. With the woman wrapped in her cloak and wearing trews, none will suspect she is not one of us."

"Unless she be shrieking and struggling . . ."

Wulf gave a low laugh. "She will not shriek nor struggle, man, that I promise you. Could you not see the wench was begging me to rescue her?"

"You?" Leif's mouth twitched. " 'Tis strange how I missed that."

In his mind, Wulf saw still the desperate message in those beautiful green tear-shimmered eyes locked on his. Soon she would be safe, but he regretted deeply that he had not prevented Ospak's claiming her. He pushed the ugly picture away. He must hold no thoughts of murder in his heart if his head was to be clear.

"As for how to find her," he said into Leif's ear, " 'twould seem this building is built like our other strongholds. Ospak's bedchamber will be the grandest, the first one behind the great hall on the left. We can enter by yon side door and—"

He gripped Leif's arm and pointed as a slender figure emerged stealthily from the door. As it hurried into the storm, bending into the wind, Wulf moved after it, beckoning Leif to follow. He ran on silent, fur-clad feet through the deepening snow and soon was upon his quarry, blocking the way.

"Hold," he said low. He was not surprised to see the maid's wide, frightened eyes gazing up at him. He had known it was she.

Brianna's heart fell. She had not heard a sound, and now a sentry stood before her, having come out of nowhere. She gasped, seeing the icy eyes, golden hair, and wild beard beneath the hood. Oh, God—Sitric's captain, and he had another with him! She was trapped. Had she escaped harm at Ospak's hands only to fall prey to these men out here in the storm? She watched, afraid to move, as the captain lay a finger to his lips. He spoke to her softly in her own tongue:

"Do not cry out, we will not harm you. I am Wulf Thorsson of Husaby. I will take you to safety."

Brianna gazed up at him stupidly. "Wh-what?"

"You will never make good this escape on your own. Ospak's sentries surround Valaberg. They will seize and return you to him and you will be punished."

"I—I . . ." Her wits had left her. Nor could she imagine why this man who had appeared to hate her was making this offer of help which she did not need nor want. She remembered

Ospak's words that the captain had slavered over her. Now she saw the lust in those fierce blue eyes . . .

"I will return you to your people," Wulf said, "but not this day. You will come to Dublin with us now." She was so like a fleeing doe in her fright and bewilderment that he was filled with a strange tenderness for her. "We have no time to talk. You may have been missed already and the guard sent out. Come, little wench, there is naught to fear." He put an arm about her.

Brianna balked, planting her feet firmly in the snow. "I do not believe you. Why wouldst you help me?"

Wulf ordered himself to be patient. "Because I would not see you in thrall. Now come!"

"Nay, I—I will not!" Brianna's voice lifted above the wind-wail. She tried to shake off his arm but he tightened his grasp, drawing her along inexorably between himself and his companion. "Stop!" It was a shriek, for she was frightened now. "I will not leave. Please—unhand me!"

Wulf gave her a shake. "Hush, you stupid wench! Wouldst have the whole stronghold know you are fleeing?" Meeting Leif's laughing eyes over her head, he ground his teeth.

Leif asked in Norse: "Was't a woman-shriek or was't wind we just heard, old friend? Ah, but then 'twould have to be wind . . ."

Wulf gave him a black look, and spoke again to the struggling thrall. "Know you, woman"—it was an effort to keep his calm—"I want naught but your safety. Think of the grand tale you can tell your folk when you return. How many others know you that have visited the king's palace in Dublin?"

Brianna did not miss the coaxing lilt in his voice. It was the way Boru used to entice her into eating her vegetables when she was small. She hated it that he minded her so of Boru, for he was the enemy, the age-old enemy, and she feared what he would do with her once she was in his power. Even more, she feared for Fin. With each passing moment, he would grow more likely to slay the first man who came near in order to escape, and in turn, would himself be slain. She had to get to the stockade and speak with him, which meant she had to change her ploy with this Thorsson. She gazed up at him, her eyes suddenly soft. She spoke beneath the wind:

"I was wrong about you, sire. F-forgive me. I see now that you mean well and want only to help me, but I pray you, let me make my own way. I know every inch of this land of mine and will be home before nightfall."

"Nay," Wulf said gruffly. "Ospak's men will find you."

"Sire, I beg of—"

"Nay. You are coming to Dublin and that is the end of it. I will buy you a fine gown there to take home with you." Seeing her beautiful eyes widen, he saw he had won her. By the gods, all it had taken was the bribe of a gown. The silly wench.

Dublin? It was as though Brianna's ears were hearing for the first time what he had said earlier. He was taking her to Dublin to the palace of the king! It was as if the pieces of a puzzle were fitting together of a sudden. Boru no longer had a spy in Sitric's court, and here she was, at the right place and the right time to be taken there to help him.

But she was a fool for certain if she thought it would be easy. It was more likely that this brute Thorsson would attempt to have his will with her and afterwards sell her to another. She of all people knew what Vikings were capable of. On the other hand, if he were honorable and truly did mean to bring her home again, what excuse could she make to stay on at the palace? And how could she possibly pretend she was a thrall, she who had never been known for her docility? And what of Fin? She simply could not leave without telling him.

They were passing the last cottage when, through the snow, Brianna saw the gray spitting sea and the great dragonship pulled onto the beach like some black gleaming sea monster. Her legs froze. Did she dare go ahead with such a hastily made plan?

"Wench, listen to me carefully," Wulf said quietly, seeing her hesitation. "Those be Ospak's men standing guard at the shore. I will tell them you are one of our men who has taken ill and would go below deck to sleep. If that is not to your liking, I will allow you to go your way. However, if you are seized and returned to your master, I will do naught to interfere. 'Tis your choice."

Ay, it was her choice, Brianna mused, gazing on the ship and the sea. And she had already made it. She would go to Dublin. But to go there without a messenger between herself and Boru was like sending off a ship without a sail. Fin had to know, but could she trust Ospak to free him? She could only hope for the best. She pulled her cloak about her more tightly and murmured:

"I will go with you, sire, but I beg your permission to speak with my kinsman first, he who was taken to the stockade." Seeing the Viking's mounting impatience, Brianna knew what she had to do. She fell to her knees, her hood hiding her burning face. "Sire, he be my only kin and he is imprisoned because of me. He followed me here to rescue me. Wouldst be so cruel as not to allow me to bid him farewell?"

Wulf bent and lifted her to her feet. "Go you then," he said gruffly, "but hurry. We will follow behind. And if you think to flee, so be it. If you value yourself and your freedom so little, Ospak can have you and welcome."

Chapter Five

It was done. For better or worse it was done, Brianna mused, and only time would tell if she had chosen the right path. After Wulf Thorsson had led her below deck on the Dublin king's dragonship, he had given her a fur-lined sleeping bag and warned her to stay close to the hull and out of sight. He and his companion had then gone back to Ospak's great hall, but before long, the whole troop of them had returned and cast off. Now, gazing up through the trap at the dramatic sunset overhead, she wondered if the turn in weather from storm to sun was a good omen. She shook her head. Fin for one would never believe that any good could come of all this.

Poor Fin. It was not fair what she had put him

through this day. He had been so gladdened to learn that Ospak had but employed a clever ruse to fool Sitric, and that he himself would soon be freed. And then, then she had told him she was sailing to Dublin with Sitric's Vikings . . .

Her cheeks burned remembering his fury and the tongue-lashing he had given her. But it was fear for her that had made him act so. Fear and his helplessness to prevent her doing what he thought was a dangerous and foolish thing. Nor could she soothe him and try to explain her reasons with the two Norsemen standing nearby glaring at her and urging her to make haste. She had only an instant to tell Fin she needed him desperately in Dublin and to beg him to follow her to Sitric's stronghold there.

Hearing sounds of activity on deck and sensing the slowing of the ship, Brianna knew the time was close to hand when she would begin her new and dangerous adventure. There came shouts and thumps as the oars were stowed and the sail furled, and then quiet. She crawled out of the bag, got to her feet, and stood tall, her cloak pulled tightly about her in the frigid air. Now was the reckoning. Would Wulf Thorsson prove to be as he claimed, a man concerned for her welfare, or had she been misled by his resemblance to the most noble man in Ireland? Suddenly he was in the opening over her head. Disdaining the steps, he jumped down beside her. Brianna's eyes widened. She had known he was tall, but not this tall—the top of her head scarce reached his shoulder.

"We have arrived, lady," Wulf said. " 'Tis Dublin."

"Ay, sire."

She anxiously searched his face for some trace of the deception and lust she feared to find there, but there was none. Her gaze lingered as the rays of the setting sun tipped his dark lashes and streaked his long, unruly hair and unkempt beard with gold. He was comely, ay, but he had a wild heathen look about him that frightened her. Of a sudden she marked a scar she had not seen before, a pale slash from his right temple to the square line of his jaw. It was a chilling reminder that she had placed herself in the hands of a Viking warrior.

Wulf scowled. "Be you all right?"

"A-ay." The word was a whisper, so tight was her throat. She nervously tossed back her hood and loosed her long hair.

Wulf's breath caught as he saw her closely and in good light for the first time. She was much younger than his own thirty winters and fair beyond belief, more king's daughter than thrall. Never had he seen such glorious hair, a deep wine-red with the last rays of the sun striking in it glints of flame and copper, and when her green eyes shuttered in a slow blink, his attention was drawn to the thick smudge of ebony lashes outlining them, and thence to her soft mouth. He imagined it tilted at the corners in a smile just for him, imagined her saying she wanted to stay with him, not return to Maun . . .

By the gods, what foolishness was this? He bent abruptly and snatched up his sleeping bag. Entrancing as the wench was, he would not be ruled by her beauty nor her plight. He craved her, ay, but having saved her from Ospak, he would do nothing to distress her further. He would return her to her folk. His plan called for nothing more.

"What be your name, lady?" he asked gruffly.

"Brianna."

Wulf gave a curt nod. "Know you, Brianna"— he rolled up his fur bag and tied it—"you be a freedwoman now. From the moment you set foot on this vessel, you were free."

"I am grateful, sire . . ." Should she drop to her knees? she wondered. Kiss his feet? Weep with joy? She was uncertain, for never had there been thralls kept at Carnane.

"For your safety, however, the king and his court must still think you belong to me. None will dare toy with you if you are mine. You will therefore share my bedchamber at the palace."

Brianna stared at him. So, there it was, just as she had feared. She was free, oh ay, but in exchange, he would have her in his bed. So much for his honor. She yearned suddenly, desperately, for home.

As he gathered his gear, Wulf saw the pink staining her cheeks. He said drily, "Nay, Brianna, 'tis not what you think. The bed will be yours alone, and as soon as 'tis possible, I will return you to your land." He damned

Ospak again, promising himself that someday he would skewer the bastard.

"M-methought you said tomorrow . . ."

It frightened her when he looked at her so. Her knees trembled. It was as if some dark shadow turned his eyes to ice and his mouth into a grim slash. Even the scar on his face seemed angry.

" 'Twill not be tomorrow," Wulf said, collecting his gear. "The king has other plans for me. Mayhap 'twill be the following day. What part of Maun be you from?"

"Jurby."

Wulf nodded. It was the fertile northwest lowland area of the isle where many of his people had settled. " 'Twill be an easy matter to get you there."

But he was not gladdened by the thought. He craved to know more about her and how she had come to be a thrall. Damnation, was he going to stand here gaping at her and brooding over her all morning? He tossed his sleeping bag and his sack of gear up on deck and gave her a smile.

" 'Tis time we got us to the palace. Be you ready for your big adventure and the gown I mean to buy you?"

Brianna blinked. "Ay, sire."

He had actually smiled. She'd caught only the briefest glimpse of teeth that were strong and white and unmarred, and his face and eyes had fair glowed with a warm friendliness. She straightened her shoulders. She would not let herself be impressed. He was sore mistaken if he thought to lull her into friendship when he was plotting against Boru. Never would he be a friend of hers.

Wulf swung himself easily up on deck. He stifled the impulse to help the maid, knowing his touch would make her shrink in fear. "This river be the Liffey," he said, "and on yonder rath be Sitric's palace."

He watched, enchanted, as the wind gently stirred her cloud of dark-red hair and her wondering gaze moved over the ice-glittered river and up to the palace, a long two-storied stronghold with snow-topped walls and watchtowers about it. Of a sudden, he craved to catch her to him, kiss her pink mouth, and carry her back down into the hold . . .

Wulf drew a sharp breath and thrust the thought away. He was damned if he would treat her as Ospak had. It was a vow he had made long ago. Never would he rape. And she was a freedwoman now. She deserved to be wooed tenderly by the man of her choice, but it would not be he. He saw clearly that she feared him and yearned only for her kin and her homeland. Nor should his own thoughts be on women and lovemaking now. All his energies must be geared to war. Nothing else was as important as the downfall of Brian Boru.

He stepped over the low freeboard of Sitric's vessel onto the rime-hardened mud of the riverbank. It surprised him that she followed so easily, agile and graceful as a young cat, and her long, slender legs in their trews near matching his own stride on the log pathway. How fair she was. It reminded him that she would not be safe for long in the palace.

"Know you, Brianna"—he hesitated, not certain how to continue without frightening her—"there be certain things you should know."

"Ay?" She looked up at him in all innocence.

Wulf cleared his throat. "In Sitric's stronghold, there will be men who will crave you . . ."

Brianna bit her lip before she could laugh. But on closer thought, there was little to laugh about. She had forgotten too quickly Ospak's effortless overpowering of her, and she was far from convinced this man himself meant her well. Only when this night was over would she know more. She was minded then of her greatest fear: how to guard her every word and gesture, to act and think and walk and breathe and talk like a thrall. But she must. Her very life could depend upon it. Lowering her gaze to the pathway, she asked shyly:

"What wouldst have me do, sire?"

"Let no man get you alone," Wulf replied. He saw her cheeks flame.

"Ay, sire." It was a whisper. "Wh-when will you return?"

"Would that I knew," Wulf muttered.

Brianna managed a smile. " 'Tis all right, sire. I will be careful."

That night there was feasting in the great hall of Sitric Olavsson. Brianna, resting briefly on a corner bench far from the king's board, watched the merriment, listened to the harpers, and marveled at the fashions of the ladies of the court. All wore white coifs to cover their hair and gowns which revealed much of their bosoms.

Brianna minded not at all her own lowly position. Because she was a thrall, few paid her heed, and it was exactly as she wished it. She had arranged her hair into two braids and donned the garb she had been given, a modest kyrtil of the coarsest pale-blue wool topped by a striped apron. Her sole duty was to wait upon her master throughout the eve, seeing that he had every comfort and tending to his food and drink.

As she made her many trips between kitchen-house and the high-board where Wulf Thorsson sat with Sitric and his nobles, she heard much in passing. It seemed this was a coming-home feast. The king had been gone many weeks rallying his countrymen and had just now returned, having won to his cause two great warriors who commanded loyalty from many men—Sigurd of the Orkneys and Wulf Thorsson of Husaby.

As Brianna hurried a fresh keg of wine to the high-board, she was struck suddenly with the absurdity of her situation. Was it but two days ago that she had been garbed as a serving-wench in her father's own hall and carrying a keg to Boru? It was not to be believed that she should now be here in the stronghold of a Viking king carrying wine to a man she called master. Wulf Thorsson sat in the seat of honor as had Boru at Carnane, and above his golden head hung his own dark-purple banner on which gleamed a silver hammer. Brianna stood meekly by his side until he deigned to glance up at her.

"What is't, wench?"

"Here be the wine you craved, sire. Shall I fill your horn now?" She marked that his once-wild hair was tamed and his beard newly barbered. It molded his chin and jaw becomingly, and made him seem far less fierce.

"Put it here on the board," Wulf ordered. Deciding that all should see how it was between them he let his eyes move over her insolently. He reached out and slipped an arm about her waist. "Sit you here and warm me."

Brianna dared not protest as she was drawn down onto his knees and pressed back against his chest, his hands locked beneath her breasts. It was like sitting on a bench of granite except for the heat of him. It radiated through his leather trews and tunic to penetrate her kyrtil and sear her flesh. As her anger flared, her entire body grew hot. Damn him! He had drunk deeply, and even a man with the best of intentions forgot them in drink. Yet she sensed no hunger in his slow, sensuous stroking of her throat and shoulder. It was as though his thoughts were elsewhere.

"You have you a beauty there, Thorsson," said Sitric from across the board. His face was flushed and his eyes, glassy from too much drink, dwelled on Brianna's breasts. If she were his, damned if he would not be tempted to divorce his wife and wed the wench—except for her low birth. It was a pity, that. " 'Twas a bold thing," he said, "your stealing her from Ospak, yet 'tis easy to see why you craved such a prize. But I fear 'twill turn the bastard against me."

Wulf laughed. "Man, I had not the chance to steal her. I found her fleeing on her own. It doubts me Ospak will connect her disappearance with us. Aside from that, the bastard is already against you. Forget him, we have no need of him."

Sitric gaped at the man he had made his captain. "Think you?"

"Ay. Never will he be yours, nor am I convinced we should plead with Brodir."

"But the two betwixt them will bring us thirty ships!"

Wulf shook his head. "Men who require fat bribes are men prone to treachery."

And men who required fat bribes were men who deserved treachery, thought Sitric darkly, minding the awful price he had paid for Sigurd's help. His throne and his mother. But then the greedy devil would never have either.

"Let Boru have the scut," Wulf said, absently stroking the rounded thighs under his fingers. "I will get you thirty ships and more from those who will gladly give them. They will need no bribes. They crave only to see Boru dead, as do I."

Brianna was reeling from his words when the doors to the great hall were flung open and the herald called out:

"Her highness, the princess Gormlaith, my lord!"

Sitric's stomach twisted into a knot. By all the gods, his witch-mother. What was she doing here? He had sent her to Wexford, and had sent his wife, Emer, and the children to Emer's kin in Limerick to be rid of them all for the winter, so what was this? Why had this woman returned? Damnation. He rose with the others as she made a regal sweep through the middle of the hall between the two fire trenches, her dark-green cloak billowing. There was a great flurry as the wenches flew to prepare a place for her at the high-board at Sitric's right. When she stood beside him, as tall as was he himself, Sitric bowed low over her shapely, perfumed hand and bestowed a kiss upon it.

"Greetings, Mother."

Gormlaith gave her first-born son a respectful curtsy. "It gladdens me we are both home again, your majesty."

Brianna gazed on the woman in astonishment. Gormlaith? This wildly beautiful creature with her hair flaming to her hips was Boru's former wife? She knew that Sitric was her son, ay, but never had she thought to find the woman here in Dublin. Brianna stared unashamedly, for the princess was ravishing. Unlike Sitric, she was pure Celt. Brianna wondered how she had ever borne the shame of being wed to a Viking. She herself could think of nothing worse.

"Mother, may I present my captain, Wulf Thorsson of Husaby," Sitric was saying. "We drank together at Sigurd's board and he rallied to our cause immediately. He is recruiting and organizing our campaign and will accept our hospitality 'til this affair be concluded."

Gormlaith's gaze flickered over the tall Norseman as she offered her fingertips. "Have thanks, sire," she said gravely. "Welcome to the City of the Black Pool."

Wulf touched his lips to the warm, scented skin and felt the lightinglike impact of her green eyes upon his entire body. It was common knowledge that Brian Boru had wed a beautiful woman of Irish royalty. Seeing her now, Wulf could not imagine why Boru had put her aside. She was magnificent, and she appeared keenly intelligent. Perhaps the Ard Ri was more fool than any thought.

"What news bring you, Sitric?" Gormlaith asked, seating herself and dipping daintily into the food put before her. "I am eager to hear."

"Good news, Mother. Wulf commands allegiance from an untold number of troops in Norway and the northern isles. He hungers for Brian Boru to lie in the dead-straw, as do we."

Gormlaith gave Wulf a sad smile. "Know you, sire, it tears my heart to think of the emperor being harmed. Him I love still, though 'tis not returned or—"

"Not now, Mother," said Sitric sharply. What a liar she was and what a consummate actress. It was Gormlaith herself who had started this whole damned rebellion. She would not rest until Boru was in the ground.

The princess fixed a resentful eye on her son. "Am I permitted to ask of Sigurd, my lord? I would not displease my lord king further."

Sitric gave a convulsive swallow. "Don't say that, Mother, 'tis ridiculous. Of course you are permitted to ask of Sigurd. He, too, has rallied to our banner. Maelmorda will be greatly pleased, I trow."

Gormlaith gave an audible sigh and leaned against the tall back of the intricately carved high-seat. " 'Tis glad I am for both your sakes, yet always will I grieve for Boru . . ." She then directed her beautiful eyes to Wulf's face where they lingered, heavy-lidded and unblinking. "I would hear about you, Wulf Thorsson of Husaby. Tell me about yourself." She took a small sip of mead and sank her teeth ever so delicately into a bit of lamb.

"There is little to tell, my lady," Wulf answered, returning her solemn gaze. He was puzzled. He had heard a strange waif-word concerning this Irish princess's excessive dealings with men, yet seeing her in the flesh, he could not believe the rumors. She seemed as noble and gentle a women as ever a man could want, though Sitric himself did not seem to appreciate her.

"My captain is far too modest, Mother," Sitric answered. "There is much to tell about him." He subdued his simmering jealousy of the Norseman, for he knew how great was his fortune in attaining Wulf's help. "Wulf Thorsson comes from a noble family which has served the kings of Norway so long as there were kings to serve. He himself was offered the crown in the southern part of Norway's land but—"

Wulf muttered, annoyed, "Olavsson, there is naught to be gained by this prating."

Gormlaith looked at the broad-shouldered Viking with undisguised interest. "You could have been king?" she asked.

"Being king has never been one of my goals, my lady."

Sitric recognized in his mother's intent gaze the familiar signs of lust and admiration for a man of power. He took a long breath and drank more deeply of his mead. It seemed she had found her next lover. If it were so, he prayed to all the gods that Thorsson would keep her so immersed in the pleasures of the flesh that she would not pester him for details of his visit to Sigurd. Eventually, of course, he must confess that he had given her to the Orkney king, but not yet. Not yet . . .

As Brianna stood by Wulf Thorsson's side, her head was awhirl with all she had heard. How was she going to remember everything when one thing stood alone in her thoughts? Boru in the dead-straw. She had shuddered so each time it was said, she wondered if the Norseman had noticed. And the fact that he himself had promised to put him there—this damned Viking who could have been king. She was so wroth with him she could have slain him then and there. And she was angry with Boru himself. How could he have divorced such a lovely woman, especially one who still openly declared her love for him? She felt Gormlaith's emerald eyes on her.

"What a pretty thing you be, my dear. When were you hired? No matter, wouldst like to be my bodyservant?"

Brianna looked to Wulf Thorsson and back to the princess. "I would be willing, my lady, but—"

Wulf said sharply: " 'Tis out of the question. This wench be my thrall, your highness, and I value her highly." He pulled Brianna down onto his knees once more, and gazed about the board at the nobles and their ladies seated there. "I would take it greatly amiss if any were to forget that."

Sensing her mother's hidden anger, Sitric raised his horn to hide his smile. Well, well. Gormlaith lusting after Thorsson, and Thorsson with eyes only for his new thrall. But he had not the slightest doubt it would be an easy matter for himself to bed the wench when Thorsson was gone gathering forces for him. After all, what woman would not choose a king over a chieftain if given a choice? But then, she would have no choice . . .

Chapter Six

Brianna stiffened as the Norseman drew her close once more. It shamed her to be stroked before the eyes of them all, and shamed her that she must accept it unresisting, yet his fingers had set her skin afire. Her breasts throbbed, and she felt herself softening, melting against him. She had never experienced such a thing before, and she yearned to leap up and run out into the wintry night, as far as possible from this man who made her feel so. But she could not. She was a thrall. She sat obedient, her eyes downcast, and bore silently her anger and the rush of hot blood through her veins. At the same time, she prayed that Gormlaith would assert her authority and demand her as a bodyservant. But it was not to be.

"Forgive me, sire," the princess said smoothly. " 'Tis my mistake entirely. Methought the wench was a new servant hired since my departure. In any event, you need have no fear regarding her. None will lay a hand on her in your absence, I promise you. I personally will see to it."

"You have my gratitude, my lady, and since I am leaving early, Olavsson, I will forego your further hospitality, pleasant though it be." Wulf released Brianna and got to his feet. He had had no excuse for fondling her again, except he could not stop himself. Nor had he missed her quickened breathing and the way she had leaned back against him.

"You are right, of course," Sitric agreed. " 'Tis time I, too, turned in for I may well accompany you. I have not yet decided."

"Then I bid you all good night." Wulf left the great hall abruptly, his berserks on either side of him.

Brianna trailed behind, her worried thoughts already on the bedchamber they would share and on the strange bed, the bedcloset, that stood there. Having noticed her staring at it earlier, the Norseman said it was where she would sleep. And when he left so she might change her garb, she had examined it throughly. Never had she seen its like before. Its headboard and far side were the wooden corner walls of the room, while the footboard, too, was of wood that reached the ceiling. The side facing the room had but a small curtained opening, making of the bed nothing but a box heaped with furs and pillows. After dressing, she had quickly secreted her dirk among the furs. Now the thought of sleeping there with a Viking in the same room frightened her. What if he came to her during the night? Did she dare use her weapon?

Wulf marked that the maid hung back shyly as he opened the door of the bedchamber, yet she gazed up at him with wide eyes and softly parted lips. His manhood stirred. This was not a thing he had planned on, bedding her, but it seemed clear she desired it. He took her arm and drew her into the chamber.

Brianna watched in dismay as he closed the door on his berserks and lowered the bar into its brackets. Returning to her, he gently pulled her into his arms. They felt so hard and strong and he held her so closely, she grew flustered.

"Sire, what are you—"

Her words were stopped by his kiss. She tried to turn her face but there was no escape. He had twisted her hair about his hand. Leisurely yet firmly he tasted her lips and explored her mouth until Brianna began eagerly to return the soft, insistent kisses he brushed over her lips. But when the kisses became longer and hotter and deeper, draining the strength from her and causing her to melt against him and kiss him with like passion, she saw her danger. He was seducing her! She twisted her head to the side.

"Sire, I—I beg of you, loose me!"

Wulf chuckled and recaptured her rosy lips. Her mouth was so sweet and fresh and yielding, he craved to drink from it the night long. As for her pleadings, he was well aware of the wiles of maids who cried nay when their eyes and bodies said ay. He paid her not the slightest heed but picked her up and carried her to the bedcloset. After placing her inside on the furs, he removed his swordbelt and sat on the bed ledge untying his boots.

Brianna's heart raced as she crawled into the shadows beyond his reach. Her head spun, so light-headed was she from his kisses, except now it seemed that more than kisses awaited her. She knew what she wanted to do—use her dirk—but nay, she must instead sit here a-tremble like a terrified thrall and wait. Pulling her knees up to her chin, she watched in silent fury as the Norseman tossed his boots aside and stripped down to a short woolen kyrtil and woolen hose. He climbed into the bed beside her.

"I will help you undress . . ."

Brianna sat frozen, knowing she could not stop him without slaying or injuring him. But then perhaps she could plead her way out of it. As he unpinned her shoulder brooches and placed them on the bed ledge, she spoke through clenched teeth: "Why wouldst do this to me?"

Wulf drew off her apron and tossed it out onto the rushes. "Is't not what we both crave?"

Brianna's eyes flashed. "I for one certainly do not!"

Wulf's laughter rang out. He pushed her gently back into the furs. "Your kisses say I be right, little wench."

She sat up abruptly and was again pushed back, this time her arms pinned beneath her. "Sire, you warned me to—"

Wulf covered her mouth with his, at the same time slipping down her kyrtil and chemise to expose her shoulder and one full white breast. He cupped it, touched the tip of his tongue to her nipple, circled it and felt it standing erect in his mouth as he bared her other breast.

Brianna hissed in a sharp breath. The last Viking to put his mouth to her breasts had caused her to scream. She was not prepared for this gentle teasing and fluttering over her nipples and the exquisite pleasure rippling throughout her entire body. Even so, it was not what she wanted. She twisted away, tugging up her garb with trembling fingers.

"You warned me to be careful, to let no man get me alone"—she spoke with what little dignity was left her—"yet you yourself would now force me. Is this the honor of Viking chieftains, sire?"

A dark flush swept Wulf's face as he gazed on her pink cheeks and the glorious hair spread across the pillow. Had he been so wrong, then? Was it fear and not desire that made her tremble and look this way? Soft, yielding, her skin glowing and the black centers of her eyes so wide and fathomless a man might well be lost in them? Nay, he had felt her hungry response. Or was it the response of a maid who knew she had no choice but to please? He hoped he was able to tell the difference by now.

"You do not want to make love?" he asked gruffly.

"Nay, I do not want to make love!" Brianna cried. " 'Tis what I have tried to tell you."

She was scorched by her anger and humiliation. Never could she continue this stupid pretense of meekness. Never. But then what other way was there to hold the advantage she had gained thus far for Boru? She bit her lip. Oh, holy angels, there was no other. She must obey her head, not her pride, and she must not forget who she was. Ospak's slave. She bowed her head.

"F-forgive me." The words near choked her. " 'Tis just that you said you would return me safely to my people. I—I believed you, my lord."

"I am not your lord," Wulf growled, his wrath soaring. By all the gods, he did not appreciate looking to be a lecherous, lying lout in those exquisite green eyes of hers. But despite his huge annoyance, it pleased him strangely that she had actually lashed out at him. It had taken more courage than he thought she had. "I am not your lord," he repeated. "Hear you?"

"A-ay . . ."

His scar showed whitely against his dark face, and his eyes burned over her so angrily that Brianna knew real fear. She struggled to sit up, greatly hampered by the long fall of hair caught beneath her body.

"I will not touch you if 'tis not your craving, lady," Wulf said crisply. " 'Twas a misunderstanding. I take all blame."

Brianna was so astonished, she felt a burst of gratitude. She blurted, "You must not. Mayhap I was—" She caught her lip between her teeth. To admit she had received even a speck of pleasure from him was the worst thing she could do.

Wulf's eyes rested on her coolly. "Ay? You were what?"

Brianna shook her head. " 'Twas nothing. Already it has slipped my mind . . ."

Wulf glowered at her. The little vixen. He knew well what she had been about to say, as did she. It had not "slipped her mind." She had been pleasured by his kisses but would not admit it. It was a thing he did not understand. Always did he tell a maid when she pleased him. But then what man could fathom the ways and the wiles of females? None he knew ever meant what they said or said what they meant when more could be gained by teasing and lies. It would seem this Brianna was no different. So be it. Women he could take or leave, and this one he chose to leave. He could not be bothered with her foolishness. The next time, if there were a next time, the silly wench would come to him.

"Get you to sleep," he said brusquely, "and have no fear that I will crave you in the night. I will not." He lifted the curtain and departed the bed.

Brianna made no answer. She sat against the bed wall gazing at the flap of dark wool. Feeling chilled, she pulled a sheepskin over her shoulders and snuggled under another. Sleep? Hah! She had no intention of sleeping. She would sit here the night through in her clothing. He had been quick to say the blame was his, oh, ay, but the scowl he had given her said the fault was hers. In no wise did she trust him. Hearing him move away, she crept across the bed.

Through a slit in the curtain, she watched unashamedly as he carried his garb to his pallet, tossed it onto the rushes, and then moved to the hearth. Clad as he was in but a kyrtil and tight-fitting hose, Brianna saw well the broadness of his shoulders and his long, powerful legs. An easy animal grace marked his every movement, and when he knelt to bank the fire, its glow cast a golden radiance over his hair and beard. She stared. He was beautiful. As beautiful as ever Boru had been to her child-eyes, although never had she seen the Ard Ri in such a state of indecency. She scarcely breathed as he moved from one wall torch to another, snuffing all but one.

"Brianna?" His deep voice broke the silence.

Brianna started guiltily and leapt back from the curtain. "Ay, sire?"

"I will have left by the time you awaken." Wulf unrolled his sleeping bag, lay it on the pallet, and slid into it. "I trow I will be gone several days."

"And you command me to be careful and let no man get me alone," Brianna retorted more sharply than she intended. She caught her breath, for the words had slipped right out.

"Ay." Wulf's lips twitched. The wench continued to surprise him. She would have little difficulty growing accustomed to her new freedom. "I would warn you especially against the king should he stay behind."

"The king?" Brianna's skin crept. How could a mere thrall naysay the man who sat on the throne of Dublin? "Sire, if the king commands me to come to him, what am I to do but obey?"

"You heard the promise made me by the princess Gormlaith. If any man distresses you, go to her." Rubbing his tired eyes, Wulf wondered if perhaps he should have announced the maid's freedom at the board this night. But nay, it was safest for her this way. Besides, as her master, he was expected to fondle her occasionally before them all. He smiled in the shadows. What a bastard he was.

"Sire," Brianna raised her voice, "I dare not complain to the princess about her own son. I—I dare not . . ."

"Lady, you had best dare," Wulf muttered. He had marked well that Gormlaith, for whatever reason, was eager to please him. For this reason alone he trusted her. Sitric he did not. Hungry as the Dublin king was for Norse warriors, his hunger for beautiful women was greater. "Understand you what I am saying, Brianna?"

"Ay. I will do as you bid me." For now she had a more immediate problem to solve. "Sire, may I go beyond the palace walls whilst you be gone?" Without such permission she would never meet Fin.

Wulf was wide awake suddenly. Dublin itself held more dangers than the palace, filled as it was with slavers and traders, yet he did not want to restrict her freedom. "If you would walk about Dublin's streets and look at the shops, I will not say nay, but there, too, you must be careful. 'Tis unsafe for a pretty woman to stray too far. Go only in the light of day."

"I will be careful." Brianna was torn between gratitude toward him and her simmering anger at who he was and why he was there—to bring about the downfall of Brian Boru. Hearing movement and realizing that he was approaching her bed once more, she leapt against the far wall. She was huddled there when he drew the bed curtain aside and fastened it.

Seeing her jade eyes gleaming wide in the shadows, Wulf muttered, "Damn me, why be you frighted still? Have I not said I will not harm you? It has occurred to me you will need this." He drew a heavy gold chain from beneath the neck of his kyrtil.

Brianna blinked at the gold disk suspended from it. It was embossed with a silver hammer and appeared to be of great value.

"Sire, what am I to do with such a thing?"

" 'Tis my seal," Wulf said, pulling it over his head and seating himself in the bed opening. He pointed to a spot beside him. "Come to me." When she hesitated, his impatience flared. "Lady, had I wanted to force you, I would have done it by now." He reached in, caught her arm, and dragged her to him. "You will wear this," he said, undoing the stiff clasp. "Lift your hair or 'twill get tangled in the chain."

Brianna obeyed, allowing him to loop it about her neck several times and fasten it. She was overly aware of his closeness and the strength in the big, rough hands brushing her throat and her nape. It sent a chill shimmering through her.

Seeing that she trembled, Wulf gripped her shoulders and gave her a gentle shake. "For the last time, Brianna, I will not harm you. I will not lay a finger on you. 'Tis not to my liking to be thought a brute and a manhandler of women."

Brianna saw his gaze linger on the medallion which rested in the hollow of her throat. Touching her fingers to it, she found it still warm from lying against his own chest. "What means it, Wulf Thorsson, that you would have me wear this?"

"It means your safety is assured. If any accost you on the street, you have but to show them this seal and say you are the property of Thorsson of Husaby. It doubts me any will molest you then." He gave her one of his sudden rare smiles before he returned to his bed on the floor.

It was not long before his deep, even breathing told Brianna that he slept, but she herself was wakeful. He was the Wolf of Husaby. A Celt-killer. She mused again what a different man he seemed when his mood was good, and she could not put from her mind the way his mouth had felt on her lips and her breasts. She allowed herself to savor the memory only for the briefest moment before pushing it away. She must plan.

Tomorrow after he left, she would go down

to the harbor and seek Fin. There was no other way to send information to Boru. And should she flee the palace, she would need Fin's help to return home. But as of now, she saw no reason to leave. Wulf Thorsson seemed to have her best interests at heart. Ay, he seemed to . . . But every Celt alive was born and raised with a deep mistrust of the conquerors of their lands, and she was no exception. Settling herself in a corner of the bedcloset, she heaped the soft furs about her. It would be cold if the fire died, and she was not about to crawl out and mend it.

Brianna was already awake when she heard the Norseman stirring. The sounds he made told her he was yawning, crawling from his sleeping bag, and quickly donning his grab in the bone-chilling cold. At the last, he strapped on his swordbelt. She did not watch, having spied on him so shamelessly the night before, nor would she show herself since he did not expect it. But she wished she knew where he was bound so she could tell Fin. As his footsteps approached the door, she had a sudden thought. She called softly:

"Sire . . ."

Wulf frowned, seeing the bed curtain drawn aside. " 'Twas not my intent to waken you."

"You did not," Brianna assured him. "I am accustomed to rising early. Methought I might prepare morning-food for you before you took your leave."

"There is no need."

"Sire, 'tis the only way I have to—thank you for your kindness." She marked that his mail was slung over the same arm that cradled his helmet, and that the hilt of his sword was of finely worked silver encrusted with gems. A sword that drank Celt blood.

Wulf shrugged. "Do as you will." He unbarred the door and nodded to his berserks, who were already on their feet and armed. "We will break fast and then go," he ordered them. "Tell Leif."

Brianna retrieved her apron from the straw, donned and pinned it with her brooches. She was glad she had realized in time that others in the stronghold would doubtless be accompanying the Norseman. There would surely be talk as to where they were going and who else they hoped to rally to Sitric and Maelmorda. But as she followed the three to the kitchen-house, she felt a stab of remorse. She swallowed and lifted her chin higher. This was not to be believed! Why should she feel so? She was but giving back a small repayment for the misery these devils had meted out to Celts these past three hundred years. It was all right what she was doing. It was perfectly all right . . .

In the smoky kitchen-house, only the serving-folk moved about in the half-light. The bread was new-baked and wheat porridge was waiting in a vat chained above the embers in a long central fire pit. Brianna was hurrying bread, cheese, and beer to the Husaby chieftain and his party when the princess arrived. She watched admiringly as Gormlaith strode to the board where the Norseman sat, unfastened her green cloak, and tossed back her hood. Her loosened hair fell in glorious disarray down over her bosom and shoulders.

"Good morning, sire." She extended a slim white hand for Wulf to kiss. " 'Tis glad I am to have caught you before you left."

Wulf stood and touched his lips to her fingertips. "How can I be of help, my lady?"

Gormlaith's green gaze measured his height and the hard breadth of his shoulders. She felt a twinge between her thighs. "You be a gallant one, Thorsson of Husaby. Already you have given abundantly of yourself to my son and my brother and taken naught in return."

Wulf's own eyes held a deadly light. "My reward will be the fall of Brian Boru, my lady. Rest assured, the day will soon come when he lies in the dead-straw and my comrades will be avenged at last."

Studying his grim face, Gormlaith felt the thrill of the hunt. She nodded. "Ay, that do I see well. 'Tis a sad thing that it has come to this with Boru, but then you men must do what you will. A mere woman cannot understand nor guide the affairs of kings and chieftains. Know you, sire, whether or not Sitric goes with you this morn?"

"I know naught of Sitric's doings," Wulf answered.

"Well, then, I will leave you to break your fast. Here be your thrall with your meal. 'Tis why I came, to remind you again not to fear for her. I will watch over her."

"Have thanks, my lady."

Wulf remained standing. Never had he seen such a tall woman, although he himself towered over her. Now he was better able to see that the princess was not as young as first she had seemed. The fragile skin about her eyes was webbed with fine lines, and there was a hint of frost in the autumn of her great mane of hair. But she was beautiful still, this woman who had been wed to three kings. From what he knew of the three, her life could not have been an easy one, yet here she stood, full of kindness and concern for his thrall. His heart warmed.

" 'Twould seem only fitting that my wench serve you in my absence," Wulf said. He saw, too, that the maid's being at Gormlaith's beck and call would help assure her safety.

Gormlaith's red lips parted in a smile. "I take that as a special kindness, sire."

Brianna had heard from a distance his threat to Boru and was silently raging. Now she grew uneasy. She did not mind serving the princess, but would Gormlaith give her the freedom she needed to come and go?

"Know you, my lady," Wulf added as though reading her thoughts, "the wench has my leave to go into the city a bit each day. This I insist upon."

"She will have my leave also," the princess assured him.

Brianna wanted to cheer, yet she wondered how long Gormlaith would remember his words once he was gone. It was obvious that the royal mind was not on thralls or their small doings.

"Where go you this day, Thorsson of Husaby?" Gormlaith asked.

"To those strongholds southwest of Dublin."

"Then you must ride Kildare, for you will be in the mountains. He is our finest mount along with Sitric's Gulbein. I will inform the stablemaster you are to have him before I return to my quarters." The full force of her gaze was turned next to Brianna. "What be you called, child?"

"Brianna, your highness." Brianna dropped a curtsy. How beautiful she was, and how warm and generous. Again Brianna felt a twinge of resentment toward Boru for having put Gormlaith aside. How unlike him to hurt a woman so . . .

"When your master leaves, come to my apartment, Brianna. 'Tis behind the great hall, the last door on the left."

"Ay, my lady."

It was not long after the princess's departure that Sitric and his berserks noisily entered the kitchen-house.

"Brianna, go you to the princess now," Wulf said in a lowered voice. "I have no further need for you."

"Ay, master." It was a pity, for now she would hear nothing further about their journey. But as she marked the king's hot eyes upon her, it seemed unimportant. Brianna fled before Sitric drew near.

112

Chapter Seven

Gormlaith's anger mounted as she paced her bedchamber. Wulf Thorsson was the most glorious thing she had set eyes on since Boru, and to have him lusting after a sniveling thrall afraid of her own shadow was not to be believed. Perhaps she could arrange her abduction in Dublin. But then she had not missed the seal of Husaby the wench wore about her scrawny neck, nor had she money enough to tempt any man to anger the Norseman in such a way. It would be more difficult, though better by far, to coddle the bitch and thereby gain his gratitude. And once that was done . . .

Gormlaith felt a familiar exquisite heat in her depths at the prospect of sharing with the Norseman many of the gray days of winter that stretched out before them. The man could not be on the road forever. Her pleasure was interrupted by a shy tapping on her door. Ah, the wench was here already.

"Enter," she called, commanding herself to gentleness as the door creaked open and the thrall, all a-shiver, stared at her with huge eyes. "Girl, I will not bite you. Come in and shut the door."

Brianna was amazed by the sight that met her. A fur-draped throne chair before the fire, rich rugs and wall hangings, a purple silken bed-covering, thick beeswax candles in ornate bronze holders. Gormlaith's apartment was a luxurious haven in the otherwise austere stronghold, and Brianna reminded herself that a thrall would be in awe.

She gasped, "My lady, 'tis so beautiful here, it fair takes my breath away."

Gormlaith had studied the girl as she gazed open-mouthed about her chamber, and now she gritted her teeth. It was a nigh impossible task she had set herself, the coddling of this wench, for she hated her. She had hated her on sight. The fires of her jealousy leapt high seeing the soft white flesh of the maid's face and throat. Her skin was so young and fresh and moist, a man would never tire of quenching his thirst there, and her mouth was as her own had once been, full, red as a berry and doubtless tasting as sweet. She carefully masked her face before speaking.

"You may braid my hair now, Brianna, and

then fetch you the water for my bath. The men will bring it from the kitchen-house."

As the girl awkwardly tugged her hair into a plait, Gormlaith commanded herself to be calm. She would force herself to gentleness and patience with this wench if it killed her. Whatever was necessary to get the Norseman into her bed, that she would do. An idea began bubbling in her thoughts that could well help things along. Sitric. She had marked his hungry gaze on the girl last eve, but was he man enough to brave the Viking's wrath by toying with her?

She watched with veiled eyes as the wench returned with several serving-men carrying buckets of steaming water. After they had hauled the wooden tub before the fire, filled it, and departed, Gormlaith spoke:

"My scent is in the glass vial on yon table, girl. Pour a thimbleful into the water."

"Ay, my lady."

Brianna lifted the stopper and scented the water. She averted her eyes as the princess disrobed and lowered her long, shapely body into the tub.

"Why dost stand there gawking at the wall?" Gormlaith said sharply. "There be my sponge and soap on the table. Bathe me." She sank her teeth into her lower lip, damning the wench for making her forget herself. She forced a smile. "Forgive me—'tis easy to see you are unaccustomed to such work. What have you done before, child?"

Brianna blinked. Why had she not thought

ahead better than this? Her mind spun. "I—I was a kitchen-wench, my lady."

"Where?" Was there ever such a frightened mouse? Gormlaith craved to shake her until her teeth fell out. "Hast forgotten?" she asked gently.

" 'Twas at C-Carnane, lady," Brianna stammered and cursed her stupidity. It was all that came to mind, and now what if the princess recalled the name, having been wed to Boru? She held her breath as she soaped and rinsed Gormlaith's soft body with its ripe curves.

"Where be Carnane?" Gormlaith murmured, leaning forward so the thrall could wash her back.

"On Maun, lady."

"This be your first time in Dublin then?"

"Ay, lady." Brianna's relief made her sigh. The dangerous moment had passed. It was followed by quiet as Brianna completed her task.

"I trow you know naught of me?" Gormlaith spoke finally.

"Only that you were wed to the Ard Ri and be the fairest woman I have ever seen," Brianna answered.

Leaning back and gazing up into the young thrall's worshipful green-gold eyes, Gormlaith wondered if her own had ever been so clear and beautiful.

"The fairest? Oh, ay," she said bitterly. "So fair I was given in marriage to three kings who craved naught but my body." She got to her feet, rosewater streaming from her long, elegantly curved limbs, and allowed Brianna to enfold her in a wrapper of cloud-soft wool. "Know you, girl," she added softly, " 'twas my doing and mine alone that ended those marriages. Know you that."

"Ay, your highness," Brianna murmured. But she marked the sadness in the princess's eyes and knew her words were not completely true. Boru, for one, had put her aside. And it was a puzzle to her. How could he have been so cruel?

Five days had passed since Wulf Thorsson had left Dublin and since Brianna had gone into Gormlaith's service. To the good, she acted her role of thrall so convincingly that all spoke freely before her and she had many things to report to Boru. The princess was wonderfully kind, having given her several gowns and some slippers—and she had kept her promise to the Norseman. No man dared touch Brianna with Gormlaith there.

On the other hand, Brianna was near exhaustion and on edge from the strain of always pretending. Pretending meekness and obedience; pretending to be awed by the palace and the tall blond nobles and their ladies who clung so tightly to Sitric's coattails; pretending gratitude to the point of tears for the clothing Gormlaith had provided, while if the truth were known, she much preferred her trews and tunic.

But these were minor matters. Her real worry was Fin. She wondered if Ospak had ever released him from the stockade, for as she had feared, she had not yet gotten to town to look for him. Gormlaith kept her too busy. And then suddenly, the princess and her retinue left for the day and she was free. She hurried to her chamber and with trembling fingers, pulled on her long, fur-lined boots and her cloak. Hastening out into the fresh-falling snow, she was brought up short by a guard at the gate.

"Who be you and where go you?" he demanded.

Brianna opened her cloak at the neck to reveal the seal of Husaby. "My master has given me leave to visit the town whenever I choose," she answered coolly, and waited while he bent close to peer at the seal.

He waved her on. "Go you, wench, 'tis all right. Wulf Thorsson told me you would be by."

Wrapping her cloak about her more tightly, Brianna hurried over the log streets into a whipping wind. As she walked toward that area where the whitewashed shops of Dublin lay huddled in the snow, her eager eyes sought her kinsman, but her thoughts were of the Husaby chieftain. Why had a Viking, pledged to the downfall of Brian Boru and the subjugation of Celts, gone out of his way to help her, a Celt? It made no sense at all, and she wondered, not for the first time, if all he had told her was a lie. If he had no intention of freeing her.

Stepping from the bluster into the dim warmth of a weaver's shop, she found herself hoping that Wulf was deceiving her. She did not want to like him, nor feel guilty about using his kindness to betray him. In fact, it would be a boon if he forced her to remain at the palace, for what other excuse had she to stay there? As she mused on it, the weaver, a short, stout man with a red beard, waddled through a curtained opening in the rear.

"Can I help ye, lady?"

"Ay. My master has directed me to look over your blankets."

"Ye'll find naught to compare elsewhere." As he spoke, Brianna was aware that another customer entered along with a blast of wintry air.

"Can I help ye, sire?"

"Ay, I'll be needing a blanket."

Brianna's eyes flew to the tall, black-haired newcomer as he shook the snow from his cloak. She hid a smile of triumph, for it was Fin.

"If this lady doesn't mind," Fin said, "mayhap she can help me choose one."

" 'Twould be my pleasure, sire," Brianna replied, and when the weaver disappeared into his back room, she whispered, "Have thanks, Fin. Methought you might cast me to the wolves in your anger."

" 'Tis not that you don't deserve it," he said crisply. "Damn me, Annie, never have I known your like. Tell me, are you unharmed?"

"Oh, ay." As she searched through the blankets, she added casually, "None dare touch the thrall of the Wolf of Husaby."

Fin uttered an oath. "You said your slavery

119

was but a ruse, and now you tell me—"

"Hush you, kinsman, and hear me out. We have little time to talk. Wulf feels—"

Fin glowered. " 'Wulf' is it now?" Of a sudden, he spied the chain and seal about her throat. "Damn me, I'll kill him."

Brianna lay her fingers across his lips. "Nay, you will not. He feels 'tis safer for me this way. All fear him and will not incur his wrath by touching me. See you, he leaves me free to come and go." She dared not tell Fin that she did not yet completely trust the Norseman.

Fin said between clenched teeth, "I am taking you home, lass, and that is the end of it."

"Nay, Fin."

"Ay, by damn." He gripped her arm, but seeing the fire in her eyes, he groaned. "What's a man to do with a stubborn wench like you?"

" 'Tis simple," Brianna whispered. "Tell me when and where we can next meet."

Knowing he was defeated, Fin released her. "Two days hence," he muttered, "at this same time. The comb shop on the next street."

"I will be there. Tell me now, how long hast been in Dublin?"

"Since the day you arrived. Ospak feared you had fled to Carnane on foot and released me immediately. I took our mounts to Shenn Valley, hired me a boat, and here I have been ever since. Know you, it has not been an easy wait."

"My father . . . ?"

"Lachlan knows naught."

"Sire, hast made a choice yet?" the weaver bawled from the back room.

"Not yet, man." Fin chose a blanket, shook it out, and spoke into Brianna's ear. "Annie, come home with me. Lachlan will have a fit when he—"

"Fin, listen well." Brianna spoke quietly and rapidly. "Tell Boru that Sigurd of the Orkneys has rallied to Sitric. Sitric commands every Viking chieftain on the Scottish main from Uist to Aran. Wulf Thorsson, who is putting together a force for him, has strongholds on several isles. Hundreds from Norway will rally to him." She added under her breath as the weaver approached: "On Thursday he and Sitric went into the mountains to rally more men—and 'tis possible they have given up on both Ospak and Brodir. They fear treachery."

"Damn me!" Fin's eyes revealed his admiration. "I will take this direct to Boru's quarters, though it doubts me he is there now. And when he comes, don't be surprised if he insists I fetch you away from here."

"Have you chosen, sire? You'll find naught elsewhere to—"

"I will take this blanket, old fellow." Fin dropped several coins into his palm and gave Brianna a grave nod. "Have thanks, lady. Your help was much appreciated."

On the eve of the sixth day, Wulf Thorsson and Sitric Olavsson and their band rode northward through deepening snow to Sitric's stronghold on the Liffey. They had traveled far into the Wicklow Mountains and rallied many Viking chieftains to their cause, but it was not on this triumph that Wulf dwelt. Instead, his mind simmered with worries.

There had been much speculation among all regarding the strength of Boru's forces and whether his twelve years of peaceful rule in Ireland had softened the emperor's fierceness. In the end, it was agreed that peace had lasted so long only because none had craved to rouse the Lion's wrath. Wulf above all knew of the blood-lust of Boru's Celts. His old wound throbbed now, reminding him of that long-ago lightning-fast raid when he and his men had been taken unawares by them. He clenched his jaw, thinking of comrades slain on the spot; of those carried off and tortured; of his battle with a copper-haired giant whose great sword had slashed his face and laid bare his right thigh-bone. Despite the cold, sweat trickled down his chest and his back at the memory. It shamed him that he would rather go to Valhalla this moment than endure another such injury.

Wulf forced his thoughts in another direction, to the vision that drew him so constantly—the soft curves of a white bosom, small perfect pink nipples upthrust toward his hungry mouth, a cloud of flame-dark hair . . . He inhaled a deep breath and shifted in his wooden saddle to ease the fullness that accompanied his memory of Brianna. His blood ran hot, ay, but little good it would do him. Never would he allow his passion to rule him.

Not since he was a lad, new-blooded in battle and wild with victory, had he taken a maid against her will. Hearing her hopeless weeping afterward, he had vowed never again to inflict such shame and hurt. Now that subject, too, he thrust impatiently from his thoughts. Was there nothing he could think on with pleasure this day? He was becoming crotchety as an old woman. Especially infuriating to him was the news Sitric had told him.

"Your face be like a war cloud, man," Leif said softly and drew his mount near. "What are you chewing on?" He suspected it was Brianna. He sensed something was brewing between the two, and in fact hoped it was. He liked the maid.

Wulf said quietly: "Sitric has promised Gorm-laith and his crown to Sigurd of the Orkneys in exchange for Sigurd's help against Boru."

Leif gave a low whistle. "Does the princess know?"

"No one knows. It doubts me Sitric himself remembers even that he told me. He was deep in drink."

"By the gods, methought Sigurd was well content, having grown so fat on the Orkney throne. 'Twould seem he be greedier than any of us knew."

"Ay, and Sitric's yielding to his demand I find stranger still. He had but to remind Sigurd of the scathe he would receive if he twiddled his thumbs in comfort whilst the rest of us fought."

Leif grunted assent. "Far better that you had dealt with Sigurd. 'Twould have spared the princess being given to yet another king. Yon Silkbeard is an ass for sure."

Brianna had just fallen asleep when she was awakened by a soft knocking on her door. She sat up, instantly awake. Was it the princess summoning her at this late hour? She climbed down out of the bedcloset, hastily donned a wrapper, and pressed her lips to the crack.

"Ay? Who is't?"

"Wulf Thorsson," came the low answer.

Hurriedly Brianna withdrew the bar and the great door swung open on its creaky hinges. She could not speak. She could only stare up at the tall warrior standing there, his helmet nestled in the crook of his arm and his mail and swordhilt glimmering in the light of the wall torches.

Wulf's blood heated as his gaze swept her pale-green wrapper and the bright hair falling over her breasts. She was the vision of his dreams . . .

" 'Twould seem I have awakened you. I'm sorry."

"I—I have only just now retired," Brianna replied quickly. Seeing his eyes linger on her mouth, she feared he would kiss her, but the moment passed. As he moved to his pallet and placed his helmet beside it, her hand flew to her lips. What had happened to make his step so uneven? "Oh, sire, you are wounded!"

Wulf said sharply, "Why wouldst think that?"

"Y-your leg—" She saw that he was in great pain, his face so drawn and pale, but it was clear she dared not pursue the subject. Besides, if he had received the hurt plotting Boru's downfall, it was deserved. She asked coolly, "Shall I fetch you food and drink?"

"Nay. Get you back to your bed. I crave naught but sleep now."

It was a lie. He craved her. Seeing her warm and pink from sleep, and remembering the honey taste of her and how soft she had felt in his arms, he wanted to lay her down and take her then and there. But he had vowed she would come to him were there ever a next time. His eyes followed her as she moved obediently to the bedcloset.

"Brianna . . ."

Brianna turned, her hand on the curtain. "Sire?"

"Did all go well for you?"

"Oh, ay. I tended to the needs of the princess"—her heart sped as she watched him unstrap his swordbelt and lay it and his weapons carefully beside the helmet—"and she gave me such pretty things in return. Gowns and ribbons and slippers—and this wrapper. Never have I had such grand things nor been treated so kindly by a lady. 'Tis glad I am you brought me here, sire." She knew she was babbling.

Wulf frowned. He had not expected such

enthusiasm. "You have not forgotten, I trow, that soon you return to Maun." He stripped off his mail and leather and placed them at the foot of his pallet. "Never had I thought 'twould take this long to get you back to your folk."

Brianna drew a shaky breath, for once again he stood there in only his short kyrtil and skin-tight hose, firelight playing over his hair and beard and the dark-gold fur on his bare arms. She looked away, feeling the heavy drumming of her heart. She should bid him a quick good night and return to her bedcloset, but she could not allow this moment to pass. It was the perfect moment to tell him she wanted to remain. She murmured:

"Never had I thought I would crave t-to stay here, sire." She craved, too, for him to take her into his arms. The very thought of it set her afire.

Wulf glanced over at her sharply. Her voice was so faint, he doubted he had heard her aright. "What? You would stay?"

"Ay . . ." She despised the way she felt—trembling, shy, breathless, her cheeks burning. She despised it. It was a weakness she could not afford and she would not allow it to master her.

Wulf marked that she could not meet his eyes and there was a suspicious bloom on her white cheeks. The tip of her tongue slipped nervously over her lips, and her breathing had quickened. Her unspoken message was so clear, he went to her, drew her into his arms, and took her mouth, gently at first, and then passionately as his hunger flared.

Brianna was stunned. What had happened? She had but thought of being in his arms and now she was bound fast to him, her body and her mouth devoured by him. She returned his hunger, reveling in it for one glorious instant before she began to struggle. She could not allow him to make love to her. It would be a total betrayal of Boru, nor could she bear the pain of his claiming her. She had promised herself she would never endure such pain again.

She twisted from his grasp and stood glaring at him, panting, her eyes ablaze. This charade had to end. He had to know she was no thrall but was daughter to the chieftain the Maun Vikings feared more than any other. But even as the words hovered on her lips, she knew she could not say them. She knew she would play this game for as long as need be. She would be a thrall, a serving-wench, she would be anything to help Boru remain emperor of Ireland. She lowered her eyes so he could not read them, for she saw suddenly what path to take—if he did not slay her first . . .

" 'Tis your right to do with me what you will, Wulf Thorsson," she murmured. "We both know I be yours, though you say I be a freed-woman."

Wulf's already-hot blood boiled over. "For the last time," he growled low, "you are your own woman and belong to none but yourself. But whilst you be here with me, this damned game must be played. And know you, lady, I tire of your tricks. Never have I seen such a changeable wench."

"If truly I be free," Brianna flung, "then I— I refuse your attentions! 'Tis not for your love-making I crave to stay here. 'Tis that—if I return to Maun, Ospak will find and seize me again."

Wulf's jaw worked. The damned little tease. Never had he been so tormented by a wench. Did she think he was some beardless lad that he could not sense a woman's need? The way she had offered her lips, her soft body cling-ing, melting against him. The memory burned within him like a bonfire.

"I understand that you would fear Ospak, but why lie about the other? A man knows when his hunger is returned."

Cheeks aflame, Brianna retorted, " 'Tis what you want to believe, I trow."

Wulf gazed on her without answer, for there was none. Not only was she a tease, she was a liar, and of a sudden his anger and his desire for her were gone. Such a wench he did not need this night nor any other. He craved a woman who was giving, one who could make him laugh and forget, just for a time, all he yearned to forget. Above all, he craved a woman who wanted him.

"Go you to Gormlaith if 'tis your wish," he muttered and turned to the warming hearth-fire. "I trow she will find a place for you."

Brianna pondered it as he stirred the fire and laid another chunk of peat in its midst.

The princess would likely keep her so busy, she could not visit Dublin daily. She dared not risk it. But did she dare stay here? She twisted a lock of hair about one finger, fretted, murmured finally, knowing full well it was madness:

"Rather would I stay with you . . ."

Wulf shook his head. "Lady, you make no sense."

She put on an innocent face. "Sire, the princess promised you I could visit Dublin daily, but only once did I s-see the shops . . ."

Wulf stared at her. How sad, that beautiful head with nothing in it but thoughts of shops and gowns and ribbons. But then why did he expect more? At least she had told him something he could finally believe.

"Stay then," he said, "but there will be some changes made." He pointed to the pallet lying on the rushes. "Henceforward you will sleep there." He retrieved his weapons and his sleeping bag, tossed them inside the bed, and crawled in after them. He was damned if he would bid her a good night.

Brianna watched aghast. What if he jabbed his foot with the dirk hidden there? Oh, God . . . She held her breath as he tossed out several furs to her, and then the curtain fell. She waited, immobile, listening, and when no further sounds came, her heart quieted. She spread the furs on the pallet and lowered herself to it gingerly. She grimaced. The pallet was wretched. It was thin and hard and filled with lumps and twigs, and he had slept there to save her discomfort. He was the enemy, ay, but he had a heart in him; this more than anything proved it. And in what a shabby way she was going to repay him.

Brianna nibbled on a fingernail and rolled onto her side. Perhaps she should be kinder to him—but he could easily misunderstand and think she craved him. And it was beneath contempt to act kind while behind his back she betrayed him. She would take care, of course, that he would never know of it, but she would. She would know. She twisted onto her other side, gazing unhappily into the flames until she finally slept.

Chapter Eight

The next day, after Brianna took morning food to the princess and had bathed and dressed her, she said gently, "My master has returned, my lady."

Gormlaith had been watching with lazy eyes as the wench tidied her chamber and mended the fire. Now she said, sighing, "And so I will lose you . . ."

"Have you no other, your highness?"

"None I treasure as well," Gormlaith lied.

"I am sorry . . ." This side of Brianna's venture was a thing she had not planned on. She had never expected to like any in this stronghold, and it was not in her to ignore kindness such as that shown by the Husaby chieftain and this Irish princess. Also, Brianna felt great compassion for Gormlaith. It was clear that Boru had wronged her, although Brianna did not understand why.

"Mayhap I can still help with your bath since my master rises before dawn and—"

Gormlaith shook her handsome head. "Nay, Brianna, never would I dream of it. The one time you were not there for him, then he would need you. I have marked well how highly he regards your services." Seeing the maid's white cheeks and bosom turn pink, she felt murderous. She was able nonetheless to ask gently, "Be he kind to you?"

"Ay, lady." Brianna cursed the quickening blood that made her face tingle. She knew she was blushing and that it looked for all the world as if she and Wulf Thorsson were lovers.

Gormlaith lowered her voice. "You be very young, and I would not see you hurt, so fond am I of you." She pointed to a chair opposite her at the table. "Sit you, Brianna, and let us talk before you go." When the maid obeyed, she continued: "You must be wary of any kindness in Viking men. 'Tis always short-lived and always for selfish reasons. After they get what they crave, they show their true selves and 'tis then too late. I was but a maid of fourteen when I was given to Olav Iron-Shoe, the Dane-king of Dublin and a man old enough to be my father. He promised my father he would not touch me until I was older, but once I was his, the promise was forgotten. I bore his child nine months later . . ."

Brianna saw the shudder the princess could not suppress. She gasped: "He—forced you?"

" 'Twas a life of rape. I despised him after the first time."

"Oh, my lady!" It made Brianna's skin crawl. More than that, it outraged her. An Irish maid handed over by her own father to a Viking, with no end to the sort of brutal treatment she herself had experienced only briefly. It was unthinkable. "I—I sorrow for you . . ." Tears brightened her eyes.

" 'Twas not for that I told you," Gormlaith said crisply. " 'Twas but to warn you. These damned spalpeens count it their right and their duty to seed every Celt virgin they encounter. Know you, girl, this Wulf Thorsson is Viking through and through, kind though he may appear. 'Tis likely he will sell you when he tires of you or gets you with child. A pregnant woman be twice as valuable to Arab slavers as a virgin. Two for the price of one." Seeing the horror in the maid's eyes, she patted her hand. "There, there. Some good doubtless will come of it, just as good came from my years with the Iron-Shoe. I am referring to my son, of course. Sitric be the joy of my life . . ." It was a lie. Sitric was an ass, a fool, and a coward, and she cursed the day she had brought him into this world.

"I am glad," Brianna said, but she was shaken.

"Sitric be more Celt than Dane," Gormlaith said softly, her narrowed eyes studying the young thrall. "He be a gentle and sensitive man.

A man with a tender heart who is interested in more than splitting skulls."

" 'Tis grand that he gives you such joy, my lady," Brianna murmured, rising. She collected the remainder of Gormlaith's morning-food on her tray. "With your permission, I had best leave now. My master—"

"Of course, go to him," Gormlaith said sweetly, but she simmered at the wench's easy dismissal of Sitric. She craved to tear out her long, glimmering red hair strand by strand and listen to her screech, but not yet. Not yet . . .

Brianna was uneasy as she deposited the things in the kitchen-house and then trod the cold, windswept corridor to her own chamber. It was ironic that just as she had begun to trust the Norseman, Gormlaith had stirred her concerns about him again. And Sitric was another worry. It was not that she feared the king himself. She could have such a man on his back with her dirk at his throat in the blink of an eye. It was the situation she feared. As a thrall, how could she refuse him if he sought her? Hearing soft footsteps behind her, she spun. Oh, nay, it was Sitric!

"Hello, my pearl." Sitric stroked her cheek.

My pearl. Brianna turned her face to hide her disgust. It was what Ospak had called her. She murmured, "Greetings, your majesty." She gave a curtsy and made to move on.

Sitric seized her arm. "What is your hurry?"

How soft she was, and what tantalizing breasts she had. His manhood stirred as he gazed on the full swells above the neckline of her kyrtil. Having no reason to restrain his hunger, he thrust her against the stone wall of the passageway beneath a guttering torch and rubbed himself against her. He then reached inside her clothing and grasped one of her breasts.

Brianna gasped, shocked by his crudeness. "Sire! I—I beg of you. My master awaits me."

"Nay, but he does not, my pearl. He has just gone to the armorer's. By Odin, what a delectable little wench you be." He kissed her roughly and then plunged his tongue into her mouth.

Brianna felt as if she were suffocating. He was pressed heavily against her, his tongue halfway down her throat, and the scented oil on his hair and beard filled her nostrils. She tried to twist away but he held her too tightly. She could only wait until he released her. When he did finally, she sagged against him, breathless, the strength gone from her.

"Your master will be leaving Dublin again soon," he spoke low into her ear, "and this time I mean to stay behind. After he goes, you will come to me."

"My lord, I—I cannot!" she protested, her mind casting about for some reasonable way to deny him.

Sitric turned fiercely royal. "What mean you, you cannot? I am king! When I say you are to come, you come, hear you? And you will say naught of this to your master."

"Ay, my lord," Brianna answered obediently, but only because a tall figure had just appeared at the end of the shadowy corridor. Seeing the man's height and his tawny hair, she felt weak with relief. It was the Husaby chieftain.

"What is this?" Wulf asked, coming upon them. His suspicious gaze went from Sitric to Brianna. "Wench?"

Brianna's instincts told her that she dared not tell him the truth. He would take her from the stronghold and her plans would be ruined.

"I felt faint, sire," she murmured, "and the king was kind enough to assist me." She dropped a curtsy to Sitric and saw him smoothly cover his astonishment. "Thank you, my lord. I—I trow I would have swooned away but for your help."

Sitric gave Wulf an accusing look. What was the devil doing back here when he had seen him leave? He muttered, " 'Twould seem you work your thrall too hard, Thorsson."

"Ay, so 'twould seem," Wulf drawled, his hard gaze taking in the reddened skin about the maid's mouth and the frightened look in her eyes. So that was it—the bastard was at her. "Since the sun be shining for a change, Brianna, mayhap you would like to visit the shops this morn. I can spare you."

"Oh, sire, thank you!" Brianna curtsied to him, to the king, and in her confusion was giving the Norseman a second curtsy when he waved her off impatiently.

" 'Tis enough of your bobbing. Go you, before I change my mind."

"A-ay, sire."

After she hurried away, Wulf's steel-cold gaze returned to the Dublin king. "So, you kindly aided my thrall when she was faint?"

"Ay." Sitric patted his beard. "Never would I withhold my help from any, not even a thrall."

"Especially one so fair . . ." Wulf returned. When Sitric reddened, he added softly, menace in his voice: "Hear me well, Olavsson. I have pledged you my right arm, my ship, and my men, but not my thrall. Hear you? I thought I had made that clear when first we arrived." The Dubliner made to protest, but Wulf tapped his chest with a threatening finger. "Think you I know naught of what you were about?"

Sitric laughed uneasily. "Come, man, you are mistaken. Why would the maid lie?" But he was chilled by the Norseman's icy eyes.

"This be my last warning, Olavsson. I would be greatly displeased were you to ignore it."

Sitric glared after the chieftain's broad departing back. By the gods, what an arrogant devil. How dare he order a king about? And what did he mean, displeased? Would he actually withhold his followers for such a poor reason? Sitric felt his hunger for the wench fast fading. No woman on earth was worth losing a war over, but on the other hand, were the wench to come to him on her own, would Thorsson feel the same? He had to admit, he was amazed by the lie she had told. Amazed and intrigued.

But enough. He drew an in-hiss of breath. He had been on his way to tell his mother of Sigurd when he was interrupted. Now he had best get it over with—but he was not looking forward to it . . .

Brianna was eager to get away, for already she had planned to meet Fin that morn. She quickly donned her trews, tunic, and fur-lined boots. It was the only practical garb to wear in such deep snow as lay outside. She had just slipped her dirk beneath her waistband when a knock sounded. She waited, silent, fearing it was the king.

"Brianna, 'tis Wulf Thorsson," came the deep voice.

Brianna hastily unbarred the door. "I was but changing my garb to go to town, sire."

"So I see." Wulf's casual gaze moved over her long legs, slim hips, and the flaming hair that she had tucked beneath her tunic. How like a lad she seemed at first glance, and how deceptive such an assumption would be.

"Know you, sire, I—was not barring you from your own chamber."

"I have no complaint with your barring the door," Wulf said gruffly. " 'Tis a good idea, considering . . ." He waited, half expecting her to admit that Sitric had frightened her. He felt a surge of anger when she did not but instead donned her cloak and gloves.

" 'Tis exceeding grateful I am for your permission to go to town, sire."

Wulf's eyes flickered a warning. "Lady, you be free to visit town whenever you choose. The permission I gave was for the king's benefit alone." He removed his cloak and flung it onto a bench.

Seeing his annoyance, Brianna sensed what ailed him. His pride was badly stung by her rejection of him last eve. She marveled that he could remain so kind and protective of her still. Although Gormlaith's warning about Viking men rang in her ears, her heart told her she need not fear the Wolf of Husaby. She smiled, minding the princess's boast that her precious son was gentle, sensitive, and tender-hearted. It was clear that Gormlaith did not know as much as she thought. Wulf Thorsson was a benevolent god in comparison to Sitric; a benevolent god who was annoyed by Brianna's continuing submissive behavior. Very well, if he craved for her to change, so be it. She strode to the bench, retrieved his cloak, and examined it.

"This be in dire need of repair," she declared. " 'Tis ripped and filled with holes. When I return from town, I will mend it for you. I will also wash your kyrtil. Kindly have it waiting for me, sire." She was gratified to see him blink.

"I like my clothing as 'tis," Wulf growled, taken aback by her forthrightness.

"Your cloak is in tatters. As for your kyrtil—" Brianna's nostrils twitched, but seeing the dangerous glint in his eyes, she said no more. She shrugged, pulled on her hood, and opened the door. At the last moment she turned. "If you should change your mind, sire, you know where to find me . . ."

With the sun shining so brightly, there were more folk on the snowy streets of Dublin than Brianna had seen thus far. Even the comb shop was crowded with traders. She was glad, for none paid her any heed as she took her time examining the wares. As she admired the various combs and spindles and knife handles, she wondered if Fin had seen her arrive. She had little news to give him this time, but she was eager to hear his news of Boru.

When after a time he still had not appeared, she began to worry. Had he been found out? She started, feeling a tap on her shoulder. It was an aged man who had squeezed in beside her. He was tall and stooped and the hood of his disreputable cloak nearly covered his face. In a faint voice, he said:

"Have ye ever seen the craftsman make his combs, lady?"

When Brianna gave him a cool stare and moved on, he followed. She said sharply: "Move along, sire, I have no interest in seeing combs made."

"Then you had best develop one quickly, Brianna," came a deep familiar voice.

Her mouth fell open as she met a pair of steel-gray eyes. Boru!

"Come along, lass," said the emperor of Ireland, taking her arm and propelling her toward

140

the back of the shop. "The shopkeeper is a friend of mine. We can talk safely here."

Brianna held her tongue as she was drawn into a curtained room, but once there, she uttered a small joyous shriek and leapt into Boru's open arms. She gave him a fierce hug which he returned, making her breathless.

"Oh, Boru, what a grand disguise. Oh, I cannot believe this!" She kissed both his cheeks and patted his thick coppery beard much as she had when she was a child. Only then did she see the ice in his eyes.

"Nor can I believe what your kinsman tells me," Brian growled. He sat her in a chair like a naughty child and stood gazing down on her, arms crossed over his broad chest. "Damn me, Brianna, what mean you by this fool trick? I will not have you at the mercy of Silkbeard."

"Never was I at his mercy, Boru, nor will I ever be," she answered quietly. "Did Fin not tell you of Wulf Thorsson?"

"Oh, ay." Brian's coppery brows drew together. "That be another thing—first Ospak, then Thorsson, and you in thrall to both bastards . . ." He opened Brianna's woolen cloak and glared at the seal of Husaby gleaming on her white throat. "By all the saints, this abomination comes off immediately. Lift your hair! Never will I understand, Brianna, what possessed you to—"

"Boru, nay." Brianna caught his big hands. "You will hear me out."

Seeing the fire in her eyes, Brian allowed her to stay his hands, but his wrath was unabated.

"You be no man's thrall, girl. Never will you go back to that viper's nest. Know you that since Fin brought me word of your whereabouts, I have had men positioned to storm the stronghold if you did not appear this day."

"Oh, Boru!"

He stood her on her feet and gave her an angry shake. "Never could I have looked your father in the eye had anything happened to you."

Brianna whispered, "My father knows?"

"For the love of God, woman, what a question!"

The emperor's gray eyes burned molten and the skin about his compressed lips was white as the streaks in his hair and beard. He was more furious than Brianna had ever seen him, and of a sudden she felt her own fury stirring. Was this how it was to end, then? Was she to be taken back to Maun in disgrace? Was she to be considered nothing but a silly woman who had endangered the lives of many men by her foolishness and who had brought grief to those who loved her?

"Was my information no help to you at all, then?" she asked stiffly.

"Now you embarrass me," Brian muttered. "Have thanks. 'Twas of greater value than ever you could know, but 'tis beside the point. I will not have you in such great danger. I will put a man there."

So. He still needed someone in Sitric's court, and she had been of help—he had just said so.

Now she had but to calm him and make him see reason. She drew a deep breath.

"Sit you and listen to me, Boru. Please." She gave him a smile. " 'Twould help if you released my arms so they did not ache so . . ."

"Damn me." Brian's handsome face darkened. He loosed her abruptly and sat himself on the craftsman's bench.

Brianna drew up a stool at his feet and perched on it. She knew what she was going to say and she wasted no time. "When last we met, you said I would always be ten winters in your eyes." Seeing those eyes mist, she added gently, "You cannot afford such whimsy, Boru. I am not a child, but a woman of twenty-three winters. You be at war and need a spy in Sitric's court. I am there already and well able to defend myself, you have but to ask Fin. And I have proven my value to you—you have just admitted it."

Brian was silent. He could not refute the maid, for her every word was true. But he did not like it. His stony gaze went to the seal of Husaby.

Reading his thoughts, Brianna said, "I swear to you, I am not his thrall. 'Tis but a game we are playing whilst I am at the palace. He says none will toy with me if they think I am his." She went on to answer his questions of the Husaby chieftain as best she could—from that moment she had first seen Wulf Thorsson until this day. She marked that the emperor, listening gravely, weighed her every word.

"Long have I heard of this Wulf of Husaby," Brian said after she had finished. "He has slain Celts without number in years past, yet 'tis said he be an honorable man." He added drily, "I myself have no proof of this."

"In the palace, they call you Brian-the-Hundred-Killer," Brianna answered softly, "and all know you be an honorable man." Seeing that he was deeply worried still and undecided, she added, "I have come to trust him. He minds me much of you, Boru. He even looks like you. He is tall and strong and—and he is gentle with me . . ."

"And he be a Viking," Brian growled.

"Ay." Brianna bit her lip and gazed at the packed earthen floor. Why had she said such a stupid thing? Naturally he would not be pleased, her comparing him to a Viking.

The emperor studied his foster daughter's red cheeks and the way her slender fingers twisted in her lap. He frowned. What was this? Was the lass smitten by this so-noble chieftain or was it her excitement at the prospect of helping him that made her look and act so? It had best be the latter, he thought grimly. An entanglement with a Viking could bring her nothing but grief.

"You have no doubt he will continue to protect you?"

"I have none. He has proven it again and again." Seeing that Boru was softening, Brianna nearly blurted that Wulf had saved her that very morn from Sitric's attentions. She caught herself just in time, for never would Boru allow her to remain in the palace if he thought Sitric was a real threat. Nor must he learn that Gormlaith was in residence. The princess loved him still, but he had no use for her.

" 'Tis settled, then." Brian rose abruptly to his feet. "You may stay."

Brianna was dumbfounded, for she had been prepared for a lengthy argument. "You will not worry?"

"I will worry every instant, but then I am not so poor a general as to turn away such a warrior as you because of it. 'Twill be a great boon to have you there. I admit, valuable time would be lost if we had to put another in your place, and time is in short supply."

"You will—fight soon?"

"All the signs say the battle will be joined this spring," Brian answered.

Five months. It seemed far off, Brianna mused, but it was not. Not when war lay at the end. The game she was playing had become reality, and soon men would be fighting and dying. She dragged her thoughts away from the horror of it and back to Boru.

"—and know you, girl," he was saying, "my men have a constant guard on the palace. Should even one day pass when you do not appear, we go in for you."

"I understand. I will show myself daily, even if 'tis just to take the air at the gate." She watched in fascination as he pulled the hood over his grizzled lion's mane and became once more that bent and aged man who had talked to her of combs. She followed him from the back room, through the crowded shop and out into the snowy street.

"You'll not forget, lass"—Brian's quiet voice held command and his gray eyes were now unmistakably those of the Ard Ri, the emperor of Ireland—"this Wolf of Husaby be your blood enemy. He be the enemy of us all."

"Nay, Boru, I will not forget . . ."

Chapter Nine

Her blood enemy . . .

Of a sudden, Brianna wanted nothing so much as to run after Boru crying that she had changed her mind. Wulf Thorsson was not *her* blood enemy. He wanted only to save her from those who would harm her, and he had made her feel as no man had ever made her feel before. Nor would she ever forget that he had slept on that dreadful pallet to spare her. Nay, he was not her blood enemy.

She put her fingers to lips that had begun to tremble. Boru was right, of course. He was her blood enemy. How could she deny it? He was a Viking warrior who had slain many of her people, and now he had sworn to slay Boru. With her own ears she had heard him tell Gormlaith his reward would come on that day when Boru lay in the dead-straw. The words chilled her, but only for an instant. After that, they served to fire and strengthen her, to remind her that he was indeed her enemy. He was the enemy of every Celt alive, and any small human kindness he offered her was as nothing compared with his own bloody goal: to slay the Lion of Ireland and keep her people oppressed.

Brianna threw back her hood, freed her hair from beneath her tunic, and lifted her face to the warming sun. Perhaps by summer there would be peace in the land again. With Boru at the helm, there could be nothing other than a Celt victory. And she would have helped. His name and face filled her thoughts as she started back toward the palace. Boru . . . Boru . . . Bo-ru . . . BO-RU. She walked in rhythm to her whispered chant, face aglow, head high, unaware of the admiring glances cast her way.

As Wulf left the armorer's, his eye was caught by Brianna's slender figure in the distance. Gazing after her, he was amused by how regally she walked, cape flying and the wind lifting her long russet hair. By the gods, how quickly she was changing. First ordering him to surrender his clothing for repair, and now this—striding along as though she owned Dublin. Or did she always turn from an obedient thrall into the lady of the manor when she came to town? Intrigued, he walked faster, narrowing the gap between them. On an impulse, he scooped up a handful of snow, packed it, and lobbed it at her.

Brianna had been marching into battle at the side of the Ard Ri when there was a sudden thud against her shoulder and a shower of snow spilled inside the neck of her tunic. She gasped. Little boys! The little wretches were the same everywhere. Whirling to confront them, she discovered, not a band of urchins, but the Wolf of Husaby. His face bore a shamefaced grin as he tossed her a salute and sauntered over to her.

"Greetings, mistress."

Brianna's laughter rang out as she decided this was a game two could play. She knelt, rapidly packed a ball of her own, and let it fly. She saw the Viking's astonishment as it thudded against his shoulder so hard it clung there. She casually brushed the snow from her gloves.

"Greetings, sire. 'Tis a grand day for a walk, is it not?"

Wulf gave a low admiring whistle. "Where didst learn to throw like that?"

Brianna's gaze was one of innocence. "Like what?" She plucked the clump of snow from his cloak. "I hope I did not injure you, sire."

Wulf chuckled and fell in step beside her. "You throw like a man. 'Tis a thing I have not seen before, a maid with a strong right arm." He brushed the crystals from off her own cloak. " 'Twould seem there is more to you than meets the eye, Brianna. Mayhap someday I will hear your story."

" 'Tis a fascinating one, for sure, filled as 'tis

with cooking and mending and baking."

She had a sudden foreboding. How long had he been following her? Had he seen her with that shambling, stooped man and recognized him as the emperor? But then such worries could drive her out of her mind. She simply must not imagine a ghost behind every tree.

"Didst find aught to your liking in the shops?" Wulf asked.

" 'Twas so pretty outside, I visited only one place," she answered. "The comb shop."

Wulf could not take his eyes off her. With her head held high and her queenly stride, he saw her of a sudden in her own manor house wearing the jewels and the gown of a lady, ay, the very gown he had yet to buy her. It would be green-gold to match her wonderful eyes and of a fabric that caught the light and every graceful line of her body as she moved. The moment was gone then and it seemed she was exactly where she ought to be—not in a manor house but by his side sharing talk with him, her long legs matching his stride and laughter on her lips. He had to blink several times to dispel the euphoria it gave him.

"—and then tomorrow," Brianna was saying brightly, "I must visit the cobbler to see his slippers and ribbons and 'tis said there is a dressmaker nearby—and a jeweler. Oh, I so love to look at all the pretty things. Dost like the shops, too, sire?"

"They be a necessary vice, I trow," Wulf muttered. "This minds me—I have not yet bought your gown. But you will have it, 'tis a promise."

Was he losing his wits, he wondered, day-dreaming of sharing his life with a wench who cared for nothing but clothes and ribbons and looking at the shops? It was laughable. Except she was ravishing. He imagined her in his bed, naked, with her long hair a silken veil wrapped around them both. He made to dismiss the delectable illusion, but it clung. He had held her close only twice, yet his head was filled with the way she felt and tasted, the fragrance of her skin . . .

"I see the logs be slippery along here," he said brusquely.

"Ay." Brianna slowed her step. " 'Tis a glitter of ice since I passed this way earlier."

" 'Twouldn't do for you to go down. Let me help you." He slid a strong arm about her waist.

Brianna hesitated. "Sire, 'tis not that I be ungrateful, 'tis just that now if either of us falls, w-we go together . . ."

Wulf laughed. "Lady, we will not fall. These feet of mine be so nimble, I leap from oar to oar whilst my men row."

Brianna giggled at the picture it made. A giggle that turned to a shriek as her feet suddenly flew out from under her. She flailed her arms before going down in a heap, taking the astonished Norseman with her. He lay beneath her, his arms about her, protecting, and her cape of hair spread across his face. She looked down on him, horrified.

"Oh, sire! Oh, 'tis sorry I am!" She began to laugh then. She could not help the laughter that pealed from her throat at the sight of him stretched out on the icy logs, her hair draped over him . . .

Wulf gave a mock scowl as he climbed to his feet and then helped her. "As I was saying when I was interrupted, I be the most nimble of the nimble—"

Brianna nodded, her merriment bringing tears to her eyes. "Oh, ay, leaping from oar to oar whilst your men row."

"Ay." His own eyes danced. " 'Tis just that on land I be not quite so agile."

They set forth again, this time more cautiously, with Brianna's gloved hand tucked inside his arm. Once more Wulf experienced a warm euphoria from having her beside him, and once more he damped it. The last thing on this earth he needed just now was to grow overfond of a Celt thrall who had given him nothing but aggravation. But there was no denying he'd been pleased to see her striding along as though she owned Dublin. And that she had insisted on mending his cloak was good, and that she could laugh with him and even tease him a bit was also fine. She was gaining a sense of worth.

Brianna yawned and slipped into her bedgown, glad that the day was finally ended. Perching on a stool and braiding her hair into one long rope for the night, she wondered when she had ever been so weary from having done so little. After adding another chunk of peat to the fire, she snuffed all but one of the wall torches, unbarred the door, and dropped to her pallet. She pulled the furs over her and yawned again. It was as though she were made of lead.

Closing her eyes, she immediately saw Wulf Thorsson's face, saw him laughing with her amid the snow and ice. How strange that he should have been so carefree with her after his anger of last night. This morn, too, he had been stiff. She sighed. The truth was she did not want to know why such a change had come about. In fact, if he turned cruel, she would consider it a blessing.

Hearing the door creak open, she lay rigid under the furs, her eyes squeezed shut. She did not want to see him nor talk to him. She wanted only to sleep and forget him, except that now her whole body was alive and tingling. Scarcely daring to breathe, she listened for the sounds of him preparing for bed. There were none. What was he doing, she wondered angrily, watching her? Her lids fluttered with the effort to remain closed, and then she gave up. Opening them, she found him gazing down on her. She swallowed.

"G-good evening, sire."

Brianna's heart was out of control. He was helmeted, his cloak flung back over one broad shoulder, and his sword and his great battle-axe hanging from his belt. Torchlight glinted in his hair and put a dangerous glitter in his eyes. The sight of him fair took her breath away.

"I but wanted to see if you slept," Wulf said softly, "and now I have frighted you."

"Nay, you have not." What frightened her was his continuing concern and kindness. She prayed he would turn cruel and tell her she was not now free and never would be free; prayed he was about to sell her to Arab slavers; prayed she might forget their laughing together this morn . . .

Wulf looked on her entranced. If ever he had seen a fairer wench, it was only in his dreams. He watched her sit up and rub her eyes, her shining rope of hair curving over one breast and drawing his gaze to the small nipples that thrust against her bedgown. He looked away. Nay, there would be none of that. She had made her wishes quite clear, and he craved at this point only to stay on good terms with her. He removed his helmet and swordbelt and placed them at the foot of his bedcloset.

"Shall I fetch food or drink for you, sire?" Brianna asked.

Wulf shook his head. "Nay." Seeing that she was fully awake, he added, "You were happier this morn than I have ever seen you."

She shrugged. " 'Twas a beautiful day to be out and about." She averted her eyes as he stripped off his leather tunic.

" 'Twas naught but that then? The beauty of the day?"

Brianna was instantly wary. Had he seen her with Boru after all? She answered through stiff lips, "Sire, I—know not what you mean . . ."

Wulf, sitting on the bed ledge to tug off his boots, said easily, "Lady, you marched through Dublin as though you owned it and then you near felled me with a snowball—and you say 'twas all because of the day?"

Brianna expelled a deep sigh. She was safe from discovery, but she must give him a more believable answer. She said quietly:

"You be right, sire. The truth is that—that ever since you freed me, I have craved to shout it to all of Dublin-town." She added hurriedly, "Of course, never would I do such a thing, seeing as how none must know." She watched in astonishment as he came and knelt by her pallet. When his hands slipped under her hair and brushed her nape, she felt a shiver of delight. She gasped, "Sire, what are you doing?" It was then that she felt the chain being removed from her neck.

"I am returning the seal of Husaby to where it belongs," Wulf said. Still kneeling, he settled the chain around his own neck. "Tomorrow all in this stronghold will know you be a freedwoman. I should have considered your feelings earlier. 'Tis only natural you would want others to know."

"Sire, you cannot fault yourself for that! 'Twas for my safety."

Wulf's jaw tightened. Oh, ay, and he had been damned quick to take advantage of the situation. "You will be safe still should you care to remain here to work."

Brianna blinked. If she cared to remain? If? "Sire, where else would I be?" she exclaimed. "I be a stranger in Dublin! Please, I—I will be your servant if you will have me."

Seeing her fright, Wulf said easily, "Of course I will have you. I but wanted you to know the choice was yours. On the morrow when I announce your freedom, I will make it clear you wish to remain as my servant and will still be under my protection."

Shame brightened Brianna's cheeks as she whispered, "You be too kind . . ."

From the very beginning, she had found every reason to doubt this Viking warrior, but she doubted him no longer. Celt-hater though he was, Wulf Thorsson had proven to her that he was a good and honorable man who craved her well-being. She was shocked now by the realization that she craved the same for him. All along she had fought her attraction for him—he was more comely than any man alive and his resemblance to Boru fascinated her—but this was different. This had nothing to do with the way he looked or the way he made her heart race. This had to do with the man himself, with his gentleness and compassion. Of a sudden, she cared desperately what happened to him, and she knew it was the worst fate that could have befallen her.

Seeing the new tenderness in her eyes and the tears that had come so swiftly, Wulf grew watchful. What was this now—was her heart melting at last? Cautiously, he touched his fingers to the soft curve of her chin and then stroked her cheek. Her skin was like satin. And when one small hand slid atop his, the other shyly touching his face, tracing his mouth, the neatly bearded line of his jaw, his temple, lingering to touch his hair, Wulf's hunger flared.

Gone, vanished like smoke, was his intention to be on but good terms with her. Long and long had he waited for such a moment as this, and before it could vanish, he kissed her mouth, a kiss as light as a butterfly wing. She returned it, her parted lips warm and sweet and giving. And when he revealed a deeper hunger, she responded eagerly before she drew back. He reined a flare of impatience.

"So, you fear me still."

Brianna shook her head. "Never will I fear you again."

Wulf caught both her hands, kissed the palms, kissed her slender white wrists. "What is't then? Never would I harm you."

" 'Tis just that . . ." She could not go on, for what was there to say? Was she to confess that she could not care for him nor make love with him because she was here to spy for Boru? She covered her face.

"Brianna . . ." When she made no answer but began to weep softly, Wulf got to his feet. " 'Tis all right, 'twill end here and now," he said quietly, but his pulsing blood was a torment. He was confused and angry. What in damnation ailed this wench? Was it that he was Norse and she

Celt? There was much of intermingling and intermarriage between their two peoples, but for some the hatred was too great to overcome. Perhaps she was such a one.

"Brianna, hush you now," he murmured low. "Never would I force you to do aught against your will."

She raised a tear-streaked face. "Sire, I know you would not."

Wulf's heart was squeezed in a vise. Even in weeping, she was the fairest thing he would ever see in this life—drowned green-gold eyes, the long lashes webbed with tears; the sweetly arched brows and white forehead; her full, trembling underlip; hair like burnished chestnut. Pondering her quiet sobbing, he thought of that time when she had first spurned his kisses and he thought her a tease. Now he knew she was not. Thrall though she was, he saw that she was an honorable maid who craved him as he craved her. That she held him off after revealing her hunger told him that something was gravely amiss. She had some deep fear which he could not fathom, but while she wept was not the time to question her. He gently drew her up from the pallet.

" 'Tis time you dried your eyes and slept, Brianna. You will feel better when you awaken." He led her to the bedcloset. "You will sleep here from now on. I am used to a pallet."

"Nay," Brianna murmured, her voice thick with tears. "I will not take your bed from you."

"You are not taking it, I am giving it."

Brianna gave her head a violent shake. " 'Tis kind of you, but I—I cannot." She did not deserve a nice bed, especially not his.

Wulf shrugged. "If 'tis your wish . . ."

" 'Tis my wish."

She returned to the wretched mat and pulled the furs up over her. Curling into a ball with her back toward him, she allowed her tears to flow afresh. She nearly strangled on them, having little experience with tears, and stuffed her fist into her mouth to stifle the sound. How had such a thing as this ever happened? She cared for him. And he cared for her. She had seen it in his eyes, felt it in the tender way he touched her, marked it in his voice when he said he would never force her to do anything against her will.

She heard him placing more peat on the fire and extinguishing the last wall torch, heard the creaking of the great wooden bed as he climbed into it and thence into his sleeping bag. Long and long she lay awake, her eyes on the tiny flames licking the peat. No sound came from his bedcloset, yet every part of her felt the heat of his craving for her, and then of a sudden there came deep within her own body a hot starburst of sensation. She gasped, realizing its meaning. She wanted him. She wanted him close, wanted his long arms and legs wrapped about her. She wanted him within her, no matter what pain it brought . . .

Turning, she gazed toward his bed with joyless eyes. It was bootless even to think of

Joan Van Nuys

such a thing. The barriers between them were too high. She could not cross them, and he would not. Never would he take her against her will. In her mind's eye, she saw herself fleeing Dublin, refusing to stay here and betray him. But what of Boru? He needed her here in the enemy's midst. But she could not stay, came her silent cry. She could not. But even as she swore it, Brianna knew that she would.

Boru she had known and loved forever; Wulf Thorsson she scarcely knew at all. He had won her gratitude and her growing concern for his well-being, ay, but more than that she could not give. It had been a grave mistake to return his kiss and let him see she cared for him. It was not fair to either of them. And if, God forbid, he ever learned of her treachery, it would be far better for them both if he hated her. But then, he must never find out. It was one more promise she made to herself.

Chapter Ten

When Brianna awoke the next morn, the Norseman's bed was empty and his clothing was gone. The sky beyond the slit of a window was so murky, it could have been eventide, and she felt as tired as if she had not slept at all. It was the same leaden weariness she had experienced the night before, and now she knew it for what it was. Dread. Pure dread for the task which lay ahead of her. She forced herself to rise, bathe in icy water, dress, and comb out her hair.

In the kitchen-house, the wenches were just then taking steaming oatmeal, cheese, and bread to the great hall for the folk to break their fast. Marking a new maid struggling to carry several tubs of clotted cream at once, Brianna moved quickly to her side.

"Here, let me help you . . ." She took two of them and hurried toward the corridor.

" 'Tis kind of you," the girl said, falling into step.

Brianna smiled, marking that she was a pretty young thing, soft and plump as a brown baby rabbit. "You'll find 'tis easier to use a tray next time," she offered.

The maid sighed. "Never had I thought of that—always have I been a bodyservant. Mayhap we can talk later and you can give me more advice. My name be Fiona."

"I'm called Brianna. There's little I know, Fiona, but ay, we can certainly talk."

Brianna made her own way then, carrying the cream to the high-board and placing one tub before Wulf Thorsson. She kept her eyes lowered. She felt such a traitor, she could not look at him. She was too heartsick to wonder even if those at the board had been told yet of her freedom.

"Shall I fetch you aught else, sire?"

"Nay, this will do nicely."

Feeling his eyes on her, Brianna wondered if he were thinking of last eve and her kissing him so hungrily before turning him away again. Or was he remembering her stupid tears and her stubborn refusal to sleep in his bed rather than on the floor? She had not handled herself at all well.

Sitric, spooning cream onto his oatmeal, said, "Your thrall is a late riser this morn, Thorsson."

"She needed her sleep," Wulf drawled. "'Tis as you said, I work her too hard."

Sitric moistened his lips as his eyes slid over Brianna. "Lucky devil that you be . . ."

Marking Brianna's blush, Wulf craved to throttle the bastard. He smiled instead. After all, he had encouraged them all to think what Sitric was thinking, but now he would right matters.

"I trow this is as good a time as any to announce I have given the lady her freedom," he said.

Sitric stared. "Man, you astonish me. Her freedom?"

"Ay." Wulf marked that all at the board heard and that they, too, stared. "As such, she is free to leave, but 'twould seem she chooses to remain here—"

"Well, now . . ." Sitric's hot gaze flickered over Brianna.

"—as my serving-wench," Wulf concluded. "Know you, Olavsson, as well as the rest of you, she be under my protection still."

Sitric nodded. "Of course. I trow we will all strive to protect her."

Wulf laughed. "Oh, ay."

His skeptical eyes rested on Sitric for a long moment and then moved slowly over the nobles seated there. Half had wives, still abed in their quarters behind the stronghold at this early hour. The other half would not protect the maid but would bed her in all haste if she allowed them. From his own experience, Wulf doubted that would be a problem. As for Sitric—he himself would handle Sitric. Marking that Brianna stood there still, wide-eyed and uncertain, he said gently:

" 'Tis all right, Brianna. Go you and break your fast now."

Brianna made a curtsy. "Ay, sire."

Wulf frowned as she left. Why did she look so wan and frightened when she should have been bright-eyed and bursting with excitement? Never would he understand women.

As Brianna hastened through the chill corridor to the kitchen-house, it seemed as if the earth were shifting beneath her feet. Thinking it was hunger that made her feel so poorly, she tried to eat, but there was no food that she wanted. She yearned to be where it was quiet so she could convince herself that she was doing the right thing. Fleeing to her chamber, she sat on a bench in the half-light, face buried in her hands, and chanted a litany of Viking outrages that had taken place in her own land.

In years past, there was not one man, woman, or child in her tribe who had not lost a loved one through death or slavery to the raiders. She could still see Con Kinrade, Fin's father, lying in the dead-straw. He had died by the blood-eagle, his chest hacked open and his beating heart and lungs pulled out to flutter and die while the Norsemen laughed.

And that one who had had his will with her, he had laughed afterwards. Never had she dreamt she would have a chance to repay the outrage. Not until now. But it meant being hard as iron and not afraid to do what had to be done. Above all, it meant not allowing her feelings for Wulf Thorsson to grow beyond her control. She was brooding over it, wondering if she were brave enough and strong enough to walk such a path when a soft knocking came.

"Brianna?"

"Ay, sire, please come in. 'Tis not barred."

Her hand went to her heart to deaden its ache at the sight of him. His brows were a golden slash over his eyes and his lips were a thin line. He was angry and she knew exactly why. She was coming to know him too well. He had resented Sitric's crudeness toward her and he was disappointed in her lack of enthusiasm at being freed. He wanted to see her happy . . . At the thought, she dug her nails into her palms. This was exactly what she had vowed not to do—allow her feelings for him to become too important.

"Are you ill?" Wulf asked. She was too pale and her eyes too big.

"I—felt faint earlier, but now that I have rested a bit, I'm fine." Brianna gathered up the sheepskins from her pallet, shook them, and then shook the pallet itself. Sensing his eyes on her, she turned and gave a shy smile. "Sire, I have not thanked you for my freedom. Know you, I be grateful." Dropping to her knees suddenly, she touched her lips to his boot. "Never have I known such kindness . . ."

Seeing her bent over his feet, the white nape of her neck so soft and vulnerable, Wulf felt a spear of red rage pierce him. By holy Odin but he hated slavery and all who practiced it. Had he in his hands that bastard who had first stolen the maid, he would have broken him in two. He grasped her shoulders and raised her roughly to her feet.

"Lady," he rasped, " 'tis the last time you will ever kneel to anyone again. Hear you?"

"Ay," Brianna whispered. She managed a smile. " 'Tis the last time, I—I promise."

Wulf held his arms at his sides rather than catch her to him and kiss her mouth. "Know you, Brianna, you have but to say the word and I will take you home to Maun."

Home. Carnane at Yuletide. That holiest of days was but one month hence and happy memories overcame her: green boughs everywhere, the Yule log burning, the bustling kitchen-house with its wonderful aromas. She forced the visions away. She must not even think on them. It was war she must think on . . .

"I will stay, sire."

Wulf nodded. "So be it. And now I trow you will want to live with the other maids."

Brianna recalled that several of the serving-wenches, Fiona included, lived on the first floor of a longhouse that stood behind the kitchen-house. Living there could have great advantages, but she dared not show her enthusiasm. She murmured:

"If 'tis where you would have me, sire."

Wulf gave her a look of exasperation. "By the gods, do *you* want to be there? 'Tis your decision to make."

Seeing his annoyance, Brianna bit her lip. " 'Twould be nice, I trow, to be with the others. Ay."

He could not have made it more clear. Any decision involving herself was hers to make. She was to leave her thralldom behind her. And while she felt a certain sadness that they would no longer share this bedchamber—she had come to enjoy his concern and his caring for her—in all ways it was for the best. And now she must get busy. She said brightly:

"I will move my things later in the day, sire, but this morn I mean to mend your cloak— nor have I forgotten your kyrtil. Hast another to wear whilst it dries?"

"Ay." Wulf stared at the roses in her cheeks and how her eyes sparkled of a sudden. Did the little wench enjoy menial tasks as much as all that? He said, teasing, "Mayhap I will bring you my sail to mend next."

Brianna's lips twitched. "You doubt I could do it?"

"Your hands seem a trifle small and soft . . ."

"Sire, there is naught I cannot do. I will be the best serving-wench you ever had." Everything considered, it was the least she could do for him.

Wulf laughed. " 'Tis likely you will, lady. You be the only serving-wench I ever had."

*   *   *

Gormlaith forced open her eyes and gazed about her with distaste. What was this? Her always-immaculate bedchamber was as dim and sour-smelling as the pig house. God's bones, what hour of the day was it? Not only was her head splitting but the fire and torches were dead and the windows still covered. Why had her wench not awakened her and tended to such duties? She was about to shriek the woman's name when she remembered she had driven the old fool out last eve and told her not to come back. Megan was the last in a long succession of unsatisfactory wenches who had tended her since she had first come here from Kincora. Now Gormlaith found herself yearning for Brianna. Much as she loathed her, the girl could at least follow directions. Hearing a familiar voice raised at her door, she smiled. Well, well, was her luck changing then?

"Your highness, 'tis Brianna. May I come in?"

Gormlaith lay back on her pillows and flung an arm across her forehead. "Enter," she called weakly. Through lowered lids, she watched the maid come in, stop, and stare about her at the cold dark chamber and the disarray.

"Your highness, what has happened!"

"I be somewhat ill today, Brianna. Doubtless 'twas the ale last eve."

"Shall I fetch Megan? 'Tis odd she has not come before this."

Gormlaith knew better than to lie. The damned old witch already would have moaned to the other servants that she had been ill-treated and driven out.

"Megan hates me, child," Gormlaith said wearily. "I told her to go and not come back. I feared she would poison me one day." She put both hands to her eyes, covering them.

"Oh, my lady, none could hate you!" Brianna gazed about the untidy chamber again. "I came for the sewing box—I must mend the Norseman's cloak, but I trow he would bid me attend you first. Wouldst have me?"

Gormlaith looked at her with pain-filled eyes. "What a question—does a caged bird not yearn to fly?"

"Then I will return with your morning-food, and I will bid the men fetch your bathwater."

Gormlaith sighed. "You be a godsend."

Brianna simmered as she hastened to the kitchen-house. The princess had had much to contend with in her lifetime, and even now she was to have no peace. Slovenly servants were the least of it. She looked so unhappy always that Brianna sensed her heart was breaking over the rebellion against Boru. But then how could one lone woman defy the wills of kings and chieftains bent on war? She could not. She could only be swept along with the angry tide. And considering her own part in it, Brianna felt compelled to offer her extra kindnesses. Thus it was that Gormlaith, still abed among her furs and satin pillows, broke her fast with hot oatmeal, cream, and fresh-baked bread while Brianna rolled up the window coverings, rekindled the fire, and tidied the room.

But Brianna herself was troubled. When she had fetched the food, the kitchen-house was abuzz with talk. It was said that Gormlaith, screaming insults and hurling shoes, had driven Megan from her chamber last eve. It was also said that Megan might have deserved a small rebuke but not the venom the princess had heaped upon her. In Brianna's eyes, the old woman was like her own beloved Maeve, half-blind, slow, and doubtless her bones ached constantly. It was a shame if the princess could not see it—but then Gormlaith's own woes were so great, perhaps it was asking too much. Brianna shook her head, unable to shake her growing uneasiness. She had marked a streak of cruelty in Gormlaith, ay, yet she had been kinder than kind to herself. It was a puzzle without a solution. She added more peat to the fire and wiped her hands on her apron.

"There, my lady, 'twill be a hot blaze by the time your bathwater arrives." She picked up a gown that lay crumpled atop the rushes.

Gormlaith, looking upon the domestic scene in contentment, murmured: "When does your master leave again, Brianna? I crave for you to come back to me."

Brianna hung the gown on a wall peg and faced the princess with a shy smile. "I have good news, my lady. As of this morn, I—I am a freedwoman."

Gormlaith stopped her chewing and gazed, stupefied, at the maid's pink face. "What? You be freed?" She swallowed with difficulty. "Why, how—wonderful . . ."

"Ay. The Norseman be a kind man after all. Never would he have sold me to Arab slavers." Seeing the princess's seeming confusion, Brianna added, "Never will I desert him, my lady, nor you. I will serve you both if you wish it." She said it wholeheartedly. She would brighten in any way she could the princess's unhappy life.

Gormlaith gave a thin smile. "Be assured, I wish it."

She lost all appetite as she wondered why Wulf Thorsson had freed the wench. Was he so fond of her as all that, or was she so wretched in bed it was not worth his while to feed and clothe her? Her heart warmed at the thought. It warmed, too, thinking that she would have a decent servant for a change. It would be an easy thing to wheedle her into doing all she craved, so desperate was the girl for her cast-off gowns and slippers. As for the Norseman—one week had passed since his arrival and it was time he had a glimpse of her charms. Smiling, she spooned into her oatmeal.

"I will have the small storage room at the end of the corridor emptied and prepared for you, Brianna," she declared. "That way you will be close to us both when we need you."

Brianna immediately foresaw danger, for Sitric's chamber was also nearby. She said hurriedly, "My lady, never would I put you to such trouble. I will dwell in the longhouse with the other maids. 'Tis fine enough for me."

"I will not hear of it. You will move in this eve."

Brianna bowed her head. "As you wish." She was no longer a thrall, but she was still a servant, and servants did not naysay royalty. As she continued to hang up Gormlaith's clothing, she saw that she had no cause to worry over Sitric's proximity. Every chamber had a bar on the door, and she had two powerful protectors, after all, the princess herself and the Norseman.

Thinking on Wulf, she felt a wave of emptiness cresting to break over her. She caught herself. Nay, she would have no regrets. She had made her choice and she would not look back. He himself had said it was ended between them, and so it was.

In the week that followed, Wulf's business for Sitric Olavsson was in Dublin, so that he and Leif were in and out of the palace frequently. Each time they came or went, they marked Brianna busily and happily going about her chores. As they swung into their saddles and headed for the smithy, Leif shook his head.

"Never have I seen the like of that wench. Everywhere we go in yon stronghold, there she is—mending, washing, baking, and scrubbing whilst the others loll about and do half the work. Either she is simple or she was born with a broom in her hand."

"She is not simple," Wulf answered drily.

"Then I trow she will make some farmer or

goatherd a good wife now that you have freed her."

Wulf's mouth lifted at the corner. "It doubts me she will ever wed."

"Methinks you're wrong. The way she stares at you, she could be yours for the asking. And I trow your manor could use a good sweeping and scrubbing when you return." When Wulf's only answer was a flinty gaze, Leif went on: "Yet never could you take to wife a wench of such low birth. But then again, why not? Never have I seen a high-born maid so fair. They all have bad teeth and stringy necks." He grunted. " 'Tis quite a quandary, that."

Wulf had given his friend free rein to tease him, marking how greatly he was enjoying himself. Now he drawled, "The quandary is yours alone, man, seeing as how I have no intention of taking any kind of wife, high-born or otherwise."

Leif shrugged. "Nor I. At least not for a while." He stroked his dark beard thoughtfully. "Hast seen the new serving-wench at the palace? The little plump one with the brown curls and brown eyes? Fiona be her name."

"I saw no new wench."

"She is there, man, believe me. It heats me to look at her."

" 'Twould seem I should pay more attention."

Wulf's thoughts returned to the only woman there who had captured his own hungry gaze. If, as Leif said, Brianna stared at him, he had not marked it. Since she had removed to her own chamber, it was as if he did not even exist for her—except when she served him. But it was all to the good. He had kept his distance, and as she had promised, she was the best serving-wench a man could ever hope for. His clothing was clean and in good repair, and his bedding smelled of wind and sun—but enough! He forced his thoughts back to his comrade.

"—then never have I known a woman with brown eyes," Leif was saying. " 'Tis said such females have a wild and wicked streak in them."

Wulf chuckled. "So I have heard. And I suppose you mean to find out."

"Oh, ay." Leif grinned. "And I hope to holy Thor 'tis true."

The talk moved to their journey north in the morn, but in a corner of Wulf's mind was a vision he could not dismiss. Brianna. A laughing Brianna walking by his side; an obedient Brianna fetching his ale and mending his cloak; Brianna in his arms, soft and sweet and returning his kisses; Brianna weeping and frightened. Damnation, why did he not dwell on those things about her he did not like? Her silly passion for shops, and for ribbons and shoes and gowns. He frowned as, unexpectedly, he decided that any who worked as hard as she deserved any simple pleasure she chose. They were harmless-enough flaws for the maid to have. He drew a deep breath, inadvertently tightening his legs around his mount's barrel and causing the beast to snort and dance sideways. Wulf stroked his glossy neck.

"Sorry, old fellow, sorry. 'Tis all right."

Leif studied his friend with amusement. He knew him better than Wulf knew himself. "Man, can you not see she craves you? And 'tis plain to see how you feel. She should be back in your bed where she belongs."

Wulf's anger flared. "Can you think of naught but women? Just because there is no fighting yet does not mean we are not at war." When Leif accepted the rebuke without protest, Wulf was shamed. Did he actually think to hide the truth from the one who knew him best? He reached out a hand. When Leif struck his palm and shot him a grin, he knew he was forgiven.

" 'Tis true I crave her," he said quietly, "but so far she has offered me naught but tears and trembling."

Leif scowled. "You mean you have not . . . ?" Seeing the warning in his captain's eyes, he shook his head in disgust. He had seen women throw themselves at Wulf Thorsson's feet from Byzantium to Oslo, and to have this damned little thrall rebuff him—why, it was not to be believed.

"I trow she has been badly abused," Wulf said.

"Then I trow she needs extra gentling and petting," Leif said hotly. "And if that fails, then feed the wench some friggja-grass. 'Twill heat her up in a hurry." Marking the stubborn set to Wulf's jaw, Leif glowered at him. "Man, there is not a maid alive who will not give herself to you, and well you know it."

"I have ended it," Wulf said crisply. "I will hear no more of it."

But Leif saw that it was far from ended. It had scarcely begun, but now was not the time to say so. He shrugged. "So be it."

Chapter Eleven

It was eventide, and after Brianna finished the last of her chores, she went to her new chamber and stretched out on her bed fully clothed. Never had she worked so hard in her life as she had these past several days. This day alone she had helped in the brew-house, the weaving-house, and the kitchen-house in addition to serving the princess and tending to the simple needs of the Norseman. And it had been a wise thing for her to take her mending to the sunny-room where the nobles' ladies sat in their finery and did their broidery. She had learned much from their chattering as each vied to prove that her lord was most favored by the king. She smiled and gave a sleepy yawn. For a fact, she had heard things in every place she worked. Perhaps some of it would even be valuable to Fin when she saw him on the morrow.

She was relieved that Wulf Thorsson was keeping his distance. He had seemed disinterested in her ever since she had removed to her new chamber. At the thought, she sighed and got to her feet. She mended the fire, dressed for bed, and then sat, chin in hands, gazing at the flames. It was strange—how could one be so lonely surrounded by people? But she was. Her heart was heavy with loneliness. She assured herself it was not because she missed the Norseman's being about.

She rose and took from a shelf the things she had collected for the coming Yuletide—some pine twigs and four candle stubs from the princess's chamber. She arranged the greens in a circle on her washstand, placed the candles inside, and then studied her handiwork. It was pitiful, but it was the most she could do to celebrate in this heathen place where even a princess of Ireland did not acknowledge the holiness of the season. Oh, there would be feasting and drinking aplenty, but Gormlaith scoffed at all else. Carrying a flame to the candles, Brianna lit one. There. It looked pretty after all, and it brought home closer.

"Brianna?"

She spun, hearing Wulf Thorsson call her name. She stared at the closed door, hating the way her heart had begun to pound. She would not answer. She would pretend to be asleep.

"Come, Brianna," came the deep voice. "I would speak with you."

"One moment, sire." She donned her wrapper and hastened to the door. Never had she thought her room was so small until he stood there in the doorway. Marking that his eyes were flinty, Brianna knew she should be glad, but it served only to deepen her loneliness.

"I will be leaving before dawn," Wulf said, coolly taking in the neat chamber and its narrow bed. "I did not want to go without telling you." Her touch was everywhere: the lively fire and fresh rushes, her few gowns neat on their pegs, a small wreath with one candle-stub burning bravely within it.

"Can I help ready you?" Brianna asked. "Wilt have food before you go or a food-pack to carry?" She knew not where to rest her eyes. His mouth minded her of kisses and his thick hair begged for her fingers to stroke it.

"I need naught," Wulf replied, "but have thanks."

His heart hammered at the sight of her. How fair she was with her white white skin and her thick mane of red hair falling to her waist. He hungered to take her into his arms and kiss her, but if he did, he would not stop with kisses. He would make love to her, and her tears and trembling would not help her this time.

" 'Twas all I had to say," he muttered. "I'll bid you good night now." He made to leave.

"Sire!" The cry flew from Brianna's lips.

"Ay?" Wulf turned, waited.

She yearned to gaze on him, talk with him, touch him. Now she looked down, terrified lest he see it in her eyes. She murmured:

"A-a fair wind be at your back, sire." Fool! she lashed herself. Did she really want to hasten him in his war against Boru? The wind at his back indeed. Rather she should pray that he fall into a bog and disappear forever.

Wulf hesitated. She was being her usual annoying self; her lips saying one thing and her eyes another. They told him she wanted him to stay. He returned to stand in her doorway. "I have been meaning to ask—be you content here at the palace? You have so many chores."

"I be content enough."

"Methinks you accomplish more in one day than all the others heaped together do in a week." He studied her face, but it told him nothing. "Know you, Brianna, that laughing maid I met in Dublin-town needs more in her life than work. Hast made any friends?"

Brianna felt a swell of guilt. She did not want his concern. She did not want him to be the most glorious man she had ever seen nor feel the hot pleasure he aroused in her. Even now it was sweeping over her. It was unfair.

"There be a new maid working in the kitchen-house," she murmured. "I trow we will become friends."

Sensing her sudden underlying sadness, Wulf urged gently, "Let me take you home. You can be with your folk for Yuletide."

For the space of a heartbeat, Brianna was tempted to accept. But then, she could not go home. She was needed here. The thought filled her with such relief that she wondered, for the first time, if this Norseman were becoming as important to her as Boru and his war. She denied it instantly. Nay, it was for Boru alone that she had to remain here with her lies. She said dully:

"Sire, I cannot return. 'Tis too soon. I—I fear enslavement again."

"I see." Wulf came into the chamber uninvited, and gazed down stonily onto the small circle of pine and the guttering candle. He was not accustomed to the feeling of helplessness that gripped him. He touched his fingers to the pine needles. "What be this wreath, lady? Is't to do with Yule?"

"Ay." Brianna hurriedly offered him a chair beside the table. She then sat on a stool, elbows on her knees, chin in her hands, flame-glow reflected in her eyes. "When I was small, my mother always made such a wreath, a big one, and she decked our house with pine boughs and lit all the candles. 'Twas a grand sight." She sighed, realizing that, for the first time, she had told him something about herself that was true.

"What mean the four candles with but one lit?"

Watching his strong, dark fingers stroke the glossy needles, Brianna yearned to lay her own atop them. She forced her eyes back to the flames.

" 'Tis to welcome the Christ-child," she murmured. "Each Sunday in December, a new candle is lit and a prophecy of His Coming spoken. I know little more than that, for my mother was the godly one in our family." After some moments, she asked shyly, "Dost have a holy day to honor your gods?"

"Ay." Wulf nodded as an old memory stirred. "I attended all the great fests when I was a lad. Well do I mind the drinking, the singing and dancing and bonfires, the blood . . ."

Brianna stared at his closed face. "Blood?"

"Ay. 'Twas Vinterdag, Winter Day, when animals were sacrificed to all the gods." His child's-heart had wept over the helpless beasts, and more than once he had gone behind the cow barn to empty his stomach. Seeing her dismay, he said easily, "Such things are no longer allowed in Norway's land, Brianna. In my valley, most are Christian now. In fact, my own folk and kin will be celebrating Yuletide. I had hoped to be with them."

She blinked. "You—be Christian?"

Wulf laughed, seeing her round eyes and the astonishment on her face. "I could say ay, for the sign of the cross be on my forehead, but 'twouldn't be true. This"—he touched the long, pale scar on his face "—be a truer sign of who and what I be. A warrior. Thor and Odin be my gods, Brianna." He craved to reach out and stroke her cheek but resisted. " 'Tis my mother who loves the White Christ. In my family, as in yours, she be the godly one. My father, though he be prime-signed as am I, prays to the old gods as well as to Jesu."

Brianna was speechless. His folk were Christian and he was prime-signed? Yet here he was, gathering an army to slay an emperor who wanted only peace and who built churches and schools and fed the poor! She was outraged.

"What of your father?" Wulf asked, his curiosity aroused. "Whilst your mother decked the house, was he out slaying the goose or the ox or whatever?"

She answered with stiff lips: "My father was out slaying Vikings. He be a chieftain." It was a blunder, but she could not hold her tongue she was so furious—with him, with herself, with everyone. Why was this war even being fought? She cried suddenly, "Oh, why must our two peoples be enemies?"

Wulf hid his astonishment over her outburst and the news of her father. It had opened more questions than it answered. " 'Tis a long tale," he replied.

" 'Twas a silly question to ask even," she said icily. "When one people is cruel enough to raid and plunder and conquer another, how could they not be enemies?"

Wulf's words also held frost. "Lady, I was not there to advise my forefathers against it."

"Yet you stay on," she answered calmly, but she was seething. "Is't not time for you all to go back whence you came?"

Wulf studied her pink face. He had wondered if it were himself she feared or his people. Now it seemed he had his answer. It was his people. She hated them. He said quietly, "There be legions of us now who be as much Celt—ay, more Celt even than Viking. Wouldst send them back also?"

Brianna forced herself to make a quiet reply but her eyes flashed fire. "I would certainly send back those who do not like the way this land is ruled—by those whose land it is. 'Tis said on Maun that the emperor of Ireland be fair to all, Celt and Viking alike."

Wulf's annoyance flared. What did she know of it? " 'Twould seem you have forgotten the good that has come of our being here."

"Oh, spare me, I pray."

"The shops you find so irresistible could not exist without Viking ships and traders."

"That I cannot believe."

"Believe it. 'Tis Viking ships that supply all of Ireland's needs. Believe, too, that without our strongholds in your own land of Maun, your coasts would be swarming with marauders."

Brianna smiled. "I see you do not include yourselves. And of course you do not demand tribute but accept it, out of the goodness of your hearts, as a gift from a grateful people."

"Our men must eat and have roofs over their heads," Wulf replied. When she emitted a scornful laugh, he added drily, " 'Twould seem you are unaware your own Celts are amongst the worst of the raiders."

Brianna's face reddened. "So you say."

He saw that his barb had hit its mark. "And so it is. Brian Boru himself would be the first to tell you that Celts make war against Celts with great regularity. His rule has reduced the carnage somewhat. Our strongholds reduce it further."

Brianna was shaken, for she knew he was right. "Celts do not kill by the Blood Eagle," she countered.

" 'Tis true. Celts prefer to nail a man's gut to a tree and drive him 'round it." Seeing her blanch, he instantly regretted his bluntness. " 'Tis bootless for us to discuss war," he said gruffly.

"Ay . . ." She was angry, he was angry, and there was no more to be said. She blew out the dying wreath-candle and knelt by the hearth. She felt his gaze on her as she stirred the fire.

"Know you, Brianna," Wulf said low, "there be many things in the past that I would change if I could." When she made no answer, he got to his feet. "I trow Ospak abused you. Know that I will avenge you for it."

Brianna gazed on his grim face in surprise. "He—did not abuse me . . ."

"Was't the other, then?" When she seemed not to understand, he growled, "Damn me, woman, I speak of that bastard who owned you before Ospak had you stolen."

Brianna blinked. Holy angels, she could scarce remember all the lies she had told him. She was going to be caught one of these days. She answered coolly:

"Neither gave me bruises nor did they bloody me, if that is what you mean." She yearned to tell him of his brute of a countryman who had forced himself on a helpless child of fourteen . . .

Wulf's jaw clenched. The little troll. It was not at all what he meant and well she knew it. He resented it that she refused to talk of it, but so be it. "I have overstayed," he said abruptly and left.

In his own chamber, he brooded as he removed his swordbelt and boots. What a damned odd interlude that had been. She had wanted him to stay, and then turned it into a battle. A chieftain's daughter, was she? He shook his head. Who could believe it? But as he drew off his leathers and tossed them to the floor, he wondered how he could doubt it. There was the regal way she walked of late, the look of calm defiance in her eyes, the way her tongue had grown suddenly bold. It had but taken her a while to become herself again, for the gods alone knew how long she had been in thrall. But he was puzzled. Why would not a chieftain go after his daughter and forcibly take her back? But then he would have to know where to look.

He grunted, crawled into his bedcloset, into his bag, and closed his tired eyes. It was too much to ponder on, nor did it matter. The wench could say and do as she chose and look as defiant as she pleased. She was out of his life and beyond his concern—yet in his dreams, he made love to her the night long. And when he

awakened in the morn, it was to an empty bed
and empty arms. And an empty heart . . .

Gormlaith was moving inexorably toward her
conquest of the Wulf of Husaby. She had sensed
that he was a man who must be dealt with carefully; never must he suspect she was the pursuer
or she would lose him. But he had a soft heart
when it came to women, and it was that which
she would use to draw him into her net. She
gave a soft laugh, thinking of her cleverness.
Not only was he grateful for her kindness to
his wench, but this morn she had stirred his
compassion—and doubtless his passion.

She had arranged to be pacing the corridor
at dawn as he was leaving his chamber. Noting
her distress, he had asked if he could be of
service—just as she had known he would. She
had thanked him, eyes brimming, and told him
that none could help with her sleepless nights.
It was a battle only she could fight: facing life
without the husband she had loved so well and
enjoyed so fully. When she had raised an arm to
push back a lock of hair from her tear-streaked
face, her wrapper had parted for an instant.
She saw his eyes fall and linger on her breasts
beneath her silken shift before she quickly covered herself.

Gormlaith smiled at the memory. He was as
good as hers. His eyes and his face had been
masked so as not to betray his lust, ay, but she
knew Nordic men. Their passions they kept hidden, but in the end they were as fiery as any. As

for his obsession with the thrall, it was cooling.
And when he left on his next journey, she meant
to put Sitric's lust for the wench to good use. She
was mulling over this when the object of her
dark thoughts tapped and entered her chamber.

"Good morn to you, my lady," Brianna said.

" 'Tis indeed a good morn, child."

As Brianna arranged her silken pillows so
the princess could break her fast in bed,
Gormlaith toyed with the exquisite thought
of the Norseman's returning to the palace and
finding his wench in Sitric's arms. Better still, in
his bed. But she could not dismiss the risk that
Wulf might slay him. Or that he might depart
in a rage. Nay, she must give this more thought,
for without the Wolf of Husaby rallying men
to their cause, they would be in dire trouble.
The truth was that Sitric's arrogance alienated
men—though he had been exceeding clever in
his dealings with Sigurd. He had actually gotten Sigurd to believe she would place herself
in his fat hands and that Sitric himself would
surrender his crown in return for Orkney aid.
She laughed aloud at the thought.

Brianna joined in as she rolled up the window
tapestries and let the sun stream in through the
horn panes. "Never have I seen you so happy,
my lady."

"I am counting my blessings," Gormlaith
answered. "I have been sour too long."

"With good cause . . ." Brianna murmured.

Gormlaith shrugged her shapely shoulders.
"Be that as it may, child, from this day forth,

I will rejoice. I will think of Boru's betrayal no more, nor his coming downfall. Him I loved and still do, but I see finally that I am better off without him. I deserve better than a whoring man."

Brianna frowned. A whoring man? That was not the Boru she knew. Always had he treated women with gentleness and respect. Not daring to reveal her disbelief, she carried the sewing box and a torn gown to where a beam of sunlight filtered onto the rushes. Putting a stool there, she sat herself down, her back to the princess. She said carefully:

" 'Twould be a bitter thing to bear . . ."

Again Gormlaith shrugged and finished her ale. " 'Tis a thing all men do, being naught but animals when it comes to a woman's body. All deem it their right as our lords and masters to take as many of us as they crave, nor do they care that we must then risk death to lie in the birthing-straw yearly. Nor was Boru any different. But no more will I accept such treatment. I have borne children enough, and never again will a husband rule me."

Once again Brianna's feelings toward Boru wavered, for why would the princess lie, after all? She herself had been but a babe when she knew him at Kincora, and children were always protected from such things. But then she pondered the coarse talk she had heard just that morn in the kitchen-house—talk of Gormlaith and men. She stitched more rapidly on the red silken garment in her hands, telling herself not to heed the gossip of serving-folk. It was their bread of life. Yet Maeve had taught her that always did the servants know things first.

"—of course, Sitric be as lusty as any other," Gormlaith was saying, "but he be different from other men in that he is exceeding generous. He loves to give pretty things to those ladies who please him. Jewelry and ivory combs and slippers of satin. Hear you what I am saying, Brianna? I know well you love pretty things . . ."

Brianna hid her annoyance. This was not the first time Gormlaith had attempted to interest her in Sitric—but why? She met the princess's eyes.

"My lady, forgive me," she said mildly, "but I have no interest in any man's bed. Not even the king's."

With great effort, Gormlaith forced herself to answer calmly:

" 'Tis a pity, that, for Sitric finds you very fair. This mother's heart sorrows, seeing his yearning for you. I had hoped only to help you both. Know you, Brianna, never would he betray Wulf Thorsson's trust by approaching you, but 'twould be a different matter entirely were you to go to him. He finds you enchanting and would heap many luxuries upon you."

As Brianna gazed at the princess, puzzling over her words, she wondered what it was that seemed not quite right. She saw it then. It was not that the words were false, it was the odd watchfulness in those beautiful eyes as they moved over her. This woman had been kinder than kind to her but now looked on her in a strange, veiled way. Had it always been thus, Brianna wondered, and she had not seen it?

"For those luxuries, your highness," she answered quietly, "the king would expect to rule me. Methinks we two are alike, you and I. I will not be ruled."

Gormlaith forced a ghastly smile. "I see . . ."

The bitch! How dared she, a mere serving-wench, a former thrall, liken herself to a princess of Ireland? And how dared she continue to dismiss Sitric as if he were some plough-hand? As the maid bathed and dressed her and coiffed her hair, Gormlaith fumed in silence. She would say no more on the subject, it was bootless, but the outcome would be as she wished it. She would simply feed the wench one of her special sweets—the ones she and her lovers ate to enhance their lovemaking. Not only would the maid give herself willingly to Sitric, she would fair beg him to take her. And never would Sitric know it was not his own virility that had brought it all about. Why in God's name had she not thought of this before? She gave the wench a smile of camaraderie.

"I admit I knew not we were so alike, Brianna," she murmured. "Methinks now you will enjoy my favorite sweets. I have just received a fresh supply." She held out a small box of creams and watched, eyes glittering, as the maid thanked her, took one, and popped it into her rosy mouth. "Have another," she urged.

Chapter Twelve

A pale sun filtered through clouds black and heavy with snow as, later that day, Brianna hurried through the streets of Dublin. She was edgy, an odd hot excitement racing through her veins. She suspected it was because she was anxious. She had not seen Fin for several days, and had many things to tell him. Now, however, her thoughts spun nervously over Gormlaith. It was as if she had looked behind those beautiful veiled eyes this morn into a dark chamber she had not known existed. She shivered, more from the strangeness of it than from the bitter wind which rushed at her just then. It lifted her cloak and blew her hair every which way as she entered the small jewelry shop chosen for her meeting with Fin. As she gazed on the gems winking up at her from the counter, the jeweler approached.

"Be you Brianna?" he asked quietly.

It startled her. Looking about, and seeing that she was the only one there, she whispered: "Ay. Is—all well?"

"The Ard Ri will answer that."

When he crooked a finger, she followed him, concerned. Boru? Here? Had something happened to Fin, then? Holding her cloak close, she trailed after him to the rear of the dusty shop, their shadows looming in the light cast from two soapstone lamps. Behind the curtained opening stood Boru in his hooded cloak. He looked hard and tall as an oak, and he wore a scowl so fierce it made her shrink. Marking well that there was to be no joyous greeting, she wondered what had she done to incur his wrath. She felt ten winters old again . . .

"Greetings, Brianna." A muscle moved in his bearded jaw.

Brianna inclined her head a fraction and said coolly, "Boru."

"I will hear your report later," he said gruffly. "Now I would hear why I was not told the princess Gormlaith is in residence at the palace."

She had anticipated he would not like it and it seemed she was right. But how had he heard? She answered stiffly, "You were not told because I foresaw you would disapprove of my knowing her."

Brian gave an incredulous laugh. "Disapprove? Disapprove? By holy Saint Patrick, 'tis your life I fear for, girl. The woman is a witch! She speaks naught but lies and brews trouble like any other brews beer."

Even one week ago, Brianna would have dismissed such words. Now, minding the shadows behind those veiled green eyes, she was not so sure.

"What mean you, she brews trouble?" she asked.

Brian sat himself at a table and threw back his hood, revealing the grave majesty of his face. "There is more to tell than there is time to tell it," he rumbled. "Suffice it to say 'twas Gormlaith who stirred Maelmorda and Sitric to rebel against me."

Brianna joined him at the table. "Nay, Boru, that I cannot believe. She loves you still. Not a day goes by but what she speaks of you."

"With curses, I trow."

"Not curses. Tears. She grieves that she had to divorce you because you be a—a . . ."

Seeing the accusation written on her face, Brian laughed. He asked softly: "A whoring man?"

"Ay." She was mad to be telling him such a thing. She looked down at her gloved hands and wished she did not feel so hot and shaky inside. Holy Jesu, was she taking ill?

"Brianna . . ."

"Ay, Boru?" Meeting his eyes, she saw that they held only concern for her, not anger.

"Know you," he said, " 'tis not in me to complain of Gormlaith to all and sundry. I tell you of her now only because you dwell with her in that vipers' nest, and not to know her true nature could bring you great harm. Hear me well, foster daughter, 'twas I who ended that marriage, not the other way around. I divorced her only after I had lost all respect for her. I loved her as I love my life—" He clamped shut lips that trembled and was unable to speak for some moments. "I would love her still had she not changed so . . ."

Brianna was shamed for having doubted him. She murmured, " 'Tis true I have heard gossip about her, but I could not believe it."

"What is said?" Brian asked.

"That she be a bitch. The serving-folk swear she is cruel, greedy, arrogant, and overfond of men." She squirmed on her seat, scarce able to sit still as she spoke. It was as though her skin were too small for her body. And speaking ill of the princess made her uneasy.

Brian showed his teeth in a wolf-smile. "Believe it all, lass. As for overfond, that hardly describes it. The wench needs men as she needs air to fill her lungs and water to drink and food to eat. She cannot exist without men. But 'tis unimportant, that. What matters is that you not cross her. Let her have her own way. And believe naught of what she utters. If she says 'tis day outside, you can be sure the stars are shining, and if she swears a thing be black, 'twill be white."

"She has been kinder than kind," Brianna protested. "She has given me her protection and showered me with clothing she no longer wears. Just this morn she gave me a pair of red silken slippers and plied me with her favorite sweets . . ."

Brian shook his head. "If she be kind, look for a reason. Gormlaith does naught which is not for Gormlaith." His pewter eyes shone like hot coals in the dim room. "Be warned, lass. 'Twould gladden this old heart to see you home again, but you be of too great value at the palace now. I depend upon you, and I trow you be clever enough not to anger the witch."

His words made Brianna smile despite the increasing discomfort within her body. "I am not fooled, Boru. You leave me there only because you have brought in someone to guard me. Who is he?" When he looked innocent as a saint, she chided: "Come now. 'Tis clear you have eyes and ears there other than my own, else how would you have known of Gormlaith?"

Brian shook his head. " 'Tis best you don't know. Know only that if you need help, 'twill be there in an eyeblink. Now, to the business at hand—what news have you for me?"

Wulf Thorsson and his band had left the palace at dawn for a three-week land journey to Meath and Oriel. They had ridden no farther than the northernmost boundary of the Kingdom of Dublin when the skies grew black and the wind began to howl. When the snow fell so thick and fast as to blind them, Leif muttered:

" 'Twill be worth our lives to go on in this, man, not knowing the land."

"I agree," Wulf said. "We'll backtrack to Holmgeir Jonsson's steading and warm us a bit. If it clears, we'll go on, if not, we'll return to Dublin. I doubt it has reached there yet. 'Twould seem it's sitting directly over us."

Leif shouted the change in plans to the men, and when all were turned south with the wind whistling at their backs, he settled in his saddle, a smile on his face. As far as he was concerned, they could return to Dublin straightaway. Three weeks was a long time to be away when he craved to learn more about the maid called Fiona. He pulled his hood forward against the flying snow and heated himself with thoughts of her.

Wulf's own thoughts were black as the swift-gathering clouds overhead. He had been looking forward to the journey, the camaraderie of men he liked and using his powers of persuasion on the warriors of Meath and Oriel who sat straddling the fence between Sitric and Boru. It gave him deep satisfaction, this large part he played in drawing them to the rebel side. And it would have been a boon, not seeing Brianna day in and day out. Now, marking the foreboding change in sky and wind in these past moments alone, he feared the arrival of a major storm that might hold them back indefinitely. He instructed Leif that they were returning to Dublin at once.

After he closed the fasteners on his hood and urged his mount to a canter, Wulf's thoughts strayed. Seeing where they were headed, he attempted to steer them, but the vision that swam before him would not be steered and was unaffected by the wind-scream and the pelting snow. Green-gold eyes, a soft laughing mouth, hair the color of a flaming sunset, a soft white body so slender yet curvesome it made his heart gallop to think on it.

Wulf shook his head in disgust. Had he been gone the three weeks intended, he would have gotten the little vixen out of his blood. Now his obsession with her was likely to continue. Not only was he more curious than ever about her, he feared for her safety and he was jealous of her. And ay, he craved to bed her. It drew a deep sigh from him as, for the hundredth time, he remembered her tears and his vow to her that it was ended. No more would he touch her. He muttered an oath, which was borne off by the wind. Leif was right. He had not gentled her for a long enough time to make her forget her fears. Leif was right, too, about women liking his lovemaking. None had ever protested before . . .

When Brianna finally left the jeweler's, the wind was keening in from the north and the snow was falling fast. As she hurried back to the palace, Boru's warning words regarding Gormlaith seemed unimportant and unreal. She could think only of herself and the strange way she felt. Here it was, the dead of winter with a blizzard wailing about her, yet her body was so hot and restless, she craved to bathe herself in icy water.

But as she passed through the gate and crossed the courtyard, she knew she must consider carefully what Boru had told her. If she were to believe him, all the princess did and said—her kindness, her smiles, her small confidences—all were for her own benefit. She wanted something in return. But what did she, Brianna, have that a princess of Ireland could possibly covet? Oh, it was too complicated for her to think on, feeling as she did. But as the palace doors slammed shut behind her, she was shocked by the thought that struck her. Did Gormlaith want Wulf Thorsson? Was it possible she craved the Norseman and actually thought he was bound to herself?

Brianna mused on it as she removed her heavy cloak, shook out her hair, and hurried along the dim corridor. The Viking was marvelous to look upon and he was of noble blood. It was only natural any woman would be drawn to him, but why would the princess need to pretend compassion for Wulf Thorsson's thrall in order to entice him to her? Brianna shook her head. It was the silliest thing she had ever heard. Gormlaith was so fair, all she need do was beckon him and he would be hers.

Oh, holy angels, what ailed her? She was so hot, and her skin felt so strange that she still craved to tear off her clothing and bathe herself.

And then if only she could sleep, she might feel better when she awakened. As she reached her door and laid a shaking hand on the latch, a tall figure loomed by her side. She froze, seeing it was Sitric. He spoke to her, his voice low as if he wanted none other to hear:

" 'Tis said you be clever with a needle, wench."

"I—I make only simple repairs, your majesty." She was fearful, seeing the look in his eyes.

Sitric pointed to a gaping seam in the purple satin tunic he wore. "I trow this be simple enough. I would have you mend it now. My mother's sewing box is within my chamber."

It was a lie. But then if she craved him as he suspected—and what woman did not?—there would be no sewing done. And if she did not crave him, he would soon make it so, being expert in such matters. Seeing her eyes widen, her luscious lips part and the tip of her tongue moistening them, Sitric wasted no time. He crushed her against him, took her mouth, and then, tormented by her sweetness and softness, lifted her in his arms.

Brianna tried to struggle as he carried her into his bedchamber, but her body was so weak and trembling she could not make her limbs obey. She was afire, and Sitric's greedy hands and lips moving over her were so cool and pleasured her so greatly, she wanted to cry out for him to touch and kiss all of her—quickly, quickly, for she could not wait . . .

The thought horrified her. This was Sitric she was responding to so hungrily. Sitric! She could not abide the man. He was arrogant, insolent, conceited, and he disgusted her. She could not believe what she wanted him to do to her—ay, craved for him to do. Dear God, what was it that had come over her? Was she bewitched? Drugged? She had heard of such things happening to maids in heathen lands. Even so, she would fight against it until she could fight no more. Never would she yield to such despicable yearnings.

Seeing that she was nigh swooning in his arms excited Sitric to the utmost. He bent to her parted lips and took them in a brutal kiss. He then tore off her apron and tugged down her kyrtil from off her shoulders. Her fairness so inflamed him that he sunk his teeth into the side of her throat, his fingers roughly squeezing the soft mounds of her breasts and her nipples. She cried out, but he stifled her, thrusting his hungry tongue into her mouth. Someday soon, he thought hotly, he himself was going to own this wench. He could not let her go.

As his teeth sought the pink velvety buds tipping her breasts, the pain roused Brianna to her peril. He was as cruel and brutal as his countryman who had raped her, and never would she let such a beast have her again. But even as she clawed and bit him, her throbbing body opened itself wide for him to claim her. She wept in her despair. She was truly bewitched, or was this her terrible punishment for the betrayal of these folk in whose stronghold she dwelt and whose food she ate? If only the Norseman were here—or the man Boru had put here to guard her. Why had he deserted her?

"So, little bitch," Sitric snarled as he deposited her in his bedcloset, "you be even hotter and sweeter than I had hoped. You will stay here with me whilst Thorsson is gone."

Brianna shook her head. "My lord, I cannot! I—I will not!" She tried to force back his head as his mouth again sought her breasts. In her weakened state she could not prevent him taking his pleasure with her. As he sucked on her, she closed her eyes, a dizzying wave of sensation sweeping over her. "Have mercy, I beg of you . . ."

Sitric raised his head and laughed low. "I am the most merciful of men, as you will see. I will pleasure you from morn 'til night."

"I—I am unable to receive a man now, my lord," she lied, desperate for an escape.

"I care naught, little slut . . ."

Fiona Corcoran was frantic. When Brianna had returned from her trip to town, she had been odder than odd. Fiona had greeted her brightly, but the maid had not even marked she was there and had walked right past her. Misliking the strange, wild look in her eyes, Fiona had followed at a distance. When she had seen Sitric accost and kiss her, and then carry her, unprotesting, into his chamber, she knew real fear. This was not like Brianna at all. She abhorred the king who pawed every wench within his reach, and in addition, he was a Viking. Never would Brianna allow a Viking to touch her, king or no!

She had raced to an unused storeroom on the second story and hung from the window a length of white cloth—a signal for the emperor's men who were but moments away. When they did not come, she knew they had not seen it for the blizzard raging outside. Oh, holy Mother . . . She wrung her hands and wondered if she should herself go to the king's chamber. She could say Brianna was wanted in the kitchenhouse. Ay, if she got the words out before the king slew her! She had just started for his chamber when the front doors flew open.

Fiona whirled, wide-eyed, as a band of men entered. Laughing and talking, they stamped snow from their feet and removed their snow-laden cloaks. She stared at the tallest of them. Holy Mary Mother of God! It was the Wolf of Husaby and his dark-haired companion, the one who always frightened her when he stared at her so hotly. But she had not the time now to fear for herself. Having marked that the blond Norseman had an eye for Brianna, it was to him she flew.

"My lord Husaby, come quickly, you are needed!"

Wulf scowled down at the little brown-haired maid, his eyes not yet accustomed to the dimness after the white dazzle of snow. "What is't, wench?"

Leif stepped forward. "Lady, I am at your service."

Fiona shrank from him, and from the berserks who also stepped toward her. She shook
her head and turned back to Wulf Thorsson.
" 'Tis you alone who must come, sire. Please,
'tis Brianna—"

"Brianna?" Every part of Wulf leapt to life.
He tore off his cloak and tossed it to one of his
berserks. "Take me to her."

With the chieftain close behind, Fiona fled
down the narrow torch-lit passage leading to
the bedchambers. She marked that Brianna's
cloak still lay in a heap before her chamber
door where it had fallen. She saw, too, that
the king's door was still open wide. She feared
to look inside. She could only point.

"In there," she choked. "Th-the king has her,
sire . . ."

Following behind the maid, Wulf had been
cold with dread. Was Brianna ill? Was she dying
even? It could explain why he had not been
able to put her from his thoughts. The maid's
words changed all that—the king had her. It
was not fear he felt now but a rage so white-
hot it fair devoured him. If the bastard had
harmed her . . . He thrust the thought away as
he approached the door on silent feet, swiftly
withdrawing his sword from its sheath.

He froze, seeing her in the devil's arms. They
were kissing, Sitric's greedy sucking mouth
sliding down over her bared breasts, her soft
throat and shoulders, and then claiming her
lips again as she writhed in his arms and made
small moans. Or was she struggling against him

and protesting? He stared, eyes narrowed, heart roaring, scarcely breathing, sword at the ready. He drew a deep breath and stepped back, sickened. What he had first thought was so. The wench was not struggling but was accepting.

So great was his fury and jealousy that he craved to slay her on the spot, slay them both, but he remained rooted where he was. His brain, coolly detached from his body's rage, told him that revenge against such a wench and against Sitric Olavsson was not worth the heavy price of outlawry. The two deserved each other; let them have each other. He thrust the Shining Death back into its sheath.

Hearing the hiss, Brianna forced open her sleepy eyes. They were so blurred and heavy-lidded that she could discern only that the figure who stood there was a tall man whose mail tunic and tawny hair gleamed in the firelight. The sight of him gave her the strength to struggle once more against the sick heaviness pulling her down.

"Wulf . . ." She stretched out a hand to him even as Sitric set her abruptly on her feet. "Help me, please . . ." Oh, Jesu, he was leaving. Why did he not help her? "Wulf, please . . ." Only then did Brianna glimpse the brown-haired maid who had been standing behind him. "Fiona, is't you?"

"Ay, Annie, 'tis me."

Fiona hurled a look of outrage at the Wolf of Husaby as he strode past her and stormed from the king's chamber. He had been no help at all. If a rescue were to be made, it seemed she herself would have to do it. She gave Sitric a similar fiery gaze as she hurried toward her friend. Men! What good were they, excepting the sainted Ard Ri, God save his blessed soul.

"Help me, please," Brianna murmured, blinking, her eyes refusing to focus.

" 'Tis all right, precious, I'm here," Fiona crooned. She pulled up Brianna's disheveled clothing to cover her nakedness. "There now," she soothed, but she was deeply concerned. Her friend seemed more ill than ever. She slipped Brianna's arm about her own neck, gripped her firmly around the waist, and started toward the door. "There, love, Fiona is here."

The parting look she gave the king defied him to thwart her. He did not. Rather he stood gaping after the two of them as they left his chamber.

Chapter Thirteen

As Fiona hurriedly led Brianna into her bed-chamber and barred the door, she wondered what awful ailment had claimed the maid. Her step was uncertain and her eyes had a hot, glassy look about them that was frightening. Was some sickness visiting her just now when she needed every bit of strength and wisdom she possessed to succeed in this mission? And for that wretch of a Sitric to take advantage of her was disgusting.

"Come, little one," Fiona cooed, as though Brianna were the younger of the two. She took her to her narrow bed and helped her lie down. " 'Tis all right. You are safe now and you're going to be just fine." Hurrying to the washbowl, she dipped a cloth in the icy water and placed it upon the maid's hot forehead. She then hurried to the hearth, jabbed the dying fire with a poker, and wet another cloth to replace the first. "There, I trow you feel better already."

Brianna shook her head. "Would that I could die," she murmured tonelessly.

Fiona stared at her, certain she had misheard. "What said you?"

Brianna turned her face to the wall. "Would that I could die . . ."

Fiona brought the basin to the bed, pulled up a stool, and sat down. "What is't, love?" she asked softly.

Brianna put both hands to her eyes and covered them. It was of no avail. The terrible scene in the king's chamber was burned into her brain for all time. Never would she forget the look of disgust on Wulf Thorsson's face.

"Methinks I have gone mad," she whispered.

"Nay, you have not," Fiona declared. "You but fell into the king's lecherous hands. 'Tis enough to make any maid ill."

Brianna stared at the younger girl with wide, wild eyes. "Fi, I—allowed him to hold a-and fondle me . . ."

Fiona smiled. "I am sure you did not. The king—"

Brianna sat up and tore the cloth from her forehead. She hurled it to the floor. "Will you not listen?" she cried. "I am telling you, I allowed him to touch me and kiss me. I—I did not want him to, yet I allowed it! Mayhap I even kissed him back, I know not. Oh, Holy Mother of God, surely I am going mad. I loathe the man!" She got to her feet but swayed dizzily and had to sink down onto the bed again. "And for Wulf to have seen us so! Oh, I am so disgusted with myself, so shamed . . ."

Fiona's tender heart swelled with pity seeing Brianna's despair. So she called him Wulf, did she? And she cared that deeply what he thought of her? She herself had never felt love, but she was not so blind as to miss it in another. And she knew a thing or two about those darker matters dealing with love, having worked for certain odd folk in days past. As she grimly retrieved the cloth from the rushes where Brianna had flung it, she wondered if the maid had been given a love potion.

"Lie yourself back down now," she said firmly. "Nay, lady, I'll not hear a word of protest. Down you go." Gently she pressed on Brianna's shoulders until she yielded and sank back into the furs. "Just you close your eyes and rest. Methinks I know what ails you and—"

Brianna sat up again. "What is't? 'Tis as if I be on fire."

"You say you craved for the king to kiss you?"

"I craved to knee him in the gut, yet I allowed him to kiss me. I cannot understand it." She shuddered, remembering Sitric's hungry mouth sucking on her breasts and his hands exploring her body. It had revolted yet excited her at the same time. "Know you, Fi, never have I felt such a way or allowed any man to touch me so before."

Seeing her distress, Fiona said quietly: "Methinks 'tis a good thing the Husaby chieftain came when he did." She said nothing of his storming from the room.

"Ay. 'Tis grateful I am."

Fiona brooded. For certain it sounded like a love potion, and the Dublin king was the worst sort of beast for having taken advantage of her in this way. And what a cruel thing it was, Brianna's loving a man she could never belong to and being forced to betray him, and now he was wroth with her. She should not have to continue on here in such a dreadful position. Fiona wondered if the emperor knew all of the circumstances.

"I trow the devil would have taken me," Brianna murmured in the deepest disgust, "— but only because my strength had fled me. 'Tis shamed I am you both saw me so." She rubbed her hot, sleep-heavy eyes and gave Fiona a mournful gaze. "Was't you who fetched the Norseman to me? It seems you were about when I returned from town."

Fiona nodded. "Ay, I was about, and when I marked you were unwell, I followed you. When I saw what was happening with the king, I—I knew not where to turn—and then there came Thorsson with his men." Her cheeks burned, remembering the dark Viking who stared at her so. She hurried on: " 'Twould seem the weather grew too treacherous for them to continue their trek north, and so they returned. And as for your being shamed, 'tis foolishness, that. You were ill, and 'tis Sitric Silkbeard who should be shamed for taking advantage of you. If Wulf Thorsson could not see that, what matter?"

Brianna was not yet ready to bare her soul. She forced herself to give an indifferent shrug. "You be right. He will have to think what he will." But even as she said it, she minded the scorn on his face and died inside.

"You look like death, little one," Fiona murmured. "Get you some sleep now." She returned the basin to the table and put another chunk of peat on the fire. "Come, love, bar the door after me and then get you to bed."

Brianna obeyed, marking that she was dizzy still. As she had talked with Fiona, an unpalatable notion had been festering in her mind. Those sweets Gormlaith forced on her this morn—could they have contained some sort of aphrodisiac? She had heard of such things, but surely the princess would not stoop so low to bring her together with Sitric. Yet it would explain her disgusting craving for intimacy with a man she detested. But nay, she was being ridiculous. Besides, Fiona seemed to know what ailed her.

"Think you I will mend soon from this illness?"

Fiona smiled. "Oh, ay. If 'tis what I suspect, you will be up and about by eventide. When next I see my older sister, I will ask her about it." Eva was in service with other noble folk in Dublin where the use of such abominations was common. If there was anything to know, she would know it. Fiona kissed Brianna on the cheek. "Soon this will all be a bad dream. Mind now, get some sleep, and I will see you at evening-food."

Brianna caught the hand of her new friend and gripped it hard. "Have thanks, Fi. What would I have done without you?" Gazing into the maid's soft eyes, she was astonished to see that they held a glint of steel.

"We be Celts," Fiona answered. "Who else have we if not each other in this heathen place?"

Returning to his own bedchamber, Wulf found that Leif had a roaring fire and a keg awaiting him. He took his friend's offering, a horn brimful of frothing ale, and after downing it, hurled it to the floor and began to pace.

Leif said nothing. He stood gazing thoughtfully at the fire and drinking his own ale, but it gave him no pleasure. What in the name of all the gods had happened? he wondered, watching Wulf stride to and fro. Fiona had fetched him to Brianna's aid, that much was clear, but why? Was it Sitric? Had he harmed her? Leif shook his head and promised himself he would hear about it later.

Wulf ceased his prowling long enough to retrieve his horn from underfoot and fill it again. As he tilted back his head and poured the biting ale down his throat, he felt Leif's hand on his shoulder. No words, just silent support. Wulf met his eyes for an instant, showing his gratitude, but turned quickly away. He did not

want his torment seen, nor did he want pity
nor compassion. He wanted only to do Sitric
violence. The bastard had been warned that the
woman was his own, yet he had gone on to
betray him. In the dark chaos of Wulf's mind,
he slew him again and again, and first he cut
the Blood Eagle on him. As for the slut . . .

A vision of Brianna swam through the
red flood of fury that careened through his
thoughts: Brianna writhing and moaning in the
devil's arms. Soft lips, soft breasts, soft hair,
soft flesh, soft soft soft . . . A man might sink
into such softness and be destroyed. He uttered
several choice oaths and wet his throat again.
He did not need softness, nor did he need her nor
her deceit. What a fool he had been to believe her
show of tears and trembling and her pretense of
maidenly purity. He had actually thought she
was frightened and in need of his protection.
He had thought she was special. He spat into
the rushes. Let the half-breed have her. Let her
destroy Sitric rather than himself. He would not
face outlawry for such an undeserving wench.

But in all truthfulness, never had she encouraged him. It was he who had pursued her. Disgust swept over him, and scorn for his own
lustfulness. Oh, ay, he had rescued the wench.
He had given her her freedom, not ill-used her,
and had protected her from others—but he had
lusted after her without cease, for she was more
beautiful than any other woman he had ever
seen. In fact, he had been unable to keep his
damned hands off her, while all along she had

set her sights on the king. Doubtless she had been laughing at him the whole time. He burned with the shame of it even as he rejoiced with every ounce of his being that he had not bedded her. He sank into the chair Leif had drawn up to the hearth and said abruptly:

"We need to talk." He raised his horn to his lips and drank.

"You have my ears," Leif answered, marking well that his captain still raged although his face and eyes shone calm.

Wulf said coolly. " 'Twould seem Silkbeard's hunger for my serving-wench is greater than for the men I can bring him."

So. It was as Leif had feared. Despite being warned, Sitric had taken the maid Wulf considered his own. And that was bad. He asked quietly, "Do we leave now or do we slay him first?"

Wulf laughed. "Whether or not we leave is our only question. The wench is not worth dying for."

Leif hid his shock. Did Wulf actually think the maid had given herself freely to Olavsson? He rejected the notion outright but held his tongue. First things must be dealt with first. He muttered, "My friend, you have but to say the word and the bastard is a dead man."

"I would not risk a hair of your head for such a cause," Wulf answered. Seeing that Leif's blue eyes burned with a dangerous light, he added, "That is the end of it, man. There will be no slaying."

"Then I trow we will go to Maun where our crew and vessel await us, and let the devil scrounge his own troops to fight his war."

" 'Tis a tempting thought except it be our war, too. It shames me it has been so long since Boru felt the sting of Viking wrath. This blow must be a mighty one which will cut him down." Only then would his slain comrades rest in peace.

As Wulf rose, feeling the need to pace once more, pain shot through his leg. It had throbbed earlier as he rode, but he had forgotten it in Sitric's bedchamber. Now it returned in full force, a sickening stab to the bone that nearly brought him to his knees. Damnation, pain during the day, and his battle-dreams had come once more to plague him at night. It was too much.

Leif's sharp eyes caught his friend's quickly hidden grimace. "What is't?"

Wulf waved him off angrily. "Naught to concern you."

"Damnation, 'tis your old Celt-wound! Sit you down by the fire again and I will fetch the ointment and lambswool."

"Stop your clucking or get you gone," Wulf said quietly.

Marking the deadly glint in those wintry eyes, Leif was minded that the tall warrior standing before him was far more than the friend of his childhood. This was the Wolf of Husaby whose Shining Death had lain Celts without number in the dead-straw. Who was he to give orders to such a man even though his face was white with pain?

Leif shrugged. "I will stop clucking, ay," he said easily, "but let us both sit by the fire a bit. I be frozen through and through from our trek." When his chieftain had sat himself, his long legs outstretched toward the healing heat, Leif continued. "I still say we cross over to Maun and let the half-breed fend for himself. Just for a week or two, man. Enough to let him see how few men he and his coward-uncle can rally without your help. There be not a Viking alive who can abide either of them."

"He will find men, never doubt it," Wulf answered. "But, like Sigurd and his horde, they would be fighting for booty, not to wrest this land of ours from Boru's hands. They would be a weak link in the chain I have been trying to forge."

Leif looked thoughtful. "You be right. 'Twould divide us at a time when all of us, Dane, Swede, and Norse, need most to be united. 'Twould be a boon for Boru."

" 'Tis my thinking."

"Then I agree with you. We stay."

"So be it." Wulf rose, and after the two struck hands, he said, "As for the wench, give the matter no further thought, nor will I."

After Leif departed, Wulf poured himself still more ale and once more sat before the fire. He gazed into it with distant eyes. He knew not which ached more, his leg or his pride—or was it his heart? While he had known that Brianna would never be his, yet he had taken great pleasure from those small things that passed between them. He shook his head sharply. Nay, he would not stir that pot again. From now on, when he thought of her, it would be to see her in Sitric's arms, her face contorted with pleasure and hunger; to hear again her small moans. By the gods, so she hated Vikings, did she? But it seemed not to extend to the king. And she had had the damned audacity to call to him for help to make it all seem right.

As he glared into the flames, it struck him suddenly that she had called him by name. He sat straighter. Never had she called him Wulf before. An icy dread prickled through his veins as he wondered if he had mistaken what he had seen and heard. Had she, in truth, needed his help? His hopes lifted for an instant before he crushed them. Nay, man, no more. She had been pleasured by the bastard's pawing and slobbering over her until she saw himself standing there. He finished his ale and was carrying his horn to the table when the butt of a sword-hilt was applied to his door. A voice came.

"Thorsson, 'tis I, Olavsson. I would talk with you."

" 'Tis open," Wulf answered crisply.

Sitric entered alone, leaving his berserks to jaw in the corridor with those of the Norseman. He quaked inside. Rather would he be anyplace else in the land but here, for what could he say to defend himself? He had been caught with the damned wench half-naked in his arms. He swallowed, forced a smile on his lips, and tried and failed to gauge the other's mood behind those flinty eyes. But then the devil would be murderous, what else? And he himself had lost a valuable warrior. He could not imagine otherwise.

"We rode to the tarn north of Holmgeir Jonsson's steading," Wulf said tonelessly, "but the snow grew so thick we deemed it best to return. We will go when it clears."

Sitric snapped shut his mouth, realizing he was gaping. He muttered, "Fine, fine. 'Tis of no import whether you go this day or another. Your safety and that of the men is what matters."

"So I thought," Wulf said drily, marking the king's white lips and nervous hands. "You say you have come for talk, Sitric?"

Sitric? The king blinked. "Ay," he murmured, wondering what the devil was up to. He could have handled Thorsson's rage or accusations or threats regarding the affair, but silence and politeness he could not understand. Did the bastard not want the wench any more? Was he glad to be rid of her, or was it some sinister game he was playing? His anger flared at the thought that they should be at odds over a mere serving-wench. She was ravishing, ay, but such a low-born wench should not come between leaders of men like themselves when war was imminent.

"I but wanted you to know the circumstances of"—Sitric cleared his throat—"of that which you saw earlier."

Wulf said nothing. He waited, his gaze unblinking as he gazed on Sitric's now-flaming face.

"I tore my tunic. Here, look you." The king pointed out the gaping seam beneath one silk-clad arm. "Having heard your wench was clever with the needle, I bade her sew it. But once she was in my chamber, I saw she was not interested in sewing." Damnation, why did the devil not speak? "The truth is, I could not resist such hunger as she displayed. Know you, Thorsson, I am a—a virile man." He nearly choked on the words. The Norseman's face and eyes remained masked. "I regret offending you and trow this will not cause you to cease your—remarkable efforts for me against Boru." God, but he hated him, stiff icy unfeeling bastard that he was.

Sitric's every word about Brianna was a dagger that stabbed Wulf's heart. He wanted to throw Sitric headlong from his chamber; wanted to shout that it mattered not in the least if he took the bitch for his own since he himself had put her aside days ago. But he could not. Even in rage, he could not utter such a lie. He knew now, and it was bitter as gall in his mouth to admit it, that he craved her as much as ever. More than ever. The gods of both their worlds be with him.

Sitric muttered, "I trow 'tis well betwixt us still. She is but a serving-wench, after all, and—"

He grew silent as the tall Norseman moved wordlessly to the door and opened it. The devil's face had grown dark red and his eyes glinted dangerously. Sitric marked well that he was meant to leave, but he was not quick enough.

Wulf rasped, "You be mistaken, Olavsson. 'Tis not well betwixt us. I know too much about you and like none of what I see."

Sitric stared. He felt the cold breath of fear and outrage on his neck. "What mean you?" he growled.

"I have not the hours 'twould take to tell you."

"Methinks you have grown too high and mighty, Norseman. Mayhap you would rule in my place?"

Wulf's lips curled. "You tempt me. Or mayhap you would rather I left . . ." Seeing the Dubliner's face blanch, he said crisply, "But then you know I will not. The fall of Brian Boru is too important to leave in the hands of such as you and Maelmorda."

"Take care, Norseman"—Sitric's lips were stiff with fury—"for now 'tis I who am tempted. I could have you seized."

Wulf's laughter erupted. "Don't act more the fool than you already be, man. And know this— when I return from this next journey, I would take it unkindly were I to hear from any that you had abused the maid further whilst I was gone."

Sitric was so wroth he could scarcely speak. "Be that a threat, Thorsson?"

"Ay, that be a threat, Olavsson."

She is but a serving-wench after all . . .

Sitric's words rang in Wulf's head along

220

with the roaring of his blood and his heart's pounding. He minded well an earlier magical day when he had thought Brianna was like no serving-wench he had ever seen before. He gave an empty laugh; she had certainly fooled him. She was no different from those others who let themselves be pawed and bedded by any man who could give them a pretty bauble or two. Now he wondered what Sitric had promised her, wondered if the wench knew she had offered herself to the worst bastard in Dublin . . .

As for himself, what had it profited him that he had taken her from slavery, freed her, and abided by her wishes not to touch her? Nothing. Nothing but an easy conscience which did not warm his bed nights nor set his loins aflame. He craved more. And if the lady preferred the lovemaking of a brute, that was what he would give her. He but needed to remember his wild young days when the Shining Death drank Celt blood daily, and he himself craved to prove his new-discovered manhood to his comrades. Ay, he could be as brutish as any. And who deserved the wench more than himself?

Chapter Fourteen

Fiona was right. Brianna had recovered by mealtime and helped to serve evening-food in the great hall. While her body had no ill effects from the nightmare she had endured that morn, her soul ached. She could not look at Wulf Thorsson as she served him but was aware that his scornful gaze followed her everywhere. Now as she prepared for bed, she was plagued by the same worry that had nagged her all day. How wanton she must seem in his eyes. How ungrateful and small in spirit after the care he had taken to protect her from every harm. Even if it fell out that she was a victim of Gormlaith's trickery, never would he believe it. In his eyes, the princess was a noble figure.

Brianna threw herself atop the furs on her

narrow bed and felt the tears gathering. But nay, she would not weep, for this very thing could be a blessing. It was a reason for him to despise her, and would save him from deeper hurt if the truth ever surfaced. Hearing a sharp knock on her door, Brianna sat up. Oh, holy Mary, was it Sitric? She had met his gaze but once as she served him this eve, and it was clear her troubles with him were just about to begin. She would not answer. Never would she let him touch her again.

"Brianna, let me in."

She gasped. Wulf! It was actually Wulf. Could it be that he was no longer angry and had forgiven her? She jumped to her feet and hastened across the room. She placed her lips to the door.

"Sire, is't—you?"

"Ay. Open the door." When she obeyed, Wulf entered and closed it softly behind him.

None but his berserks knew he was there, and them he had left in his own chamber. Now he looked on Brianna with icy disdain. Little whore. All creamy silken smoothness and scented softness. So much beauty it made his heart pound to look upon her—and soon she would be his. He ignored the guilt that gnawed him, told himself he had not wanted it this way. It was she who had chosen this path, she who had chosen to sell herself.

Brianna's heart soared. How it gladdened her to see him, no matter what his reason for coming. As he threw off his cloak, she delighted once more in his height and the strength of his body, in the way the torchlight glinted red-gold in his hair and beard. And then she marked his ashen face and that his eyes burned storm-dark. She stepped back.

"Sire, I—I know what you must think—" His quick burst of laughter silenced her.

"What I think, lady, is that 'tis time I claimed that which you be offering. 'Twould seem I have already paid for it in full." When she gazed at him in disbelief, he growled, "Had I but known you were for sale, I would not have taken such trouble to guard you."

"Never have I been for sale!" Brianna cried.

She knew then that he had come there to take her. But surely he would not, he had always been so gentle. As her thoughts flew over the ways she might defend herself, she was pulled to him roughly and crushed against his chest. It forced the breath from her lungs.

Wulf felt nothing but rage. He wanted to punish her, repay her for having played him for a fool. He heard her small moan as he claimed her mouth and his fingers sunk into the soft flesh of her arms. When the glow of revenge he craved did not come, he gathered her to him yet more closely, burying his face in her throat.

"Wulf, nay—y-you do not mean this. You be a—a gentle man."

This could not be happening. Never would he harm her, yet his teeth and lips were hurting her, bruising her flesh, and his hands moved roughly over her body. When he carried her to the bed and threw her down on it, his face was savage, that of a man she did not know. She wondered suddenly if she would live the night.

"Sire, h-hear me, I beg you," she began as he tugged off his boots. "Never would I have accepted the king willingly. 'Twas the strangest thing that"—he tore off trews and tunic and hurled them to the rushes—"that came over me this morn. I—I grew ill. I was so weak and dizzy that I—" Her breath caught as he ripped off his kyrtil and hose, and stood scowling down on her in the dying firelight, his manhood fully extended.

"Take off your clothes," Wulf said gruffly.

Realizing that he had not paid heed to one word she'd said, Brianna exploded. "Didst hear me?" she choked. "I—I was ill this morn. Some strange sickness overtook me and I was not myself. 'Twas as if I were given some—" In the instant she hesitated, fearful of telling him her suspicions about Gormlaith, he lifted her out of the bed and set her sharply on her feet.

"Didst hear *me*, wench? Take off your clothes." When she made no move but glared her defiance, Wulf grasped her bedgown at the neckline and tore it down the middle. If the bitch craved a brute, she would get a brute . . .

Brianna struck out at him with her fists. "Bastard! You dare do such a—stop, damn you!"

Her chemise he dealt with in kind, ripping it up the front, tearing it off her, and hurling it to the rushes. He gazed coolly on her fury and her nakedness. When she tried to cover herself, he forced her arms behind her.

"Nay, wench." He sealed her wrists together with the fingers of one big hand. " 'Tis only right that I look on you. Have I not taken you out from slavery and freed you and guarded you well, even from myself?" Marking the pink that suffused her beautiful face, his eyes grew mocking. "But then, 'twould seem you did not need nor want guarding." With the fingers of his other hand, he traced the shapeliness of her breasts. "Know you, lady, 'tis ended. I will have you this night, and henceforward you can fend for yourself with any who crave you."

For an instant, she glimpsed a strange flickering in his eyes. She knew well that he was in a jealous rage, but what was this other? Pain? Had it hurt him to see her with Sitric? Him, a Viking warrior? She could scarce believe it. Nor could she believe he would actually carry out his threat to take her. She struggled as he lifted her into his arms.

"Sire, d-don't do this thing . . ." Despite her fright and anger, the feel of his warm naked body against her own, the taste of his lips as he harshly claimed her mouth were like manna to her. Oh, Jesu, how unfair. How unfair that she should crave a man about to force her . . .

As Wulf sank to the bed, holding the wench close, his resolve was steely. He would take her quickly and without mercy or tenderness. She deserved neither, nor did he himself expect any pleasure. He craved only vengeance. But as he lay back on the furs and pulled her down beside him, her white face and the fear in her eyes touched him. He had to tell himself sternly that he was glad she was frightened. No more would she think he was so soft she could play him for a fool.

He placed her neck in the crook of one arm and threw his leg across her lower body. With her thus securely imprisoned, he began roughly to explore her nakedness, tasting and savoring her mouth and breasts. But hearing her small moans, he soon realized it was not in him to bruise her so. He was still angry and hurt, ay, he was crushed by her, but he could not punish her as he had planned. Not when she was hungrily returning his kisses with lips wet with her tears. Of a sudden, he thought of her in Dublin-town . . . hurling a snowball . . . the two of them falling with his arms about her . . . their laughter. Damnation, why would he think on those golden moments now of all times? What was this accursed hold she had over him? He thrust the memories away. It was time to get on with this thing. He was hungry. He had been hungry from that moment he had vowed to make her his.

Brianna's thoughts were a tumble of confusion. She resented such harsh treatment even though he had grown more gentle and his kisses excited her. But he was only doing this to punish her. Yet she understood his fury, he had every reason for it—but oh, if only he had listened to her and believed her! She thought then of her treachery of which he knew nothing. Was this to be her punishment? For there was no way she could stop him short of using her dagger, and that she would never do. She squeezed shut her eyes. Perhaps if she did not see his face, she could pretend his fierce hunger came from love for her. She wondered, would the pain this time be as terrible as before?

Of a sudden, he parted her thighs, his own legs entwining them so that her body lay open to him. She gasped as his fingers lightly touched her there, there in her secret place. It was as a small flame at first, hot, flickering, teasing, but then he was on top of her, and no longer were his fingers teasing her, but his shaft. Without warning he plunged, scorching, deep within her. It was as if she were ripped in twain. The shock of it caused her to scream.

"Oh, Jesu, help me . . ."

It was a cry that tore Wulf's heart, but there was no turning back. The passion consuming him and demanding release was a primal thing he could not control. As he suspected, she was not a virgin; he could not have pained her too deeply. Yet his heart made itself heard even as his body was held in the ancient savage grip of a hunger that would not be denied. How small she was; how soft and tender and helpless. The power in his hands had felled strong men, so what must it be for her? And the weight of his body must be nigh to crushing and suffocating her . . .

He rolled abruptly onto his side, keeping her sealed to him still, but giving her the freedom to move and breathe as he continued to thrust within her. Slowly, inexorably he moved up the fiery mountain, so bright and shining it seemed to vanquish all of the black fury and hurt raging within him. Suddenly he craved for her to share it with him, though it was not a thing he had intended nor wanted. He took her mouth, kiss after small kiss without anger, ran a gentle hand over her wet cheeks, tucked a damp tendril of silken hair behind her ear, murmured against her soft breast:

"How beautiful you be, Brianna. How fair . . ." As he moved within her, the fire building, he trailed kisses over her breasts and throat, nibbled the thick fringe of her lashes, kissed her lips again, and gently, gently teased and coaxed her tongue to meet his own. He groaned, his movements growing faster, deeper as he neared the summit.

Brianna opened her eyes, astonished that he had grown so very gentle. The first great rush of hurt was gone. Now she was experiencing a blossoming warmth in response to his tenderness, to the insistent tantalizing movement of his shaft against her inner walls. Deep within her, she tightened around him, writhing unexpectedly and arching her back to bring him closer. How dark-skinned and hard and comely he was with the shadows flickering over his body. His mouth tasted of mead and honey, and the fresh tang of winter-wind clung to his

229

skin and his hair. Winter-wind . . . leather . . . smoke. He was Man . . .

Her heart lifted as if on bird-wings as a glow began to spread through her body, warming every part of her. So this was how it felt, this magic between man and woman that she had never thought to possess . . . She had not been ruined by that first rape after all; she could be pleasured much as any other woman. Marking the Norseman's face, the fluttering of his closed lids, his quick guttural breathing, the moans slipping from his contorted lips as he thrust more and more violently within her, Brianna knew well that she gave pleasure in return. But she felt envy. It would seem Wulf Thorsson's wild ride was a thing not given to women but only to men.

After, as he lay drained and quiet, eyes closed, his breathing deep and even, Brianna studied him. She craved to smooth his tangled hair and stroke the dark-gold curls on his chest and forearms, kiss his partly opened lips. Above all, she craved for him to put his arms about her and pull her close. She craved to lie beside him, their bodies touching, and sleep, and then she craved to wake up with his arms still about her, craved for him to talk with her, laugh with her . . .

But none of that was going to happen, she warned herself sharply. None of it. She must not dwell on it nor think of it ever again. At the realization, the heat fled her body. Seeing that the fire was near dead, she shivered.

Wulf opened his eyes and looked stonily on

the wench by his side. She met his gaze unblinking, but he saw the fine trembling of her body. Doubtless she feared he would take her again. Remembering her cry as he had claimed her, seeing the dark marks on her arms where he had grasped her so roughly, he felt disgust for himself. He had punished her, ay, but he felt no better for it. Rather he felt less a man than he had been before; he had broken his vow never to rape. Yet she had ceased resisting him and had even returned his passion.

He rose from her bed and silently gathered up his clothing. Who knew what it meant? He did not. He had ceased to wonder or to care what went on in her head. She had forfeited any right to his concern when he found her in Sitric's arms kissing the bastard and being mauled by him. Despite himself, Wulf saw red again, felt again the ugly sting of hurt and resentment. He dressed slowly, silently, deliberately allowing her to see the evidence that he craved her still.

Brianna met his gaze without flinching. This was the memory she would hold of him, his scorn and contempt, not that brief interlude when his gentleness had surfaced amid his fury. She watched in mute defiance, chin high, as he took up his cloak and tossed it over his shoulder. Only after the door closed behind him and she was left with the cold and the silence and the dying shadows did she face the truth. She loved him. This Wolf of Husaby, this enemy of Boru and her people was the man she loved. And he

hated her. What punishment for her treachery
could be more fitting?

Leif marked that Brianna was white as death
the next morn. And when he learned that Wulf
had saddled his mount and gone off before
dawn, his concern deepened. Never would he
poke and pry where he was not wanted, but
this could be a serious matter. This maid was
special to Wulf, even if he denied it, and it was
plain to see she cared deeply for him. He could
not imagine her giving herself to a bastard like
Sitric, yet Wulf had washed his hands of her.
He knew not what it was that had happened
between them but he was going to find out. The
little Fiona, whom he had not yet approached
but who had come to be a glow in his heart and
a fire in his loins, was the key. When she served
him, he said to her low:

"I would speak with you, wench. My chamber
is above, the second door on the right."

Fiona's cheeks turned red. "Know you, sire,
I be a good girl and not one to visit a man's
chamber!"

" 'Tis an order," Leif growled. "I will expect
you shortly. Bring a sewing box. I have—I have
damaged my cloak."

Fiona stared. His cloak? She had thought
he was sweet on her. But now his face and
manner were so stern, she doubted he had a
dalliance in mind—especially at this hour when
folk were coming and going. She felt a twinge
of disappointment. He always stared at her so

admiringly, she had come to expect it—not that she would ever respond to him, certainly!

"Hear you, wench?" Leif snapped when she made no answer.

Fiona bobbed, aware suddenly that if she displeased him she could well be dismissed. "Ay, sire. The sewing box. R-right away, sire."

Upon reaching his chamber, Leif barely had time to tear open the hem of his cloak before a knock came, followed by a muffled voice.

"I be here to mend your cloak, sire."

"Enter."

Stepping into his small, dim chamber, Fiona, wide-eyed and suspicious, clutched the sewing box to her breasts. The Norseman pointed to a heap on the floor.

"There be my cloak, girl." He lifted a stool and carried it to where a thin ray of morning sun slanted through the horn pane of the window. "Is't enough light for you to see, think you?"

"Ay."

As Fiona retrieved his heavy cloak and settled herself on the stool, her heart fluttered like a bird beneath her breast. She felt his dark presence so strongly that she knew she was blushing. It angered her. She marked well that he craved her, but for herself even to have noticed that his eyes were heaven-blue and danced much of the time, and that his dark curly hair and clipped beard minded her of her own brothers—She gave her head a brisk shake. She had no business noticing such things, nor enjoying his admiration. He was a Viking.

"Why do you shake your head?" Leif asked. "Can you not mend the thing?"

"I can mend it," she answered crisply. She took a needle from its case, threaded it, and bent to her work. Hmphh! It would seem he had taken his own hands to rend it apart—doubtless to put herself at his mercy. Well, he was in for a disappointment. She would not yield. Feeling his gaze on her still, she gave him a disdainful look. " 'Tis annoying, sire, your standing there staring at me so."

Leif hid a smile. He had been wondering how to bring up his real reason for calling her there. Now, seeing that she was no longer frightened, he decided to go right to the point. He cleared his throat.

"Lady, I—would speak with you."

Fiona gave him a direct brown gaze. " 'Twas unnecessary to rip open your cloak to do so, sire."

When his laughter filled the chamber, her face grew hotter still. It was plain to see he more than craved her, he liked her! He was not even angered by her bluntness. And never had she heard a Viking laugh so; the others here were so cold and brooding, it fair made her shiver to look at them.

Seeing that he had pleased her, Leif quickly pulled up another stool and sat opposite her. "You be a friend to Brianna," he began, "and I be a friend to Wulf Thorsson. I would know what went on betwixt them when you fetched him to her aid."

Fiona gave him a look of astonishment. This was not at all what she had expected. She murmured, "Sire, I—I would feel uncomfortable gossiping so—and it doubts me Brianna would want the world to know . . ."

"I am not the world," Leif answered. "I be Wulf's best friend." He laid a dark hand atop hers and spoke low in her own tongue: "Fiona, lass, I need to know, for I crave to help him. In turn, I trow 'twill help Brianna. In the name of holy Jesu, tell me for both their sakes . . ."

Fiona blinked. He knew her name and that of her god and he spoke her tongue in a way that charmed her. And when his hands, so big and warm and strong, cupped hers and he looked deeply into her eyes, she fair melted down over her stool onto the floor. In a small voice, she murmured:

"T-tell me again, sire—what is't you would know? I have forgotten . . ."

Leif's blue gaze widened, marking that her pretty face glowed and her soft pink lips were parted. He had known maids enough to see that, of a sudden, she was intrigued by him— but why? What had he done? He wished he knew so he could do it again. He said gently:

"You fetched Wulf to help Brianna, but I know naught of what went on. Only that Wulf returned in a killing rage. What happened, Fiona? I must know."

Fiona blinked, murmured, "H-how know you my name?"

Leif smiled. " 'Tis a lovely name—Fiona." His

deep voice was caressing. "And why would I not learn the name of the fairest maid I have ever seen?" He did not lie; it was the truth.

Fiona could only stare. His teeth were a dazzle of white in his dark, bearded face, a face that had such kindness in it, and what a marvel, the way he said her name. Never had it sounded so soft and lilting. So romantic. She watched, mesmerized, as he drew nearer. Oh, holy saints, how blue his eyes were, heaven-blue, a-and they were making love to her. She closed her own eyes then, her lips parting for his kiss . . .

Not until later in the morn did she realize she had been bewitched. Nothing else could explain it. She had gaped at the man like a lovesick calf, she had blathered on and on about the king's lechery and that Brianna had been given a love potion, and then, then, the most shameful thing of all, she had allowed him to kiss her again and again and had eagerly kissed him back. By all that was holy! And she could not even berate him for his wickedness, for he had left Dublin. Even as they had kissed, Wulf Thorsson's berserks came banging on his door. Their chieftain had just returned from scouting the land to the north and it was passable. They were to leave immediately.

Fiona fair burned with shame as she did her chores. She had had compassion for Brianna, marking that the maid had given her heart to the enemy, but secretly she had thought her weak. Never would she herself be so soft or so foolish. Now, all of that had been changed in the blink of an eye. She was besotted by a black-haired Viking! And she had betrayed her best friend to boot, for God alone knew what the man would do with her tale of lechery and love potions. He might even go to Sitric with it. And she dared not tell Brianna what she had done; she could not worry her further when the maid had such grave worries of her own. Nay, all she could do was pray to the blessed saints to have mercy on them all.

Chapter Fifteen

The king of Dublin prowled the corridors of his palace with ill-concealed impatience. Where was Brianna, and why was the damned wench rarely about when he sought her? Had he not known her lustful feelings for him, he would have said she hid herself from him deliberately. Perhaps that was her game, the clever slut. Having gotten him obsessed with her, was she now tempting him beyond endurance playing cat and mouse? Was it but her way of making their inevitable mating the more delectable for the waiting? His mouth watered, remembering how she had felt and tasted.

By damn, he would have her. He would have her in his bed this day, and there was nothing and no one to stop him this time. Wulf Thorsson was gone; he would not be breaking in on them again. Even if the devil were here, it made no difference. He was not frightened by the fellow's outrageous warning and threat, for he had seen his complete disgust for the wench. It doubted him much the Norseman cared enough for her any longer to guard her even were he about. And now to find her—doubtless she was in the weaving-house or the brew-house. He would send a berserk to fetch her.

As he grew heated contemplating the delights that lay ahead, he marked a woman emerging from the great hall. Brianna? As she moved toward him, the throbbing deep within him intensified. He frowned then, seeing that the wench was far too tall to be Brianna. By all the gods, what abominable luck. It was his witch-mother.

Gormlaith hastened her step, spying Sitric at the end of the corridor. "Hold!" she called. "I would speak with you."

"I cannot tarry, Mother," Sitric answered testily. "I have much to do."

Gormlaith's green eyes narrowed. "Yet 'tis always Wulf Thorsson who tends to the doing of it."

" 'Tis little you know," Sitric retorted.

"Ay," said the princess coolly, "because you tell me naught. Methinks we will rectify that right now. Come into my chamber, Sitric."

When the royal eyes glittered so, the king knew better than to argue. He followed his mother into her chamber and sat himself sulkily in the carved throne chair nearest the fire.

"What wouldst know?" he muttered and stroked his beard. All of his thoughts were on the wench soon to lie in his bed. Silken skin . . . rose-petal lips . . . those milk-white breasts he meant to devour . . .

"What wouldst know?" Gormlaith mimicked, glaring at him. " 'Tis a marvel you need ask. There be but one subject dear to my heart."

Sitric returned her glare. "There be two subjects dear to your heart, lady, but I trow 'tis Boru you would talk of and not the seduction of my men."

Gormlaith's laughter chimed out. "You be right. Have you aught new to tell me?"

"I was not aware I must report our every move," he said stiffly.

"Then be aware of it now," the princess snapped, her mood changing on the instant, and her red lips drawing back in a snarl. "This be my war, Boru be my blood-enemy, and 'twill be my triumph when he lies in the dead-straw. From now on, I would know the news as soon as it arrives. Hear you?"

"I hear," Sitric answered coolly, but he shivered. It was glad he was the wench was not out for his own blood. "From now on, you will be the first to know. This past week, the northern O'Neills and the O'Ruarcs allied themselves with us."

"Good. 'Twas Wulf Thorsson's doing, I trow."

Sitric clenched his teeth. " 'Twas my doing, mother. Long have I known their hatred for

240

Boru rivaled our own."

Gormlaith marked the muscle jumping in his jaw. "I salute you. And have you further news of Sigurd, my future betrothed from the Orkneys?" She laughed aloud at the thought. " 'Twas clever of you, son, to snare him so. Again I salute you. Has the fat devil brought in the others he promised in exchange for my hand?"

"—and my throne," Sitric growled, but he, too, could not help but laugh. "Ay, the word from Sigurd is as we agreed earlier. With him come his chieftains from all the isles on the Scottish main. And Thorsson has garnered us more men betwixt Waterford and Dublin and inland beyond the Barrow to Tullamore. Our forces grow."

Gormlaith rubbed her jeweled hands together. " 'Tis lovely to hear, that."

From the corner of her eye she saw him fidgeting with his crotch and hid a smile. She was well aware he had mistaken her for Brianna at first glance and that he lusted for the maid even as they talked. She wondered, had the friggja-grass she gave the wench yesterday worked its magic and Sitric made her his? She was wildly curious. She herself had been with a lover and so knew nothing of what had gone on. Perhaps now was the moment to question him.

"I thank you for giving me your time, son," she murmured in a gentle dismissal. "I know you be consumed by many worries and crave to be on your way."

Sitric rose. "More than you will ever know." He gave the fire a black scowl. " 'Twould seem your wench is haphazard in her duties. Your fire needs mending."

Gormlaith hid her smile. "Brianna be a good wench and a prompt one. She will be along soon. By the way, have I told you that she—admires you?"

Sitric stayed his hand on the door latch. "What mean you, she admires me—how know you that?"

Gormlaith poured herself a horn of ale. "She is ever discreet, of course, but a woman can tell these things. 'Tis a certain hot look she gets in her eye when I speak of you. Methinks she is intrigued by you, as well she should be."

Sitric shrugged. " 'Tis a thing I have known. In fact, already she has offered herself to me."

Gormlaith stared at him over the horn rim, her glittering eyes level with his own. "And . . .?"

Sitric's gaze was icy. "Am I now required to report to you my personal life as well as war matters, Mother?"

Gormlaith swallowed a sharp retort. She could not abide such defiance. She craved to lash him with the truth—that the wench had come to him only because of her own doing. But she dared not. It would spoil everything. She forced her lips into a stiff smile.

"Your personal life be your own, Sitric. 'Tis but a mother's curiosity . . ."

Sitric burned to boast that already he had

made the wench his. And why should he not when soon enough it would be so? He gave another shrug and said casually:

"You may as well know, the wench came to me so burning with desire I took pity on her. When she comes to mend your fire, tell her I await her in my bedchamber."

"I will tell her," Gormlaith murmured, suppressing her jubilation. Only after the door closed behind him did her shout of laughter rise to the smoke-blackened rafters. How all things came to those who plotted for them . . .

As Brianna returned to the palace after meeting Fin, she could not put their talk to rest. She had mentioned to him that Boru had a man in the stronghold guarding her, whereupon Fin laughed and said, ay—the emperor knew most every bite she ate and every step she took. Thinking on those men she saw daily, Brianna rejected every one. Who on earth could it be to know such things?

It was an intriguing puzzle which momentarily took her mind off the worries gripping her. But they returned in force as she entered the musty gloom of the stronghold and the door clanged shut behind her. Her greatest fear now concerned Sitric and how much longer she could hold him off. As she walked toward her chamber brooding on it, Fiona fell into step beside her.

"So there you be, Annie. Didst enjoy the air of Dublin?"

Brianna returned her smile. "Ay, 'twas good to get out for even a bit."

It gladdened her that Fiona was always about. The maid did much to lighten her spirits, and it was amazing that she had actually rescued her from Sitric yesterday. What would she have done had Fiona not marked her distress and fetched Wulf Thorsson to Sitric's chamber? And it was Fiona who had learned for certain she had been given a love potion. She had told her of it this morn.

Brianna stopped in mid-stride to stare at her friend, and Fin's words rang in her ears: Boru knew most every bite she ate . . . most every step she took . . . She frowned. Fiona? Was it Fiona who had been watching over her all this time? And all the while she had been looking for a strapping Celt male in the guise of a Viking! But then why not Fiona? Yet how could a mere maid protect her, and why had Fiona not told her? Why such mystery? She caught the girl's slender arm.

"I would have a word with you, Fiona Corcoran."

The young serving-wench blinked, but went along obediently to Brianna's chamber. Once inside, Fiona looked up at her with wide brown eyes. "Is aught wrong, Annie?"

Brianna barred the door and crossed her arms. "We be Celts, you and I, Fiona. 'Twas you yourself who said we have only each other here in this enemy stronghold."

"A-ay." Fiona blinked at the change in the

maid. She seemed taller of a sudden and there was no sign now of servility in her demeanor. "Annie, wh-what is't?"

"I would know the truth," said the daughter of Kinrade of Carnane sternly. "How comes it that you who hate the enemy are here in this Viking stronghold? Who sent you?"

So penetrating was Brianna's green-gold gaze that Fiona knew better than to lie. Nor did she want to. She was prouder than proud of having been chosen by the Ard Ri for this job and she had yearned to tell Brianna the truth. She straightened her shoulders.

" 'Twas the emperor himself who sent me. He said you be his eyes and ears here, but he fears for you. I am to signal from the loft-room above if you be in danger; a white cloth in the window by day and a candle by night. A great swarm of men can be here in moments—excepting yesterday the snow flew so thick, none marked my signal. 'Twas then that I fetched Wulf Thorsson and—"

"Did the emperor tell you aught about me?" Brianna asked.

Fiona shook her head. "Only that you be a trusted servant like myself and are here to spy for him." For the first time, she understood why. Brianna looked a veritable lioness. Never would Fiona have believed that Brianna's gentle voice could hold such crisp command. In fact, she doubted much that the maid had ever been a serving-wench at all. She added, "The emperor says we two be here where Celt men cannot tread. He says we be the bravest of the brave . . ."

Brianna smiled, minding how Fiona had whisked her out from under Sitric's very nose. "For a fact, you be brave," she said. " 'Tis glad I am the Ard Ri chose you to watch over me. How came you to know him?"

"My folk serve at Kincora as did I—'tis his palace near Killaloe." Fiona giggled. "He heard me moan that 'twas dull as dishwater there with no comely men about, so he brought me into service at his secret quarters near here."

"Near here?"

"Ay. North several miles. When we talk next, I'll tell you where 'tis, but now I must leave. Annie, methinks 'twould be best he not learn that you know about me."

Brianna nodded. "Methinks you're right. He would worry that the two of us would chatter about things no maids should know and be overheard. Of course we will not. We will chatter only of household matters and the weather and—"

"—and men." Fiona's cheeks turned bright pink. "I—I need your advice."

Brianna laughed. "I be the last person to ask for advice about men! And now 'tis time I, too, was on my way. The princess awaits me." She caught the girl's hand before she left. "Fi, have thanks for everything. 'Tis glad I am you're here."

Sitric had dozed off in his throne chair before the fire when a sound at his door waked him.

"Enter," he growled. Seeing it was Brianna, he remained seated.

"The princess gave me your summons, my lord," she murmured.

"It is time you got here, wench. Bar the door behind you, and then sit you here." He pointed to the stool at his feet. "I would speak with you. Lean back against my chair."

Brianna obeyed. She settled herself on the stool, her back toward him, and gathered her skirts about her ankles. Her calm face belied her uneasiness and the rapid beating of her heart as she wondered what the king was about. Why must she lean against his chair? When he lay a heavy hand on her nape and began caressing it, she knew.

" 'Tis time we had an understanding, you and I," Sitric began, having decided he would not allow Wulf Thorsson to thwart him. He would have this wench as often as he chose, and he would find some way to lock her lips. The Norseman would never know. He continued smoothly, "Since your former master saw us together, I trow he no longer cares about you nor protects you. Therefore—"

Brianna turned wide eyes toward him. "Sire, that is not so!" In truth, he was right, but she hoped to keep the fact hidden as long as was possible.

"Silence!" Sitric's long fingers tightened their grip. "You will hear me out."

"Ay, sire." She ordered herself to sit quietly, assuring herself there was no situation she

247

could not handle, not even this dangerous one.

"Therefore," he continued, "you will do my bidding from now on." He resumed stroking her nape, feeling its silkiness and longing to sink his teeth into it. "You will be available to me at all times. This means that if you have chores in the brew-house or the weaving-house, you will tell me earlier where you be. No longer will I search the entire town for you when I have need of you."

Brianna swallowed a sharp retort. "Ay, sire."

Her gaze was on the hearth fire, but she did not see the merry flames dancing there. She saw herself forcibly disrobed by him, carried to his bedcloset, mounted by him . . . But nay, it would never happen. The question was, how to deny him and still be allowed to remain in the palace. She had no answer, but deny him she must, not only this time but every time. Never would she allow this man to bed her.

Even as she vowed it, he tilted back her head and his mouth plundered hers. His marauding hands caught both her breasts and plundered them, too. It was some moments before she managed to twist free, only to have the king seize her wrist cruelly.

"Nay, wench, I mean to have you now. You have proven you crave me as I crave you." He rose and pulled her after him toward the bed.

Brianna stiffened and resisted. "Never have I craved you."

She expected laughter, but Sitric did not laugh. His face reddened.

"You dare deny it? You dare?"

Despite his fury and his crushing grip on her wrist, she forced herself to be calm. Think! She must think. If she was to be saved from him, it would be by herself alone. Fiona knew nothing of her danger, and Wulf Thorsson was far away. Even had he been here, he would not have helped her. She moistened her dry lips and prayed for Jesu and all his holy saints to come to her aid. She said quietly:

" 'Tis shamed I am, sire, that I behaved so with you, but I was not myself. A—a cruel prank had been played on me."

Sitric's fair brows drew together. "What mean you? What prank?"

Brianna took a breath. "I was given a love potion. I—I know not how nor where nor by whom, but—"

Sitric groaned. "By the gods, it gets worse. Now you dare insinuate your passion was naught but the result of some damned aphrodisiac?"

She met his gaze directly. " 'Tis no insinuation but the truth, sire." She held her head high. "My body was not my own to command. I swear it before holy Jesu and all his saints."

Sitric waved off her words. Talk of the White Jesu always made him nervous, for never had he given up the gods of his father. He said impatiently:

"We will speak of it no further, for 'tis of no importance. What matters is that you are here now, and I crave you." He lifted her in his arms.

The insufferable ass! Brianna fought to keep his red wet mouth from claiming hers. Pushing fiercely against his bearded face, she twisted her own from side to side, foiling his every attempt to kiss her.

She gasped, "Sire, you put us both in terrible danger if you think Wulf Thorsson no longer protects me."

"You lying bitch! He cares naught for you. He has washed his hands of you."

"That is not so, I swear it. Before he left he—came to me. He be my protector still and he be wildly jealous. He raged so after finding us together, methought he would slay me—and you." Marking the flicker of fear in the king's eyes, she added, "I trow 'twas but the grace of God that spared you. I—I thought to see you in the dead-straw this day . . ."

Sitric contained a shudder, remembering the devil's warning. Suddenly it seemed more ominous. "Damn me, woman, 'tis you who will lie in the dead-straw if you cannot control your wagging tongue." He tossed her into his bed. "Now lift your damned skirts and open your legs." He sat on the bed ledge and began to tug off his boots. Feeling her eyes on him, he turned. She had not obeyed but sat glaring at him. "Didst hear me, wench?"

Brianna could stand it no longer. She hissed through clenched teeth: "I will not lift my skirts nor will I spread my legs. Slay me if you will." Her eyes glittered a deadly challenge. "Or if you can . . ."

Sitric blinked. In the name of all the gods, what was this? How dare she defy him? He reached out to seize and shake her but she leapt beyond his reach. He snarled, "Raise your skirts, damn you. I command you. I am king."

"And I am the daughter of a chieftain of Maun." Brianna's voice was thick with rage. "I raise my skirts for no man."

She was so fury-filled, she could have slain him. Ay, she yearned to slay him, but in the midst of the fury, she saw that she had jeopardized everything by her rashness. Everything. And since she could not take back her words, she must somehow soften them though it choked her. He must never suspect he had just seen her real self.

"Not always have I been a thrall and a——a serving-wench," she gasped, tears rolling down her cheeks. "Know you that, sire."

Sitric gaped at her, his own rage vanishing as he absorbed this astonishing revelation. What? Was this the truth? She was a chieftain's daughter? Which chieftain? How long since she had been enslaved? And could he demand ransom for her return or, better still, gain allegiance from her tribe? But all of that could come later. First he would have her. Gazing down on her angry face, he saw well that he would have a battle on his hands. He felt a hot stab of jealousy. How had Thorsson gone about taming her? Or had he . . . ?

By the gods, it came to him plain as day. The Wolf of Husaby was a fiend in battle, ay, but it was said he was gentle with women. And now here sat this wench who boasted she raised her skirts for no man. Suddenly Sitric knew in his heart, in his bones, that the devil had never taken her but all the while had led them to believe she was his in every way. By the gods. Well, he himself would have her, make no mistake. But he saw now that he could not use force on the daughter of a chieftain of Maun. Not if he would later have the man for an ally. Nay, nay, rather he would use guile . . .

Chapter Sixteen

Sitric placed his boots on the floor and hastily pulled off his trews. "Know you, my pearl, chieftains and their kin are treated with great respect under my roof. 'Tis a pity you did not speak sooner of your father's importance. Who be he and from what part of Maun?" When she made no answer but stared at him with fathomless eyes, he shrugged and said easily, " 'Tis of no import. What matters is that I seek a wife and you be the fairest maid these eyes of mine have ever seen." He knew from long experience that the least hint of marriage made a wench as good as his. There was not a woman alive who would not spread her legs for the promise of a crown.

Brianna said stiffly, " 'Tis said you already

have a wife, sire. The daughter of the emperor himself."

Sitric damned the ever-flapping tongues of the palace gossips and covered his irritation with a smooth lie. " 'Tis true, that, but what is not said is that I mean to put her aside. I have sent her to Limerick to winter with her kin as a first step."

He removed his tunic and upon entering his bedcloset stretched out on his side to gaze upon the wench at his leisure. She sat rigid, her back straight, staring at the furs and the silken coverlid beneath her. Sitric inhaled a shaky breath. Already he could taste her, and his hunger burned hot within him. He had thought of nothing but her for days now, even when he lay abed nights with another wench pressed close against him. He patted the furs by his side.

"Come, Brianna, lie you here alongside me. Be you not shy." He reached out, pulled her to him roughly, and lay back down again, her soft body pressed close to his. Holding her fast, he slipped his eager fingers inside the neck of her kyrtil and began fondling her breasts. "Know you," he murmured against her hair, "never could a king wed a mere serving-wench, but a chieftain's daughter, even though taken in captivity and made a thrall—now there, my sweet, there is another thing entirely."

Brianna was shaken. Was he serious, or was he but another Ospak who would go running in the opposite direction if she said ay? Terror drove the question from her mind as she felt his hard shaft throbbing against her. Her thoughts raced over the many dark things she had heard about Sitric of Dublin, whispers of his cruelty and treachery and lies, of the women he had claimed without end. She feared she would be one of them unless she found a way out of this, but she knew not how. No longer could she defy nor insult him, and she dared not slay him, for his berserks would surely be close by.

She closed her eyes as his heavy hands moved over her more insistently. Was she actually meant to sacrifice her honor to him for Boru's cause? She could not believe it—in fact, she absolutely would not. She began to struggle.

" 'Tis useless to resist, my silky wench." Sitric pulled up her skirts and slipped his hands along her thighs, seeking the treasure between them. "I mean to wed you, sure enough, but know you, never will I bind myself to a female whose charms I have not tasted. I am king, after all."

Brianna's eyes widened. What? He would not bind himself to any whose charms he had not tasted? She felt a burst of fury. Had there ever been such an arrogant ass? Yet it was his very arrogance which suddenly pointed the way for her to follow. Yes . . . it might work . . . but she must play the game carefully, carefully. Pouting prettily, she said:

"You be cruel to tease me, sire. Never wouldst marry me."

Sitric laughed. "We will wed, lady, be assured of it. You be the fairest wench I have ever seen, and I crave you as I have never craved another."

Marking the heat in his blue eyes, and minding that he had looked on her hungrily from the very first moment he saw her, Brianna knew that this at least was true. He did crave her. She hid her revulsion as he pulled down her kyrtil so that her breasts were exposed.

"Holy Odin . . ." His breathing was heavy.

"Sire, I—I would speak with you—"

"Later," Sitric growled.

She shuddered when he lowered his mouth to one breast, hungrily kissing it and sucking the nipple. She wanted to be sick, but she steeled herself.

"Sire," she persisted, " 'tis flattered I am that you find me comely and w-would wed me." When his mouth sought her other breast while his hands roved over her greedily, she cried, "My father, too, will be pleased by my great good fortune—but he be a particular man, my father. He will wonder, have I your respect in addition to your admiration? He holds in high esteem that man who respects his woman . . ."

Sitric raised his head, drunk and dazzled by his voluptuous feeding, and gaped at her. He scowled. "Respect? By all the gods, certainly you have my respect. Why wouldst even ask such a stupid thing? Take off your damned gown, woman, 'tis in the way."

"Sire, I be a high-born maid—"

"Of course you be. 'Tis evident to any with eyes in their heads." He fell on her again, not caring whether the silly wench cast off her gown or not. He himself would tear it off very soon now.

"You truly mean to put aside your wife?" Brianna raised her voice. "You promise to marry me?" She was certain he would not, it was but a trick to seduce her.

"Damn me, of course I do. Ay!"

"But you insist I lie with you first . . ."

Now Sitric raised his head and fixed her with a warning stare. "Lady, 'tis unwise to naysay a king. Know you, I grow weary of your chatter."

"I—I will obey, sire," Brianna said quickly. "I will lie with you . . ."

Sitric grunted. "Never did I doubt it." It followed as the day the night. Mention a crown and the wench, be she high-born or low, yielded. Silly bitch. He slid his questing fingers between her thighs, only to have them grasped by her own which minded him of steel.

"But first, sire," Brianna said sweetly, "you will divorce your wife. In my presence. Then will I lie with you. I trow my protector, Wulf Thorsson of Husaby, will not think I am unreasonable to insist on such assurance."

Sitric looked on her in disbelief. He said thickly, "You jest."

Brianna shook her head. "Nay, I do not, your majesty. I have told you, my father be a particular man and I be his only daughter. If I am to be your queen"—she was amazed by the bold words coming from her lips—"we must do this properly." Marking the uncertainty on his face, she knew she had saved herself from rape. At least this time. It was all she could ask, that for each encounter with the king of Dublin she be given the strength and the wisdom to overcome his determination to have her.

Sitric masked his anger and befuddlement. He knew not what madness had come over him these past weeks; he knew only that his loins burned constantly for her. His head was ever spinning with schemes to talk to her and touch her, whereas his wife he thought of not at all. And the wench was high-born, the daughter of a chieftain of Maun. By all the gods, why not wed her? Why not? All of this maddening game-playing would then cease once and for all, and Thorsson could hardly object if his intentions were honorable. She would then be his to command, to have any hour of the day or night he chose. And if she did not give him the great pleasure he anticipated, why then she, too, he would put aside. What could be more simple?

He thought suddenly of another aspect of the matter that fair made his mouth water. Brian Boru had coldly and cruelly divorced Gormlaith, making her more of a troll than ever. What could be more fitting now than for himself, Sitric, to divorce Boru's daughter the same way? Never had he cared for Emer in the first place. He smiled at the deliciousness of it as once more he fastened his narrowed eyes on the wench in his bed.

He marked that she was frightened, though she hid it well. It was a good thing, that, fear in a woman, for it made them more biddable. He caught her breasts roughly in one big hand and compressed them so that there was a deep valley between them. He slid his tongue there, licking the soft flesh and feeling her tremble. He whispered, his mouth on her:

"So be it, lady. I will divorce Emer before your eyes. Know you, 'twas my plan to bring her here and put her aside even before you asked it." He scarce knew how to tell the truth any more, but what matter when lies dripped so easily from his lips? " 'Twill give me the greatest pleasure to cast her into the street and let her find her way back the many miles to her father's palace."

Brianna hid her horror. She had misjudged completely Sitric's hunger for her, for she saw now that it was not a mere craving but an obsession. While she herself was in no real danger—she would flee before Emer arrived—she feared for Sitric's queen. This daughter of Boru would be the object of his revenge. Never had Brianna intended such a thing.

"I will send a messenger to her immediately," Sitric said, "but she need not come until after Yule. I am not so cruel as to separate my children from their mother during the holy season."

"Children?" Brianna whispered. Holy Jesu.

"This will not concern you. You may go now." He rose, and as he donned his clothing, he watched her cover herself and slip quickly from out his bed. "Mind you," he ordered, "henceforward you will tell me exactly where you be should I—need you."

"Ay, my lord."

"And say naught of this to any, not even the princess Gormlaith. I would not have her know yet nor have the servants gossiping. Hear you?"

"Ay, my lord."

8 December

The great hall of Knut Haugen of Oriel lay quiet finally. After a long night of feasting and talk and, in the end, agreement and handsala, the striking of hands, the Oriel chieftain was gone to his bed. His guests snored in their sleeping bags on wall benches and on the floor. Only Wulf Thorsson and Leif Karlsson remained awake, both gazing gloomily down their long legs into the central fire pit that still held flames enough to toast their feet.

Leif studied his captain with thoughtful eyes. In the days since they left Dublin, Wulf had effortlessly garnered a host of chieftains to their side. Leif marveled on it now, musing that it was more to Wulf the men had rallied than to any cause, even so great a one as the overthrow of Brian Boru. Men loved Wulf and would die for him—so how came it that he had such trouble with one small wench?

Ever since Leif had coaxed the truth from Fiona, he had sawed back and forth over whether to speak to Wulf about a thing not his business. At an earlier time, he had been bold enough to make light of Brianna's balkiness and urged Wulf to woo her. But this was different. His first thought had been to keep quiet and trust the storm to pass; never had Wulf Thorsson brooded for long over any maid. And it was not a thing Leif relished, admitting to Wulf all that he knew, and that he had coaxed it out of Fiona by the most ungallant means. But that time was past. Now, in the stillness, Leif saw that the deep hurt in his friend's eyes had not gone away. If anything, it was greater than ever. He must speak. Gathering his courage, he said:

"How much longer will we be gone from Dublin, think you?"

"Be there any good reason to return?" Wulf answered low, so as not to waken the others.

Leif tossed a sprig of straw into the flames, and then another and another. "We both know there is, man," he answered, his eyes on the fire.

"Then you speak for yourself, not me," Wulf grated. "I have no craving to look on Sitric's face 'til need be. I thought to move on up the coast awhile yet and gather yet more men."

"Ah." Leif's heart thundered as he commanded himself to say what had to be said before he lost the wisp of courage he had. Already it was vanishing. He pulled in a breath and released it. "I—talked with Fiona before we left . . ."

So that was it. The Celt wench. Wulf allowed his annoyance to show, saying crisply: "She will

261

still be there, I trow, when you return."

A ghost-smile hovered over Leif's mouth. "How comes it, my friend," he asked softly, "that you who direct your men never to assume anything, do so yourself?" When Wulf looked up, his eyes hooded, Leif plunged on. " 'Tis not about Fiona I would speak—'tis about Brianna."

"Then find other ears to listen." Wulf got abruptly to his feet.

Leif caught his wrist in a steely grip. "Sit you, man," he growled, "and hear what I have to say."

"There is naught you can tell me about the wench that could interest me."

Leif grinned. "Wouldst care to bet? The Shining Death be mine if you be wrong."

Wulf gave him a long, black look before lowering himself to his chair once more. He would give anything in the world to be wrong about Brianna. Anything but his sword. He muttered, "Well you know I am not a betting man."

"But you will listen?"

Wulf glowered. "I am here, am I not? Get on with it."

What in damnation was this? He had said as little as was necessary to Leif after returning from Sitric's love-bower. Only enough to explain his sudden murderous mood. Had that damned wench, Fiona, gabbled it to all who would listen? It was just like a serving-wench to gossip about such a thing until her tongue fell out. Thor's bones . . .

262

"I know what you saw and what you think—" Leif began.

Wulf gave a harsh laugh, but quickly lowered his voice to a scornful whisper: "Man, you know naught. You know only what that wench said. Why wouldst believe her?" He resented the sudden twinkle in his friend's eyes.

"Because I know women, my friend," came Leif's quiet answer, "and I know a practical, level-headed maid when I see one. She says Brianna was given a love potion, and I have no reason to doubt her."

Wulf's shoulders shook with silent laughter. A love potion? "Oh, ay, 'twould explain it all, I trow."

"I think it would," Leif said gravely. "The maid was already weak and dizzy when Sitric summoned her to mend his tunic. In no wise could she control her actions when he made his first advance. She tried to fight him, but the damned potion fair overcame her. Fiona said that after, Brianna wished herself dead and feared she had gone mad. Why else allow a man she feared and loathed to fondle and kiss her?" Leif watched with satisfaction as Wulf's face blanched. He saw that he was touched with uncertainty.

"Doubtless he filled her head with promises . . ." Wulf muttered, his own head filled now with what this could mean.

"Come, man. Fiona said she grieved that you had seen her so and that you thought 'twas of her doing."

Wulf's stomach knotted. A love potion . . .
Why had not Leif told him sooner? But nay,
he would not put the blame on Leif. He said
low, "Was't friggja-grass, think you?"

" 'Tis likely," Leif answered grimly.

"By all the gods . . ." It was one of the most
potent of the aphrodisiacs and was easily mixed
in food and drink. "Who?" he muttered, wanting
to slay the culprit. "Sitric?"

Leif shrugged. "Or one of his nobles or any
jealous serving-wench minded to play a prank.
You know how they be."

Wulf shut his eyes. Brianna had tried to tell
him of the strange sickness that had claimed
her, but he had been so full of hurt and rage
that he had not even listened. Over and over he
had brought to mind his finding them together,
growing angrier each time. Now he saw that
he was not the one wronged, she was. She had
cried to him, her protector, for help, and he
had abandoned her—and then he had returned
and taken her. Forced her. Remembering her
muffled shriek of pain, he groaned, shook his
head. Holy Thor . . .

The fire died as long and long he sat, brooding, flogging himself for his callousness and
brutality. He had to start for Dublin this day,
now, not to seek forgiveness, never could he
ask forgiveness, but to tell her he was sorry and
that he understood. Finally he understood. He
looked up when Leif gripped his shoulder.

"Man, have you sat here the whole night?"
Leif asked, just having risen from his sleep.

Wulf's brows drew together as he gazed about him. He was surprised to see the men beginning to stir. "Is't morning already?"

"Ay."

Wulf rose and stretched his taut muscles. "Wake the men," he ordered. "We leave for Dublin as soon as they have broken fast."

For days, Brianna had tormented herself with the unexpected turn of events with the king. Now, as she helped the other serving-folk clean the palace in preparation for Yule, she was at peace. She was not to blame for Sitric Olavsson's putting aside his wife. He would have done it in any event. Nay, her only demand had been that he divorce Emer in her presence. The poor thing would be better off without such a man anyway. As for Emer's having to make her own way back to Kincora—it was foolishness. Kincora was miles and miles away, and Boru's men, their eyes ever on the stronghold, would carry her to safety immediately should they find her cast out onto the streets.

Brianna was at peace, too, knowing that Sitric no longer dared lay a finger on her. He had tried, oh, ay. The day after their talk, he had summoned her from the brew-house to paw and slobber over her, whereupon she had declared her father would not accept such behavior from a future son-in-law. Sitric, his face terrible to look upon, had yielded.

As Brianna carried the bed gear out from the bedclosets and burned the straw and washed

the bed walls, she was ever planning ahead.
Rather than guess when the queen might arrive
from Limerick and flee beforehand, she decided
to wait until Emer came. She could then slip
into Dublin during the excitement and never
return. But she would not tell Fin any of this,
for he would insist she leave now. As for Boru,
he must make do with whatever news Fiona
gleaned for him in the great hall where most
of her work was centered. And as for Wulf
Thorsson of Husaby . . .

Brianna pondered the Norseman with sadness as she carried the bed furs to the bathhouse to bake. Climbing the steps to the loft and
spreading them on the floor in the stifling heat
above the steam room, she brooded on those
last moments she had spent with him. She saw
again his storm-dark face and eyes, the grim
set to his jaw, his clenched fists. Beyond any
doubt he hated her, and it tore her heart. But
all had fallen out as it should; never could they
be lovers, nor even friends. They were enemies.
They would always be enemies. She prayed she
would never see him again, for the pain would
be too great.

As she descended the narrow steps to the
steam room, she marked through the thick haze
that a man stood just inside the door. Seeing
that he was tall and his hair and beard golden,
Brianna froze. Sitric. Would he never leave her
alone?

"Hello, Brianna . . ."

Hearing Wulf's deep voice, she bounded down

the remainder of the steps to stand gazing at him, wonderstruck. Never had she expected to see him again so soon—nor had she expected him to seek her out. It was as if he had just this moment returned. He still wore mail, his helmet, and a sword at his side, and there was a light in his eyes. How tall and strong he was, and how she had missed him, worried over him, yearned for him, grieved over him. How she loved him . . .

"Greetings, Wulf," she spoke softly. Never more could she call him sire, this man she had held in her arms and cherished within her own body.

Chapter Seventeen

Wulf drank in the sight of her. He had not known he was so starved for her, nor had he remembered that she was so fair. All his memories of her, until his talk with Leif, had been dark ones. Now he stood rooted there, dazzled. Her face was rosy from the heat of the bathhouse, and the moisture, like thousands of tiny diamonds, glittered in her long, autumn-hued hair. Her lips were parted in surprise and her eyes, more gold than green in the mist and shadows, held a strange light he had not seen before. It would seem she was glad to see him despite his ill treatment of her, but he did not want to speak of that now. He craved only to hold and kiss her, comfort her. After, if she would hear him out, he would tell her he was sorry . . .

Brianna was too bewildered to speak as he came to her, took her in his arms and held her, tenderly yet so tightly she could scarce breathe. She wondered what had wrought such a change in him, but only for an instant. Marking his eyes on her lips, she lifted them willingly for his kiss. It was warm and insistent, wildly hungry, yet so gentle she soon was lost in it and in him.

She knew not how long they clung together, their mouths sealed, her hands stroking his face and hair, his hard body and the strength of him warming and thrilling her. She wondered suddenly if she had never awakened this morn and was but sleeping still. It would explain so much. His being here at all . . . his tenderness instead of rage . . . But it was not a dream, and though part of her was happier than she had ever been before, she knew it would soon end. It must end. She withdrew from his kiss, not meeting his gaze.

"Others will be coming to steam and bake the rugs," she murmured.

"I would be alone with you," Wulf said gruffly. He could not make himself release her but held her close, stroking back the dark, flaming hair from her damp face, yearning to kiss her again. Temptation overwhelmed him. His lips sought her white temples, the dimple beside her mouth, the soft skin beneath her ear. He craved to rain kisses over her, make love to her, guard her, bestow upon her her slightest whim no matter how foolish.

Brianna uttered a soft moan, knowing that her resolve was once more slipping away. Her body and heart were not hers to command when she was in his arms with his lips caressing her so. Resisting the impulse to draw his head down to her breasts, she pushed him gently away.

Wulf released her. His hunger was growing, and he dared not hold her any longer. "We must talk, Brianna."

She sensed what he wanted to say, sensed his regret at what had gone on before and that he craved to make things right between them again. But she must not let it happen. She murmured:

"There is naught to say."

"There is much to say," Wulf countered, low. "I know now I accused you wrongly . . ."

Brianna could not speak, her thoughts were in such turmoil. Moving to where a heap of wet stones steamed atop the embers, she gazed down on them, her hands at her throbbing temples. Why? Why had this happened when it had been over between them? She was gladdened that he knew the truth, ay, yet now she must struggle further, and he must be hurt again.

"It stabs me to the heart that I hurt you so," Wulf muttered. "I ask no forgiveness, for 'twas unforgiveable."

Brianna turned. "That's not so. I—I forgive you . . ." Oh, nay, she had done it again! Why had she not just kept silent?

"You be too kind, lady," Wulf answered gruffly. "Myself I will never forgive."

End it now, Brianna told herself. End it and leave. End it.

Wulf watched in hungry silence as she drew on her hood and moved to the door. "I will come to you later," he said.

Brianna hesitated, her hand on the door. She dared not look at him. "You must not . . ."

Wulf frowned. "What mean you, I must not?" After the kisses they had just shared he meant to have her in his arms this night. He meant to show her that he was not the raging, raping brute he had been the last time. When she did not answer, he turned her around, lifted her chin. "What is't?"

Oh, holy angels. Never would she love any other as she loved him, for there was not another like him on this earth. The way he looked and walked, the deep sound of his voice, his strength and grace, his height, all thrilled her. But it was far more than that. It was that he had been good to a maid he thought but a thrall. He had guarded her and been caring and kind, and when he had made a mistake, he was strong enough to admit it and not blame another.

"Is't that I harmed you?" Wulf asked quietly. "That I could understand."

The steam was smothering her, suffocating her. It blurred her vision and filled her nose and mouth so that breathing was difficult. In truth, she would have welcomed the dead-straw at that moment.

"I am—going to wed the king," she whispered.

Wulf stared, at first uncomprehending and then in astonishment at her ashen face. He said, "Is this some jest?" Even as he said it, he saw that it was not. She was going to wed Sitric Olavsson.

He released her as if stung. He was minded to give a shout of laughter, let the little troll see his scorn and disgust, but he felt his mask lowering, felt the seething of instant full-blown rage. What a fool he was. Had he but trusted in his own judgment of her and not in that damned wild tale of Leif's about friggja-grass, he would at this hour be where he should be—in Ulidia gathering men. But he had wanted to believe in her, so here he was, being humiliated for the second time. He would not be so witless again, he vowed.

Brianna died inside, seeing his quickly covered hurt. It shamed her to her very soul that he should think she craved such as Sitric over himself. How stupid and greedy she must seem, and how ungrateful. He had proven over and over that he cared what happened to her, and his regret at forcing her had been deep and heartfelt. He had been filled with tenderness toward her. Now all of that was forgotten. She whispered:

"Wulf, 'tis—sorry I am."

Wulf's gaze was scathing. "Oh, ay, that I can see well—yet 'twill not hamper your wedding the bastard."

"I—I . . ."

Wulf shook his head. "You be a freedwoman now and need explain your reason to none. 'Tis my hope only that it be a damned good one."

She took herself in hand then, saying firmly, "I trow 'tis good enough. I would wear a crown and sit by his side." Her cheeks brightened, thinking how despicable that sounded.

Now Wulf could not contain an explosion of laughter. First she had craved gowns and ribbons and shoes, and now the king. "Here methought you were an innocent maid in need of guarding."

Brianna lifted her chin. "And now?"

"Now I know not whether you be conniving or merely stupid. Or gullible."

The words so stung that she made herself taunt him. "Gullible I am not. He means to divorce his wife and we will wed s-soon. He has promised . . ."

Wulf was amazed by her naiveté. "Lady, if you think to share the throne with the bastard, you will first have to wrest it from the Orkney king."

Brianna blinked. "What mean you?"

Wulf misliked it that his anger had loosed his tongue. Never did he talk of private matters outside of council, and then only with his comrades, but what matter? Already he had heard the men jawing about it over their ale for the serving-wenches to hear. Now he craved for this silly wench to see what manner of man she had promised herself to.

"What I mean," he lowered his voice, "is that Sitric has given his crown and his mother to Sigurd of the Orkneys in exchange for his help in the war."

Brianna kept her face composed. It was she who had told Boru of Sitric's alliance with Sigurd, but she had not known the price that Sigurd had exacted for it. It would interest Boru greatly. But what of Gormlaith? Did she know of this? Brianna had been wary of her since eating her tainted creams, but even so, the princess's being given to yet another Norse king with no voice in the matter was a harrowing thought. Brianna could not help but feel compassion for her.

"Be he a kind man?" she asked softly.

Wulf scowled. "Who?"

"Sigurd. Will he be good to the princess, think you?" She damned the tears that filled her eyes.

Seeing them, Wulf shook his head. Never would he understand this wench. "The gods only know," he answered.

Brianna met Fin one time more to give him the news of Sigurd, and then the Yule season fast approached. As the days flew by, she was too busy to go to town. Along with the other servants, she was hard-pressed to serve the many extra guests who feasted and drank day and night in Sitric's great hall. She mused that in no way did the celebration compare with Yuletide at Carnane, for this was mere revelry. There was no priest to tell them of the Christ-child, no Yule log nor green boughs decking the hall, no story-telling nor harpers playing nor singers nor jugglers—only visiting chieftains talking of war and glutting themselves on food and drink. It was the most dismal Yule she had ever spent.

Immediately after the holy day, Wulf and Leif and their small band departed for Meath while Sitric lay about yarning and drinking with those guests who hung on. Fiona, pale and with dark circles under her eyes, was too tired to chat, so that Brianna was left to her chores and her own thoughts. She attended Gormlaith daily as usual, and though all appeared the same between them, it was not. Even if the princess had not fed her those treacherous sweets, Boru's warning and her own strong instincts would have made Brianna cautious. More and more she sensed that the princess was but pretending to like her.

She minded that all throughout the holy day, Gormlaith had gazed on the Norseman with narrowed green eyes. She lusted for him, there was no doubt of it, and Brianna was filled with wrath imagining them in each other's arms. She thrust the thought away. Nay! She would not be jealous. What right had she? As she carried the remains of Gormlaith's morning-food to the kitchen-house, Fiona fell into step beside her.

"Can we talk?" the maid whispered.

Marking her white face and worried eyes, Brianna had a sudden fear that someone suspected them. It would explain why Fiona had looked so wretched these past few days. She looked up and down the corridor before answering softly:

"Go to my chamber. I will meet you there."

When she entered, Fiona was huddled on a stool by the hearth, her face buried in her hands. Brianna pulled up a second stool and joined her. When the maid did not look at her but began to weep quietly, Brianna whispered:

"Fiona, what is't? Does someone know of us?" When the girl shook her head, her shiny dark curls bobbing, Brianna said, "What then, for the love of God? You must tell me."

Fiona's brown doe-eyes were drowned in tears. "I—I love him . . ."

So great was Brianna's relief, she nearly laughed aloud. She bit her tongue and put an arm about the girl's shoulders. "Why should love be so terrible a thing? Why are you not happy?"

" 'Tis the Viking," Fiona gulped. "Leif Karlsson, the dark, wonderful one who m-minds me of my brother, Des." She began to sob outright. "Oh, Brianna, 'tisn't fair that you and I have fallen in love with the enemy."

Brianna looked on her in shock. "Fi, never have I said I was in love!"

"Never did you have to!" Fiona cried. " 'Twas written all over your face. Oh, holy Mary, now what do we do? We are betraying them! I can think of naught else." She stood and began to pace to and fro.

Brianna rose and caught her hand. "Come, little heart, sit you down with me again and let us talk, there's a good lass." Her soothing voice had a calming effect on the maid, but Brianna herself felt far from calm. It was bad enough that she herself had fallen into such a snare, but for this child now to be trapped—yet if it was to be, she judged that Leif Karlsson was a man who would not take advantage of Fiona. Brianna had always sensed kindness in his smiling eyes.

"Methought to solve this myself," Fiona murmured, wiping her eyes on her apron, "but I cannot. Know you, Annie, the Ard Ri and my land and my people I would die for, but now—"

Brianna gripped her hand.

"—now I have found me the man I've waited my life for a-and saved myself for. In the little time I have known him, he has fair stolen my heart. And he be the enemy." She shook her head. "I know not what to do."

"What would your heart have you do?"

"Wed him and live with him 'til the day I die," Fiona murmured.

Still holding the maid's hand, Brianna asked softly, "Did he ask you to wed him?"

"A-ay."

That was that, thought Brianna. Fiona could not possibly remain here, torn as she was between her loyalty for Boru and her love for Leif. She was strong, but not that strong.

"I will tell Fin you must leave," Brianna said. "If you can live with your sister, you can still see Leif each day."

"Nay," Fiona declared, a stubborn tilt to her chin. "Never would I desert you."

"Come now, 'tis not as if you slipped off in the dead of night with no warning, after all. 'Twas my idea. Besides, it doubts me I need guarding any more. The king knows his great charms are wasted on me."

Fiona's eyes showed a glint of hope. "You would not lie about such a thing?"

"Nay, I would not lie," Brianna lied, knowing it was the only way.

"Then I will do it! Oh, I will do it! Oh, Brianna . . ."

Brianna returned her fierce hug, rejoiced in her radiance, and then watched her turn grave once more.

"But I fear for you still, Annie," Fiona said. "I cannot help it."

Brianna smiled. "You must not. I'm fine."

"What of Wulf?" Fiona whispered. "Loving him as you do, how canst continue on here for the emperor?"

Brianna gently led her to the door. "Just as you have made your choice, Fi, so have I made mine. Now I had best get busy . . ."

"You are sure?" Fiona misliked the odd look in her eyes.

"You silly thing, I am sure. Now go you."

That eve, Brianna's spirits were low as she left the kitchen-house and started for Gormlaith's chamber to freshen it for the night. Already she missed Fiona, and the maid had not even left the palace yet, and Wulf—oh, Jesu, Wulf she missed with such a sick sense of loss that he might as well lie in the dead-straw. Never would she recover from it. But to dwell over and over on his angry face and the words exchanged between them was bootless. She must put her mind on other things and keep her hands busy. She had therefore come early to fluff the princess's bedding and mend the fire and light fresh candles so she could begin sewing on the great pile of mending that awaited her. But as she laid her hand on the latch of Gormlaith's door, she marked that it stood open a crack. Hearing Sitric's voice within, she turned to go. Sitric she could not bear to see this night. But then she heard that he spoke of Brodir.

"He be a devil, that one," Sitric was muttering. "I know well he hates Boru, but his demands be outrageous. And methinks, as does Thorsson, that he is not to be trusted. Him we can do without."

"That may well be," the princess declared, "but his men and his ships we cannot do without."

"Damn me, woman, what wouldst have me do?"

"I would have you use your head, you ass," Gormlaith hissed. "Offer him riches he never dreamed of—the same you offered Sigurd. Give him Dublin, and give the greedy fool my hand . . ." At that, she burst into laughter. "What matters it when they are but words and the thing itself will never happen?"

"What a schemer you be," Sitric said, joining in her merriment. "Very well, lady, 'twill be done."

Brianna stood motionless. Had she misunderstood? But she knew she had not. Gormlaith was not a helpless pawn at all, but knew everything that was happening. This news could well be the most important she might garner for Boru. It was for this that she was here, for this that she had turned away the man she loved and made him despise her. Even fate was on her side, for Sitric's berserks were nowhere to be seen in the smoky torch-lit passageway. Hoping to hear more, she drew closer, her ear to the narrow opening. She heard the crackle of fire, the slosh of ale being poured into the horns, heard Gormlaith's lowered voice, smooth as honey.

"I have never asked—how mean you to safeguard the throne and myself from the bastards?"

"Surely you know there be only one way . . ."

"Slay them?"

Sitric chuckled. "Ay. In the thick of battle, arrows go astray."

"Tragically so."

"Damn me, what if Brodir has heard already of the offer to Sigurd? 'Tis secret, but these things happen."

"Then you will have one less arrow to lose, for Brodir himself will take care of Sigurd. I mind that the two hate each other."

"There be not one amongst the Viking chieftains who does not hate all the others."

"Excepting Thorsson of Husaby," said Gormlaith pleasantly. Seeing her son's instant irritation, she twisted the knife. "Him they admire and respect, and 'tis easy to see why. He be the loyalest and the bravest of warriors, the Wolf of Husaby." And the most tempting. She would lose her mind if she could not soon coax him into her bed.

Sitric stifled a biting retort. Two could play that game. He had news that would make her choke on her venom. He poured himself more ale, settled himself before the fire, and drawled:

"Have I mentioned, Mother, that I am taking a new queen?"

"You have not, but 'tis about time. Never could I abide that mouse Boru gave you. You will mind I said so at the time. Who is't you have chosen?"

"Brianna," he replied, smiling.

Brianna, a darker shadow among the shadows in the corridor, held her breath waiting for the princess's reaction. It came instantly: a sharply indrawn hiss.

"What game is this you play with me? Brianna be naught but a serving-wench."

"Nay, Mother, Brianna be the daughter of a chieftain of Maun." Sitric greatly enjoyed the spectacle of his mother attempting calm in the face of rage.

" 'Tis impossible!"

Sitric smiled. " 'Tis so. Never fear that I would marry any but a high-born wench. I have sent for Emer so I can divorce her before an assemblage

281

of my nobles. She should arrive shortly after Yule."

Gormlaith gritted her teeth so she would not catch up the poker and strike him. God's bones, she had wanted him to *bed* the wench, not wed her! And now she must look daily on the bitch's blooming dew-fresh beauty while her own showed the cruel fingering of age. It was diabolical.

"Why Brianna, may I ask?" She managed a half-smile.

"Since 'twould serve no purpose, you may not," said Sitric, rising. "And now I bid you good night, lady."

Brianna fled to her own chamber before he could see her. Not until her heart had quieted did she return to Gormlaith's chamber to tend her.

Chapter Eighteen

Brianna stood without the princess's chamber door for an endless time fearing that her face and eyes might betray what she had just over-heard. But then she had had much experience these past weeks in hiding who she was and how she felt. She tapped, entered, and found Gormlaith in her fur-draped throne chair before the hearth. She curtsied.

"Good evening, your highness."

"You be late," Gormlaith answered.

Brianna made no reply but went directly to the hearth. In silence and with the princess's eyes upon her, she tended the fire, replaced the burned-down candles with fresh ones of beeswax, lit the wall torches, and lowered the tapestries over the windows. She then went to the bedcloset and was about to fluff the bed-skins and pillows for the night when the princess said sharply:

"Stop your fussing and sit you." She pointed to the chair opposite her. "I would talk with you."

"Ay, my lady." Brianna sat herself, neatened her skirts, folded her hands, and looked at Gormlaith, politely attentive, but a shiver coursed through her.

Gormlaith gave her a long, pointed gaze, taking the time to sip from her horn. "I have just talked with my son," she said, finally, "and what he said fair amazes me. 'Twould seem after all this time, I know naught about you, Brianna. Why is that?"

Marking the watchfulness of those marble-green eyes, Brianna warned herself to be careful. " 'Twas not my place to speak of myself, my lady. I am but here to serve you."

"You led us to believe you were a thrall."

"Never have I called myself a thrall," Brianna replied evenly, "though I was stolen from my family and forced into servitude."

"By Ospak?"

"By another, your highness. Ospak stole me from my first captor, and then Wulf Thorsson claimed me as I fled Ospak . . ." She thrust away the ever-painful thought that, from the very first he had sought only to help her.

Gormlaith stretched her stiff lips into a smile. "And now you would be queen."

" 'Tis blessed I am to have found favor in

his majesty's eyes," Brianna said carefully. She blinked, widening her own. "Oh, my lady, I—I hope you approve. I know he be king, and I be but a chieftain's daughter . . ."

Gormlaith clenched her teeth. The bitch could lie and fair melt her way through a block of ice. But she had made a grave mistake. While she might not call herself thrall, she had carefully called attention to her lowly estate: tearful gratitude over the most wretched castoffs, the trembling and eagerness to please. What was behind this game she played? Whatever it was, two could play it. And always had she herself been superb at games.

"If I seemed curt," she said smoothly, " 'twas but my great surprise over this matter. One day you be naught but a thrall, the next you would appear to be the high-born daughter of a Maun chieftain and hand-fasted to my son."

As her narrowed eyes moved over the girl, her jealousy smoldered anew. Never would Sitric take this wench to wife, she would see to it. Now that Wulf Thorsson no longer showed interest, she could make plans. It would be easy enough to find an eager buyer for such a wench. She bit her lip, remembering then that it was the dead of winter and few traders were about. Mayhap it would be more profitable to ransom her to her chieftain-father, if indeed there were such a person.

"Who be your father, Brianna?" she asked, her face carefully guarded.

Sensing that Gormlaith was as angry with

Sitric as herself, Brianna decided that instant to stir the pot. It could only help Boru if there were greater enmity than usual between the two. She said quietly:

"My lady, forgive me, but I—I would wait until after the divorce to speak of my father. His majesty has not pressed me on it." She wondered then if she had been too bold. Yet what could the woman do? Her son was king. He ruled her as surely as he ruled his nobles.

Gormlaith felt scathe for Sitric's weakness even as she felt a grudging admiration for the wench. She said softly, " 'Tis brave you be, Brianna. Mayhap you indeed be the daughter of a chieftain."

Brianna met the princess's eyes. "Let there be no doubt, my lady. My father be a great man in my own land."

Gormlaith's own gaze glittered. The cocky bitch. More than ever she craved to sell her to the highest bidder, and then see how proud she would be. Or should she gift Maelmorda with her? How he would relish her. But she dared not, for were Sitric to find out, and he surely would, it would be disastrous. Once more, she studied the maid's slender body and the lustrous dark-red braid curving over her bosom. She favored her with a smile.

"Methinks you will be an asset to my son, Brianna. You be a great improvement over the mouse he now calls wife. She gives him no pleasure whatsoever, though he be as virile a lover as any woman could want." Returning her stare to the fire, she raised the horn to her lips. "I trow you have discovered that by now."

Brianna's smile went unseen. The woman was consumed by curiosity, and now Brianna would give the pot another stir. She murmured, "I—I have not, your highness. 'Twould not be seemly were I to lie with the king before his divorce. He agrees, of course."

What? After the wench had been used by however many Norse chieftains, Sitric still had not had her? Gormlaith kept her gaze on the flames while her fingers grew white-knuckled from clutching her horn. She bit her tongue. In God's name, had there ever been such a calculating slut? It seemed clear now that netting Sitric had been Brianna's goal ever since she set foot in the palace. It would serve him right, the silly ass, for not bedding her immediately but allowing her instead to twist him about her little finger and extract a promise of marriage. It was unheard of. And now Gormlaith herself must be civil to the witch and not reveal her wrath. Never must she be suspected in the slightest way when Brianna disappeared, for it was in Sitric to send her away as had her husbands. Men! They were all alike. She turned to the girl, her mask securely in place.

"It gladdens me that you be a maid of such high scruples. 'Tis fortunate for you that Sitric is in agreement."

Brianna nodded. "Well do I know it, my lady."

"I tire now, Brianna. You may prepare my bed."

"Ay, my lady."

As Brianna plumped the furs and pillows, she knew that the princess followed her every move. She marveled at how quickly things had changed in but the blink of an eye; both of them now playing a game, both pretending, both wearing velvet gloves with the other. It was just as well, for she had no desire to meet Gormlaith in open combat. Not yet.

In the six weeks that followed, Brianna had never felt so alone. Having driven Wulf away filled her with the worst emptiness of all, and it pained her that the woman whom she had admired and grieved over had never really existed. Gormlaith's charade had been as great as her own. And with Fiona gone, she had none to laugh with nor confide in. Purposely she had made no other friends in the palace, for she feared they would want to accompany her to her meetings with Fin—and Fin she saw rarely now. After telling him the shocking news of Brodir and Sigurd, she'd had nothing to report with Wulf's being gone. What remained to her was Sitric. He had taken to waylaying her in the dark passageways and demanding kisses. When she had first resisted, he reminded her sharply that she was soon to be his wife. Or, if she wished to call the whole thing off, she could leave.

Brianna's decision had been an easy one to make. His disgusting attentions were a small price to pay for the satisfaction of helping Boru.

She gave nothing of herself in return and soon she would be gone. But she had another deeper problem which seemed to have no solution. She craved to tell Wulf, upon his return, of the treachery to his cause planned by Gormlaith and Sitric. He deserved to know, yet it was all to Boru's good if she said nothing. She should be content to let the enemy destroy itself from within by its own deceit. But on the other hand, might not Wulf, if he knew, decide that Boru was by far a better ruler than such as Sitric? Her pulses quickened, thinking he might even change his allegiance.

It was at this point that she always threw up her hands in frustration. Never would Wulf Thorsson betray his countrymen to fight for Boru. Besides, she could not plan on being here to tell him the tale. Sitric's men were long overdue from their trip to Limerick to fetch Emer and could arrive at any time.

When they finally did return on the fifteenth day of February, Emer was not with them. Hiding in the shadows, Brianna learned that the queen, unhappy with her Limerick kinfolk, had long since traveled with her retinue to Kincora, her father's palace. Sitric's men declared they were not about to go there, to the very center of the enemy's holdings, to drag her away!

As Sitric's wrath exploded, Brianna stole to her chamber and shook with relief and silent laughter. Who would have thought such a wonderful thing might happen? She was safe! But was she really? Why should Sitric change his stripes and turn honorable of a sudden? Perhaps she should flee on the morrow and not await Wulf's return . . . But when the Norseman and his band arrived at eventide on that very same day, Brianna saw it for a sign. It was meant that he know of the treachery of Gormlaith and Sitric . . .

Upon his arrival at the Dublin stronghold, Wulf called for an immediate meeting with Sitric. But before it could take place, he was summoned to the chamber of the princess Gormlaith. Clad in a dark-green fur-trimmed gown and seated in her throne chair before the fire, she was the essence of Irish royalty. Her husky voice held a promise of intimacy.

"Welcome back, Wulf Thorsson of Husaby." She gave him her hand.

Wulf touched his lips to her fingers. "Have thanks, my lady." He was taken aback by this first sight of her apartment. It held the scent of roses and was filled with the richest of satins, brocades, and furs, a sumptuous contrast to the remainder of the stronghold.

"I but wanted to tell you of my deep appreciation for your effort. Tomorrow night we will feast in your honor."

Wulf shook his head. "There be no need—"

"But there is." Gormlaith lay a jeweled hand atop the deep swells of her bosom, and saw his eyes drawn there. "The Wolf of Husaby be a hero to all here, and I would give you a hero's welcome before you go off again." Rising languorously, she stood before him, and tall though she was, her eyes came only to his bearded chin. Desire shot through her. "Wilt not yield, sire?" she asked, low. "For me?"

And so Wulf had yielded—and now the feast, which had gone on for hours, showed no sign of ending. Clad in his richest garments, he sat opposite Sitric in the seat of honor, his purple and silver banner mounted over his head. His belly was filled with the finest food and drink Dublin had to offer, and his ears rang with the music of harpers and with praise for the new banners he had gathered for the king. Even so, he craved nothing so much as quiet and solitude. Into his mind stole the memory of a snowy morn in Dublin-town and a laughing pink-cheeked maid pitching a snowball. He sighed. Where was she this eve? He had half-expected to see her in the high-seat beside Sitric. He grew aware then that the princess was speaking.

"You be far away," Gormlaith said with a slow smile.

"Ay."

She savored his regal appearance. He wore a tunic of rich burgundy wool bordered with gold, and the great seal of Husaby gleamed on his broad chest. She mused that a crown atop his head would become him . . .

Wulf marked that the gaze of the princess had scarce left him throughout the meal. He saw now for a certainty that which he had suspected for some time. She craved him. It would seem he had but to say the word to have her in his bed this night. He drummed the board with his fingers, considering it. He had thought to hold her above such things in deference to her position, but now he sensed that the rumors about her were true. By the gods, if she were an easy piece, why should he not enjoy her? She was fairer than most, and it had been weeks since he had had a woman. Not since Brianna . . .

Abruptly he shuttered his mind to the bitter-sweet memory. It still stabbed him to the heart what he had done to her, and that she would wed such a bastard as Sitric stung him just as deeply. She had been out of his life these many weeks now, so why could he not put her out of his thoughts? It galled him. And when he met Gormlaith's slumberous eyes once more, he made his decision: He would bed the wench. It was said that when she gave herself to a man, he forgot all but her.

He appraised with deliberate slowness her softly parted red lips and the lush white curves of her throat and bosom. When she met his gaze unblinking, a glimmer of excitement in her green eyes, he gave her an imperceptible nod. He put down his horn and got to his feet.

"I will bid you good night, Olavsson. A thousand thanks. Your hospitality is unexcelled."

"A thousand thanks for the banners you bring us," Sitric answered with false warmth. He knew not how the devil had done it; Grisine of the Flemings, Gresham of the Normans, and the

Earl of York were but a few. But Brodir Sitric had won on his own. Greedy bastard. Sitric smiled thinking on their secret pact that would never be honored.

"My lady"—Wulf bowed to Gormlaith. " 'Twas a gracious welcome. Have thanks for your kindness."

Already Gormlaith could imagine those strong dark hands moving over her flesh, and her heart fluttered in her throat. "The pleasure is mine, sire."

As Wulf and his berserks left the great hall and moved through the torch-lit passageway toward his chamber, a maid slipped suddenly from out the shadows and approached them. He tensed, marking the long, gleaming braid that hung outside her shawl. It was Brianna.

"Sire, I—I beg of you. I must see you before you journey forth again. May we talk in private? 'Twill take but a moment."

Wulf was minded to continue on without answering, but seeing that she was frightened, he could not. "Where?" he asked gruffly.

Brianna pointed overhead. "I now be on the second story in the loft-room at the end of the corridor."

Certain the princess would not expect him until the palace slept, Wulf nodded. "I will come shortly."

In his chamber, he splashed water on his face, rinsed his mouth and combed his hair and beard. Leaving his berserks at the foot of the steps, he ascended to the second floor, pondering what she might tell him. Had Sitric abused or betrayed her? Neither would surprise him, but then it was the path she herself had chosen. As he applied the hilt of his dirk briskly to her door, he reminded himself that his heart must be hard as a plank and twice as unyielding where she was concerned. He would not soften no matter what woes had befallen her. When she opened the door and bade him enter, he did so in lordly silence.

Brianna had melted when she saw the Norseman seated in the great hall beneath his silver-purple banner. He had looked like some far-northern prince in his gold-bordered garb, but in no wise had she been prepared for the great rush of feeling that swept over her now. Had ever a woman been so lucky, having such a man care for her? Or so unlucky as to be in the position she was now in? Though she had been assigned to the far end of the hall, she had scarce been able to keep her eyes off him.

Now, having him there before her in her small loft-room, she was overwhelmed once more. This was her love, this strong golden Wulf of Husaby, but never would he know it. In his eyes, she was but an object of scorn and disgust—and hatred. And she had made it happen. She had done her job well.

"I can stay but a moment," Wulf said curtly. "What is't you would tell me?" Marking that her face and lips were pale, he felt concern and damned himself for it. What manner of trouble had the little troll gotten herself into while he was gone? "Has the bastard harmed you?" he asked.

"Nay." Brianna did not miss the concern that had flickered across his face. Oh, Jesu, did he still care? That instant, she resolved he would know the truth about Sitric and herself. She could not bear it otherwise. "Know you," she murmured, "never did I intend to wed the king, and this be the truth before my God. I despise him . . ."

Wulf's brows drew together. What joke was this? He could still hear her saying the words that had driven him to fury and despair: She would wear a crown and sit by the bastard's side. He barred the door and returned to her.

"Lady, dost ever mean what you say?" When she stepped backward, he grasped her by the arms. "Nay, wench, stand you right there and tell me what you are about. Now." Her softness and warmth beneath his hands scorched him. He released her instantly.

Brianna craved for him to hold her close, just for a moment, but if he did, she feared that never could she let him go again. Instead she must make him understand why she had done what she did, yet not disclose the real reason. It seemed nigh impossible.

Wulf's anger and his hunger for her were taking a toll on his breathing. "I am waiting . . ."

Brianna met his skeptical gaze. "The king tried to force me," she began, "b-but I told him

I raised my skirts for no man, I be a chieftain's daughter. He then said he would wed me but I must lie with him first. I felt 'twas but a ruse. I said I would lie with him only after he divorced the queen in my presence. I—I hoped he would not dare anger a chieftain of Maun, and that he would let me alone—but h-he agreed!" She shook her head. "Never did I think he would divorce his queen to wed me!"

Wulf laughed. " 'Twould seem you two connivers deserve each other." He had meant to hurt her, but he was not prepared for the tears that filled her eyes.

"I saw no other way to save myself than to pretend I would wed him," Brianna answered with quiet dignity. "I meant to flee as soon as the queen arrived."

Wulf crossed his arms. "Why didst not tell Gormlaith who has always protected you?"

"The princess is—not as she seems . . ."

Wulf's eyes narrowed. "Why didst not tell me the truth of the matter? Or am I, too, not as I seem?"

She did not remind him that in his fury he had withdrawn his protection. She said faintly, "You be exactly as you seem." As for the truth of the matter, she shook her head. Never would he know the truth—that she had planned on his hating her . . .

He was standing so close, she had but to stretch out a hand to touch him. She minded how crisp his hair and beard felt beneath her fingers, the way he kissed, the taste of him . . .

She felt cold of a sudden and pulled her shawl about her more closely.

"Mayhap you feel I cannot guard you well enough," Wulf said stiffly.

He was fury-filled with her and with himself. Here she stood, white-faced, trembling, telling yet another tale the rationale of which he could scarce believe. And all he could think of was that damned day in the snow and that laughing maid who had seemed to own all of Dublin-town.

"Always did I feel safe with you," Brianna answered. "Safer than ever I felt in my life." Her teeth chattered she was so cold, and there was an odd buzzing in her ears. "The end of this tale be that Sitric's men arrived this morn without his queen. I must leave here soon, but first I craved to talk with you . . ." She could not resist touching her fingers to his lips and tracing them. Wulf, Wulf, how I love thee . . . The shadows closed in on her then.

Wulf caught her in his arms as she fell. By the gods, the little wench had fainted dead away. It seemed he had been too hard on her. And had ever a maid got herself into more predicaments than did this one? And what was this foolish talk of her leaving? He would not allow it. He would return her safely to her father if it was the last thing he ever did. And before he departed again, he meant to have another talk with yon Sitric. This time he would hold the devil's treacherous dealings with Brodir and Sigurd over his head to insure Brianna's well-being. It would well-nigh ruin the Dubliner if word of it ever got out.

Gazing down on Brianna, marking her closed eyes, the lashes lying so thick and dark against her pale cheeks, Wulf knew that he craved her still. Always would he crave her. It was a curse. He held her close, cradling her against his chest. His lips still tingling from the touch of her fingers, he gently kissed her temples, her damp cheeks, her hair, her mouth . . . She would never know, and he would be gone by the time she awakened. But when he lowered her to her narrow pallet, he saw that her eyes were open.

Chapter Nineteen

Brianna was shamed. She had swooned, ay, but she had recovered instantly—and feeling Wulf's tender kisses and his holding her close, she had but pretended oblivion. It seemed to be her way of life now, pretending. It was all she knew. And gone now was the bone-chilling cold she had experienced earlier. His touch had brought her alive and afire.

Seeing her gazing on him, Wulf's face grew warm. He muttered, " 'Twould seem I have overstepped—"

"Nay," Brianna answered quietly. "I—wanted you to kiss me . . ."

Kneeling by her side, Wulf saw her face regain its color; saw in her green eyes a light that had not been there before. Warning himself to be wary, he asked low, "Why wouldst want me to kiss you?"

"I know you have scathe for me and that there can be naught between us, but I—I craved to be close to you one last time . . ."

Wulf shook his head. "Methinks you crave something, lady, but not that," he replied crisply. "What is't you want of me? And why wouldst lie to get it when I would give you freely anything in my power to give? Is't my protection? You have it. Never have I withdrawn it, though I said I would."

Once more tears stung her eyes, infuriating her. Why was she so weak? No more could she look at him nor speak to him without their spilling down her cheeks. She cursed them, dabbed them, but down they flowed, aggravating her resentment toward him.

She choked, "Damn you, Wulf Thorsson, 'tis no lie!" It had not been easy for her to admit she wanted to be close to him. Now she craved only to strangle him.

Wulf looked on in bafflement. What in the name of all the gods was a man to do with a wench who kissed him one time and turned her back on him the next? Never did he know where he stood with her. He knew only that never had she been more fair than she was at this moment, and he yearned to make love to her. But no more was he such a fool. Her beguilement of him was as great a threat to him as was a Celt with a blade in his hand. Greater even. A warrior he could slay, whereas the memory of lovemaking with her would scorch him until he lost all reason and all command of his senses.

But then he saw reason . . . Having her one more time might well give him the peace he craved. Always had it been so in the past—his hunger for a maid vanished with familiarity. Why should it be different with her? Or had it come to pass that he could no longer take his pleasure with any woman without brooding over her like some love-struck lad? Damnation, never had he been so weak, nor was he now. He wanted her, and if she craved him, for whatever the reason, why not?

Seeing the way his eyes were moving over her, Brianna sat up. Never had she meant to let this go beyond a kiss. She said quickly, "Methinks 'tis time I told you why I summoned you. I know you be eager to leave." He seemed not to have heard. He took her thick rope of hair in his fingers and toyed with it.

"Meant you what you said?" His voice was husky. "That you craved to be close to me one last time?"

When he lifted her braid to his lips and kissed it, Brianna could no more lie than cease breathing. "A-ay."

"Then I would make love with you if you will have me—and then 'twill be goodbye. I will not come to you again nor will I look back, Brianna. Not this time. You have said there can be naught between us, and I see 'tis so." When she made no answer but gazed on him with huge eyes, he asked softly, "What say you, my lady?"

She murmured, "I know not."

She was remembering his strength and tenderness, the way his hands had thrilled her as they moved over her body. For that very reason, how could she make love and then give him up? Yet how could she not? She was hungering for him. And if he were willing and knew it for what it was, the end—and if afterward they said goodbye for a certainty . . . Oh, how could she not?

She allowed him to unbind her hair so that it cascaded over her breasts, allowed him to draw down her kyrtil to uncover one shoulder. He bent over it, and she felt a searing shock of pleasure as he pressed his lips to her flesh.

"Know you, Brianna," Wulf murmured, "never will I hurt you again. Rather would I die, your God be my witness . . ."

One last time, she mused, her blood running so fast and so hot she could scarce bear it. One last time. Delight winged through her as his tongue touched the taut nipple thrusting against the fabric of her kyrtil. His lips next sought her throat, the corners of her mouth, her lips. She was breathless when he finally raised his head.

Wulf's hunger was mounting, but he willed himself to patience. He traced the curve of her other breast with his long fingers, cupping, gently kneading, pressing kisses on it.

Brianna hissed in a breath as his lips sent a sweet fire shooting through her, from her breasts to the very center of her womanhood.

"What say you?" Wulf whispered. "Wilt have me, my lady?"

"Ay, m-my lord. Please, ay . . ."

In a daze, she watched him rise to his feet, felt herself lifted easily to stand beside him. As she struggled with trembling fingers, undoing pins and ties, she marked that he had swiftly stripped off his boots and outer garments. He captured her hands and kissed her palms and wrists, kissed each finger before lowering her arms to her sides. Realizing he meant to undress her, she blushed.

"There is no need, I—I am quite able to—" He stopped her words with a kiss.

After, she could but stand there wordless, allowing him to remove her kyrtil and feeling his warm lips brush her shoulders and arms. When he drew off her chemise and hose, she saw the heat in his eyes and heard the change in his breathing. Yet his caresses were slow and gentle, cupping her breasts, bending to them, the tip of his tongue touching her nipples. When he kissed each one deeply before suckling her, Brianna gasped. Never had she known such pleasure existed—and it was he who was giving it to her, allowing her to savor it and not plunging into her instantly to gratify his own hunger. She was touched to the heart, for she had seen that he was fully aroused.

Wulf took her tongue gently between his teeth, nipping and kissing it, and felt her arch against him. How sweet she tasted, sweeter than ever he had remembered, and how hungry she was, kissing and caressing him so that he knew her need was as great as his own. He felt a sudden terrible regret, knowing he would never have her again, but it vanished when unexpectedly she touched his hardened shaft with shy fingers, stroking and fondling him so that his barely controlled passion blazed. He groaned, caught her up into his arms, covered her face and breasts with kisses, and then lay her on the pallet. He tore off his inner clothing, stretched out beside her, and pulled her close, feeling her soft naked body heating his bare skin. He shuddered. Holy Thor, only in his dreams had he ever felt so. He smiled, marking that she clung to him tightly, her eyes glazed and half-closed. She was panting lightly. She was ready. Long and long had he himself been ready—since that first moment he laid eyes on her. He put a finger to her lips, felt the soft moist tip of her tongue touch it.

"Wilt have me still, Brianna?"

"Ay—dost want me still?" She heard his soft chuckle, felt his arms tightening about her.

"What a silly little wench you be . . ."

Gormlaith had burned with impatience as she ate the last of her food, drank the last drop from her horn, and talked and laughed leisurely with those about her. Fools, she thought with the deepest of scathe. Stupid boring idiotic fools. Her body smoldered as she contemplated the evening that lay ahead. At long last she would have Wulf Thorsson in her bed. At long last. After an interminable interval had passed, she deemed it proper to leave and patted a delicate yawn.

" 'Twould seem I be wearier than I thought," she murmured. "I cannot hold my eyes open another instant."

"Then by all means, get you to your bed." Sitric lifted his horn to her. "We will somehow manage without you."

He had not missed her frequent heated glances at his captain throughout the feast, and he foresaw a night-long orgy for the two of them. It was good. She had been more of a bitch than usual of late and doubtless it would sweeten her temper. As for himself, he meant to have Brianna later this night. Since his men had had the audacity to return without his queen, no more would he concern himself with the wench's silly scruples nor veiled threats of her father's displeasure. He had been too patient for too long as it was. As he brooded on it, his mother rose from her chair. All at the high-board stood.

"I bid you good night," Gormlaith said. "Return you to your merry-making."

She passed through the crowded hall and hastened to her bedchamber. She doubted the Husaby chieftain would come before the palace slept, but then he had looked on her so hungrily, he might arrive at any instant. She smiled at the thought as she stirred the fire and lit fresh candles. She quickly removed her feast-dress and the many chains and bracelets adorning her, and with trembling fingers touched scent to her body, to all those places a starving man sought. She then slipped on a deep-red gossamer gown, combed and scented her hair, and stood before the fire. He would see her thus when he entered, her body showing like porcelain through the cloudlike fabric and the fire glowing behind her . . .

But when the candles had burned low, he still had not come. Gormlaith, bundled in fur against the chill, paced her chamber, brooding and sipping horn after horn of mulled wine that simmered over the flames. Where was he? Had she mistaken completely that bold gaze he had given her? She shook her head. Nay, she knew well the look of a buck in rut. He had craved her and meant to have her. Perhaps he had intended for her to come to him. But why then had he not sent a man for her? She shook her head, cursing the precious hours wasted. She slipped into the dim corridor and tapped on his door. When there was no answer, she pushed on it, swinging it open onto emptiness—black shadows flickering on walls and floor from the dying fire.

Gormlaith lay a hand over her pounding heart as a thought struck her for the first time. Brianna. Was he with Brianna? She did not want to know, but she had to know. Hastening toward the steps that led up to the storage rooms, she froze. Were those shadows or were two men sitting there? She crept forward, hugging the walls, and when she heard the murmur of voices, her heart crashed against her ribs. They were Wulf Thorsson's men, the berserks of the Wolf of Husaby. And there could be only one reason why they guarded the steps to the loft-room. Their master was trysting with his former thrall. The serving-wench who would be queen . . .

A-tremble and fair burning with rage and hatred, Gormlaith stole back to her chamber. She had had enough of the damned wench, but what to do about her? It was God's own grace that Brianna was not now queen of Dublin. But how long before Emer was finally brought here and divorced and the marriage performed? Sitric would not wait forever. And Gormlaith's own plans had been foiled. Winter storms and the coming war had kept traders away, so the bitch could not be sold—nor could she be ransomed without her father being known. And the Wolf of Husaby had not helped matters by Brianna once having worn his great seal. Now none craved to harm her in any way, thinking she wore it still. It was not fair. Not fair.

Gormlaith then remembered a thing she had marked earlier and wondered at greatly. When Wulf Thorsson was gone from the palace for weeks on end, Brianna rarely went into town. Only when the Norseman returned, or was coming and going, did she make her daily trips. It struck a strange, almost sinister note in Gormlaith's mind, and from tomorrow henceforward, she vowed, she would instruct her serving-man Regin to follow the witch when she went out. God's bones, how she prayed he would find her up to some nasty mischief.

As she leaned against the wall, eyes closed, she heard the creak of Sitric's door. Stealing a look, she saw that he walked toward the loft. She threw back her head in a silent laugh, and thought with relish of the shock he was about to receive. At least she would not suffer alone.

Wulf opened his eyes and was instantly awake. He knew not how long he had slept, but Brianna was asleep in his arms still. The fire burned low and her small chamber was chill. He pulled a skin more closely about her and gazed down on her face, so peaceful in sleep. He took a gleaming lock of her hair spread out over the fur and stroked it. It minded him of a dream he had had once, or perhaps it was a daydream—making love to her with the fragrant silken veil of her hair wrapped about the two of them. He held it to his lips, caught himself, tenderly released it . . .

Their time together had been magical but now it was over. He felt as he had hoped he would—as if a burden had been lifted from him. No longer did it matter that he did not trust the maid nor understand her. He neither expected to nor did he want to. He was satisfied that his need for her this night had been one of hunger alone, and when that need came again, there would be other maids to warm his bed. This one could go her way and tell her lies and her wild tales to another. But one thing still remained for him to deal with. Her safety. Her plan to flee the palace was a foolish one, for where would she go and what would she do alone in Dublin? Nay, here she must stay until he could get her back to Maun.

Gently he disentangled himself from her warm arms and legs twined about him and hurriedly dressed. He would awaken her, give her his seal, and leave, for what was left for them to say to the other? Never could he tell her of the rapture he had found with her. Seeing that the hearth fire would soon die, he lay more twigs upon the embers and blew on them softly. As he lay more peat on them, he heard her sigh. Turning, he found her gazing at him.

"Have thanks for mending the fire," Brianna said softly.

Wulf nodded and looked away. He ordered himself to forget that she was naked beneath the furs. And she was smooth and soft and warm and she had taken him to a paradise he'd not known existed. That, too, he ordered himself to forget.

"I was about to leave," he said.

"Nay, not yet." She sat up, clutching a fur to cover herself. "Please, wilt give me my wrapper?"

Wulf handed it to her and turned away as she rose and donned it. "I can stay but a moment . . ."

" 'Twill be enough to tell you what I intended."

Wulf frowned. " 'Twas not of you and Sitric?"

"Nay, 'tis of the king and his mother," Brianna answered. She drew a stool before the fire, sat and hugged her knees. " 'Twas when you were gone that I overheard them. Methought their talk was strange, but then doubtless you know of it already . . ."

"Doubtless." Curious, Wulf came to the hearth and waited, his arm resting on the mantelpiece.

Brianna twisted a strand of hair about one finger. "I—was about to enter her highness's chamber when I heard the king. I could not help hearing him speak of Brodir. When he said Brodir's demands were outrageous, the princess said t-to offer him the same as Sigurd—his throne and herself in marriage." She dared not look at him.

Wulf felt as if he had been stabbed in the gut. He did not approve of the Orkney king's bargain with Sitric, but it was unthinkable that the Dubliner would make the same offer to Brodir. Or was it? Or was the maid making it up? But nay, now he was being unreasonable.

Gazing on the flames, hearing Wulf's long fingers drumming the mantelpiece, Brianna murmured, "There be more . . ."

"I would hear it," Wulf muttered.

She stole a glance at his face and saw that it was watchful and angry, a look she knew well. She swallowed. "The princess asked Sitric how he meant to safeguard her and his throne from Sigurd and Brodir. Sitric said there was but one way . . ."

"Ay? Go on."

"They agreed the t-two must be slain." She looked up, gauging the redness of his face before adding: "They—laughed about it."

The blood pounded in Wulf's head as he looked down on her. Why had the little wench remained there listening, and why had she brought the news to him? He said low, " 'Tis a marvel you heard so well and so much, lady."

"Brodir be a name from my own land and I—I wanted to hear," Brianna retorted. "I make no apology for listening."

"Nor do I want one," he snapped, "but in no wise will you speak of this to any other. Hear you?" He foresaw a calamity within their ranks if either Brodir or Sigurd got word of it.

Brianna nodded. "You be the only one."

"As for the princess," he growled, " 'tis likely you misunderstood what she said."

"She is not what she seems," Brianna said stubbornly.

Wulf studied her with narrowed eyes. So she had said before. He had ignored the gossip about Gormlaith, but now it seemed time he paid it some heed. He stiffened. Holy Thor, Gormlaith! He had forgotten completely his tryst with her. And now this damned news coming out of the blue . . .

Brianna was steaming. It was happening exactly as she thought it might. It was herself he was angry with, not Gormlaith. In his eyes, the princess could do no wrong. She cautioned herself to remain silent, but she could not. She would choke on her fury if she did. She rose from the stool.

"Know you, Wulf Thorsson, I did not misunderstand what the princess said. I have told you her exact words. Oft have I heard of Sigurd of the Orkneys as I move from board to board in great hall. 'Tis clear to me your king and his mother mean to betray and slay him and Brodir, too."

"Sitric is not my king!" Wulf rasped.

"Well then, all things considered, 'twould seem your honor and bravery be wasted in such an allegiance." She held her head high.

Wulf's every sense was alerted. The maid had puzzled him from the very beginning, but never so much as now with this bold talk of hers. He said softly, "Why wouldst care, lady?"

She yearned to tell him those things about Boru which she had told Ospak, but such was impossible. She said instead, "I be Celt, after all, and 'tis said in my land that the emperor of Ireland be an honorable man. 'Tis clear Sitric be a treacherous one. Were I a man girding to go into battle, I would want to march behind a man of honor."

"I see." Wulf studied her gravely. So there was more after all in that beautiful head besides ribbons and gowns and jewels. Somehow he had known there would be. "Have thanks for your concern—and as for this odd business of yours with the king, I have my own concerns. Yet 'tis safer here than for you to wander about Dublin." He removed his seal from around his neck and held it out to her. "I would have you wear this again as evidence of my protection."

Brianna's face turned pink. She clasped her hands behind her and shook her head. "I will not burden you so." In truth, she did not deserve his protection.

"You will burden me if you do not," Wulf answered crisply. "You be my responsibility until I place you safely in your father's hands." Without touching her, he slipped the chain over her head. " 'Tis time I went." He unbarred the door.

"Wulf . . ."

"Ay?"

She bit her tongue. It was over. Ended. She could not tell him of her love for him nor tell him how his caring and his gentleness had given to her a trust in men she never thought to have. She certainly could not tell him how she grieved over betraying him . . .

"I but wanted to say goodbye."

For a moment she thought he would kiss her, but he did not. He touched his fingers to his forehead in a brief salute and then was gone. She stared after him, his seal clutched tightly in her hand and his image still before her. If only she could do as she had bade Fiona do—leave here. But no longer did she have an excuse. The seal of Husaby would protect her, and Boru's need for her to be here was as great as ever.

Chapter Twenty

16 April 1014

Spring was in the air, and in the city the merchants had placed their wares on tables outside their shops. As Brianna made her way back to the palace after meeting Fin, she stopped to finger some brightly colored bolts of fabric and try on several rings and bracelets. But her heart was not in it, nor did she receive enjoyment from the warming sun and soft breezes. Fin had said the battle could be joined as early as May, and with her own eyes she saw it was so. The Liffey was clogged with the swan-necked dragonships of the enemy coming and going, and Fin said that on the plains men were practicing war play.

She had just given her kinsman the latest list of kings and chieftains rallying to Sitric, and told him it was the last news she would bring. And told him why. No more could she betray Wulf, although long ago the damage had been done. Dear Fin. He had not made her feel guilty for loving a Viking, but had embraced her and admitted that he and Boru had suspected it all along. Boru was exceeding grateful that she had stayed as long as she had. Fin had then stunned her by saying she should leave for Maun on the morrow. He would make all the arrangements. Brianna was musing on how strange it would be, living on her father's steading again, when a familiar voice cried:

"Annie, wait! Wait for me!"

"Fiona!" Brianna's spirits lifted on the instant. "How grand! It's been weeks since I've seen you in town!"

" 'Tis because I've found work, and my new mistress is not so generous as be your Wolf of Husaby. I get to town only when she has a fancy for new ribbons or some such. The other servants do the marketing."

"How go things with you?" Brianna asked. But she knew the answer, seeing her friend's pink cheeks and bright eyes.

"Never have I been happier," Fiona said, and then lowered her voice. "Leif visits me nights at my sister's when he be in Dublin. Oh, Annie, I love him so. In my heart, we are wed, and when this is over, he will take me back to Norway's land with him. He be ready to work his farm

315

a-and raise a family . . ."

Thinking of the coming battle, Brianna caught Fiona close and hugged her. " 'Tis glad I am for you, Fi. I wish you every joy."

"What of you and Wulf?" Fiona asked. "Not a day goes by that I don't wonder and worry about you."

Brianna shrugged. "Things are no different. There can be naught betwixt us." Marking the maid's crestfallen face, she added gently, "Never could it be, Fiona. Always have I known it."

"Dost love him still?"

"Ay. More than this tongue can tell."

"Oh, Annie!" Fiona blinked back the tears. "Has he—made you his?"

Brianna laughed. Who but Fi would ask such a question? And she deserved an honest answer. "Ay, he has made me his—or mayhap I made him mine. Whatever, 'tis over now. We both agree it cannot be." She took the girl's hand. "Nay, Fi, don't weep for me. 'Tis all for the best. On the morrow I sail home to—"

"The morrow!"

"Ay. At midday I will meet Fin and he will see that I get on a vessel that takes me to Maun. I trow I will soon forget all about Wulf Thorsson." She knew it was not so. Never in this life would she forget him, but she would not burden the maid with that sadness, too.

Tears now flowing, Fiona threw her arms about Brianna's neck. "If I never see you again, y-you be the best friend ever I had, Brianna. Go with God . . ."

* * *

It had been some weeks since Gormlaith bade her man Regin to follow Brianna on her trips to town. Always he had reported, to her great disappointment, that the maid did nothing more than look at the wares in the shops. However, this early afternoon when she admitted him to her bedchamber, his face told a different story.

Gormlaith's eyes gleamed with anticipation. "Speak, man, do not keep me waiting!"

"After the wench took your shoes to the shoemaker, she went to the fish market," said Regin. " 'Twas there she met a tall black-haired man who looked Celt."

"A man?" Gormlaith's every sense came to life. "Didst hear what they said?"

"Nay, for they talked low whilst pretending not to be with the other." When the princess smiled and clasped her hands, almost prayerful, he added, "Thinking on it, I know I have seen the fellow before." He stroked his sandy beard. "In fact, methinks I have seen them together before."

Gormlaith's hopes burned bright. It grew better and better. A lover, clandestine meetings . . . "Where and when?" she prodded.

Regin shook his head. "I cannot recall, but I'm sure 'tis so. And there be another thing, lady—"

"Ay?" She held her breath.

"The wench bought a fish which she threw into the Liffey after she and the fellow parted.

She looked about as if to make sure none was looking."

Gormlaith chuckled. "Did she now?" So. She had gone to the fish market to meet a man, and had bought a fish to hide the fact.

"There be one last thing," Regin said. "Fiona, a former serving-wench here in the palace, accosted her and the two chattered for a while."

The princess waved that off. " 'Tis of no import. The other, however, intrigues me greatly. When you follow her on the morrow, take Corm with you. If she meets the fellow again, seize him. I would know who he be."

"Ay, my lady." Regin bowed and made his departure.

As Gormlaith barred the door after him, her excitement mounted. So the little slut had a man, had she? A Celt she met daily. For a certainty, Brianna was ashamed of the fact, else why keep it secret? Doubtless it was a lover, and when Wulf Thorsson learned of it, he would see her for the sly conniver she was. Not that he bedded her any longer. He did not. Gormlaith knew because she had him watched. Nay, it was his continuing protectiveness toward the wench that was such a thorn in her side. Brianna had taken once more to wearing his seal in plain sight. Never could any be bribed to abduct a maid who wore the seal of Husaby.

Gormlaith sighed thinking of that hideous night in February when she had thought to make

love with the Norseman, but it had not come
to pass. Never had he said anything of it, nor
had she. She was too proud. Since then, Sitric
had sent Wulf riding far and near seeking help
from every kingdom in the land. Always when
Wulf returned from his journeys, as he had this
very day, he held himself politely aloof from all,
herself included. He was a loner, was the Wolf
of Husaby. It made him more tantalizing to her
than ever, but now time was fast running out.
If she was to have him, she must do it quickly.
War drew near, and soon he would be returning
to Norway if he were not slain beforehand.

That eve, as Brianna carried food to the
boards from the vats and grills over the
fire trenches, she marked an odd, hushed
excitement in the great hall. Returning to the
corner bench where she sat in the shadows
with the other wenches, she turned to the maid
beside her.

"What is happening, Elin?" she whispered.
"Has someone died?"

Elin put her mouth to Brianna's ear. "Nay.
'Tis only that all be wary of the two wizards
who now sit with Sitric at the high-board. They
have been consulting with him since midday."

Staring toward the far end of the room,
Brianna marked that there were indeed two
dark-robed stranger-men with long white hair
and beards sitting on either side of Sitric. It
made the war seem closer, for often had her
father and uncles consulted those men who

read heaven-signs when a battle was about to take place.

"Have they prophesied yet?" she murmured.

Elin drew her shawl closer. "I know not, nor do I want to know. I wish only that 'twas not my lot to serve that board this eve."

"I have no fear of them," Brianna said quietly. "Wouldst trade places with me?"

"Oh, ay. Oh, have thanks, Brianna."

She had told Fin she would bring him no more news, but if there had been a prophecy, Boru must hear it. She went to the vat, ladled out a crock of veal stew, and carried it to the nobles' board where she refilled their trenchers. Wulf's eyes never left her, whereas Sitric paid her no heed at all but divided his attention between his wizards. His hushed voice was heard by her eager ears.

"—so your heaven-signs say this: If we strike on any day other than Freya's Day, all who fight Boru will die. Is't so?"

" 'Tis so," said the ancient on his right.

"But if you indeed attack on that day," said the ancient on his left, " 'tis the emperor himself who will die."

" 'Twould seem clear the gods have spoken, since you both received the same signs," Sitric breathed. "We are meant to attack on Freya's Day. Dost agree, Thorsson?"

"I agree," Wulf said quietly. "We strike then or not at all."

Brianna forced herself to continue serving the men although she felt numb. Freya's Day

was Good Friday. April twenty-third. Boru was
to be slain and would lie in the dead-straw on a
holy day but one week hence! Holy angels. She
could think of nothing else as she moved up
and down the long board, patiently replenishing
trenchers and horns. She chided herself then.
Never would it happen, because she would not
allow it to happen. It was why she was there.
She would tell Fin, and Fin would tell Boru's
captains, and never would they allow him to
go into the field that day. She wanted to run
off with the news that instant, but she could
not. She must wait until the following midday
when she left for Maun.

When finally the long hours had dragged by,
Brianna hurried to the woodshop where Fin
awaited her. The wares were displayed under
the spring sun, and she marked him admiring
a stack of bowls as she drew near. She picked
up one with trembling fingers.

"Annie," Fin began low, "the ship has not
yet—"

Brianna gasped, "Kinsman, hear me, the
Vikings attack on Good Friday! Sitric's wizards
have divined that Boru will die if he be in the
field that day!"

Fin was calm. He nodded. " 'Tis good to hear
it verified, for last eve our own diviners gave
the same message."

"Canst keep him from harm's way, think you?"

Marking that they were observed, Fin examined a polished trencher. "Hush you, Bri-

321

anna. We are watched." After the fellow moved off, he said low, "You are not to worry. Brian is bent on leading his men, but we will not hear of it. We will insist he hand the reins to Murrough."

"Oh, Fin, I—I so fear for you all—for him and you and father . . ." And for Wulf, and Leif. She pretended interest in the wooden drinking horns but she was nigh sick to her stomach she was so frightened.

"Come, lass," Fin said gruffly. "You cannot wilt after being so strong for so long. We will give the devils a battle they'll not forget. Boru's forces measure twenty thousand strong under seventy banners." He gave her a brief mocking grin. "Know you, Olaf Ospak has just come to us with his ten ships and says 'tis all your doing."

Brianna blinked. "You tease me."

"Nay. You swayed him mightily. He still craves to wed you, by the way."

Brianna smiled. The old clown, never would he wed. No more than would she.

"He brings word, too," Fin continued, "that Brodir's entire fleet has panicked because of portents these past nights."

She looked about to see if any paid them any heed, but none did. She whispered, "What sort of portents?"

"Blood raining from the sky, swords and battle-axes fighting without hands to hold them . . ."

"Holy Jesu." She crossed herself. "What means it?"

"It bodes ill for the rebels—there be another prophecy Sitric does not bandy about. 'Tis said the Irish will take this battle." But he was concerned. Sitric and Maelmorda between them also commanded 20,000 strong since Brodir had brought them 1,000 mail-clad Norsemen. He feared the casualties on both sides would be great, but never would he tell his worries to Brianna.

"Where will the battle be?" she asked, her voice small.

"North of here betwixt the Liffey and the Tolka. Doubtless you will be able to see it if you stand on the palace battlements . . ."

Brianna shook her head. "I will be gone by then, nor would I watch if I could. Am I to leave this day as you said?"

"Ay, but not 'til later in the day." Fin tested the feel of a horn in his hand. "Meet me at the jeweler's when the sun be halfway down. I will take you to the vessel and see you safely off."

Brianna nodded. " 'Til later then, kinsman."

"Ay, Brianna,'til later . . ."

After she departed, Fin entered a drinking place where a comrade waited and gave him instructions. He was to tell those men watching the stronghold that when Brianna left later in the day, she would not be returning. They could abandon their posts. He knew it would be welcome news, for all were champing at the bit to report to their commanding officers what with the battle nearing.

*   *   *

It was mid-afternoon when Gormlaith again saw Regin. "Did the wench meet her lover again?" she asked eagerly.

"Ay, my lady, and we seized him as you ordered. When Corm saw the fellow, he minded he'd seen him other times with men we know are Boru's."

The princess stared. "Are you telling me that he be one of Boru's men?"

"There seems little doubt."

"By the gods," she whispered. "Think you the wench be conspiring with him?"

Regin marked well that the princess craved for the maid to be implicated, and it was to his good to keep her content. " 'Twould seem likely," he replied. "However, you know the maid better than do I, my lady. Think you she could be in Boru's employ?"

Gormlaith carried her horn to the fire and lowered herself into the throne chair. Sipping her wine, she mused that the shaking, sniveling wench she had at first thought Brianna could never have been so clever nor so brave. But when she outfoxed Sitric, her true colors had been revealed. The bitch was capable of anything.

"It doubts me naught she be a spy," she murmured, her breathing gone heavy.

"What wouldst have us do? Seize her also?"

"Nay, the wench you can safely leave to me. What did you with the man?"

"He be in the souterrain, bound and gagged."

"Good." Her eyes moved slowly over Regin's tall, powerful body. Never had she sampled him, but she had contemplated it. Perhaps some night soon. She waggled her jeweled fingers at him. "Go you now."

"Ay, my lady."

Gormlaith dismissed him from her thoughts and sat staring at the flames and savoring her wine, savoring telling Wulf Thorsson the news of Brianna. If she slept with him this night, she would tell him afterwards. She smiled. If? If she slept with him? It was absurd. Never had she been denied any man of her choosing until Wulf Thorsson entered her life. She would not allow this ridiculous impasse to continue any longer.

That night in the great hall of Sitric of Dublin there was feasting, drinking, laughter, and the harpers played. Soon the story-telling would begin. Surrounded though Wulf was by his comrades and their merrymaking, he was alone. Even had Leif been by his side and not with Fiona, he would have been alone, for his thoughts were on war and strategy and numbers. He reckoned their forces great enough to put the Kingdom of Dublin into Viking hands once again and enough to return Leinster to Maelmorda. It would bring to an end the crushing tribute demanded by Brian Boru, and in Dublin the Vikings would once again have a safe and permanent trading station that was theirs alone. Then, and only then, could they begin to think of the conquest of all Ireland.

Oh ay, Wulf brooded, and who among them was fit to rule the land once it was in their hands? Sitric with his bent for treachery? An increasingly greedy Sigurd? Maelmorda, who had yet to show himself in Dublin and who was well known for showing the white feather in battle? Or perhaps Brodir, who was known best for his ferocity and the length of his black hair? That was another thing—Brodir and Sigurd. Had Sitric given the Maun chieftain the same pledge he gave Sigurd? Wulf was inclined to believe Brianna's tale. But when he had confronted Sitric with it, the devil had sworn he knew nothing of any such promise to Brodir. It was a thing Wulf intended to question Gormlaith about very soon.

Drumming the board with his fingers, Wulf minded an earlier time when he had not cared why any had fought Boru; he had cared only that they topple him. But considering the caliber of Viking leadership nowadays, he saw darkly the aftermath of a Viking victory; the horror and confusion that would follow the overthrow of Boru's stable government. But then, war was war, and such was to be expected. In due time, all would be put to rights.

As he always did when he thought of the coming battle, Wulf closed his eyes and sent up a prayer to Odin to grant him and his men bravery and good fortune. The gods help him if he felt then as he did now, hot and cold at the same time and with a trembling in his legs

he had never experienced before. He wiped the
sweat off his brow and found Gormlaith's jade
eyes on him when he opened his own.

" 'Tis wearying, is it not?" she murmured, and
yawned. "And so warm in here I be nearly asleep
in my chair."

Wulf gazed on her soft red mouth and plump
tongue, her white skin and the swells of her
breasts above the low neckline of her gown. He
gave a silent groan, for she was ravishing. Why
in damnation had he never bedded the wench
in all this time, when it was clear she craved
him? His shaft thrust forth throbbing at the
thought.

"When we spoke earlier," he said thickly, "you
indicated you had a matter of some urgency to
discuss." She had been entering her chamber
as he passed, and had drawn him in. She'd fed
him a cream and made but a brief moan to him
before he went on his way again. "Why do we
not go to your chamber and discuss it now?"
he muttered.

Gormlaith was hesitant. "Sire, never did I
mean to take you from your meal and an
evening of—pleasure with your comrades. Our
skald is just about to begin his tales."

Wulf got abruptly to his feet. He could think
only of the princess's wet red lips and soft
breasts. He would go into battle soon, why
should he not have her? He growled, "We will
go now."

Gormlaith obeyed. Her body had grown hot
and weak at the thought of being mastered by

the Wolf of Husaby and already her love-juices flowed. She stood meekly behind his broad back as he instructed his berserks to stay on at the feast and enjoy themselves.

Brianna had not left Dublin for Maun as planned. Long and long she had lingered near the jeweler's, browsing in all the shops close by and walking up and down the street, but never did Fin come. She had not worried, there were all manner of reasons for his delay, but finally she could wait no longer. Chancing upon Fiona hurrying home from work, she gave her a message for Fin should she see him. It was that she would meet him at the same place and the same time on the morrow. She had then returned to the palace.

Now, marking Wulf and Gormlaith leaving the great hall together and feeling her jealousy flare, Brianna wished with all her heart that she had left. She could not bear seeing them so. Yet what concern was it of hers if he bedded the witch? She herself had no claim on him, nor he on her. There was nothing between them. Nothing. She swallowed, put her attention on the meat she was carving, and felt the heat of jealousy sweeping through her—jealousy, rage, hurt, and ay, a black hatred for them both. She could not help it; she meant to blister him with a scorching look as he drew near. But when he passed by the carving table, it was without even seeing her.

Brianna stared at the streaks of sweat on his flushed face. And how unlike him to look neither right nor left, but straight ahead. Her breath caught as she marked the distant gaze in his eyes and his unsteady step. Oh, nay! Had Gormlaith tricked him with her abominable sweets to lure him to bed? Surely she would not dare, and surely he was wise in such ways so as not to be trapped as Brianna had been. But then the palace gossip about Gormlaith had not ceased to shock her since she had opened her ears to it. If the princess craved a man, she would stop at nothing to have him. Brianna put down her carving knife and sought Elin. She found her on the corner bench.

"Elin, I need a favor," she whispered. "Canst help me?"

Elin caught her hand. "Ay. Never will I forget you served the wizards in my place."

"I feel—unwell of a sudden. Canst do my work and your own, too?"

"Ay. 'Tis no problem. There will be naught but drinking and singing from now on. Go you and lie down."

"Have thanks."

Catching up her skirts, Brianna fled, but once in her small loft-room, she did not lie down. She tore off her apron and kyrtil, swiftly drew on trews, tunic, and boots, and tucked her dagger into her waistband. Her heart beat fast as she pondered what she had seen. If the Wolf of Husaby craved to bed Gormlaith of his own choosing, that was one thing—but never would she allow the princess to lure him to her bed by trickery. She minded all too well how her own body had burned with an unquenchable fire after she had eaten those drugged creams. As she crept down the narrow steps and through the shadows to Gormlaith's bedchamber, she did not allow herself to dwell on what danger might face her. She would simply do what had to be done, and then she would leave this place behind her.

Chapter Twenty-One

One thought burned in Wulf's mind as he rose from the board and moved through the great hall. He wanted Gormlaith. He craved to part her white thighs and plunge himself within her and stay there the night long—ay, the week long. Never had he wanted a woman so. When he left behind him the smoky haze, music, and laughter and stepped into the damp corridor without, he craved her still. But the cold wind whistling about his ears blew some of the cobwebs from his brain. Now he could wonder at himself. When had he ever been so lust-filled that he must rush headlong from a meal and into a wench's bed without so much as a farewell to his companions?

Gormlaith tucked her arm into his and

pressed herself against his side as they walked toward her chamber. She whispered, "Your boldness be to my liking, Wulf Thorsson . . ."

Wulf made no answer, but caught her jeweled hand to his lips and kissed it. He was afire. But it was an arousal such as he had never experienced before. The intensity fair sickened him, and he felt himself sway against her. Not only was his head spinning, his damned legs felt as if they could scarce hold him. He followed the lady into her chamber. It was warm, silken and scented with rose oil, the shadows leaping on the walls from torch and hearthfire making it mysterious and seductive as a harem. He hesitated. Always had he heeded the small, quiet voice that came sometimes from deep within to warn him of danger. It came now.

"Bar the door, sire," Gormlaith murmured, removing the shawl she had worn throughout the feast in the chilled hall.

Wulf's breath caught as she dropped it to the rushes. She wore a blood-red gown, and as she stood before the fire, her long hair falling to her hips, he could see the whiteness and the voluptuousness of her body gleaming through it. His shaft stirred, pulsed, yet he felt a strange uneasiness—enough so that he but pretended to bar the door. He left it open a crack, and then moved toward her.

Gormlaith stood tall and majestic, head high and her jade eyes glowing. She favored him with a slow smile, ruby lips parting over her small white teeth as she marked the lust in his eyes. But if he thought she was an easy piece, she had a surprise for him. He would have to wait for her, and when he was nigh mad with desire, then would she make him work to over-power her before she yielded. Her eyes glinted in anticipation of the imminent battle.

"Sire, I pray you, remove your cloak." She touched a cool white hand to his cheek. "My chamber be warm and you seem overheated." As he did her bidding, she poured a horn of wine and brought it to him. "Sit you here by the fire, my lord Husaby, and drink you. I will join you."

Wulf sat himself in one of the throne chairs, but only because he was too shaky to stand. His passion simmered. What in damnation was this? Her eyes, her manner, the way her body moved, all were seductive and told him she wanted him to bed her instantly and voraciously, and now she bade him sit. Women! With burning eyes, he watched her pour her wine and glide toward him, her shapely breasts swaying beneath her gauzy gown. As she sat herself gracefully by his side, he was nigh to exploding with hunger for her—but it was not to his liking to feel as he did, like a stallion in full rut. And he was damned if he would be the first to reach out if she were playing some game. He would use the time she dallied, teasing him, to force himself into some semblance of control.

He drew a long breath, raised the horn to his lips, scowled into the fire, and thought, not of the soft desirable woman by his side, but of war.

Boru's days were numbered. The Viking fleet was multiplying fast and was anchored between the mouths of the Tolkay and the Liffey with Dublin Bay behind them. Soon his own vessel and men would come from Maun. Already Sigurd had arrived, bringing with him not only his Orkney-men but his chieftains and troops from the isles along the way. Brodir of Maun had come with his thousand men and his twenty ships, and the two had their encampments side by side. Two powerful men, each certain the crown of Dublin and Gormlaith was his own. He shook his head at the irony of the thing if it were indeed so. He had no proof, but this night he would learn the truth of the matter if he did nothing else. But not now. Now he wanted Gormlaith for himself. He left off staring into the flames and met her eyes, his own hooded.

"Your thoughts be afar, sire," Gormlaith murmured.

" 'Twould be an easy thing to bring them near." His voice was thick with desire.

She smiled. "Dost find me so fair then?"

Wulf wet his lips. "Ay . . ."

But not nearly so fair as another. He minded how it had been with Brianna, the fire burning hot and bright and fierce between them. But this . . . He frowned and returned his gaze to the flames. He was aroused, ay, but he was sluggish and leaden. It would seem he had eaten and drunk too much, and he was nigh overcome by the heavy scent of roses which permeated the room and the princess's white skin.

Gormlaith rose, took up her box of creams, and returned to her throne chair. She popped one into her mouth and charmingly touched her tongue to the residue on her finger. She then chose another and, leaning forward, brushed it, teasing, across the Viking's lips.

"Have another, my lord . . ."

Wulf lost all patience. He caught her wrist. "Lady, I did not come here for sweets nor to prate with you. I came to make love to you. Either we get on with it or I will be on my way."

The faint odor of the sweet remained cloying in his nostrils, stirring a long-forgotten memory. It was as though lightning ripped through his brain. Friggja-grass! By all the gods, the woman had given him friggja-grass. No wonder he craved her with a hunger that would not cease.

"You be—magnificent . . ." Gormlaith breathed. The pain and the sight of his dark, steely fingers gripping her wrist was causing her love-juices to flow again thick as honey. She was open and ready for him, but she craved for him to overpower her. Never could she gain satisfaction otherwise.

Wulf released her and rose, his eyes burning over her. He lusted for her, ay, but how much was real and how much was the damned sweet he had consumed earlier? It was a lucky thing he had eaten only the one. He gritted his teeth remembering Leif's words that Brianna had been given a love potion, remembering Brianna herself protesting that she had been weak and dizzy. Was this how she had felt when he had found her in Sitric's arms? And was it Gormlaith who had given her the accursed stuff? But why? And why had she felt a need to give it to himself, for that matter? He could not think nor reason, he could only feel a huge resentment and a growing rage. He kept it hidden. There were too many things he craved to learn before he left here this night. But one thing had become clear even as he stood there brooding. Any desire he had for this woman was a result of the weed she had given him.

As Brianna stole ever nearer to Gormlaith's door, she was certain that these moments would be the last she spent in this stronghold. If it was necessary to overpower the princess to get Wulf safely to his own chamber, she must flee afterwards. There was nothing else she could do. She thanked the holy angels guarding her that his berserks had remained in the great hall drinking. Spying a shaft of light penetrating the gloom, she knew she was doubly blessed. Gormlaith's door was not barred but was slightly ajar. She pressed her ear against the opening and heard the princess's low voice.

"Know you, Wulf Thorsson, long and long have I craved for you to make love to me . . ."

Wulf grunted. " 'Twould seem you crave to prate more than you crave lovemaking."

"Nay, 'tis only that I—would not have you think me overbold."

Unwilling Betrayer

Wulf held himself rigid, determined not to sway before her like some damned puppet on its strings.

"I see you be angry," she whispered. " 'Twas never my intent to anger you. Sire, never have I had such admiration for any man. 'Tis by your own great efforts that this kingdom and that of my brother will be saved from Brian Boru."

"You speak too soon," Wulf muttered.

More and more he wanted to leave, to breathe in the cool, damp air beyond her door. Any questions he had could be asked later. But when she came to him, laying her perfumed hand on his chest and caressing him with light fingers, he knew he would stay. He caught her hand, raised it to his lips, inhaled her rose scent, and hated himself. He wanted her. He fought it, ordered himself to take up his cloak and leave, but he was rooted there. Sweat grew on his brow as he told himself it was the drug stirring his passion, not the woman, but there was no doubt she was ravishing. Her skin was silken and without blemish, red lips glistening, her breasts perfect globes showing whitely beneath her gossamer gown. He warned himself that if he did not leave then, it would be too late. As he stepped back, she wound her arms about his neck, her warm breath fanning his face. She smelled of wine and of the treacherous sweet she had just consumed.

"Have you not seen that I craved you these many weeks, Wulf Thorsson?" she whispered.

"And now—now you will soon be gone, and I cannot bear the thought."

"My lady," Wulf said gruffly, "I have had time for little but war preparations since my arrival here. In fact, my mind is so taken with war this eve, methinks 'twas a mistake to come."

"Never!"

He made to remove her arms from about his neck, but her fingers were locked in a death-grip. "Come, Gormlaith, loose me . . ." When she did not, but remained close against him pressing kisses on his chest, he forced her to loosen her grasp and then bound her wrists with iron fingers.

Gormlaith moaned, nigh overcome with delight at the pain. She sagged against him. "What's a powerful brute you be, my lord."

Wulf was stirred by the soft breasts crushed against him, but it was of Brianna that he thought. Brianna—her eyes glazed with passion, rosy lips parted, her breath clean and sweet as a breeze of summer, not tainted with wine and friggja-grass.

"My days have been filled with thoughts of you, my lord Husaby," Gormlaith murmured. "Of plans for us . . ."

"What mean you? What plans?"

" 'Tis you who must rule Dublin . . ." She slid her hands slowly, sensuously down his back, up his arms, across his wide shoulders. "This kingdom can be yours. None is more fit to rule it than you."

Wulf hid his amazement. He was sure she

had never given thought to the subject until this moment when she feared losing him as a bed partner. Now, seeing that this might lead to talk of Sigurd and Brodir, he answered, his voice lowered to intimacy:

"Your words interest me greatly, lady, but it doubts me they would please Sitric. What of him?"

"Sitric!" Gormlaith spat the name. "Wouldst care yourself to be ruled by such as Sitric?"

"I would not, but then it matters little, since he has admitted that his crown and yourself will go to Sigurd when the battle is won. Dost know that, Gormlaith?"

In the corridor, Brianna held her breath, and when Gormlaith made no answer, her concern mounted. What was happening? Did Wulf need her? Oh, if only she could see within the chamber. She minded then that the door, although a noisy one, creaked only at a certain point. Slowly, slowly she pushed on it, and then froze, seeing they were in each other's arms. Gormlaith was tracing Wulf's lips with her long white fingers. They kissed, and such a wave of jealousy rushed over Brianna she nigh drowned in it. She yearned to slay them both. She reminded herself sharply then that he was drugged, she was certain of it, but he seemed not to need her help yet.

"Heard you what I said, my lady?" Wulf asked.

Gormlaith sighed and murmured, "Oh, ay, I heard, my wonderful one. But Sitric should not concern you. Him I will deal with. 'Tis you alone who will have me and the throne of Dublin. 'Tis a promise."

"What of Sigurd?" Wulf persisted.

Gormlaith laughed. "Sigurd will be rewarded . . ."

"And Brodir?" He did not miss her surprise, nor that she covered it quickly and smoothly.

"Brodir, too, shall be rewarded," she whispered. She took Wulf's face between her hands. "I burn for you, Wulf Thorsson."

Wulf's lips held a half-smile. Never would he have believed her capable of such deviousness and treachery. Brianna had spoken the truth. Neither Sigurd nor Brodir would have the throne if the battle were won. Both would die. Of a sudden she sickened him.

"Come, bed me." Gormlaith stood on tiptoe and touched her tongue to his. "Come . . ." She caught his hands and lifted them to her breasts, urging him to cup and fondle them.

Wulf felt himself sway. He had learned what he craved to know, now he had but to force his legs to move, to carry him out of here.

"All Ireland can be ours," she whispered, rubbing her soft body against him and attempting to flutter her skilled fingers over his manhood.

Wulf swallowed a groan. He knew not whether it was pleasure or disgust. He roughly caught her hands and forced them to her sides. "Lady, you tempt me for naught. My mind be on war this night."

"Why dost lie, Thorwulf? You burn for me as I do for you."

Wulf said nothing; it was bootless. He would not waste breath in argument when he needed all his strength to push air in and out of his lungs, to remain upright and resist her. She was a siren, and she would surely lure him to his doom unless he kept his eyes and his mind off her red lips and swaying breasts. He ordered his legs to move, first one, then the other, but she placed herself in front of him. He closed his eyes to shut out the sight of her opulent curves, but her scent filled his nostrils. Holy Thor, what a troll-woman. She had turned this into a test of wills, and he was damned if she would win. Brianna . . . he must keep his thoughts on Brianna . . . on how she looked and walked and talked and laughed . . .

Gormlaith said huskily, "Why spill your seed in the straw when an Irish princess is at hand? Is that not the dream of every Viking?"

Wulf tightened his lips. With Brianna's face before him, he moved heavily to where his cloak lay in the rushes. The blood throbbed in his head as he bent to retrieve it. When he turned, Gormlaith cried:

"Look on me, my lord Husaby!" She tore open her gown, not caring that she destroyed it, and thrust out her magnificent breasts. "Look on these and tell me if you have ever seen any more fair. You have not, for I be the fairest woman in all of Ireland . . ."

Wulf marked in her green eyes the wildness and the abandon that came from the drug she had consumed. He felt its effects in his own

341

loins and racing blood as he gazed on her beauty, on her hair like flame against her white skin. He clenched his teeth and turned from her. He willed himself to deny her, willed himself to hear Brianna's low voice and her laughter, to remember how she had felt in his arms. Even as he dwelt on her, he marked that the princess was naked.

"Damn thee, woman . . ."

As Gormlaith slid her arms about his waist, his gaze was drawn to movement in the shadows. Someone was entering the chamber. He blinked, recognizing a familiar slender form, the long legs in trews and boots, the veil of gleaming mahogany hair falling to her waist. Brianna! But this stalking Valkyrie was not the Brianna he knew. He gazed in wonderment at her stealthy warrior's crouch, the glimmer of a dagger in her hand, its needle-fine point gleaming as wicked as any he had met on the battlefield—nor did he miss the deadly light in the green eyes fixed like those of a cat on Gormlaith's naked back.

By all the gods in Valhalla, who was this maid really? And what was she doing here in Gormlaith's chamber? He had been holding her in his thoughts, and now here she was. He was overjoyed, for the very sight of her shocked him to his senses. But it also aroused his deepest fears for her. If she had come to protect him, now it was he who must protect her. Gormlaith must not see her. She would have her thrown into a cell in the souterrain.

Brianna had come in low, her weapon extended should Gormlaith turn suddenly and find her there. She gave a silent sniff of scorn, marking that the princess was too drugged and too far along in heat to do anything but writhe and slobber kisses over Wulf's broad chest and throat and any other part of him she could reach with her lascivious lips. Brianna did not consider herself prim, but Gormlaith's brazenness shocked and infuriated her. And her jealousy burned bright. She would not use her dagger, nay, but she yearned to seize the wench by her hair, slap her arrogant face, and knock the wind out of her. Oh, holy angels, how she craved vengeance. Perhaps it would be a fitting punishment to make the witch swallow the whole box of her own damned sweets.

And Wulf—how grand to see his astonishment turn to relief and joy, his eyes glowing . . . But she had no time to think on it; she must get on with her task. Seeing that Gormlaith was nigh stupefied by lust and still unaware of her own presence, Brianna decided on a sharp blow to her head. She stole closer, reversing her dagger, taking firm hold of the haft so its butt would be the instrument sending the woman into oblivion. Ay. She pinpointed the exact spot above the princess's right ear . . .

Wulf held Gormlaith closer, pressing her face against his chest while his other hand shot out a warning for Brianna to leave. Pointing to the door, he motioned for her to go, ordered her to go. Go!

Brianna studied him with narrowed eyes, jealousy nigh overwhelming her. Did he mean what she thought? Did he actually want her to leave before she had accomplished her purpose so he could remain with this witch? She pointed to herself and then to the door, her gaze questioning, indignant. He nodded, still holding Gormlaith close. When she saw that his eyes were clear and that laughter danced in them, she knew what he was about. He was in command once more and would now deal with the woman in his own way. In her heart she was relieved. In truth, she would not have enjoyed harming the princess, much as she deserved it. And now she would leave as she had planned; there was nothing more to hold her here. She moved to the door on silent feet.

Wulf willed her to look at him. There was no doubt in his mind now that she had come here for him. It was a sacrifice he could scarce believe she had made, and his gratitude was boundless. He would tell her so before this night was over. When she gazed back at him as he had hoped she would, he pointed to himself, to her, and to his chamber. He saw the widening of her beautiful eyes, her grave nod. She gave him a warrior's salute, and then she was gone.

Wulf shook his head and grinned. Women. Never would he understand them. For he had seen now what he had not known before. Brianna was jealous. Jealous! It was a thought which he craved to savor, but not now. Now he must deal with Gormlaith. She clung to him

still, and he marked that she was dazed. Small
wonder, since he had seen her swallow at least
three creams this day. He grasped her shoulders
and gave her a shake.

"My lady . . ."

Gormlaith's tongue felt clumsy. She mut-
tered, "Let us wait no longer, my Wolf of
Husaby." She made to fondle him but he
caught her wrist. Seeing the steel in those
Nordic eyes, she was instantly alert. She gasped,
"You—would not leave?"

"I must," Wulf said.

She shook off his hands, swayed, cried shrilly,
"Know you, I am a princess of Ireland. I—I will
not be cast off!"

Hearing the sob in her voice, Wulf felt unexpected compassion. Three kings had craved her
and wed her and all three had put her aside.
Now he understood why. No more did he think
Boru was a fool.

"Never would I cast you off, Gormlaith," he
said gently. " 'Tis just that my thoughts be on
war this night. I could not enjoy your charms
nor could I give you the pleasure you crave."
Still gentle, he stroked back a tendril of hair
from her burning cheek. " 'Twould seem your
sweets were wasted on me, my lady."

Chapter Twenty-Two

Brianna thought to linger outside the princess's door for a bit, just to make certain all was well with Wulf—but what if she were seen? What explanation could she give to be dressed thus and loitering in the corridor instead of tending to her work in the great hall? Deciding the risk was too great, she went to Wulf's chamber as he had bade her. She promised herself that if he did not come soon, she would go back and fetch him. She did not realize how frightened she was for them both until she stoked the fire and saw that her hands shook. Unable to stop their trembling, she poured herself a swallow of ale, and then another as she pondered what she would say to him. She was pacing when he came in.

Wulf closed and barred the door and then

stood leaning against it, gazing on Brianna and feeling the heavy pounding of his pulses. He had feared she would not be there, so firm and final had been their last parting. That she was actually waiting for him filled him with exuberance. Like a man perishing of thirst, he drank in the sight of her: the shadows and fire accentuating the softness of her body in the lad's garb, her cape of russet hair, the mystery in those fathomless green eyes, her grave, unsmiling lips.

It was as if a hand squeezed his heart. He drew in a sharp breath of astonishment. He loved her. He was nigh exploding with love for her, and why it had taken him all this time to realize it, he knew not. He craved to shout out the wondrous news, and then tell her again and again, a hundred times over. But nay, he had been stung by her too many times to bare his soul so. Yet what manner of warrior was he to fear risk? She herself had risked greatly to come seeking him, ready to defend him with her naked blade. But why had she? Perhaps when he had the answer, and the answers to a hundred other questions, then would be the time to confess to her how he felt. He threw down his cloak and took the horn from her hands, his fingers brushing her own.

"Sit you there by the fire and let me replenish this for you." After filling both their horns, he sat facing her, musing on how exceeding fair she was. In her earth-brown garb, her eyes wide and watchful, she minded him of a doe poised to flee to the safety of the woods. He knew well that if he did not tread carefully, he would lose her. Let the questions be for later; for now, let her know he had been wrong about Gormlaith. He said easily, "So, I have met the real Brianna at long last . . ."

Brianna gazed at him over the rim of her horn. She answered quietly, "Ay."

She sat stiff and unmoving as the peat snapped and cracked and the flames danced. She feared that now he would ask more questions which she could not answer, and she must somehow hide her longing for him. She had been mad to come.

"I have also met the real Gormlaith at long last," Wulf said. "You were right. The lady is not as she seems."

Brianna felt the warmth of satisfaction. Marking that a muscle twitched in his jaw, she knew it had not been an easy admission. "I heard the talk betwixt you," she murmured, "and I trow her offer was from the heart. You could have her and Dublin, too."

Wulf chuckled. " 'Twas on the spur of the moment she threw me that bone."

Brianna's anger flared on the instant. Was he blind? "Canst not see that she has only scathe for Sigurd and Brodir? 'Tis you she wants!" Her face grew hot minding how the witch had torn open her gown and bared her breasts to him.

Wulf hid his delight, seeing again her open jealousy. But why was she jealous? Was it a passing thing, or did she truly care for him? He burned to ask, yet what if he were wrong? What if it were not jealousy at all but hatred of Gormlaith? He would look a presumptuous ass. Damnation. He could not abide this sitting on the fence teetering back and forth. He wanted her. He loved her. So overwhelmed was he by his love, he envied the horn from which her soft lips sipped, envied the chair and the furs cradling her slender body. He said low:

"Why didst come for me, Brianna?"

Brianna sat straighter. This was one question she would answer with relish. But first she had one of her own. "Didst eat one of Gormlaith's creams?" she asked.

Wulf nodded. "Ay."

She drew a deep breath. It was all she needed to know. "They hold a love potion," she said crisply. "I had eaten two of them on that day you found me with Sitric. The princess saw to that." When he frowned, she snapped, "Is't so hard to believe, considering her other treachery? The truth be that she threw me to Sitric because she thought you w-wanted me and she craved you herself. 'Tis common knowledge she has craved you since first she clapped eyes on you!"

Wulf laughed. So he had been right. She *was* jealous. She was blazing with jealousy.

Brianna leapt up. She stamped her foot. "You find that amusing? Or mayhap you find me amusing—or is't that you be so stupid you know not that you were drugged!" When he made no answer, merely gazed on her with twinkling eyes, Brianna choked, "Know you, you great oaf—when you left the feasting, you were unsteady on your feet and your eyes were glazed. You were pale as a sheet. She fed you the same diabolical potion she fed me!" She sucked in a deep breath for she was not finished. "And if you crave to go back and bed such a wicked wench when you are in full possession of your senses, so be it. But I would not have her seducing you when you were too weak to resist!"

Wulf savored the sweet taste of triumph. He asked softly, "And why is that? Why wouldst care, Brianna?"

Taken aback, Brianna murmured, " 'Tis that y-you have been kind to me, of course. Why else?" What was that strange smile on his face? As though he were playing some game with her and had just won.

Wulf chuckled. "That be your only reason? I have been kind?"

Brianna flushed. "I fail to see the humor . . ."

"My lady, you disappoint me. I had hoped 'twas jealousy that made you brave such danger as you faced this night."

"Wh-what mean you?" Had he seen that gladly she would have pulled out Gormlaith's hair, strand by strand? She watched his features turn suddenly grave. His gaze locked hungrily on her face, her mouth.

"If you were jealous," Wulf said quietly, " 'twould tell me you crave me as I crave you. I have craved you since that day I first saw you weeping at Ospak's feet, Brianna. Always will I crave you."

He gazed on her with such love in his eyes that Brianna despaired. It could not be. It must not, dare not be.

Wulf rose, placed their horns in stands on the table, and returned to her. He drew her up into his arms, his every gesture tender. "Know you why I can think of naught but you day and night?" His voice was rough with the intensity of his emotion.

"Wulf, do not t-tease . . ."

"Know you why I be so jealous I would slay for you?"

Brianna shook her head. She tried to twist away. "I do not want to know . . ." But his face and his eyes told her. Even as she reveled in the strength and warmth of his arms, in being pressed to him so closely, she felt cold.

"Brianna, look at me."

She could not. She murmured, "Please, Wulf, I must go."

Gently Wulf cupped her chin, lifting it so that she must look at him. He whispered, "I lov thee."

Raising wet lashes, Brianna saw the glitter of unshed tears in his own eyes. Love. He had said he loved her. Loved her! It was wonderful and it was terrible. When he lowered his mouth to hers in a soft, insistent kiss, she returned it hungrily, craving only to hold and taste him and be close to him, forcing all else from her thoughts as they exchanged kiss after hungry kiss. But then she minded the promise they had made before they had last made love: There could be nothing between them. It burned her like a brand, as true now as it was then. There could be nothing between them. Not ever.

Wulf saw that she craved him, of that there was no doubt. And he knew now that what she felt for him was more than mere hunger. She cared for him deeply. But why then was she so unhappy? He stroked her pale cheek.

"Why dost weep, Brianna?"

"I—I be so happy," she choked, "and so s-sad." A river of fire was roaring through her, cresting, flaming, and no longer could she contain it. She murmured, "Oh, Wulf, I love thee, too. I love thee."

And what a despicable way she had shown it. Her efforts for Boru had heightened the chances that Wulf Thorsson would be slain in battle. Jesu forgive her. She buried her face against his chest, felt his big hands cradling her, smoothing back the tendrils of hair, felt his warm mouth kissing her lips, coaxing her to kiss him back. Imagining that gray day when he might no longer be there, she felt such emptiness that she cried out:

"I love thee! Oh, Wulf, I love thee more than this tongue can tell!" She brought his face down to hers and covered it with hungry, frenzied kisses, his mouth, his temples and eyelids, his cheeks, his strong dark hands.

Wulf returned her starving kisses, holding her so close they might even then have been one.

It was as if he had been waiting his whole life for this one moment. That he had found love was wondrous enough in itself, but never had he expected such words to come from her own adorable lips nor expected this outpouring of passion. She loved him . . .

He craved to give a battle cry, for now he could do anything, conquer anyone—yet still she wept. Not openly, but tears shimmered, unspilled, in her eyes as though some terrible fear lurked within her. It was but one more thing he did not understand, and it filled him with unease. He would ask her about it later, for he had many questions. But one thing he knew for certain: No more would he listen to her protest that there could be nothing between them. No more. She was his now, and never would he give her up.

" 'Tis all right, I am here," he whispered. He saw that she was not comforted but clung to him all the tighter, kissing him as if he might disappear from the earth. He chuckled. It was the answer to a man's dreams and the firestorm was building within him. " 'Tis all right, my heart's treasure." He stroked her face and then untied the laces of her tunic and drew it off. Brushing his lips over her throat, feeling her body tremble with passion, Wulf forgot the coming war and the treachery surrounding him.

Brianna shivered with pleasure. When he held her close and looked at her so, his warm lips brushing her skin, she could think of nothing but the perfect joy of being with him, of how she hungered for him. All else disappeared but his beguiling face before her, his hands exciting her, the beauty and strength of his body. She untied the laces of his tunic, slipped it off, and caressed his wide shoulders and his chest beneath his kyrtil. She slipped her hands around his waist and up his back, delighting in the play of his powerful muscles and the feel of his polished skin.

"I love thee," she whispered.

Wulf answered with a deep kiss and held her closer. He gently lifted her chemise over her head and, last, removed the seal of Husaby which hung between her breasts. He then helped her to remove his own kyrtil. As she pressed kisses over his naked chest and ran wondering fingers over its crisp mat of fur, his hungry hands and mouth explored her—the softness of her white flesh, the swelling pink-tipped breasts and slender rounded arms and shoulders, the thick cascade of mahogany hair. It spilled gleaming over his hands as he raised it to his lips and buried his face in its silken fragrance. She was the most perfect blossom— and she was his. She was his woman.

"I love thee," he whispered, his whole body afire with his hunger.

He lifted her, carried her to his bedcloset, and placed her on the furs. Removing the rest of her clothing, he slid his hands slowly up and down her long, smooth legs, kissing every inch, kissing, caressing the silken triangle between her thighs. He could not wait much longer . . .

With shaking hands, Brianna helped Wulf doff his remaining garb. She gazed on him with shining eyes, her breathing quickening. "How beautiful you be, Wulf Thorsson."

She paid no mind to his soft laughter. What did a man know, after all? He was beautiful; tall, powerful, his hard-muscled legs and arms shadowed with dark-gold fur, a lean, flat belly and narrow waist, wide wide shoulders. As passion seared her, she knelt beside him, smoothing back the wild tangle of golden hair that hung to his shoulders and mingled with his cropped beard. Scars lay white on his dark arms and chest; a great one marked his thigh. She kissed each of them, thanking Jesu that his wounds had not killed nor maimed him.

Wulf gave a low growl, caught her and laid her on her back. His deep kiss and burning hands melted her. As he parted her thighs and prepared to mount her, Brianna reached out, caressing him, guiding him . . . She gasped at her hot, shuddering spasm of pleasure upon his swift plunging entry, heard his own indrawn breath. She spiraled down, down into a vortex so wild, so deep and delicious she wanted never to leave it.

"Oh, Wulf, never have I felt so . . ."

The fire that had burned so hotly within her was banked now. Lying in Wulf's arms, Brianna minded that it was this sweet quiet time she had so yearned for between them. Holding each other close, his hands and mouth moving over her gently, tenderly, easy talk between them about small things. Husband and wife talk. Husband and wife . . . She shied from the thought abruptly.

Wulf murmured, "What is't, little beloved? What are you thinking on?"

Little beloved? Little betrayer, were the truth known. But beloved betrayer never could she be. Never could a betrayer be a lover in his eyes, and it fair broke her heart. It was long moments before Brianna trusted herself to speak. "I'm thinking on you," she whispered. "On how wonderful you be."

This time with him had been like a perfect dream, but now she must awaken and face reality. She had intended to flee this night, and so she would still. He would be hurt and angry, ay, but far better that than to have for his beloved a woman who had betrayed him. And now she should tarry no longer, it would only make the parting harder. And yet—yet what would a few more precious moments matter . . .

Gormlaith stretched out languorously in her bed and opened her eyes. It would seem she had dozed. Feeling the wetness between her thighs, and that a weak pulse fluttered there, pleasurable still, she sighed. Her heavy-lidded gaze moved over the naked man who still slept by her side. His eyes were closed, his mouth was open, and he snored. Her own mouth curved, partly in scorn. There was no doubt that Regin's size and strength titillated her, but the great ox feared her. It was she who had led, she who had ridden him to a summit that lacked excitement and danger—but then the night was yet young. They would make love again and yet again before the sun rose, for she had many things to teach him. But for now, let him sleep. She had other things to accomplish this night.

She rose, donned her heavy cloak over her nightgarb, and silently unbarred her door. Moving through the passageway toward Wulf Thorsson's chamber, she rehearsed the tale she had meant to tell him earlier, the tale of a maid who regularly met a tall, dark Celt who was known to consort with the men of Brian Boru. She smiled, contemplating his rage, and it gave her the keenest pleasure to imagine Brianna's horror when the wench was dragged down to the souterrain to confront her bound and gagged ally.

It would be intriguing indeed to discover what deviltry the two had been up to, and she intended for the Norseman to be there for the questioning. At his door, she lifted her hand to knock but hesitated upon hearing a woman's voice. Brianna? By the gods, it was. Hearing low murmurs, those sounds that lovers made after their passion was spent, she clenched her hands. The clay-eating bastard! He had lied to her. He had lied in order to sleep with a damned serving-wench. Was there no one in this whole accursed palace she could trust? She returned raging to her chamber and shook Regin's shoulder.

Regin blinked, seeing the princess standing over him, tall and with a frightening look to her eyes. Good God, never did he know what to expect from this woman. He muttered, "What is't, your highness?" He remembered his nakedness then and what had gone on before between the two of them, and his face turned white. For sure she was sorry for it now. Doubtless she craved to cut out his heart.

"Cease your gaping and get you dressed," Gormlaith hissed. "There is work to be done."

"Ay, my lady." He touched his forehead in respect.

Gormlaith paced as if caged while he fumbled with trews, boots, and interminable ties. When he was dressed finally, she snapped, "Go you to the chamber of Wulf Thorsson and hide you nearby. Brianna is with him—she whom you followed into town. When she leaves his chamber, seize her and throw her in the souterrain. But in a cell separate from the Celt, hear you?"

Regin hesitated. "My lady, the Viking will slay me if he learns of it."

"I will slay you if you do not! Besides, 'twill be the bitch he will soon crave to slay." As he turned to go, she whispered, "Regin . . ."

Regin marked the husky change in her voice, the way her eyes slid over his chest and shoulders. His pulses responded instantly. "Ay, my lady?" His own voice was thick.

"Return to me after." The gaze she gave him smoldered. "I will be waiting for you . . ."

Chapter Twenty-Three

Wulf lay in paradise, soft furs beneath and atop him, a soft maid snuggled in his arm close to his heart. Thinking on her alone and on his new life with her, he brought her small hand to his lips and kissed it. He kissed the fragile skin on the back, kissed each finger, her palm, her wrist. He shook his head. How smooth and white and delicate a hand it was, and how perfect its shape and symmetry. He smiled at the absurdity, the reality of how skillfully it had wielded a dagger.

"Always have I thought of you ruling your own manor house," he murmured, pulling her closer. "Now I know why . . ."

"Why?" Brianna whispered, gazing on his face and marveling on the contentment she saw there. And never had she herself been so content. She felt so safe and warm, she could not force herself to take the first step toward leaving his arms. Not yet . . .

" 'Tis my own manor house you will rule. Husaby. 'Tis a nice enough dwelling, but it needs a woman's care. Methinks you will like it. The blue sea in front, gray fells behind, rich fields between, and the sea birds and sun over our heads . . ." When she made no answer, he said low, "Lady, you are returning to Norway's land with me, know you that. We will not live in Ireland nor Maun. I will bring you back here to visit if 'tis your desire, but Husaby will be our home."

Brianna closed her eyes. There it was. She had known this moment would come. In the blink of an eye, she had gone from warmth and safety to sinking in a bog of her own making. Never could she wed this man nor be mistress of his steading.

Wulf sat up and studied her. He frowned. "I see this does not suit you."

Brianna, too, sat up, her long hair veiling her nakedness. She lifted a strand of it and would it about her finger. "How canst even think of wedding when war looms?" she murmured. "I—I cannot." She slipped from out the bedcloset then and began donning her garb. But in her thoughts was Husaby. Husaby with the sea before it, the mountains behind, and sea birds wheeling and crying overhead. Husaby, shining with the care she would have given it. There came a great lump to her throat, for she loved it already. Vikings! She felt a stab of resentment. Why could they not live in peace? Oh, it was not fair . . .

"Rather would I think of wedding you than of war," Wulf answered quietly, drawing on his own garb.

"Never would I have guessed it, so busy have you been gathering troops for the occasion." As she tugged on her boots and tied them, she ordered her tongue to be still, but it would not obey. "You be the Wolf of Husaby, after all, the slayer of Celts without number." After the words were out, she stared, stricken, at his grave face. She shook her head, got to her feet, muttered, " 'Twas uncalled for. 'Tis sorry I—I am . . ."

Wulf watched as she slid the jeweled dagger inside her waistband. She avoided his eyes. "What is't, Brianna?"

" 'Tis just that I—I so hate war." She tried to smile. "I must go now."

Wulf moved between her and the door. "I think not. Not yet," he said gently, and then: "Who be you, Brianna? Who be you really? I mark well you are a chieftain's daughter—none other would hold a blade so skillfully nor have so bold a tongue—but long and long have I been curious. How came you to be captured and your father not win you back? Who be he? 'Tis time I knew."

Brianna stared at him helplessly. These were questions she dared not answer, for if she mentioned the name Kinrade, she might as well tell all.

"What matters it?" she asked, her voice small.

Wulf regarded her curiously. "Lady, 'tis the man I will soon call father-in-law. I trow 'tis of some minor importance—or do you not think so?"

Her face grew hot, thinking how silly she must seem. "Oh, ay, but—can we not discuss it later?" And later she would be gone from here, never to see him again. Oh, God . . . She made to move past him but he caught her arm.

"Dost imagine I would harm your father, Brianna?" he asked sharply.

"Never had I considered such a thing!" But she knew an answer must be forthcoming. She shrugged. "Very well, he be Dugald. Fin Dugald. And now 'tis really time I went."

Wulf noted her quickened breathing and nervous glances toward the door, her tongue flicking over lips gone suddenly dry. They had made love, confessed their love, and now this. She was lying. Did the little troll ever speak the truth? In fact, had she spoken one true word since he had known her? He asked softly, "Why dost lie to me, Brianna?"

Brianna saw his doubt. The light was gone from his eyes. She caught his hand to her lips and kissed it. "Wulf, I love thee, know that." His face minded her of granite. "I—I pray you, don't look at me so . . ." At that, he gripped her arm, roughly marched her to one of the chairs before the hearth, and sat her down so hard her bottom stung. She would have lashed out, but he looked so dangerous he frightened her.

"Who be you?" he growled. "The truth this time."

Brianna blinked. "I—I told you. I be the daughter of Fin Dugald of Maun."

Wulf shook his head in disgust. "Never doubt I will keep you here until you speak the truth, Brianna—if Brianna indeed be your name."

She closed her eyes, felt the trap closing. But then what matter?—war would start within the week and she had told Boru all she was going to tell. And she was so tired of lies, so tired of hiding and sneaking and pretending. She yearned to confess all, tell him who she was and what she had done and have it over. The most he could do was slay her, and at this moment it seemed not such a bad thing. Never would he believe she could love him and at the same time do what she had done. And in her heart she had known that never would she escape punishment.

Her eyes still closed, Brianna drew a deep breath. She murmured, "Brianna be my given name."

"Your father?" Wulf asked curtly.

Another deep breath. "Lachlan Kinrade."

It was as if an icy hand touched Wulf's spine. Lachlan Kinrade? Never had he expected this. The man was high chieftain of Maun, the lion of his island nation much as was Brian Boru the lion of Ireland. It was said the two were as brothers. But then how was Wulf to know whether this was not just another of her lies? He sat himself in the chair facing her, his fingers drumming the arm.

" 'Tis clear you know little of Lachlan Kinrade," he said. "Never would such a man have allowed his daughter to remain in bondage."

Brianna opened her eyes to his angry gaze. "Never was I in bondage."

Wulf masked his shock. He leaned forward, elbows on his knees. "Not in bondage?"

"Nay."

"How can this be? Ospak called you thrall, and with these eyes I saw him mistreat you."

Brianna shook her head and looked away. "He did not, I assure you. The truth be that a Viking—forced me when I was a-a young maid, but never did Ospak harm me."

The color left Wulf's face as her words and their terrible implication sank in. Rape. She had been raped by a Viking. It was as if he himself had been cut down. No wonder she had trembled so at his touch. And then he himself had seen fit to force her. He grimaced. It would always gnaw at him, but it was bootless to dwell on it now. He said gruffly:

"It grieves me to hear of your misfortune, but now I would know more of this strange business with Ospak. Why would you both pretend you were his thrall?"

"So he need not explain the real reason for my presence at Valaberg." Brianna stared down at her hands, for his eyes frightened her.

"And what reason was that?" he asked softly.

There was no turning back. She wet her dry lips. "I had gone there to ask for ships and men—for Brian Boru. We had spoken but a short time when you arrived."

It sent Wulf reeling though he was sitting in a fur-draped chair. Boru. His enemy of all enemies. Had the words come from the tongue of a man, he would have drawn his sword and demanded satisfaction then and there. Instead his lip curled. "So, Boru uses soft young maids for such work, does he?"

"If he did, is that so wrong?" Brianna flared. "As it so happens, he knew naught of it nor did my father. 'Twas my own idea and a good one. Ospak has since rallied to him, as I trow you already know."

"It has reached my ears, ay," Wulf answered drily. "And now it wonders me greatly—why didst come here, Brianna? Had you chosen, I would have left you to go your way that stormy day on Maun, yet 'twas your decision to come with me. Why?"

Her White Jesu help her if her reason this time was as contemptible as the other. She would need her God in any event, for he was so rage-filled that he craved to throttle her. But the thought of a world in which she no longer walked nor talked nor laughed nor lived so terrified him that he trembled. He was cursed for certain. He could live neither with nor without her. Through clenched teeth, he muttered:

"I ask you again, Brianna, why didst come here to Sitric's stronghold with me?"

The time for lies was over. Brianna answered simply and without hesitation. "I came to spy for Boru."

"Holy Thor, Brianna." It was a half-cry that escaped Wulf's lips before he clamped them shut. The woman he loved as life itself, and the man he was sworn to slay . . .

Brianna knelt by his side. She yearned to hold him, comfort him, but she dared not even touch him so wild were his eyes. "Wulf, please, hear me. Boru I have known and loved since my childhood and—"

Wulf got to his feet. " 'Tis enough!" He wanted to smash and rend asunder everything at hand. Instead he strode to the table, filled his horn, and took a great gulp from it.

"He be my second father," she explained. "He fostered me those years my mother lay dying, and long and long have I craved to repay him for his love and kindness."

"And so you betrayed me!" Wulf slammed down the horn and stalked toward the door.

Brianna ran ahead and flung herself across it, blocking his way. "I ask no forgiveness, only that you listen. As I once listened to you . . ." When he did not thrust her aside, but crossed his arms over his chest and waited, his eyes burning, she went on urgently. "I came here, not to betray you nor any other, but to help Boru win a war he neither started nor wanted. He had brought peace to this land." Her eyes shone with sudden tears. "Oh, Wulf, never did I want to fall in love with you. I—I fought it . . ."

"Love?" So sick and empty did Wulf feel, he could not even mock her. " 'Tis not what I call love, lady."

Lies. Lies without number. He could not count them there were so many, and now he saw clearly the answers to those things that had long puzzled him. Things that made no sense when he had thought her a helpless maid in need of guarding. And tonight, though she had come to his aid with blade in hand and her eyes aflame, it was not because of love. Doubtless it was her hatred of Gormlaith. And all this time she had been watching, listening. And those daily trips to town—of course she would have an ally who carried her news to Boru.

The black thought smoked and smoldered within him as he pondered what to do with her. He knew not. He knew only that he would not put her into the hands of Sitric and Gormlaith. Perhaps he could keep her on his vessel—ay, that would do. His crew was newly arrived from Maun, and she could be held there until he decided what was to become of her.

"If you have said all you have to say," he said gruffly, "I am taking you from here."

Never had she been so miserable. "Know you, I love you," Brianna cried out. "Believe that if you believe naught else. God help me, I love you above everything, and I grieve that I have hurt and betrayed you. Never will I forgive myself for that."

Of a sudden, it was as though she looked upon a stage in her mind's-eye, a terrible brightly lit stage, and on it she saw his long mail-clad form lying surrounded by bushes and trees. His life's-blood flowed from a gaping wound in his head, matting his hair and beard, and round about him stood his grieving men weeping and beating their breasts. Her breath caught at the sight. He was going to die! Oh, Jesu, nay! Oh, please, nay, she prayed. Watch over him . . .

Marking the terror in her eyes and her body swaying, Wulf steeled himself. So be it. If she would not come with him willingly, he would carry her. He fetched her cloak and settled it over her shoulders.

"Come, we are leaving."

"Wulf, y-you are going to die," she gasped.

" 'Tis possible," Wulf agreed. He caught her hand, drew her toward the door, and was shocked when she broke his grip and moved beyond his grasp. It was the evasive movement of a warrior, and he approached her with caution. "Come, Valkyrie, that trick will not work twice." He blinked when she threw off the cloak, drew her dagger and crouched, her blade at the ready.

"You are going to hear me out"—it was a fierce whisper—"unless you crave to go into battle already wounded."

Wulf laughed. He drew closer, himself crouching, arms extended, hands itching to grasp her and spank her bottom until she screeched. Her blade flashed then, so quick he had no chance to thwart it, and there came a hot stinging on the back of his hand. He stared at the scarlet streak glistening there. He hissed in a breath, expelled it, and looked on her with increased respect.

Brianna crouched still, wary, waiting, yet tears stood in her eyes. She said softly, "Now you will hear me out, Wulf Thorsson." Her lips quivered so that she could scarce form the words, but what matter when he would not heed them? "Heard you this coming battle will go to the Irish? 'Tis prophesied by your own seers." When he said nothing, she added urgently, "Wulf, you will die if you fight against them. I feel it in my heart."

Wulf smiled. "I do not fear death, Brianna." In Valhalla, there will be no women to be won nor lost nor grieved over. There will be only battles to win.

"Think on the many Norse other than Ospak who are fighting for Boru," she added. "Christian Norse who have thrived in the peace and the good he brought to this land. 'Tis not too late for you and those men you have rallied to join them." Marking the steely calm in his eyes, she raised her voice. "Wulf, you be so like him! You be kind and loyal and honorable. Never have you belonged with the treacherous likes of Sitric and Gormlaith!"

He answered quietly, "I know well there be much treachery about me . . ." He was pleased to see her flinch.

But her words filled his head with a thousand warring thoughts. He agreed, grudging, that the peace under Boru had been a boon, yet the devil's grasp on every Norse city in the land was an iron one. Those Vikings who lived under his rule had protection and prosperity, ay, but in exchange for their pride and freedom. And Wulf's own reason for not resisting the Lion these past twelve years shamed him. He was a coward. He had leapt at the chance for vengeance against Boru's Celts, who had wounded him so terribly, but never had he lost his terror of them. Always in his nightmares he emerged from battle half a man.

Now, as his angry gaze raked Brianna, he knew his Celt-fear was gone. She had made a fool of him, and his fury had set him free. He felt a lad once more. He was lifted on the wings of Odin's ravens, invincible and ready and eager for the Shining Death to kiss Celt throats. He would demolish every accursed Celt he encountered. He hoped especially to meet the giant who had nigh killed him so long ago—never would he forget that face. And this time, this time he would lay the bastard in the dead-straw.

Seeing the battle-light in his eyes, Brianna felt the hope go out of her. She had lost him, but then never had she expected otherwise.

"So you still fight for Sitric?" she asked quietly.

"I fight against Boru," Wulf corrected her. "You could not have expected otherwise."

She shook her head. "Nay, but I had to try . . ." She returned her dagger to her belt.

Wulf retrieved her cloak from the floor, held it for her. "We go now."

"Where?"

"You will know when we get there."

Gripping her arm tightly, he propelled her from his chamber, down the corridor, and out the front door. The watchman nodded as they passed through his gate, and then they were headed toward the Liffey under a bright moon.

Brianna stumbled, hard put to keep up with his long, angry stride. "Must you grip my arm so tightly?" she protested.

Wulf said nothing, but instead clasped her small hand securely in his. He would not give her the chance to flee into the shadows.

Brianna soon saw that they were on that same path they had trod when first she set foot on Irish soil. "We are going to the harbor?"

"Ay."

Wulf's heart broke to look on her. She seemed the same as when he had brought her here— the same lad's clothing, her long hair lifting in the wind, her eyes wide and frightened. But she was not the same. No longer was she an escaped thrall he had sworn to guard, a sweet maid who had captured his fancy. She was the daughter of a dangerous man, and herself a dangerous threat—and he loved her. He knew now that nothing would ever change that. As they neared the harbor, he said:

"You will be placed under guard on my vessel for now. Give me your weapon."

"But—"

"Now," Wulf ordered. "My men will not harm you." As she obeyed, withdrawing the dagger

371

from under her tunic and handing it to him hilt first, he marked what an exquisite little thing it was, silver-worked and with inlaid jewels winking in the moon-glow. The sight of it was the last thing he remembered . . .

Brianna knew terror as she lay on hard-packed earth in pitch-blackness. The thongs that bound her hands and feet were cruelly tight, and the rag stuffed in her mouth was nigh to choking her. She knew not who had struck Wulf down and seized her, for the man had been hooded. He had gagged her before she could make a sound, had trussed and hooded her, and then carried her to this damp hole.

She could not cease shivering as she wondered who was behind it all. Gormlaith? If that were so, she was doubtless in the souterrain beneath the palace. Oh, God, was she to be left here alone and helpless to starve in the dark? Was she to be tortured? She started as the bar on the door was suddenly slid back and the door flung open. She was near blinded as a man entered bearing a fir-root torch which he fastened to the wall. She blinked. Regin? It was. It was Gormlaith's man.

As Brianna struggled to a sitting position, she saw that her cell was no more than a closet—or a coffin. Of a sudden, Gormlaith herself was there, white-faced, taller than tall in a black cloak and with her red hair long and wild. She gazed down on Brianna with her lips drawn back.

"Spy!" she hissed. "So this is how you repay my kindness?" She dealt Brianna a back-handed blow across the face.

Gormlaith's rings raked Brianna's cheek and bloodied her mouth. Even so, Brianna gazed back, defiant.

Gormlaith laughed. "My, how fearless you be. But then we will see how you fare several days hence. We will talk, you and I, when you be a bit hungrier and thirstier and not near so brave." She snapped her fingers, and when Regin appeared, she said, "We go now."

"Wouldst have her unbound and her gag removed, my lady?"

"Nay, I would not."

With that, they departed. The door slammed, was barred, and Brianna was left once more in darkness.

Chapter Twenty-Four

Dublin slept under a high-sailing moon as a horse and rider thundered toward the stronghold of Sitric Olavsson. Those few Vikings still about on the empty streets stared and shuddered as the pair passed. And with good reason. They had seen a great stallion, gray and foam-flecked, and riding tall in the saddle was a black-garbed figure, gaunt and white-faced, a battle-ax strapped to his back, sword at his side, and his cape and grizzled hair and beard flying wild. His terrible eyes, like live coals, marked no one but looked straight ahead. All swore they had seen Odin. With the coming battle but three days away, it was whispered that the god of war had come to consult with his chieftains.

But it was not Odin who rode so swiftly in the moon-bright night. It was the emperor of Ireland and he had not war on his mind, but murder. He feared greatly for Brianna, and he vowed over and over, white-lipped, that if any had harmed her, that one would lie in the dead-straw before the sun rose.

All that day as Brian moved among his swiftly gathering troops, he had thought on her with gratitude. Because of that brave maid in the very center of the enemy stronghold, he had known the size of the forces confronting him and had planned accordingly. And he had grieved over her personal sacrifice. Fin had long ago warned him of Brianna's love for the Viking chieftain Wulf Thorsson. But then she was young, she would find another love in her own land. That he had thought her finally safe at home at Carnane had made his heart lighter than it had been in a long while. And then he learned she had never returned to Carnane.

Visiting his Dublin quarters at dusk, Brian had found confusion and fear. His men had earlier received a worried visit from Fiona. That maid, returning home from a day's work, had happened upon Brianna. Fin had not met her at the appointed place and time to put her on the vessel bound for Maun; Brianna was therefore on her way back to the palace. Neither maid had been overly worried at the time, but realizing finally the oddness of it, Fiona had ridden straightaway to Boru's secret quarters with the news. His men had immediately ridden into Dublin. When Fin was not to be found, all knew he had been taken. It was feared that Brianna herself had been seized when she returned to the palace.

It was Brian's decision to go there alone to fetch her—if indeed she were there. He wanted no great throng of men howling and battering down the door and forcing those within to use the maid as a shield—or to slay her in retaliation. Nay, he would deal personally with his former wife and her puppet son. They would not dare defy him. And if Fin were hidden there, him too he would find. But holy God, so much time had been wasted.

Little Brianna . . . Brian drew a shuddering breath as her sweet face rose before him. He felt such great fear for her that he scarce had the spit to swallow. What if he were too late? How would he tell her father? How would he tell Lachlan, even now at the battle site with his men, that he had allowed his only daughter, the light of his life, to be slain? Seeing the palace lying ahead, ghostly in the moon-rays, he slowed his mount. He would tether him and walk the rest of the way. He did not want to startle the sentry . . .

Wulf opened his eyes. He lay stretched out on the ground under the open sky and the moon. He remembered well that he had been escorting Brianna to his vessel and had just taken possession of her dagger when there came a starburst inside his head. Someone had struck him from behind. Sitting up, he was rocked by pain. Firing a battery of oaths, he climbed to his feet and looked about him. It was as he knew it would be. She was gone. Nor had he a doubt that, whoever the devil was, Gormlaith's hand had guided him. It meant that Brianna was being held in the palace, doubtless in a cell in the souterrain.

His fury with her was as hot as ever, but the little troll did not deserve to be in the souterrain. She would be terrified. His heart turned over as he imagined her shut up in one of the cold, damp cells in blackness and silence. He would have done anything, anything, to spare her that. He would have gone there in her place, but nay, he had managed to get himself knocked on the head and had practically given her away. He shot an angry fist at the sky and a howl exploded from his chest. But he had no time to waste on the luxury of rage.

Moving uphill swiftly toward the palace, he marveled that his legs worked as well as they did despite friggja-grass and a crack on the skull. But as the rath came into his sight, he slowed his step to stealth. It was some moments before he realized what it was he was seeing: a figure, unseen by the sentry, was fast approaching him on foot. Before Wulf could give warning, there was a lightning skirmish between the two and the guard was downed. As the victor then made to enter the gate, Wulf gave a shout:

"Hei, you! Hold there!" The Shining Death hissed as he drew it from its sheath.

He broke into a run across the uneven turf and within moments was face to face with the intruder, a tall Celt. Wulf's skin crawled marking the death-light in those gray eyes and the great battle-ax strapped to the fellow's back. Seeing his long, grizzled hair and beard, Wulf was shocked. This was an old man. He was lean and hard, ay, but how much fight could he have in him? As Wulf tore off his cloak and wound it about his left arm, the two warily circled one another. The fellow matched him well in height and breadth, but that great ax— and himself without a shield . . .

Even as Wulf thought it, the other slid the monster from out its sling, ceased his circling, and stood motionless. Wulf, too, stood watching, waiting. As the other's burning eyes studied him, he quickly made a battle plan—close in and keep close, confine that deadly ax to short chops, aim his own point up and under the chin. The fellow's being so old, it would not take long. It *dared* not take long, for Brianna needed him.

Sensing the Viking's sudden lack of concentration, Brian gave a low growl and came on like a battering ram, his ax forward in both hands. Swift as lightning, he swung at the other's sword to break it. At the last instant, the Norseman stepped aside, and then crouching low, knees bent, rushed him. Again and again he rushed him, thrusting upward, aiming for his throat each time. As Brian parried the strokes, he saw well that his opponent was a worthy one.

Wulf continued to carry the fight to the Celt, but the effects of the drug and his head pain were hindering him now. Nor could he believe that a man so old would come on again and again like a whirlwind. As Wulf sidestepped his lethal swings, forever thrusting with short jabs toward throat and heart, he felt a growing frustration. He had to down this devil and get to Brianna, yet he knew that his impatience could defeat him. Watch his eyes, he commanded himself, and when they target the next thrust, go in for the kill. Watch his eyes, man. His eyes . . .

Wulf blinked, hammer-struck, as he realized of a sudden where he had seen those death-gray eyes before. Holy Odin, it was on the battlefield in Maun. And he had felt the razor-sharp blade of that great battle-ax that seemed everywhere at once. Remembering caused the hair to rise on his arms and his nape. By the gods, this was the same damned devil who had near slain him so long ago. This was the face that had haunted his dreams for years—never would he forget it. The fellow had fought like a demon then and he did still, aged though he was.

But what was he doing here, alone, and in the middle of the night? For what conceivable reason was this Celt chieftain—for a chieftain he was, no mistake—here at Sitric's stronghold so near to battle time? Again Wulf felt the hair stir on his body. There was only one man who fought so. Only one man it could be. Brian-the-Hundred-Killer. The emperor of Ireland. And he must have come for Brianna. There could be no other reason . . .

Brian was close to despair. His arms and legs ached and his muscles burned like fire with the bone-splitting jolt of each parry. He was getting old. Never before had he met a foe who so stubbornly defied his every attempt to down him—and that it should be now of all times. The damned spalpeen! As he withdrew, but only to catch his breath for a greater effort, he saw a thing he could scarce believe. The Viking was lowering his sword . . . he was sheathing it. Brian stared, scowling, at the younger man. What in damnation was this, some trick? He looked about him, expecting to see an enemy horde surrounding him on the moon-bright turf, but they were alone still. He watched, suspicious, his ax held ready as the tall Norseman approached. Marking his long, powerful legs and easy stride, the way his mane and beard shone gold as the moon struck them, Boru felt such a pang that he wanted to cry out for time to move backwards. This was himself thirty winters ago. Young and vital and comely to a maiden's eye. It kindled a memory, some small thing Brianna had said . . .

Cautiously Wulf drew near, his gaze locked on the cold eyes of his blood enemy, the man he was sworn to slay. Always would he hate him, but he felt a huge grudging admiration for him. That the emperor of Ireland had himself come alone to this enemy stronghold for a maid showed the mettle of the man. It was loyalty and bravery of a sort Wulf had not known before. It was why Brianna could give nothing less than her all in return. Damnation, why had not the devil been born a Norseman? He extended his hands, palms up.

"Boru?"

"Ay," Brian answered gruffly. "And you be Thorsson."

"Ay," Wulf said low.

The Wolf of Husaby. Brian put away his battle-ax and touched the Viking's hands with his own. This was a man he had reason to hate even as he hated Sitric and Maelmorda. It was Thorsson's efforts more than theirs that had rallied such a huge Viking force against him. But him he could not hate. Brianna loved him, and in his tall, strong body and wild mane of hair, Brian saw himself in days long gone.

"Know you," Wulf said low, "we have better things to do than fight each other."

Brian's eyes flickered. "Where be she?"

"I fear she is in the souterrain."

"Lead the way." Seeing that the Viking's gaze rested on the downed guard, Brian laughed softly. "Nay, man, he be gone for the night. He will sound no alert. What of the others?"

"All should be sleeping soundly," Wulf whispered as they crossed the courtyard. "There was great revelry this night."

Brian said drily, "Doubtless because there will be scant cause for it later."

" 'Twas but an early celebration," Wulf said crisply.

Brian grunted. "Oh, ay."

He had no fears for himself as he followed the Viking into the stronghold and as together they trod the dim passageway to the kitchen-house. Even had a drunken pall not lay over the stronghold, still he would have felt no fear. It was for Brianna that his heart clamored against his ribs. As Thorsson removed a bog-fir torch from the wall, and they descended the narrow earthen steps to the pitch-black souterrain, Brian's terror for her nigh suffocated him. The poor lass . . . the poor darling lass . . .

Brianna had cried herself to sleep, and waking, she was seized with fresh horror. It had not been a nightmare. She was still bound hand and foot and a rag stuffed so far back into her mouth that she feared it would creep down her throat as she swallowed. Holy Mary, was this how she was to die then? Would she starve and rot here with none but Gormlaith and Regin knowing, or would they torture her first?

But wait—if this was the souterrain, perhaps there was hope for her after all. Daily the servants came there to fetch casks and supplies from the storage rooms. If she made some sound, perhaps they would hear her. She attempted to squeal, and knew instantly that the rag would choke her. She could make no sound at all.

Her frantic thoughts went to Fin. Had he too been seized and was he down here even now, or had he been alerted to danger and hid? Perhaps he would find her! Or perhaps he was slain . . . As her tears flowed once more, she told herself she would be brave later. She would go to her death with Jesu by her side, ay, but for now she needed to weep and rage. For herself, for those who would grieve for her, and for what might have been . . .

She saw clearly in the blackness the dear faces of those she loved and who loved her. Her father, Fin, Maeve, Fiona, Boru . . . Would they ever know how her end came? She gave her head a violent shake. Nay, if truly she were meant to die here, it was best they never learned. Never would they have any peace, for it was as if she had been walled up alive. At the thought, sweat drenched her body so that she felt the cold and the damp penetrating to her very bones.

Amid her terror, she thought of Wulf. Would he ever know? And knowing, would he care? She shivered more violently, remembering his fury. For certain he would feel it a just punishment for her. Oh, why had they not met another time and another place? Why did it have to be now? Wulf, beloved . . .

Wulf could not walk upright in the low tunnels beneath the palace. Bent over, and followed by Boru, himself hunched low, he thrust his sputtering torch in each of the rooms as they passed them. Impatiently he looked on the great bins of root vegetables, grains, and casks before moving on. It was those damp holes at the far end of the passage that he sought. The cells for prisoners. His heart in his throat, he quickened his step. What would he find there? So little time had passed, she surely would be safe. Frightened but safe. But then life was so fragile, it could be snuffed out in an instant. Hearing his teeth chattering, Wulf clenched his jaw. Coming upon the first cell, he unbarred the door quietly, steeling himself. Already he could see her in death—cold, white, nevermore to laugh with him nor sass him. But she was not there. He shut the door, moved to the next cell, quietly unbarred it, shone the light in and—His heart fair stopped, marking the wide green eyes staring up at him from where she lay crumpled on the floor. She lived.

Brianna had not heard the door open, so silently was the bar slid back. When the room was flooded suddenly with torchlight, she knew terror. Was it Gormlaith or was it Fin? She blinked, seeing it was neither who bore the light, seeing golden hair, angry blue eyes . . . Wulf! It was Wulf who had come for her!

Thrusting the torch at Brian Boru, Wulf knelt by Brianna's side and with his dagger slashed the cruelly tight gag binding her mouth. As he tore out the filthy rag and hurled it from him, his rage was so hot and so red it nigh overcame him. He promised himself that the devil who had done this would die.

"Be you all right?" His voice was a rasp.

"A-ay. Just fr-frighted. Oh, Wulf, Wulf . . ." Over and over Brianna murmured his name as he cut the thongs binding her and tenderly rubbed her wrists and ankles.

" 'Tis all right, I am here," Wulf said gruffly. He brushed back a lock of hair clinging to her tear-streaked face. So great was his relief on finding her alive that he felt completely drained. He wanted only to sit there cradling and comforting her, but he had not gained her safety yet. He had to get her out of there—and so he would, with the emperor of the land by his side.

Brian had remained in the passage, quiet, unseen, content to allow Thorsson to free the maid before he took the light and searched for Fin. Marking the rage and anguish on the Viking's face upon seeing Brianna, and the tenderness with which he smoothed back her hair, Brian was wrenched. They were lovers. It minded him of how glorious was the journey he had once traveled with Gormlaith. In those first halcyon years, never would he have believed she would betray him with others, nor threaten him with death, nor stir a war against him.

Brian's mouth curved. The war she would lose—but his own death was a certainty. Gormlaith would have that satisfaction at least. He had told no one that two nights past he had heard the Banshee of the Dal Cais, her whose wail had foretold the deaths of Dalcassian princes for as long as the tribe had existed. And this Thorsson—what had the Fates decided for him? Was he to live, or was

Brianna to be left alone, perhaps with his babe growing next her heart?

" 'Tis time we left," Wulf said, helping Brianna to her feet. "Canst walk?"

"Ay, but first I would see if—" Brianna forgot Fin completely as she saw the leonine figure who stood so silently in the passage, torch in hand. She cried, "Boru!"

Brian caught her to him, held her close, and whispered, "There, there now, girl, 'tis all right. We will talk later."

Brianna felt a leap of joy. Had the two joined forces then? For what other reason would they be here together?

"I trow I have another kinsman in this hell-hole," Brian growled.

"Here he can stay," Wulf muttered.

"Only if I be slain first," Brian countered, reaching for his dirk and handing the torch to Brianna.

Seeing that she was mistaken and that their stubbornness was wasting time, Brianna moved to the next cell. Quietly she slid back the bar and opened the door. There sat Fin, trussed, gagged, and furious.

"He is here," she called softly, and the two came. When the Norseman looked down on the raging Celt with little sympathy, Brianna said, "Wulf, please, 'tis my kinsman . . ." She knew well that Wulf would consider this no reason to release him. By his lights he should not have released *her* just now. She could only throw herself on his mercy, on any love he felt for her. "Please?" she murmured.

"Take him then," Wulf muttered, "but quickly."

He was bewitched, he thought bitterly, as Brian Boru swiftly cut through the thongs binding his man. This wench had cast on him some accursed Celt spell from which there was no escape. How else explain that he had in his hands the Ard Ri of Ireland and was permitting him to ride off into the night with two of his spies? Odin help him . . .

After Brianna had greeted and embraced Fin, she whispered to Wulf, "Come with us."

"You know I cannot," Wulf answered stiffly.

Yet etched in his mind was the shining image of Brian Boru coming alone to Sitric's stronghold for a maid and a man. In silence, he led the three up out of the souterrain and into the night. The sentry, as Boru had promised, lay where they had left him.

"Go you and get your mount, Fin," Brian ordered, his voice low, "and then come to me straightaway." He drew Brianna along with him as Fin blended swiftly into the shadows. "My mount is over yonder." When Brianna hesitated, he muttered, "Girl, we have no time to waste." To the Viking, he said, "Have thanks, Wulf Thorsson. You I will not forget."

Wulf gave the ghost of a smile. "Nor I you, Brian Boru."

Looking up, Brianna was stunned to see how tired and lined was the face of the emperor. Her heart fair cried out, seeing it. Why, he was an old man! How could that be? When had it happened that he had grown so old? And Wulf, who was so like him—now he was as her child-eyes had remembered Boru at Kincora. A tall, gentle warrior-god who was kind to her. So kind. Gazing on the two, she saw respect and admiration for the other on each of their faces.

"Brianna, hurry you. We can tarry no longer," Brian said, leading her toward his mount.

"Ay . . ." Brianna looked back at Wulf, her eyes beseeching. She saw that his own glistened. "Please, wilt not come with us?"

"Brianna, for the love of God," Brian growled, "you torture the man. He cannot betray his people. Here, you"—he interlaced his fingers, forming a low stirrup for her—"mount! Hurry!"

Brianna obeyed. When she was in the saddle, Boru sprang up behind her. He threw Wulf a salute. Knowing it was the last time she would see her beloved, Brianna began to weep. As Boru spurred, she threw out her hand as if to caress the last breath of air to pass the Norseman's lips. She called back:

"Wulf, I love thee . . ."

After Brianna's departure, Wulf felt such a loss he was numb. But he had the presence of mind to carry the felled guard to his quarters and replace him with another before returning to his own chamber. When Leif appeared, Wulf marked on his face the signs of heavy drinking. He frowned. "What is't, man?" Now he looked at him more closely, minding that earlier he had been with Fiona. "How long have you been back?"

"Since the feasting."

"You drank alone?"

"Ay, and now I be here to drink with you. You look as if you could use it. I came by earlier but you were gone." He shook his head. "Man, never will you believe the tale I heard from Fiona—not in a thousand years."

Wulf drew him in, barred the door, and brimmed a horn with ale. He offered it to Leif. "Sit you, man, and drink up." He stirred the fire, filled a horn for himself, and joined his friend.

"—never in a thousand years," Leif muttered.

Wulf stretched out his long legs to the fire. He sighed. Fiona . . . Brianna . . . He shook his head. Leif was wrong. Nothing would surprise him, seeing that the two women were close friends. Wulf up-ended his horn and took a hefty swallow.

"This tale of yours, old friend, wouldst have aught to do with Brian Boru?"

Leif stared, his horn halfway to his mouth. "You know, then?"

Wulf gave a glum nod. "Ay. And I wager my tale be wilder than yours. For sure, none but you will ever hear the damn thing."

Chapter Twenty-Five

Brianna's heart was heavy as Boru's great steed thundered away from Dublin and carried them into the silvery countryside. She was grateful to be away from that black hole of a prison and from Gormlaith; grateful to be breathing the sweet night air. But she was not happy. Never would she be happy again. She had left behind in Dublin her only reason for living. Minding the terrible vision she had seen, of Wulf lying slain and his men weeping and beating their breasts, she shuddered. She offered a silent prayer that it would not be so, and that he would be spared.

Brian's thoughts were of war. Most of his troops were gathered except for those who felt the need to burn and pillage Viking homesteads as they drew near Dublin. Soon they, too, would be camped on the plain between the two rivers awaiting the dawning of Good Friday. It was none too soon, for already battle-heat warmed his men. Of a sudden his attention was drawn to Brianna when she shivered in his arms.

"Be you cold, lass?"

"Ay," Brianna answered quietly.

Anger for himself flared as Brian reproached himself. Where was his heart? The maid had just been to hell and back—nay, she was still in hell—and all he could think of was battle-lines. He said, soothing as he could:

"I am taking you to my quarters outside of Dublin for now. 'Twill be safe there whichever way the battle goes." When she answered with a small nod, he added, "Brianna, no amount of thanks are enough for all you have done."

"You are wrong, Boru. 'Tis but a token of what I long craved to give you—and this night, you gave me my life, you and Wulf . . ." She gulped back the tears. Just speaking his name was torture.

Brian's heart broke, hearing how high and small her voice was. Once more she was his little Brianna. He tightened his arms about her and wished that sparing her from grief were as easy as saving her from harm. He said gruffly:

"Know you, lass, your Wolf of Husaby I would be honored to call kin and comrade."

Brianna was overwhelmed. She murmured, "And I saw his admiration for you—" She began to weep.

"There, now . . ." Brooding, Brian stroked her hair. What a damnable thing this was. "I pray he be returned to you," he muttered. "Know you, lass, gladly would I exchange my own life for his to have you happy again."

"Oh, Boru . . ." She caught his big hands holding the reins and squeezed them.

He had told the God's truth, Brian thought darkly. He would give his own life for her happiness excepting he was in no position to bargain. His days were at an end. He prayed only that he died with a sword in his hand.

"Dry your eyes, Brianna. We are here."

Brianna quickly dashed away her tears with her fingers and stared as they drew nigh a cozy-looking dwelling by the side of the road. "I—I don't understand. This be an inn . . ."

Brian chuckled at her astonishment. "So it is. And as such, no attention is paid to folk coming and going or to how many there be or how long they stay. Over the years, hidden rooms have been added behind the storage rooms in the souterrain, and there be a passage that tunnels to a deep ravine off to the right, and over there—" He stopped to greet several men who had appeared, and then said to Brianna, "I would talk with them, lass. Go you inside and get warmed. I will join you soon."

As the men talked in low voices, Brianna dismounted, handed over the steed to a waiting stable-lad, and went in the front door. She found an empty room, empty sleeping bags on the wall benches, and a bright fire crackling on the hearth. As she knelt, holding her hands to the warmth, a far door opened and a girlish voice cried:

"Annie! Oh, the saints be praised, he found you!"

Brianna turned. "Fi! Oh, Fi!"

The two flew into each other's arms and were hugging and laughing when Brian, followed by his men, entered. Marking the majesty of his face, Brianna knew it was as emperor that he stood before them, yet his gray eyes glittered with love and warmth.

"You maids be two of my bravest," he said. "I thank you, my men thank you, and Ireland thanks you."

Brianna grew pink with embarrassment. She would have protested again but she saw that it would be ungracious to refuse such thanks. She said quietly, " 'Twas an honor to serve you."

"I—I, too," Fiona blurted and turned red.

When Brian caught them to him each in turn and held them close and signed a blessing over their heads, Brianna was shaken. She knew it for a farewell. "Y-you are leaving so soon?"

"I must."

Brian knew that never again would he see this precious maid nor this place where he had long received shelter and camaraderie; never again would he ride the silvered countryside with his men. Unable to speak further for the tightness in his throat, he walked to the door.

Brianna cried out, "Boru!"

Brian turned. How young she was, and how

fair. And how sad and frightened. "Ay, lass?"

"Promise me—promise you will not go into battle on Good Friday . . ."

Now Brian smiled. "Already have I made that promise to my men. 'Tis Murrough who will lead my Dalcassians." Even so, Death would find him. He felt her standing by his side, riding with him through the night wind. Ay, never did the Banshee of the Dal Cais weep for her princes without good cause. But for now, he lived. For now, he would return to where his armies were massing, and on this day dawning he would visit and encourage and thank those men under the seventy banners serving him.

24 April 1014, Dawn

Gormlaith was a-tremble as hastily she bathed, dressed, and donned her cloak. She had scarce slept at all for gloating, for this was the day when she would have her sweetest revenge. This was the day when Brian the Cowking would die. She regretted only that it would not be by her own hand. Hurrying through the palace and across the courtyard, she climbed the ladder to the tallest watchtower. There she found Sitric gazing to the north where the Liffey and the more-distant Tolka lay like orange-gold ribbons in the dawn mist. Thrusting her windblown hair beneath her hood, she moved to her son's side.

"Has't started yet?"

"Soon," Sitric replied tersely, annoyed that

she was there. She would be filled with woman-talk and questions when he craved to be alone.

But Gormlaith stood silent with narrowed eyes, content to watch as the men of both sides began to advance to battle positions—the Irish facing the sea, the Vikings with their backs to their ships which rode at anchor in the bay. Her mind flew ahead to that delicious moment when she would descend to the souterrain to tell Brianna that her efforts had been of no avail—that the Vikings were the victors and Boru was dead. She would then tell her that she would be there the rest of her days—she would lie there until she rotted. Smiling, Gormlaith looked out across the spring-green fields to where the banners of the gathering forces waved so bravely in the pale sun.

Near the Tolka, she made out the all-black banner of Sigurd, a Raven with outspread wings, and there was the Three-Legs Courant belonging to Brodir of Maun. She laughed aloud that the two battalions should fight side by side when both men expected to receive herself as part of their booty. Fools! She marked Boru's black and scarlet Lion banner in the center of the line, and opposite it, on higher ground, the green-blue colors of Maelmorda. Closest to her was the Silver Hammer of Wulf Thorsson and Sitric's blue and gold stripes. Her eyes narrowed further as she studied the scene. She said to Sitric:

"How comes it that both forces be stretched out in such a long, thin line? Is that not a dangerous thing? Should not our own forces be massed?"

"Woman, you know naught," Sitric growled, but he himself was growing anxious.

The idea had been his to have the battlefront nearly two miles in length, stretching between the river Liffey and the fishing shallows of Clontarf. How else protect from the enemy both their fleet in the bay and the vital Liffey Bridge into Dublin? He had been surprised when both Sigurd and Brodir agreed on his strategy—but Wulf Thorsson had been strongly opposed. And now, observing how frail seemed the line of men, and how long, Sitric's heart thumped in his throat. Thorsson had worried, too, that the tide would come in during battle and cut off the men from their ships. Yet none but Thorsson had thought the battle would go on so long. All thought it would be over and done before the tide turned. But would it? Sitric now wondered.

"Were I you, Sitric," Gormlaith said sharply, "never would I have approved of such folly. And were I a man"—her eyes flashed her scathe—"I would be over there leading my troops, not here in the watchtower!"

"Damn me, woman, 'tis hardly necessary for me to explain myself, but I will. Soon I will ride over to the garrison where the reserve forces await me. Not all need be in the thick of battle at the start, know you. We will be fresh for later on." When she gave a scornful snort, he warned, "You tire me, Mother. Cease your tongue-wagging or get you below."

He seethed. Why should he, the king of Dublin, put up with the constant scoffing of such a venomous female? By the gods, henceforward he would not! No more. Before this day was over, he would make other arrangements for his lady-mother. She would not like them, but what matter? She was but a woman.

He forgot her when the lur horn sounded. In an eyeblink, what had been two thin lines of men waiting in silence became a great surging sea of sun-glittered shields and weapons—swords, spears, and battle-axes—and from it came the terrible sounds of battle. Shouts, grunts, the clash of metal on metal, screams. His heart galloped as Boru's Dalcassians met head-on the downhill charge of Maelmorda's mail-clad Leinstermen. The Dalcassians were quickly cut to ribbons.

Gormlaith, seeing her brother's banner go victorious into the first charge of the battle, felt a thrill of triumph. Nevermore could Boru put Maelmorda's bravery to question. "Did he fall?" she gasped.

"Who?"

"Boru! Who else, you stupid ass?"

Sitric's wrath churned. "He will fall this day, now or later, woman, be assured. It is prophesied. And now ask me no more stupid questions. I will have silence."

As the hours and the battle wore on, Sitric's mood brightened. If his men continued to fight so, Dublin would be theirs before the day was much older. It was time he went to the garrison.

Gormlaith called after him as he started down the ladder: "A strange light has just filled the sky. Come you and look."

"Whatever it be, I can do naught about it," Sitric muttered and continued his descent. Before he left, he would first give Regin orders regarding his mother. He was going to put her away, and why he had not done so before this, he did not know.

Long and long Gormlaith stood in the watchtower and gazed, frowning, at the sky. Never had she seen such an odd sight, and it fair chilled her to the bone. It was neither sunrise nor sunset but seemed a blood-red mist that hovered directly over the battlefield. And when the wind blew from the north, it brought to her nostrils the stench of hot blood. But Sitric was right for once. Naught could be done about it. All that mattered was that if Boru's banners continued to fall as they had, there could be little doubt as to the victor.

Gormlaith could wait no longer to cast her good news into Brianna's face. She hastened down the ladder, across the courtyard, and into the palace. Marking how quiet it was, she realized that the serving-folk, along with all of Dublin, were watching the battle from hills and rooftops. But then it was just as well to have no one underfoot. This way, none would wonder at her going into the souterrain. Snatching a torch from the kitchen-house, she descended the narrow steps into the pitch-blackness and marched to the end of the passageway. Hands shaking with eagerness, she threw back the bar, flung open the door, and held the torch high.

Gormlaith gaped, seeing that the cell was empty. She went in, holding up her skirts from the damp, but there was nothing to be seen. How could such a thing be? Or was this the wrong hole? In a frenzy, she entered the other four cells on the corridor, but all held nothing but air. The wench and the Celt had vanished. Her breathing grew fast as she returned raging to the first cell. Regin was the only other who knew they had been there, and if he were behind their disappearance, his head would roll. She started as a figure loomed beside her. Seeing it was Regin, she faced him with blazing eyes.

"Where is Brianna? What hast done with the bitch?"

Regin frowned. "What mean you?"

"Bastard, you dare tell me you know naught of this?" She indicated Brianna's empty cell.

"I know naught, my lady. I was down here last with you." He took her torch and himself peered into the cell. He looked bemused. "For a fact, she be gone."

"Fool! Of course she is gone." Gormlaith frowned as he stuck the torch in a wall bracket and approached her. Misliking the look in his eyes, she drilled him with a frigid gaze. "If you think to bed me down here in this hell-hole, you are much mistaken. And mistaken if you think to play some hide-and-seek game with me regarding my prisoners. I will not have it, hear you?"

Regin said nothing. He felt a certain sorrow at what he was about to do, for the bitch had a fine body and she craved him. But he was a practical man. Given a choice as to whom he must obey, there was no choice when all was said and done. He would obey the king. He grasped the princess between his big hands as though she were a wisp of gossamer.

"Whoreson, unhand me!" A hideous fear was growing within Gormlaith as she fought back with all her strength. "What are you doing? Hast gone mad?" As he thrust her into the black hole, she caught his arm and clung to him with steely fingers, her heart careening. "Regin, nay!"

"I'm sorry, my lady."

"You cannot leave me here!" She began to tremble.

"My lady, resign yourself. 'Tis the king's orders." Regin loosed himself and held her at arm's length.

"Sitric? *Sitric?* That damned snake-vomit! What orders? Know you, I am a princess of Ireland!"

"Ay, but he be king of Dublin, and here you stay until you can be carried to the convent in the mountains."

Gormlaith gasped, nigh suffocated by the panic swarming over her. A convent? Oh, the bastard. And she knew just the one he had chosen. It was walled and guarded day and night and filled with naught but whey-faced

women whose men no longer wanted them.
She would die there just as surely as if a
dagger were driven into her heart. But then,
she could easily bend the guards to her will—
she doubted not they would help her escape
if she offered certain favors . . . But to be here
in this hideous place waiting, dependent upon
Sitric's whim. And what was to say he would not
just leave her here forever? Oh, God . . . Once
more the panic flowed over her. She clutched
her bodyguard with desperate fingers.

"Regin, nay, do not leave me here!" She
screamed as he thrust her from him so roughly
that she fell to the damp floor. It was then that
she saw the glitter in his eyes. "Regin, know
you," she gasped, wrapping her arms about his
legs, "I will give you money, jewels, I will give
you anything if you do not leave me here."

Regin laughed. "You tempt me, my lady. Coax
me some more . . ."

When his eyes moved over her with lust in
them, Gormlaith, too, laughed, for she saw that
she had won. She rose and said huskily, "Let
us go up to my bedchamber, you great brute.
Scented silk be more to my liking than this
damp moldy earth." Once there, she would slay
the bastard, for no more could she trust him.

"Nay, nay, my lady, no bedchamber," Regin
answered, vastly amused. "I care naught for
scented sheets. You will satisfy me greatly right
here. Here and now." And if luck were with him
at all, he would have the use of her for several
weeks before she was carried to the convent. His

manhood stirred and thrust forward fiercely at the thought.

"Maggot-heap!" Gormlaith screeched as he came at her. She struck him across the face, but then his big hand clasped her throat and squeezed, and she went to her knees gasping. She was unable to prevent his tearing off her cloak and all she wore.

Regin's hot eyes savored the voluptuousness of her naked body for but an instant before he shoved himself into her. She screamed and screamed but there were none to hear as he plunged and ground to a climax that left him panting for more. Afterwards, he left her cursing in the blackness.

And on the fields of Clontarf, blood fell from the sky . . .

Brian was greatly anguished at being kept from battle. It was the hardest thing he had ever done, allowing himself to be sequestered in his tent in Tomar's Woods, not far from the fighting. When the forces were first met and he heard the shouts and the din, muted by distance, he chafed, paced, agonized, and then came the first runner gasping:

"Brian, your Dalcassians are falling to Mael-morda and—"

A roar broke from Brian's throat. "I am going to them!"

"Nay, Brian, the prophecy—"

"The prophecy be damned."

As he quickly strapped on his sword and

battle-ax, a shield-burg of armed men formed quickly about him, more to protect the emperor from himself than from the enemy.

"Brian," said his banner bearer quietly, " 'tis early on. Let us put it in God's hands. Know you, Ireland will prevail, for He is with her, but what will it profit her if she lose her king? Think on it, man . . ."

Brian groaned. If he bent them to his will and he died in battle, never would they forgive themselves. He sank his head in his hands, and when he raised it, all saw that he had aged before their eyes. He nodded. "You be right, old friend. I will not go."

From that moment on, he resigned himself to prayer and the reading of his psalter. As the hours passed, he prayed outside on his knees surrounded by his shield-burg, or he retired to his tent and read. He ceased his reading and praying only long enough to listen to the dire reports of his runners. And then toward sunset came news he had awaited the day long: The battle had turned for the Irish. The arrival of fresh and unwearied troops led by Malachi of Meath was throwing the exhausted rebels into confusion and scattering them. Murrough, rallying the now-heartened Dalcassians, was attacking the Vikings so furiously that already Brodir had fled into the woods leaving his own men to be well-nigh cut to pieces.

Brian rejoiced. Ireland would indeed prevail, and, God willing, he himself would lead her to greater peace and prosperity than ever. He would pray that the Banshee was wrong. Taking his prayer cushion outside, he once more fell to his knees in praise. The men in his shield-burg also gave thanks, dropping to their knees and lifting their faces to the heavens. They did not see the red glow that had come of a sudden into the sky south of them, nor did they know that Brodir's flight through the woods had led him and his men close by.

Brodir was nigh to exploding with rage and fear—and confusion. What in the name of the gods was he to do—continue his flight to safety, or join Sigurd who was rallying his men in another part of the woods? The thought of losing the throne of Dublin and the bitch, Gormlaith, was a pill almost too bitter to swallow, yet if a Celt blade kissed his throat, he would lose them anyhow. Damning Boru unto all eternity, he continued stealthily through the brush, his few men behind him. He was stopped short by the sight suddenly before him: In a small clearing was a pitched tent, and amid a circle of kneeling men was an old man on his knees.

Brodir studied them impatiently, muttering finally, " 'Tis some damned priest, I trow. We will stay clear of them."

His lieutenant stared, said low, his voice shaking, "Man, that be no priest—'tis the Ard Ri himself."

Now Brodir, too, stared. "Be you sure?"

"Ay, canst not see the great gold badge of kingship hanging about his neck?"

Brodir sucked in a breath and wet his lips.

He saw the accursed thing now, a-gleam in the waning sun. "We take them," he growled. "Boru is mine."

Hearing the hiss of metal, Brian leapt to his feet. Uttering a hoarse battle cry, he took his sword in hand, but his kneeling men were disadvantaged. The shield-burg was soon forced, and facing him was six feet of Viking rage. He recognized Brodir whose long black hair was confined beneath his belt. Brian slashed, catching his enemy in the leg, but already the devil's battle-ax was descending. The last thought of Brian Boru, emperor of the Irish, was of Brianna. It saddened him that she would grieve . . .

As the Ard Ri sank to the grass in his own life's-blood, Brodir shouted to all who would hear:

"Now let men tell that Brodir felled Brian!"

So filled was he with his own triumph that he did not see his doom approaching until he was surrounded by a wall of Celt spears.

Chapter Twenty-Six

Wulf Thorsson and Leif Karlsson bent to the
steering oar of the *Sea Serpent* as she was rowed
out of Dublin Bay under a rising moon. Behind
them, in the water and on land, lay vast carnage,
both Viking and Celt.

"What happened back there?" Leif whispered,
his face white. "Hast any idea?"

Wulf shook his head. His face, too, was pale.
He was remembering the blood raining from
the heavens and remembering his countrymen
fleeing in panic to vessels drifting out to sea in
a tide running full. He was remembering the
hundreds who drowned . . .

"I trow 'twas the gods we fought as well as
the Celts," he muttered.

He thought back on the sight he had seen one

night in the Orkneys, weapons fighting weapons
in unseen hands. At the time, he had not known
if it were dream or portent. Now he knew. It had
been a warning. He bowed his head, weary unto
death and sick at heart. The brave ones were
gone. Half of his crew . . . Sigurd . . . Boru . . .
Ay, Boru was gone. Because of the prophecy,
he had not fought, yet he had been slain by
Brodir not far from the battlefield.

Wulf felt a loss he had never expected as he
realized, too late, that Brian Boru had been the
best ruler for Ireland. It had been wrong to
interfere with the plans of the gods. He covered
his face with his hands, thinking of the irony
of it. The Celts had won, ay, but now all of
them, Celt and Viking alike, were saddled with
Sitric. That stalwart, safe in his garrison, had
been granted immediate Irish pardon when he
had turned away those of his Viking comrades
who were not slain nor drowned. Once their
usefulness was over, he had no further need
for them.

Wulf flung a wild laugh to the night sky.
Damned if they were not back where first they
began. Sitric, king of Dublin. Wulf was not sure
but that they all had gotten exactly what they
deserved. And now he must tell Brianna about
the fate of Brian Boru. He could not let her hear
it from any other. As their vessel emerged from
the bay and turned north, he said to Leif:

"Where be this place Fiona spoke of?"

"She said 'twas straight inland four miles
from Howth Head. 'Tis a wayside inn."

Wulf nodded, and fell into gloomy silence. In his mind, he played over the battle again and again, wondering all the while how they could have made it work. But it was not meant to work. It was the beginning of the end, this, and no more would Vikings rule in this part of the world. He felt it in the very depths of him. The glory days had passed. And while he felt a certain sadness at the thought, he was glad, for no more did war satisfy him. He craved to hold a soft hand rather than a sword, craved a smile and laughing green eyes more than all the booty the world had to offer. But he feared it was too late to claim the one he loved.

Leif said quietly after several hours of rowing, "Man, we are here."

They beached the vessel in a shallow hidden cove, and then the two had a walk ahead of them through greening hills and dales that were silvered with moonlight. The smell of spring filled Wulf's nostrils, wet, warm earth and soft air, but it gave him no pleasure.

" 'Twill be all right, man," Leif said when they had walked long in silence. "She will understand."

"Why should she?" Wulf asked sharply. "I have hurt her before, but never like this."

" 'Twas not your hand that killed the man."

" 'Twas my vow to lay him in the dead-straw. What matter that it was not my hand that did it?"

Leif said softly, "She will understand."

"Nay," Wulf muttered, his step and his heart leaden.

"Ay," Leif answered. "You she loves . . ."

Brianna stirred the fire and then sat on a stool before it. She wondered, for the hundredth time, what had happened on the field at Clontarf, yet she was afraid, so very afraid, to know. She thrust away from her every thought of that which frightened her the most—that her loved ones were slain. All of them slain . . .

Since Boru and his men had departed, she and Fiona and the two old inn-folk had been the only ones remaining. Last eve, she and her friend had talked the night long, and Fiona had confessed tearfully to telling Leif of this secret place. Oh, she knew she should not have, it was a betrayal of Boru, and she felt wicked and guilty about it—but she had to. She trusted Leif. And if it happened that the Vikings were driven from Dublin, he had promised to come here for her afterwards.

As Brianna gazed on the maid sleeping so peacefully on the wall bench, her fears mounted. She worried not that Leif might betray them. It was just that no one, neither Celt nor Viking, had yet come to them with news of any kind and it was well past moonrise. Surely the battle was over by now. Surely. Oh, dear Jesu, what if—? She fought panic, gritting her teeth, her nails cutting into her palms. Nay! She would not think the worst. She could not bear to. She drew on her cloak, pinned it, and went out into the night. She had fair worn a path to the door, she had so often gone to stare toward the south. She told herself to enjoy the moon, the air fragrant with the aroma of warm, wet earth and growing grass and springtime . . .

Her gaze narrowed as she detected movement in the distance. Was it someone coming over the fields? Someone coming not from the south but from the east where lay the sea? She saw then that it was so, and saw that it was not one but two hurrying figures. She stood quietly, afraid to swallow or breathe or blink for fear they would disappear when she wanted so much for them to be there. Let it be Wulf and Leif, she prayed. Oh, Jesu, please . . . She saw the moon strike their hair, saw that one was fair and one dark.

"Brianna!" Wulf called. He had seen her when first she came out of the dwelling and stood gazing to the south. Now, hearing her happy shout and seeing her wave, he broke into a run, Leif close on his heels.

Brianna flew across the field as if her feet wore wings. She could scarce believe her good fortune. He lived! And Leif, too! Oh, Jesu have thanks, she whispered over and over—Jesu have thanks. And then she was caught up in Wulf's strong arms and nigh crushed against the moon-glittered mail covering his chest.

"Beloved . . ." She had time to speak only the one word before Wulf's mouth took hers in a hungry kiss.

Leif continued on to the inn, and as he knelt beside the sleeping Fiona, his heart brimmed.

He kissed her parted lips and smiled as she stirred, made a small noise, and burrowed deeper into her sleeping bag. He smoothed back her tangled brown hair and kissed her forehead.

"Lass . . ."

Fiona's eyes flew open. She gasped, "Leif!" and gave a happy shriek. She, too, was lifted into strong arms and kissed until she was breathless.

Entering, and seeing the two, Brianna was happy for them, but she knew there was an untold tale waiting to be heard. The very fact that the men were here meant that the news was bad for the Vikings. She doubted that it was safe for them to stay long. She said gently:

"I trow you have much to tell us. Wouldst eat and drink first, beloved?"

Beloved . . . Wulf shook his head. He had not the heart for either. She was going to hate him when she heard his news. "We cannot stay," he said. "We came only for Fiona—and for you, if 'tis your wish after we have talked." Already he felt the dark emptiness of a life without her.

"If 'tis my wish!" Brianna protested. "Where else would I want to be other than with you?" Of a sudden she saw in his eyes a look that chilled her. Fiona and Leif had ceased their fondling and were listening.

Wulf said low, "I bring you bad tidings, Brianna."

She stared at him, her lips and her face drained suddenly of color. She whispered, "My father? F-Fin?" But he could not possibly know

411

of them. She put a hand to her heart. "Oh, Wulf, nay, not Boru . . ."

"Ay. He is gone, Brianna." Wulf stood rigid, watching as the words reached her. He craved to hold and comfort her, but the look in those green-gold eyes froze him. She was a wounded lioness, and it was he who had brought this pain down on her head.

"Where?" she whispered.

"In a grove in Tomar's Wood."

Tomar's Wood. A forest. Brianna saw again her terrible vision, the tall form lying so still amongst trees and bushes, the men weeping and beating their breasts. She had thought it was Wulf who would be slain this day, but it had been Boru. Boru! Oh, God . . . She was aware that Fiona wept noisily in Leif's arms, and now she herself was seized with weeping. Nevermore see his gray eyes smiling nor hear his booming laughter? And the land—what would Ireland do without him? He had won the war and not lived to see the victory! Of a sudden, her weeping was with rage.

She shrieked, "He promised he would not go into battle! He knew he would die if he did! How dare he do such a stupid thing?" She pounded her head with her fists, and then her fists she pounded together until she thought her bones would break.

Wulf caught her hands, fearing she would do herself injury. He held her close. As she wept against his cloak, he said quietly, "He did not break his promise; he was some distance from the battlefield. His Dalcassians were led by his son, Murrough." Murrough, too, was gone, as was Murrough's own son. Ireland had lost her finest princes this day.

"Then how?" Brianna sobbed. "How could it have happened?"

Wulf grated his teeth. He might as well get on with it, for the tale would grow no better with waiting. "He was on his knees praying," he answered gruffly. "His men, in a shield-burg round him, were praying also when they were taken unawares."

Brianna's eyes burned wild. She tore herself from his arms. "Praying? 'Tis not to be believed! Who would be so low as to slay a man at prayer? Tell me so I might slay him myself!"

" 'Twas Brodir, and you be too late. Boru dealt him a terrible wound and your Celts finished him. 'Twas not an easy death . . ." Wulf ached for her. Gladly would he have borne her grief on his own shoulders, but none could bear it but herself.

Brianna moaned, murmured low as if to herself, "I hate war . . . I hate hate hate it . . ." She began pacing, twisting her hands together. "Never do I want for there to be another war as long as I live."

"Nor do I." Fiona gave a wail and clung the tighter to Leif.

Brianna's devastation went to Wulf's heart where it joined his own despair. He had been wondering, might the rebellion have died a-borning but for himself? Would Sitric and

Maelmorda have had men enough to fight had he not spent these past five months garnering troops from far and near? It was a thing he would never know. When Brianna sat on a bench before the fire, he sat beside her and took her hand. It was some moments before he could bring himself to speak.

"Know you, Brianna, I—was wrong. I have been wrong from the beginning."

Brianna turned to him, blinked. "A-about what?"

"Boru," Wulf answered. "I see too late that none could rule this land nor our two peoples as well as the Lion himself. And now I see your suffering . . ."

She saw for the first time the anguish on his face. So drowned had she been in her own sorrow, she had not marked his own. Nor had she considered the courage it took for him and for Leif to come to these enemy quarters where they could have been slain. And he was praising Boru, the man he himself had vowed to slay. Now it was she who took his big hand between her own. She raised it to her lips and kissed it, searched for words to comfort him.

"Wulf, beloved—"

Wulf shook his head. "I—have made a terrible mistake. I be as responsible for Boru's death as if I had wielded the battle-ax myself."

She wanted to cry out that nay, it was not so, but she saw that he would not be swayed. His guilt was a thing he must live with. Just as she must live with hers; her betrayal of him.

414

"He saw through to your soul," she offered softly. "He said he would be proud to call you kin and comrade and prayed you would be returned to me."

The words of the dead man were but another blade in Wulf's heart. " 'Tis but further proof that I had for an enemy one who would have been the staunchest of friends, and had for friends those who made better enemies."

"You could give naught but loyalty to your people—'tis your way . . ."

"Ay." His smile was bitter. "As 'tis yours."

Brianna's eyes glistened. "Ay."

Wulf was overwhelmed by the depth of his love for her. He would protect and cherish her all of his days, and he had wanted to give her all of life's pleasures and treasures. Instead, he had given her the greatest grief. He drew her onto his knees and held her close, his arms about her, his head to hers, his body swaying slightly from side to side as though he comforted a sad child. He stroked her hair, her damp cheeks, gently kissed her lips.

Brianna lifted his hand to her breast, cupping her own over it, wanting him to feel the quickened beating of her heart. She kissed the back of his hand, the golden hair so crisp against her lips, kissed each strong dark finger. She traced the thin white scar that once had frightened her, traced his nose, his wide brow, his grave mouth, stroked his thick mane of hair and the beard that had grown unruly once more. She whispered:

"How I love thee, Wulf Thorsson. This tongue cannot begin to tell thee . . ."

Wulf cupped her hands in his, brought them to his lips and kissed them, kissed her mouth, again and again. He said low, "You will wed me, Brianna Kinrade."

Brianna's lips curved. "Is't a command, sire?" she asked quietly.

Wulf buried his face in her hair. "Never will I let you go."

"Wouldst carry me off if I said nay?"

"Ay."

She smiled, for she saw well that he meant it. He was a Viking. But it was all right, for never would she have allowed him to go off without her. She slipped her arms about his neck and pressed her cheek to his. "I will wed you, Wulf Thorsson, ay." He was silent for so long, she murmured, "Wulf, what is't?"

"Know you, Brianna, I want naught but your happiness. If 'twere in my power this moment to give you but one thing in this world"—his voice broke—"I would give you Boru."

Brianna gazed on the Wolf of Husaby with wonder. Marking a lone crystal tear stealing down his cheek, she took his face between her hands. "Methinks he is with me still."

Of a sudden, Leif stood over them scowling. "Man, 'tis not safe to tarry any longer. They could return at any time."

Wulf nodded. He rose and set Brianna on her feet. "Be you ready to leave?"

"Ay. We are both ready, Fi and I."

Fiona said, "Go you all outside. I will waken the inn-folk and tell them our men have come for us . . ."

As the four hurried across the moonlit countryside toward the sea, Brianna was faced with new worries. How could she just sail off with Wulf without a word to any? She could not. She craved to go home and see if all was well with her father and Fin—she prayed it was—and she yearned to see Maeve and she needed clothing and other necessities to take with her. But doubtless Wulf would want to be on his way back to Norway immediately. Minding his earlier words about his steading, she sighed. The thought of Husaby did not lighten her heart as it had before. Not this night. This night she yearned for Carnane. Wulf's deep voice interrupted her thoughts.

"We will go straightaway to my stronghold on Maun, Brianna, and in the morn I will take you to your folk." He smiled, seeing the surprise on her face. "If it be your wish, my heart."

"Oh, ay, it be my wish!" She caught his hand as they walked and held it tightly. "And it be my wish for us to walk side by side always, just as we are this night. Whatever lies ahead, we will meet together." Her eyes shone, love-filled, as she gazed up at him. " 'Tis more than my wish, 'tis my vow. I will walk by your side henceforward."

Wulf's laughter lifted to the night sky as he caught her up in his arms. He was minding a snowy day, a maid with dancing eyes and long legs striding by his side, the wind in her hair. And now she was his. He marveled at his turn of fortune.

"My people have lost a war, but you I have won," he declared. " 'Tis that victory I will think on when I remember this day. I won you, Brianna Kinrade."

"This day I lost the dearest of my friends," Brianna replied quietly, "but I count it as triumph because I have you. You be mine now, Wulf Thorsson." Someday she would tell him how like Boru he was. How very like Boru . . .

Epilogue

June 1014

The *Sea Serpent*, her sail hungry for the sea wind, made the journey from Maun in eleven days. As she drew near the shore of Norway's land, Brianna stood in the prow with her husband's arms about her. She gazed on the sight with wondering eyes, for never had she seen anything so magnificent. In the distance towered great mountains, blue-purple with haze, their peaks snow-capped, and from them plunged white streams in vast plumed waterfalls. A green blanket of hills and valleys stretched from the mountains down to the sea, a sea so blue and sun-glittered it fair pained her eyes to look on it. When the lur horn was sounded, from all along the shore came the call of horns answering, welcoming the travelers home. It was so exciting and beautiful a moment that Brianna was nigh overcome.

Wulf frowned, seeing his bride's wet eyes. He had thought all was well. Her father and kin were safe, and they had had a long visit and a small but perfect wedding at Carnane, so what was amiss?

"What saddens you, Brianna?"

Brianna looked up at him in astonishment. She laughed. "Naught saddens me! I be happy. I be so happy!" Looking back at Fiona and Leif in the stern, she marked Fiona, too, wiping her eyes on the hem of her skirt. It seemed they both felt the same way about their new husbands and new land. Returning her excited gaze to the steadings that had begun to appear, Brianna pointed.

"Oh, Wulf, look on that one! How beautiful it be."

Beside the dwelling place that looked onto the sea there stood a great birch, and near the farm buildings ran a silver ribbon of water that had tumbled from the far mountains and grown tame before spilling into the sea. Shielding her eyes from the sun, Brianna marked that the house was a large and stately manor with many horn windows. A grand balcony stretched around the second story, and both balcony and eaves were wondrously carved. On the turf roofs of the outbuildings grew tall grass and wildflowers of every color, and nearby was an orchard in blossom. The fields showed the soft green of new growth.

" 'Tis beautiful," she breathed, wistful, and hating the envy she felt for the lucky folk living there.

"That old place?" Wulf shook his head. "It needs a lot of work. I know it well."

"No matter," Brianna said softly, " 'tis the most beautiful place these eyes have ever seen."

Wulf's arms tightened about her. " 'Tis glad I am you like it, Brianna, for 'tis yours."

She looked up at him, startled. "Wh-what?"

" 'Tis Husaby."

Brianna was stunned. "Husaby? Oh, Wulf!" She cried to Fiona then: "Fi! Look you ahead to the right—'tis Husaby!" She returned wide eyes to Wulf Thorsson's face, touched her fingers to his laughing lips. " 'Tis paradise, husband."

Wulf caught his wife's small hand and kissed it. " 'Twas a lonely place before, but you be right, Brianna. With you here with me, 'twill be paradise."

UNWILLING BETRAYER is based loosely on fact. Brian Boru was indeed the Ard Ri, the emperor of Ireland, in 1014. Gormlaith, Sitric and Maelmorda were all part of the richly-woven historical tapestry of the time as were Sigurd of the Orkneys, and Ospak and Brodir of the Isle of Man. There was a Kincora, and there was a great battle at Clontarf, also known as Brian's Battle. This Irish uprising was the most splendid ever made by a wrathful nation against the Viking menace.

I have spun this tale around the fictional characters of Brianna and Wulf, and Fiona and Leif. Since nothing is known of the fate of Gormlaith after the Battle of Clontarf, I have supplied her with a fitting one.

I loved writing **UNWILLING BETRAYER,** and I loved, I still do, the characters, good and wicked alike. If they touch you as they touched me, please drop me a note at P.O. Box 905, Sharon, PA 16146. I value highly the response from my readers. It always helps me do better.

Joan van Nuys

Chapter One

Swords, a village north of Dubh Linn, Ireland 988 A.D.

Thomas Lachlann wiped wet, dark curls away from his sweating forehead as he slowly straightened up from the water barrel in front of his mother's small hut near the edge of the forest. Drops of water glistened on Thomas's broad, naked chest and dripped down the waistband of his rough-spun black breeches. He dried his sun-browned, flat torso with lazy circular motions that belied the intensity in his narrowed green eyes as he watched an oncoming rider. The rider cut ruthlessly across the front field, churning up the neat, newly mounded rows that Thomas himself had planted but yester eve. He watched as the man flailed the beast mercilessly until the snorting, trembling gelding finally slid to a halt in the dust before Thomas.

"Flee, Master Thomas, flee!"

"Whoa!" Thomas reached for the bridle, his strong arm muscles flexing as the skittish roan gelding tried to dance away from him. "You rode this beast too hard, mon!" His eyes glittered in anger as the sinewy man slid off the horse's back.

"Couldna be helped," retorted the other as he drew himself up in front of Thomas. He wiped his furrowed brow hurriedly, his breath coming in quick pants.

Thomas saw the fear in the man's eyes and went still. "What has happened, Caedmon?" he asked in a low voice, stroking the gelding's nose to calm him. " 'Tis not like you to treat a beast so, nor to ride carelessly across a newly planted field." He added wryly, "That is more my brother Aelfred's manner."

"Master Thomas, 'tis your father! Lord Harald is dead with this morn's sunrise. And your brother rides this way with armed men! He seeks to kill you!"

Thomas compressed his lips and his green eyes glittered. So, it had come to this. His father had finally died, God rest his perfidious soul, and now Aelfred was seeking to destroy the one person who stood between him and the Viking overlordship of Swords—his bastard Irish half-brother, Thomas.

"He seeks to steal your birthright! You are the eldest son. The land should be yours." Caedmon's wiry body tensed with his words. "He steals from you!"

Thomas fastened his gaze on the panting Caedmon.

"Steals?" He laughed, a falsely light-hearted sound in the little clearing. The sound brought a woman to the door of the hut, and she stood watching the men whilst she dried her hands on an old rag. "Steals from me?" Thomas repeated. "Why, Aelfred cannot steal my birthright, Caedmon. He was *given* it. By my *father*." Thomas upper lip curled as he sneered the last word.

Caedmon glanced from the young man's bitter face to that of the woman leaning against the hut's doorframe. And, as was the custom for so many of the local people, he turned to her. She wore a gray, shapeless dress with a gray woolen shawl over her shoulders to keep off the chill spring breeze. Her hair stood in a great black and gray knotted mass around her head, and her green eyes, the same green eyes that she had passed on to her son, held Caedmon as spellbound now as they ever had before her accident.

"Caedra," Caedmon breathed and touched his forelock in a gesture of respect.

Thomas glanced sharply at him, hearing the loss, the sadness, and knowing that Caedmon longed for the past, for the time when Caedra's vast family, the Lachlanns, were the powerful ruling family at Swords.

Caedra nodded regally, the gesture some half-forgotten vestige of what her parents had taught her in the long-ago days before the coming of the Vikings.

"Lord Harald's dead," said Caedmon and waited.

Caedra stepped into the yard, her first steps uncertain. A shadow crossed her face as she tilted her head curiously. "Dead?" she asked, a quaver in her voice. "It is certain?"

"Aye," Caedmon assured her gently. "He is dead, Caedra. He is dead." The two old ones stood there looking at each other, so many unspoken words between them.

Caedra's shaky steps brought her to stand at last next to her green-eyed son. She looked at him. "Thomas," she murmured, and 'twas as though she spoke in a dream. "Thomas, you are the new lord, the new lord of Swords!"

He looked at her, his eyes softening. "Aye, Mother, by right of being the eldest son, I should be the new lord." His eyes took in her faded face, the still generous mouth, the green eyes now framed by lines. As he looked at her, he felt the pain knot deep in him that he would have to leave her and she knew it not. "But," and his voice lowered, "it is not to be, Mother."

"Not to be?"

She looked startled, unbelieving, and he cursed the fall she had taken—the one that had given her the vague, staring look that told him she could no longer understand his words as well as before.

"But you are his son!" She clenched her fist and reached for him. "I bought you that birthright! I paid for it with my own blood! My own pain!"

"Mother." Thomas winced at hearing her speak of what had happened—even in front of Caedmon, trustworthy though he was and knowing every word of the story, Thomas's story. "Mama, 'twas long ago." He stroked her forehead and patted the mass of her hair, and she calmed, as the gelding had calmed under his same sure touch only minutes before. "Mama, I must go."

"Go?" She reached for him and clutched his hand, her face again wearing that vague, startled look.

In irritation, for Caedmon's eyes warned him there was little time, Thomas said, "I must go. Aelfred seeks me."

At the mention of his half-brother's name, a cunning look crossed her face. "Aelfred? Oh, aye, Aelfred." She turned to him, her eyes clear once more. "Go my son, flee!"

In relief, Thomas hugged her. He turned to Caedmon and placed his hand on the old man's. "My thanks, Caedmon, for your loyalty in bringing me word."

"Hurry, master, *hurry*! You may yet save your life!"

"Aye, I intend to do just that," muttered

Thomas grimly. He would waste not a moment in taking possessions with him. He had known that when this time came he would leave and take nought with him but his weapon.

He ran to the small hut and emerged only heartbeats later, looking paler and grimmer than before. His naked torso was now covered in a handwoven, oft-mended black cloak, and he clutched a small bundle of food. At his side swung the silver filigree-handled Viking sword, *Thor's Bite*, the sole legacy of his Viking father.

Caedra gave a small shriek when she saw the sword and then quickly stuffed her fist in her mouth to let not another sound escape.

Thomas neither glanced at her nor halted in his rapid strides to the roan, but he had heard her cry and it pierced him to the heart. He wanted to assure her that 'twas a necessity that he take this sword, the one that he had secretly oiled and sharpened when he thought she was not looking. He would need it now, both as a weapon and as a desperately wanted sign of his father's acceptance, when all other acceptance had been denied him in his life.

This sword was all that he had of his father, and he still remembered the day Lord Harald had come to the hut, suddenly standing there in the doorway, blocking the sun. 'Twas on Thomas's twelfth birthday and his father had at first merely stood there, awkwardly it had seemed then to the young Thomas. At last, Lord Harald had entered, though Caedra had not bidden him do so. Thomas remembered her leaving her place by the fire, running to a corner of the hut, and throwing her apron over her head when she realized 'twas Lord Harald come to call. 'Twas after her fall, when she had hit her head so severely that her behavior had become strange.

His father had looked at him and then asked him to come out into the light. Thomas had done so, heart pounding in fear, but he had followed the one man who had so marked his life, the man whom he had seen but a handful of times previously. While they stood outside the hut, Lord Harald staring at Thomas, Thomas's attention had been drawn to the beautiful black stallion that stood pawing the dust, impatiently waiting for his master to mount so that they could be off and running through the fields once more.

Lord Harald, seeing the boy's interest, had invited him to sit atop the horse. He had laughed as he lifted Thomas onto the black horse, showing him where to place his foot, where to grasp with his knees. Then Lord Harald had stepped back.

Thomas, eyes shining, breath held, had urged the stallion forward. The beast took several steps, then suddenly reared up, nostrils wide, eyes rolling. Thomas had landed butt-first in the dirt. Lord Harald had stood there laughing heartily at the boy sprawled in the dust.

Humiliation ran high in Thomas at that. In a fury, Thomas had lunged to his feet and run at his father, slamming into Harald's stomach with his head.

The attack on his father, far from enraging Lord Harald, seemed but to delight him. With great whoops, his father had then proceeded to beat Thomas to a pulp. Thomas, his nose bloody, his arms bruised, his stomach scraped, had only ceased fighting when Lord Harald stood over him with a sword at his throat. With one final laugh, the big, bearded blond man had grinned and thrown the sword into the dust. "*Thor's Bite* is yours," he had said then, gesturing at the magnificent weapon. "And so are my lands, *if* you can take them." And with this parting remark, tossed casually over his shoulder, Lord Harald had strolled over to his horse, though Thomas now saw he had to limp to do so.

Lord Harald had swung up onto the stallion and surveyed Thomas once more, from bleeding head to dusty toe. Thomas stood with sword in hand, glaring at Lord Harald who, laughing, pulled tightly on the reins. The horse reared, spun on its heels, and galloped back across the fields to the manor where Lord Harald dwelled.

Thomas had watched him go, and in that moment he hated his father to the depths of his heart for the violation of his mother, for the humiliation of himself sprawled in the dirt, for the years of indifference. But mostly he hated him for that tiny spark of yearning, for that desperate desire for his father's love and acceptance—while he received neither. The love and acceptance had gone to Aelfred, the son who lived behind the manor walls with Lord Harald—Aelfred, the legitimate issue of Lord Harald's marriage to Lady Ingrid.

As Thomas watched Lord Harald disappear that day, he swore that he would find a way to take his father's land from him. Or from Aelfred.

Thomas' brooding thoughts brought him back to the present. One look at Caedmon's concerned face and Caedra's worried one convinced Thomas that he must lose no more time.

Caedmon handed him the reins of the sweating, sorry-looking nag that he had managed to steal from Harald's—now Aelfred's—stables. " 'Twas the only horse I could fetch," he mumbled apologetically to Thomas.

" 'Twill do, Caedmon," Thomas assured him, swinging himself up onto the beast. Thomas's black hair shone in the sun and his large frame dwarfed the thin horse he perched atop of, its ribs showing through the dull red coat. Yet Thomas looked every inch the lord that his father had denied he was by rights these many years.

Horses ridden at a pounding gallop raced over the rise in front of the hut.

"Too late!" cried Caedmon.

Aelfred Haraldson and three of his henchmen yanked their lathered horses to a stop. Thomas watched, green eyes narrowed, as Aelfred swayed precariously atop his horse. 'Twas his father's black stallion. Aelfred tightly held the reins on the beast, pulling at the sensitive mouth, and the horse tossed his head several times, eyes rolling.

"So. You have heard," grunted Aelfred, walking the skittish black over. The stallion stood taller than Thomas's nag and Aelfred obviously enjoyed the advantage the height gave him. He sneered down at his older brother and waved a hand deprecatingly at Caedmon, who had joined Caedra in the doorway of the hut.

Thomas sat his nag stonily and looked up at his brother with an impassive face.

"Our father died. This morn." Aelfred's cold blue eyes watched Thomas.

"And you have wasted no time in taking his horse," observed Thomas.

" 'Tis *my* horse." Aelfred frowned. "My horse. *My* lands. *My* village." The black took a step closer. "And what are you still doing here? Why did you not run like he"—Aelfred pointed to Caedmon—"told you to do?" Aelfred's lips twisted in a grin. "Or were you just on your way?"

Thomas eyed his half-brother coldly. "I know you do not want me here."

"I want you dead!" spat Aelfred.

"Then why do you not try and kill me?" Thomas was surprised. 'Twas not like Aelfred to warn a man before he killed him.

"Because," spoke up a cynical voice behind them.

Thomas turned to look at Helmut, a Dane swordsman who had recently attached himself to Lord Harald's manor. Obviously the man thought well of himself, well enough to interrupt his new patron, Aelfred.

Aelfred gaped at Helmut, then relaxed and grinned. He turned back to Thomas. "I do not kill you because Lady Ingrid specifically forbade me to kill you. *This* time."

Thomas raised an eyebrow. "How unlike your mother to be so kind."

"Oh, 'twas not kindness at all," chortled Aelfred artlessly. "She thought that if I killed you, the men and women on our lands would rise up and attack the manor house in revenge. Lady Ingrid did not want that."

"Mmmmmm. 'Twould prove inconvenient," observed Thomas cynically.

Helmut, a hardened man whose scars indicated he had survived several battles, walked his horse over and sneered, "Get out, Lachlann. Get out and do not return."

"Or what?" Thomas's face flushed at the man's impudence.

"Or else we will kill your mother and"— Helmut nodded negligently in Caedmon's direction—"and anyone else we care to. Anyone who is of your kin. Anyone who names you friend."

Thomas turned to Aelfred. "You let this—this outsider—speak for you?" Rage swelled in his voice.

Aelfred grinned happily and nodded. "Aye. He is a good fighter. A good planner."

And Helmut planned to take over Swords and

the manor, Thomas saw in an instant. He glared at Aelfred. "You are a fool, Aelfred. Do not let this man guide you. He will take everything he can—"

"I said get out!" Helmut's sword was in his hand and he slashed the air within inches of Thomas's face. Thomas read his deadly intent in the man's pale gaze.

Thomas glared at Aelfred, cursing his half-brother's stupidity, his ambition, his ignorance. Thomas knew that if he said but another word, Helmut would slice him through.

"Thomas!" 'Twas his mother's voice. Thomas slumped in the saddle. For himself, he could fight, but what of his mother, his cousins, his friends? He could not protect them all against Aelfred, Helmut, and their deadly ilk.

"Go, Thomas," cried Caedra. "Your brother will be here any moment!" There was an urgency in her voice.

Aelfred smirked. "Still as crazy as ever, I see."

Thomas felt humiliation wash over him at the amused look in his half-brother's eyes and at the smug looks of Helmut and the other man. His mother could not help it that her mind was not quite right since her fall.

Thomas drew himself up straight in the saddle. He could not, would not, discuss his mother or her affliction with Aelfred. "See that she is not hurt," he said tersely. "And if word ever reaches me that you have harmed her, I will return and kill you. All of you."

Aelfred's mount took a step back, responding

to the icy coldness in Thomas's voice. Aelfred himself looked taken aback at Thomas's words. The half-brothers glared at each other.

Caedmon slapped the thin flanks of the nag in a desperate effort to get the roan moving and to get Thomas away and out of danger. "Ride!" he entreated.

Thomas reined in the nag and looked down at the trembling man. His green eyes steadied with purpose. "My thanks, Caedmon!" he said. "I willna forget your help!"

"Master, ride!" The desperate pleading in Caedmon's voice reached the youth on horseback.

"Aye. Get!" sneered Aelfred. The men with him laughed coarsely.

With one final nod, Thomas kicked the spindly flanks of the sorry roan and moved slowly off toward the forest.

He looked backward once.

"And do not return!" cried Aelfred.

His voice reminded Thomas of a petulant child's.

"If you do, I will kill you!" Aelfred's words, however, did not belong to a child.

Insolently, to goad his half-brother and Helmut as much as to communicate with his loved ones, Thomas waved at his mother and Caedmon, a last farewell. His mother waved back and finally Caedmon, too, lifted his hand in a sad, disheartened gesture of farewell.

Thomas swung around and kicked the horse harder. The gelding, though sorry, was not without heart, and he broke into a rolling canter, every stride taking Thomas farther away from the raucous laughter of his half-brother and his companions.

Shuddering, red-faced in anger and humiliation at the coarse taunts, Thomas's fists clenched the reins. He guided the horse into the forest and onto one of the many trails that crisscrossed the woods in a fine network like so many veins on a leaf. Within heartbeats, Thomas was swallowed up by the dense forest.

Chapter Two

"You asked to see me, Ivar?" It was dusk as Thomas Lachlann stepped into a large military tent, ducking his head to avoid the ornately carved dragon's head that adorned the top of the tent frame.

Ivar Wolfson swung around on the stool he was sitting upon. A large, slow-moving man, he dwarfed the stool. His eyes were set in a web of lines from squinting for years in the sun of hotter climes. His short blond hair betrayed his Norwegian heritage, and his skin was ruddy from those same years in the sun.

Two of Ivar's lieutenants were with him. Thomas saw the wide parchment with the black outlines in Ivar's hands and knew the three had been discussing the strategy for yet another battle. Ivar nodded, then jerked his head silently toward the tent's opening. Without a word, the lieutenants left the tent, Ingolf with a smirk and Dirk the Dane with a wink.

"You too, Jasmine," said Ivar. "Out."

Thomas watched as a sinuous, dark-haired young woman slowly unwound herself from the thick pile of pink, blue, and turquoise pillows in one corner of the tent. A dark bundle of rags in the other corner moved, got to its feet, and revealed itself to be an old woman who hobbled after the younger woman, who ignored her. She pouted and glanced angrily at Ivar through the thick lashes of her almond-shaped black eyes; then she busied herself in wrapping a voluminous black robe around her shapely contours until naught was visible but her lovely eyes. With one last unreadable glance at the commander, the young woman left the tent. The old woman shuffled after her.

Ivar waited until they had gone. "Sit," he ordered.

Puzzled, Thomas sank down onto the richly patterned Moorish rug that covered the ground in Ivar's tent. Ivar had gained the beautiful carpet, the pillows, the small, elaborately carved table, the flickering lamps, a taste for luxuries and his lovely concubine, Jasmine, during profitable military campaigns against the Moors in southern Spain.

Thomas waited for his commander to speak. Yet still Ivar said nothing, his blue eyes watching Thomas almost dispassionately. Nevertheless, Thomas perceived an intensity to the look that almost took his breath away. He swallowed once, and waited.

At last Ivar said gruffly, "You have been with me for ten long years."

Thomas waited.

"During that time you have fought for me. Risked your life for me. Pulled me out of battle when I thought I was half way to Valhalla with a Valkyrie on each arm."

Thomas said nothing, but the memories flooded over him and he nodded. The battle that Ivar spoke of had been the first time Thomas had ever met the man, though he had soldiered for him nigh on half a year. Ivar's life was being threatened by three rock-hard fighting Irishmen who had attacked him as one, and Thomas, not liking the odds, had chosen to even them. Half-naked and howling like a berserker of old, he had descended upon the three, *Thor's Bite* swinging. He had killed the Irishmen in several hacking blows. Ivar looked up from where he had been pinned to the earth and said, "I want you in my personal guard."

And so Thomas had been with Ivar as one of his bodyguards ever since that day. Thomas liked the prestige that went with the position. And he knew he had gained a reputation as a ferocious fighter, not only from that fight but from countless others against both Norse and Irish. His growing reputation served Thomas well; the other soldiers of Ivar's command, always a rough lot, gave him a respectful distance when he had need of it.

"Never asked from whence you came . . ."

Thomas was about to speak but Ivar held up a strong hand. "And I will not ask now."

Thomas subsided, silent. Mayhap 'twas best if even Ivar knew nothing of Thomas's past.

Ivar paused, as if assessing his man. At last he said, "I have contracted a bride."

Thomas started. This *was* news. Ivar, to be married?

Ivar was quick to spot the incredulous look on his bodyguard's face before Thomas could wipe it off.

"Do not look so. Even *I* have need of a wife. Of a son."

Thomas nodded slowly. Ivar was carving out a large territory around Dubh Linn, ostensibly to help King Sitric Silkenbeard. In return for Ivar's loyalty, Silkenbeard left him much power. And some land. Ivar had fought hard for Silkenbeard. But there were ferocious contenders, Norse and Irish, for Dubh Linn and were Ivar to die, his efforts would come to naught. It seemed natural to Thomas that Ivar would want to pass his command on to a son or sons. And though Ivar's concubine, Jasmine, was lovely, she had so far proved infertile. She had been with Ivar for as long as Thomas had known him and had not produced a child, boy *or* girl.

"Another concubine?" suggested Thomas delicately. Verily, he thought, his brow sweating, he had no experience in advising military commanders about such things, but surely a woman was all that was needed. No need to marry her, he thought dismissively. "A wife might find the field living difficult . . . too rough. . . ."

Ivar frowned. "I have thought about it. A wife is what I need. No contest for legitimacy that way."

"Ah," said Thomas, suddenly bitter. Indeed, Ivar would not want his illegitimate son fighting with the legitimate one for power and land. The irony was not lost upon Thomas. Why, 'twas the very situation that had driven him from Swords village. Lord Harald had sired Thomas upon an Irish woman and Aelfred upon his legal wife. Thomas clenched his teeth. 'Twas ten years later, and he was no closer to fulfilling his vow to claim his father's land today than he had been on the day he fled from Aelfred. "Aye," agreed Thomas shortly. "You have the right of it." How well he knew that!

Ivar nodded. A little silence grew between them; Thomas was lost in his thoughts.

Ivar continued, "I have arranged a ship for you. I want you to sail to Greenland and bring back my bride."

"Greenland!" Thomas' interest quickened. He had heard of such a place. As a boy he had once met a man who claimed he had sailed there. Why, 'twas at the ends of the earth! "Greenland!"

"Her name is Yngveld Sveinsdatter."

Thomas stared at his commander, pulling his thoughts forcibly back from the sea.

"Her father," continued Ivar, "is Svein Skull-crusher, an old comrade-in-arms of mine. We fought together many years ago." A shadow crossed Ivar's face and for a moment he looked cruel. Then the look was gone. "The betrothal agreement is there." He nodded at a yellowed, rolled-up parchment wrapped in a red ribbon that sat on the delicately carved Moorish table. "Take it. 'Twill convince Svein that you are my emissary."

Thomas took the scroll gingerly and barely glanced at it.

"Svein should be expecting you," said Ivar. "I sent a message two years past, by ship, to remind him of the betrothal and to tell him that I, or my representative, would come to Greenland." He eyed Thomas. "Unfortunately, I cannot get away at this time. Too much fighting—'tis a critical time." He sighed. "The Irish are in rebellion again. Brian Boru is gathering more men."

Thomas nodded. Brian Boru was a powerful Irish warrior and had enjoyed much success in raids against the Norse.

"I have chosen you," Ivar went on in a gruff voice, "because of all my men, I trust you the most."

Thomas started.

" 'Tis true," said Ivar. "I trust you as my bravest

444

and most loyal man. I want a man who can bring my bride to Dubh Linn safely."

Thomas swallowed, cognizant suddenly of the immense responsibility of his mission. "I will do my best," he assured Ivar.

"See that you do." Ivar watched him carefully. "You may have your pick of forty men to take with you, except for Ingolf and Dirk the Dane. Choose any man you think will fight hard and sail straight. Choose loyal men. You will have need of them."

Thomas nodded, his mind racing. Whom to choose? There was Caedmon's son, Neill, who had searched until he had found Thomas in Dubh Linn, stayed, and was now a presentable soldier. Thomas would take him. And Torgils—he fought well and he, too, was half-Norse, half-Irish bastard like Thomas, and also from Swords village. And what of Connall, another trusted friend? No, Connall he would leave at Dubh Linn. Mayhap Connall could make one more visit to Swords and give Caedra the few gold coins that Thomas had saved. Connall had done this regularly for Thomas over these past years. 'Twas too dangerous for Thomas to go in person. Aelfred had not stopped searching for him. And each time Connall returned, he had brought truly disturbing reports about Aelfred's treatment of the Swords peasants. 'Twas most unsettling.

Ivar was looking at him.

Thomas shook his head, coming out of his thoughts. He said, "Very well, I will choose."

Ivar answered, "Good," and nodded several times.

Thomas would need a cargo to sell so the voyage would bring a profit. And he must get a huge supply of food, though doubtless he and his men would catch fresh fish to supplement their diet.

Ivar interrupted, "There's talk of finding nine men hanging in Odinn's grove of trees."

The change of subject caught Thomas unawares. "Men? Hanging? Oh, aye, aye, so I have heard."

"Know you about it?"

Thomas shook his head, slowly coming round to the topic. "I do not have confidence in Odinn—or any of the Viking gods. I do not sacrifice to him."

For the first time Ivar's face split in a grin and he slapped Thomas on the back. "Aye, I know that well enough, my friend. Who do you sacrifice to?"

Thomas shook his head. "No one," he answered sullenly. 'Twas a sore point between him and his commander. Ivar favored the old gods, but Thomas could find little use for them *or* for his mother's Irish Christian god. He knew many of the Dubh Linn Norse sought and found the favor of Thor, Odinn, Frey, or whoever could be of help to them, but he himself did not choose that route. "No one," he said again.

"Well," said Ivar, getting to his feet. " 'Tis of little importance. I but wondered who had done it, 'tis all."

At Thomas's inquiring glance, he added, "Seems we did very well, very well indeed, the next day in our fight against some ratty Irish rebels." He grinned. "Mayhap the sacrifice worked."

"Mayhap," said Thomas noncommittally. The joke did not set well with him. He moved to rise.

"Get some rest," advised Ivar. "You leave a sennight hence."

Seven nights! Little enough time to prepare a ship, and men.

Something of Thomas's thoughts must have shown once more upon his face, for Ivar said, "The ship is ready. And has supplies enough. I have made a deal with an honest merchant of the town." He snorted. "Somewhat of a rarity! He assures me the ship is seaworthy."

Then with a wave of his hand, Thomas too was dismissed from Ivar's tent.

Thomas had just lifted the tent flap when Ivar's voice halted him. "Thomas Lachlann!"

Thomas turned.

"I want Yngveld Sveinsdatter brought to me virgin!"

Thomas smiled, a slash across his rugged, good-looking face that did not quite reach his hard green eyes. "You shall have your bride," he answered shortly. "Untouched."

Ivar nodded.

Thomas turned once more to leave.

"Tell Jasmine to get in here," said Ivar to Thomas's back before the tent flap closed. "I want her. Now."

FORBIDDEN PASSION

THERESA SCOTT

Bestselling Author of *Bride of Desire*

"More than Viking tales, Theresa Scott's historical romances are tender, exciting, and satisfying!"
—*Romantic Times*

Ordered to Greenland to escort his commander's betrothed to their Irish stronghold, Thomas Lachlann is unexpectedly drawn to the beguiling beauty he was sent to find. Bewitched and bewildered, Thomas knows that if he takes Yngveld as his beloved his life will be forfeit—but if he loses the golden-haired enchantress his heart will break.

__3305-4 $4.50 US/$5.50 CAN